Disney · PIXAR

TOY STORY

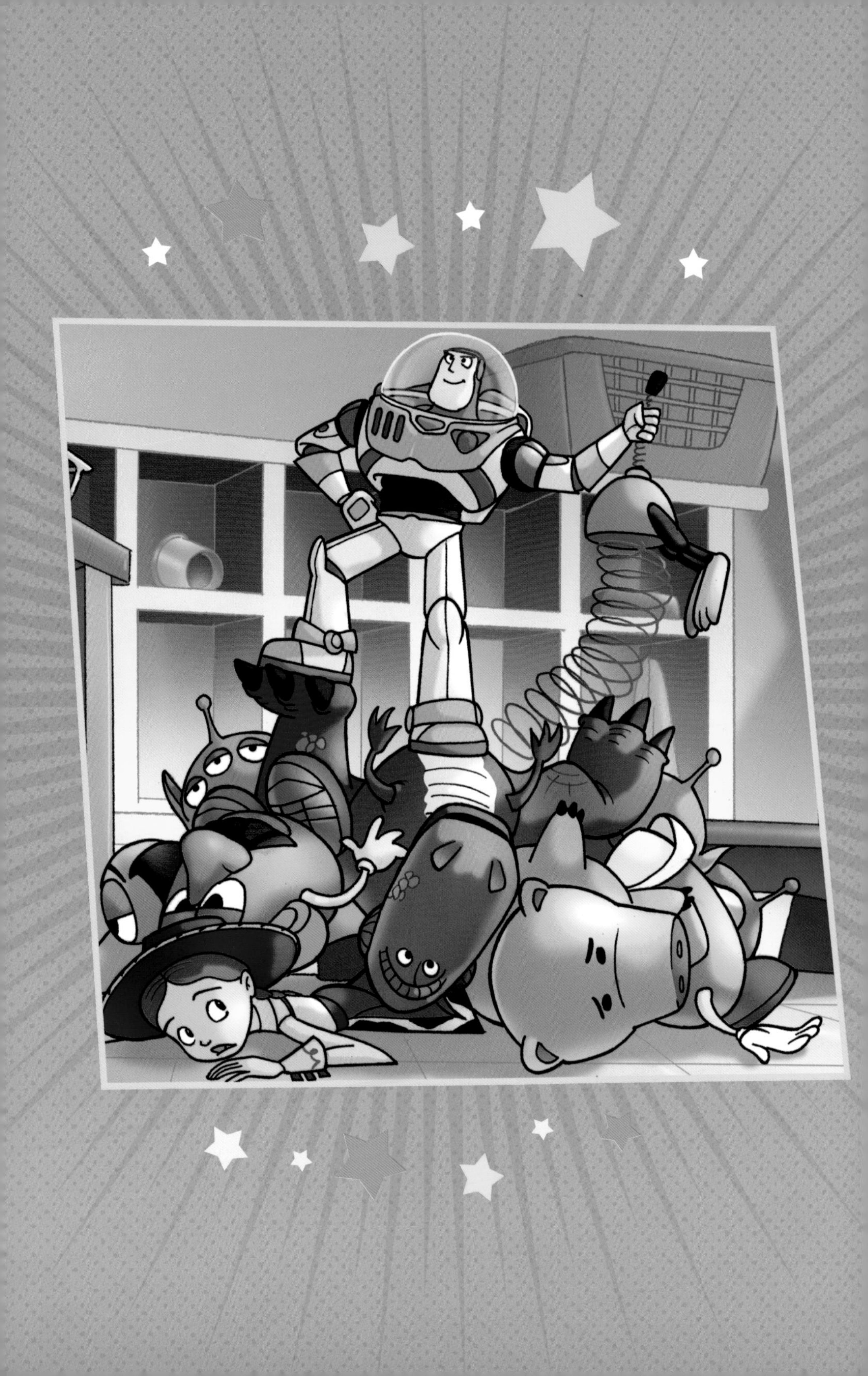

THE STORY OF THE MOVIES IN COMICS

DARK HORSE COMICS

DARK HORSE BOOKS

president and publisher **Mike Richardson**
editor **Shantel LaRocque**
assistant editor **Brett Israel**
designer **Anita Magaña**
digital art technician **Samantha Hummer**

Neil Hankerson Executive, Vice President • Tom Weddle, Chief Financial Officer • Randy Stradley, Vice President of Publishing • Nick McWhorter, Chief Business Development Officer • Dale LaFountain, Chief Information Officer • Matt Parkinson, Vice President of Marketing • Cara Niece, Vice President of Production and Scheduling • Mark Bernardi, Vice President of Book Trade and Digital Sales • Ken Lizzi, General Counsel • Dave Marshall, Editor in Chief • Davey Estrada, Editorial Director • Chris Warner, Senior Books Editor • Cary Grazzini, Director of Specialty Projects • Lia Ribacchi, Art Director • Vanessa Todd-Holmes, Director of Print Purchasing • Matt Dryer, Director of Digital Art and Prepress • Michael Gombos, Senior Director of Licensed Publications • Kari Yadro, Director of Custom Programs • Kari Torson, Director of International Licensing • Sean Brice, Director of Trade Sales

DISNEY PUBLISHING WORLDWIDE GLOBAL MAGAZINES, COMICS AND PARTWORKS

PUBLISHER Lynn Waggoner • EDITORIAL TEAM Bianca Coletti (Director, Magazines), Guido Frazzini (Director, Comics), Carlotta Quattrocolo (Executive Editor), Stefano Ambrosio (Executive Editor, New IP), Camilla Vedove (Senior Manager, Editorial Development), Behnoosh Khalili (Senior Editor), Julie Dorris (Senior Editor), Mina Riazi (Assistant Editor), Gabriella Capasso (Assistant Editor) • DESIGN Enrico Soave (Senior Designer) • ART Ken Shue (VP, Global Art), Manny Mederos (Senior Illustration Manager, Comics and Magazines), Roberto Santillo (Creative Director), Marco Ghiglione (Creative Manager), Stefano Attardi (Illustration Manager) • PORTFOLIO MANAGEMENT Olivia Ciancarelli (Director) • BUSINESS & MARKETING Mariantonietta Galla (Senior Manager, Franchise), Virpi Korhonen (Editorial Manager)

Library of Congress Cataloging-in-Publication Data

Names: Ferrari, Alessandro, 1978- author. | Gula, Ettore, artist.
Title: Toy Story 1-4 : the story of the movies in comics / script
  adaptation, Alessandro Ferrari ; art, Ettore Gula.
Other titles: At head of title: Disney/Pixar
Description: First edition. | Milwaukie, OR : Dark Horse Books, 2019. |
  Audience: Ages 8+ | Summary: The four Toy Story films retold as comics
Identifiers: LCCN 2019027516 | ISBN 9781506717197 (hardcover)
Subjects: LCSH: Graphic novels. | CYAC: Graphic novels. | Toys--Fiction.
Classification: LCC PZ7.7.F46 To 2019 | DDC 741.5/973--dc23
LC record available at https://lccn.loc.gov/2019027516

Published by Dark Horse Books
A division of Dark Horse Comics LLC.
10956 SE Main Street
Milwaukie, OR 97222

DarkHorse.com
To find a comics shop in your area,
visit comicshoplocator.com

First edition: December 2019
ISBN 978-1-50671-719-7
Digital ISBN 978-1-50671-720-3

10 9 8 7 6 5 4 3 2 1
Printed in China

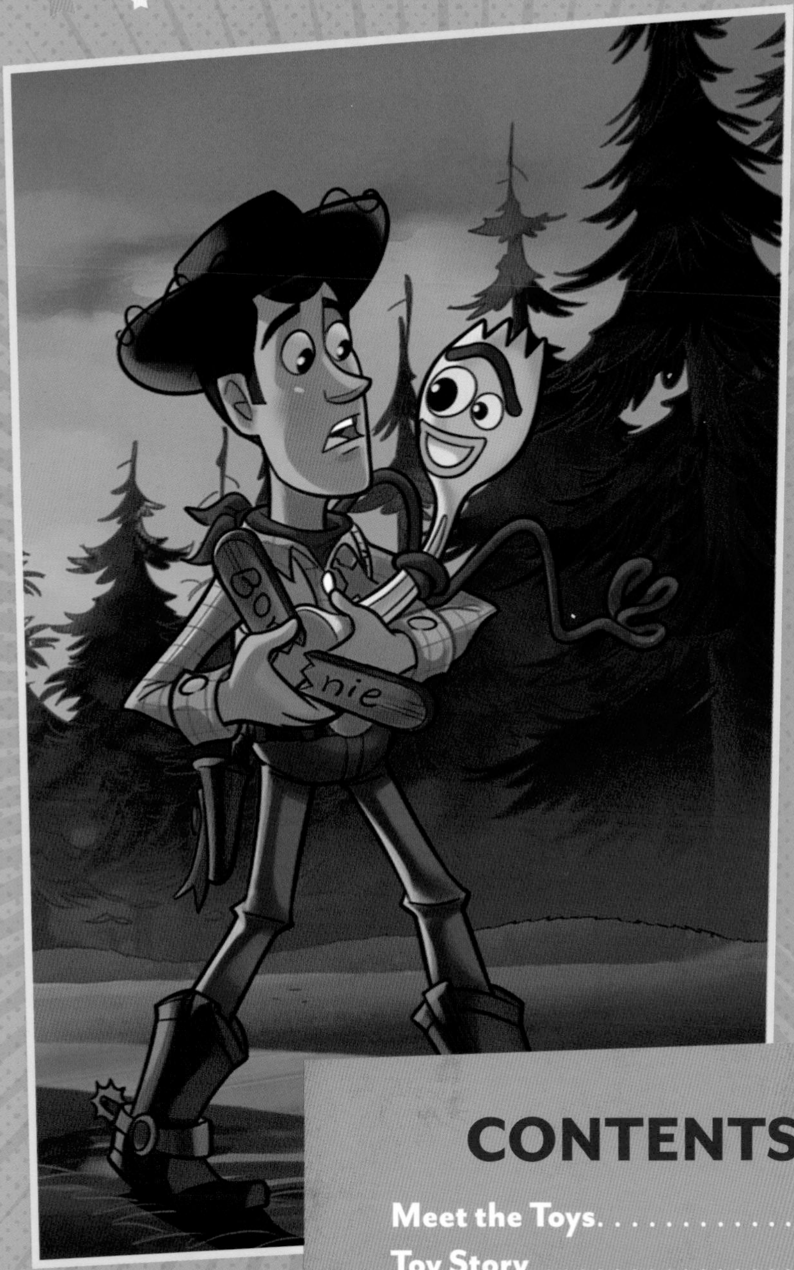

CONTENTS

Meet the TOYS

WOODY

A loyal and fearless cowboy, **Woody** used to play with his kid **Andy** for hours every day. He was his favorite toy. Though Woody didn't want that to change, Andy eventually grew up and handed down his toys to **Bonnie**, a sweet five-year-old girl. Bonnie has an active imagination and loves to play with both her old and new toys, taking them everywhere. But Bonnie doesn't like Woody the same way Andy did, and the cowboy struggles to find his place in the new room.

BUZZ LIGHTYEAR

Brave and heroic, **Buzz Lightyear** is an action figure who once believed he was a real space ranger. When Buzz first arrived in Andy's room, Woody was his biggest rival. The cowboy feared that with Buzz in the picture, Andy would forget about him. He was wrong. Eventually, the two toys became best friends. Buzz knows that Woody feels neglected by Bonnie, but he doesn't know how to help him.

Bo Peep

Bo is a porcelain figurine who was made to sit in the base of a children's lamp, along with her sheep **Billy**, **Goat**, and **Gruff**. She used to belong to Andy's little sister, **Molly**, before she was given away. Bo later ended up in an antique store, where she sat on a shelf for years. Now she travels from playground to playground as a lost toy, enjoying a life full of adventure. Though being a lost toy is Woody's worst nightmare, Bo likes that she always has new kids to play with.

ANDY'S TOYS

Jessie the cowgirl, **Bullseye** the horse, **Rex** the T. rex, **Hamm** the piggy bank, **Slinky Dog**, and the three **aliens** once belonged to Andy. Now they belong to Bonnie, but they will always consider Woody their leader.

BONNIE'S TOYS

Led by **Dolly** the rag doll, Bonnie's toys include **Trixie** the triceratops, **Buttercup** the unicorn, and **Mr. Pricklepants** the hedgehog. They gave Andy's old toys a warm welcome, and together formed an even bigger family.

New FRIENDS

FORKY

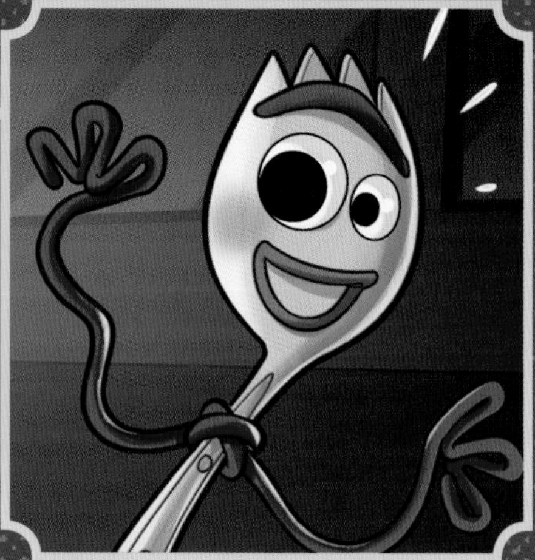

Forky has trouble accepting he's a toy. In fact, he thinks he's trash—maybe because Bonnie created him using a spork and craft supplies. But to Bonnie, Forky is not trash at all. She sees him as the best kind of toy: a friend who helped her get through kindergarten orientation. Forky needs the help of a more experienced toy to understand how important he is to Bonnie.

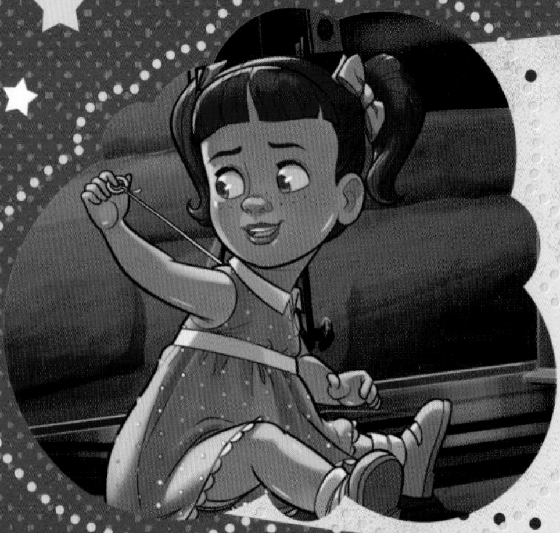

GABBY GABBY

Being there for a child is the most noble thing a toy can do. But **Gabby Gabby**, a doll from the 1950s, doesn't know what that means. Displayed in a glass cabinet inside the antique store, Gabby Gabby's only companions are mute ventriloquist dummies. With a broken voice box, Gabby Gabby has never belonged to a kid. She dreams of being loved by a child every time she sees Harmony, the store owner's granddaughter.

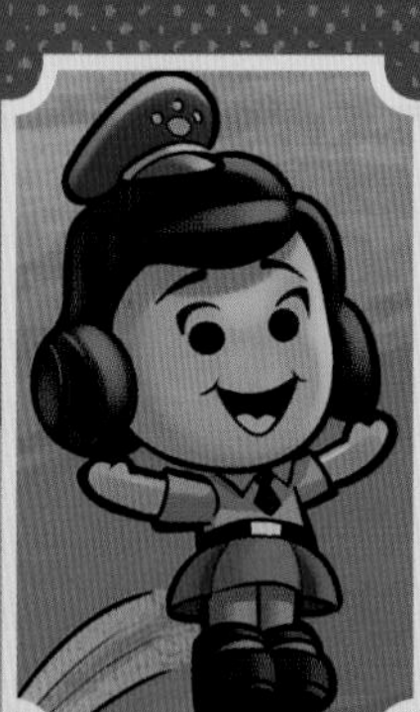

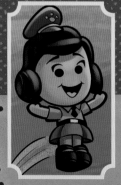

GIGGLE McDIMPLES

Pet Patrol Officer **Giggle McDimples** is a lost toy, and she loves it. Since leaving the antique store, Giggle has become Bo's closest confidant and companion. And yet, she doesn't know all the details of Bo's life with Woody and Molly.

DUKE CABOOM

A toy version of Canada's daredevil celebrity, Duke lives in the antique store but stays away from Gabby Gabby and the humans. He prefers to spend his days with other toys inside a vintage pinball machine. A proud stuntman, Duke has never gotten over the loss of his kid, Rejean, who gave him away.

DUCKY and BUNNY

Ducky and Bunny have been carnival prizes for three years, hanging from the prize wall of a game booth and waiting for a kid to win them. Connected at the hand, Ducky and Bunny are full of personality—and jokes—and will do anything to belong to a kid.

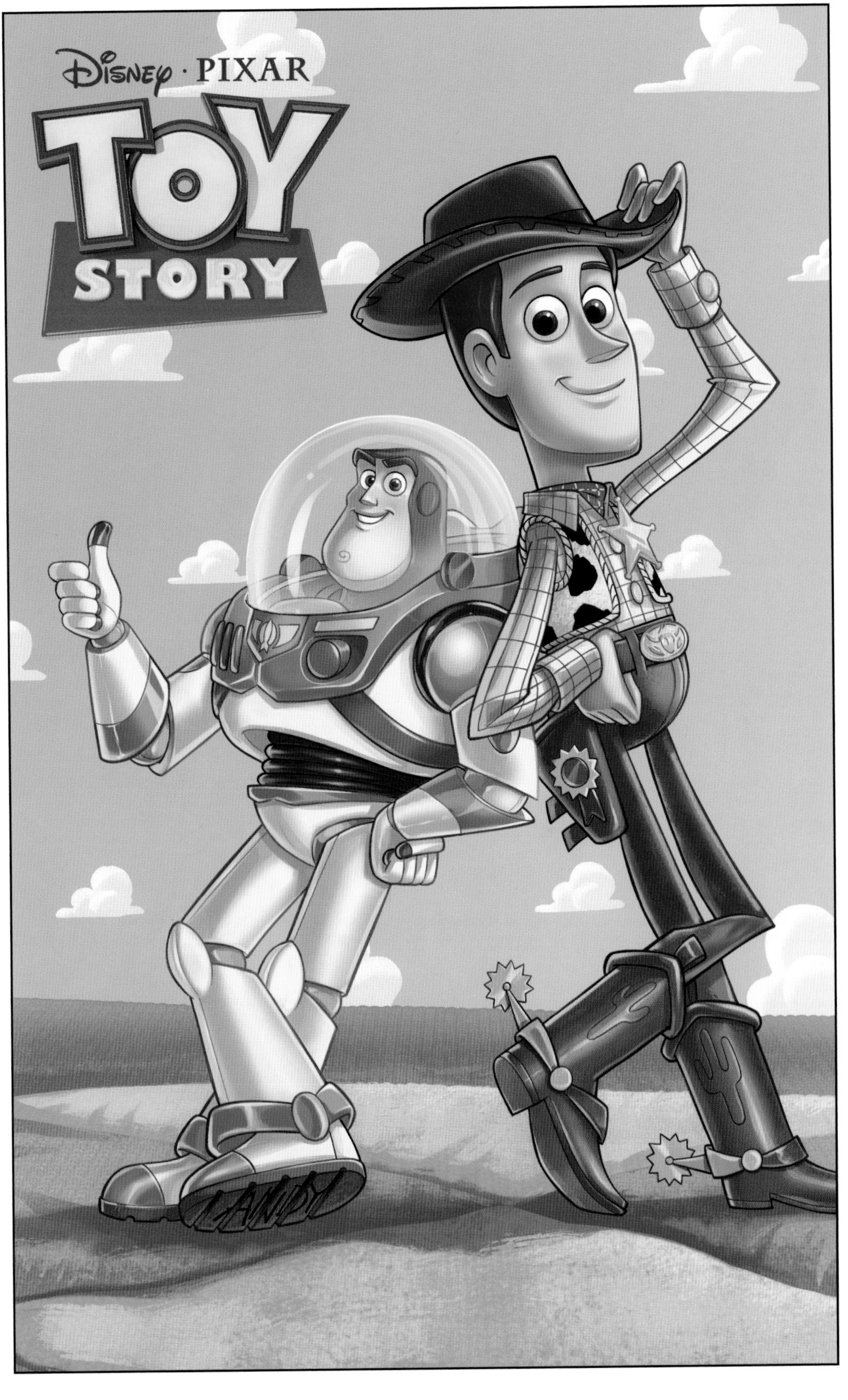
Disney · PIXAR
TOY STORY
ANDY

script adaptation
Alessandro Ferrari

art
Ettore Gula

paint
Kawaii Creative Studio
Lucio De Giuseppe
Maurizio De Bellis

art optimization
Stefano Attardi

editing
Kawaii Creative Studio

contributor
Elisabetta Sedda

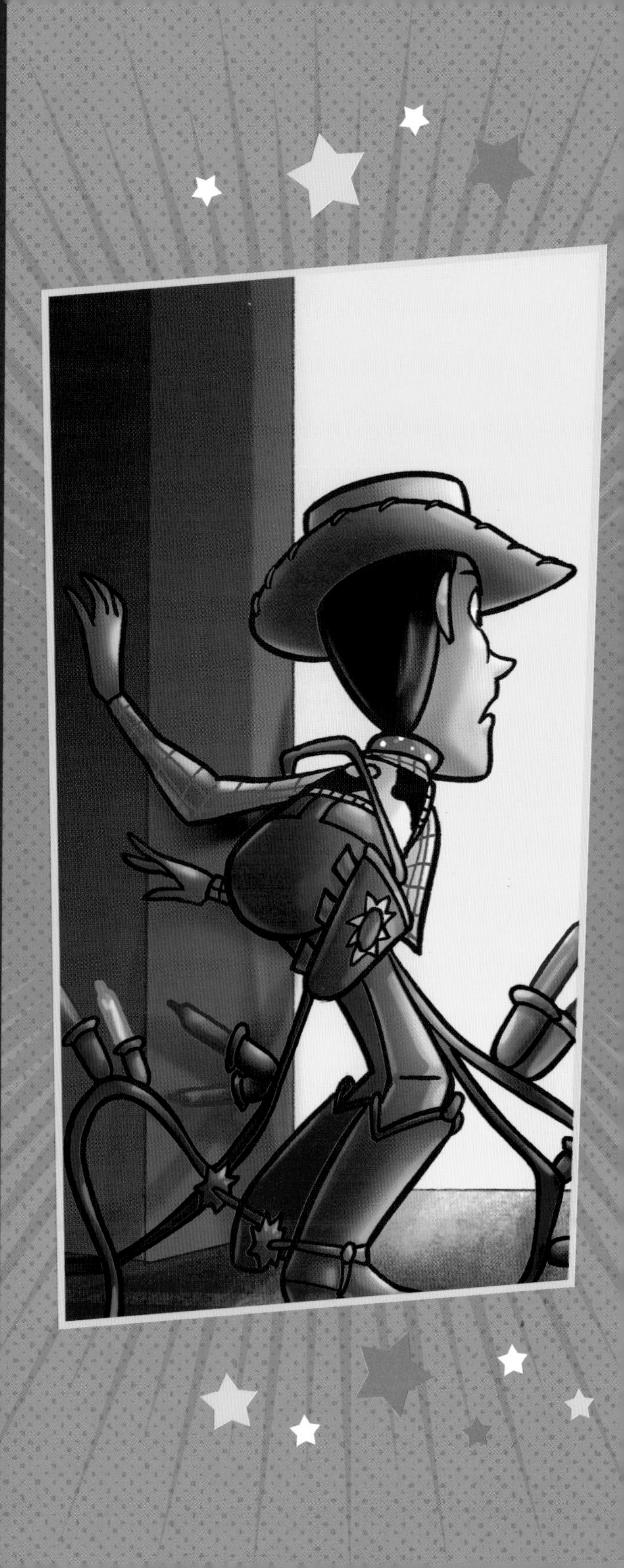

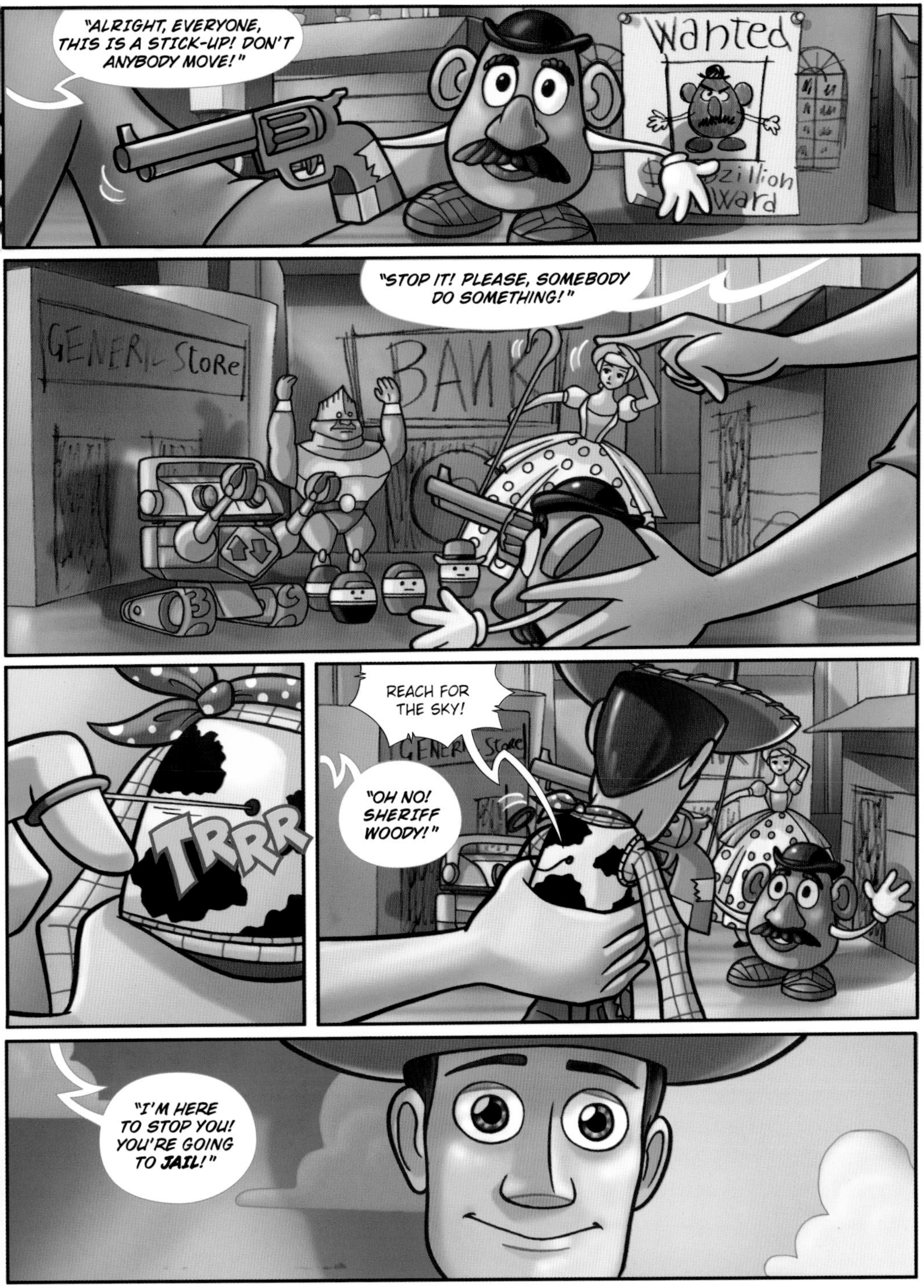
"ALRIGHT, EVERYONE, THIS IS A STICK-UP! DON'T ANYBODY MOVE!"
Wanted
zillion
ward
"STOP IT! PLEASE, SOMEBODY DO SOMETHING!"
GENERAL Store
BANK
TRRR
REACH FOR THE SKY!
"OH NO! SHERIFF WOODY!"
"I'M HERE TO STOP YOU! YOU'RE GOING TO JAIL!"

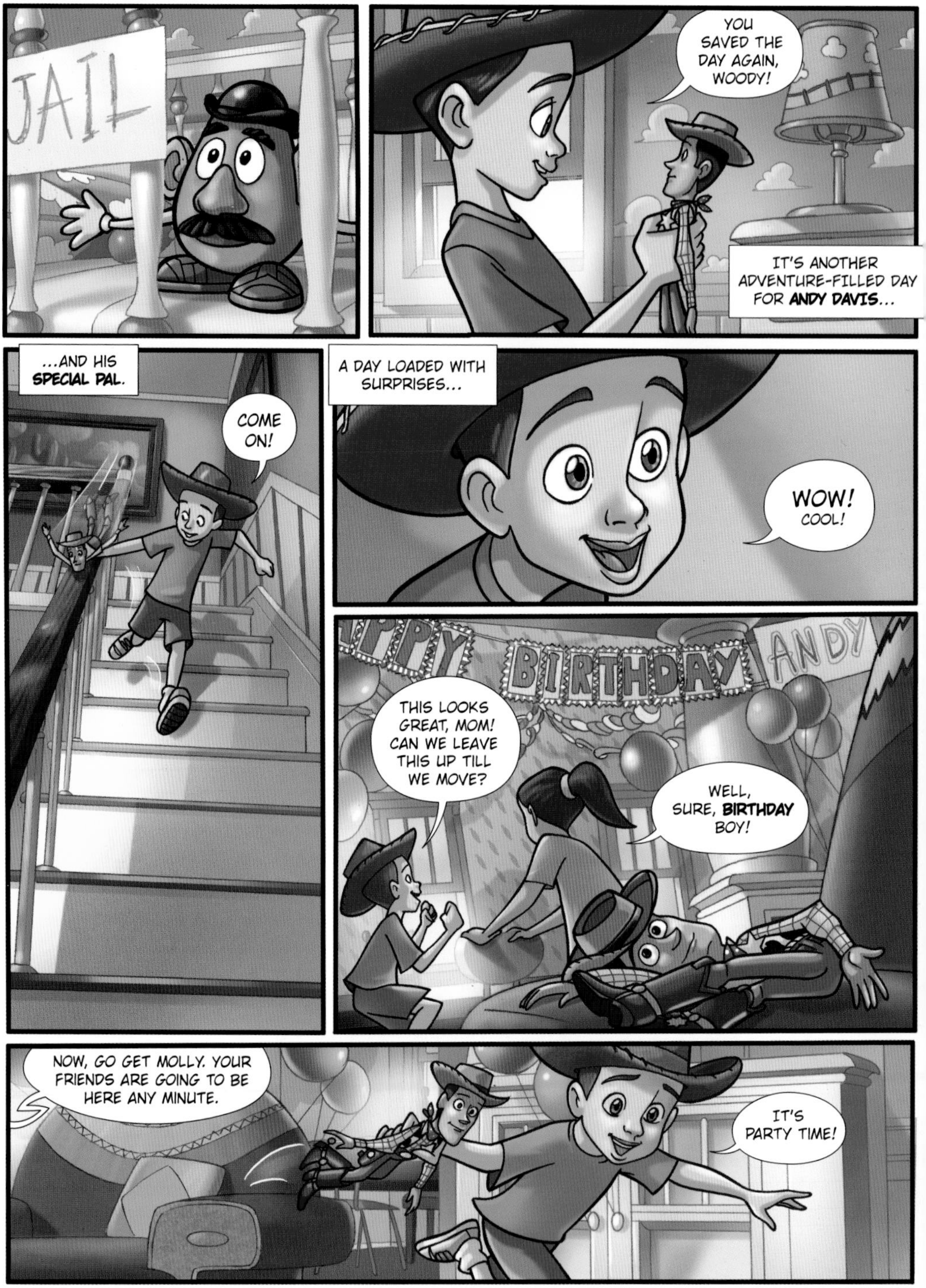
JAIL
YOU SAVED THE DAY AGAIN, WOODY!
IT'S ANOTHER ADVENTURE-FILLED DAY FOR **ANDY DAVIS**...
...AND HIS **SPECIAL PAL**.
COME ON!
A DAY LOADED WITH SURPRISES...
WOW! COOL!
BIRTHDAY
ANDY
THIS LOOKS GREAT, MOM! CAN WE LEAVE THIS UP TILL WE MOVE?
WELL, SURE, **BIRTHDAY** BOY!
NOW, GO GET MOLLY. YOUR FRIENDS ARE GOING TO BE HERE ANY MINUTE.
IT'S PARTY TIME!

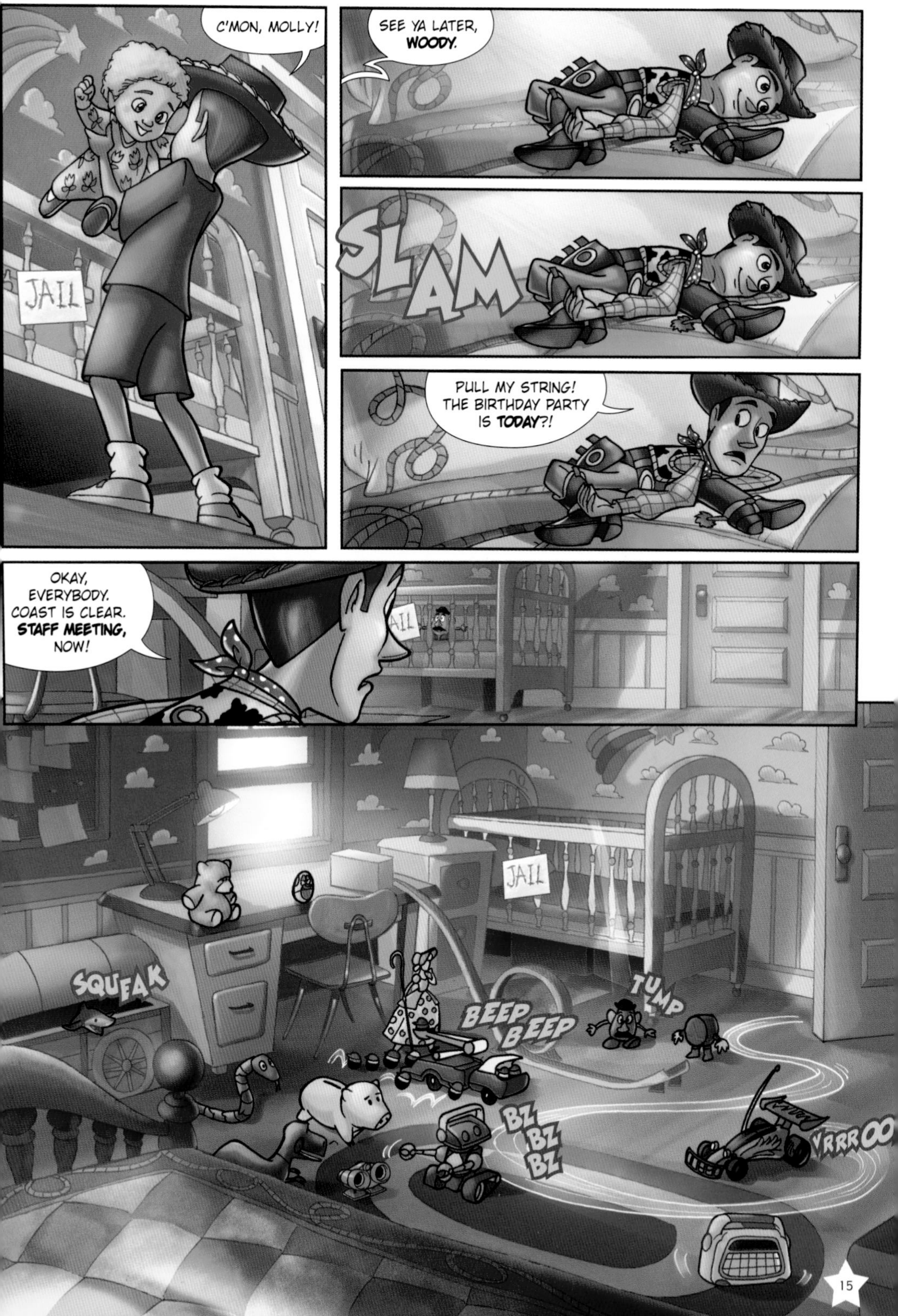

C'MON, MOLLY!
JAIL
SEE YA LATER, WOODY.
SLAM
PULL MY STRING! THE BIRTHDAY PARTY IS TODAY?!
OKAY, EVERYBODY. COAST IS CLEAR. STAFF MEETING, NOW!
JAIL
JAIL
SQUEAK
BEEP BEEP
TUMP
BZ BZ BZ
VRRROO

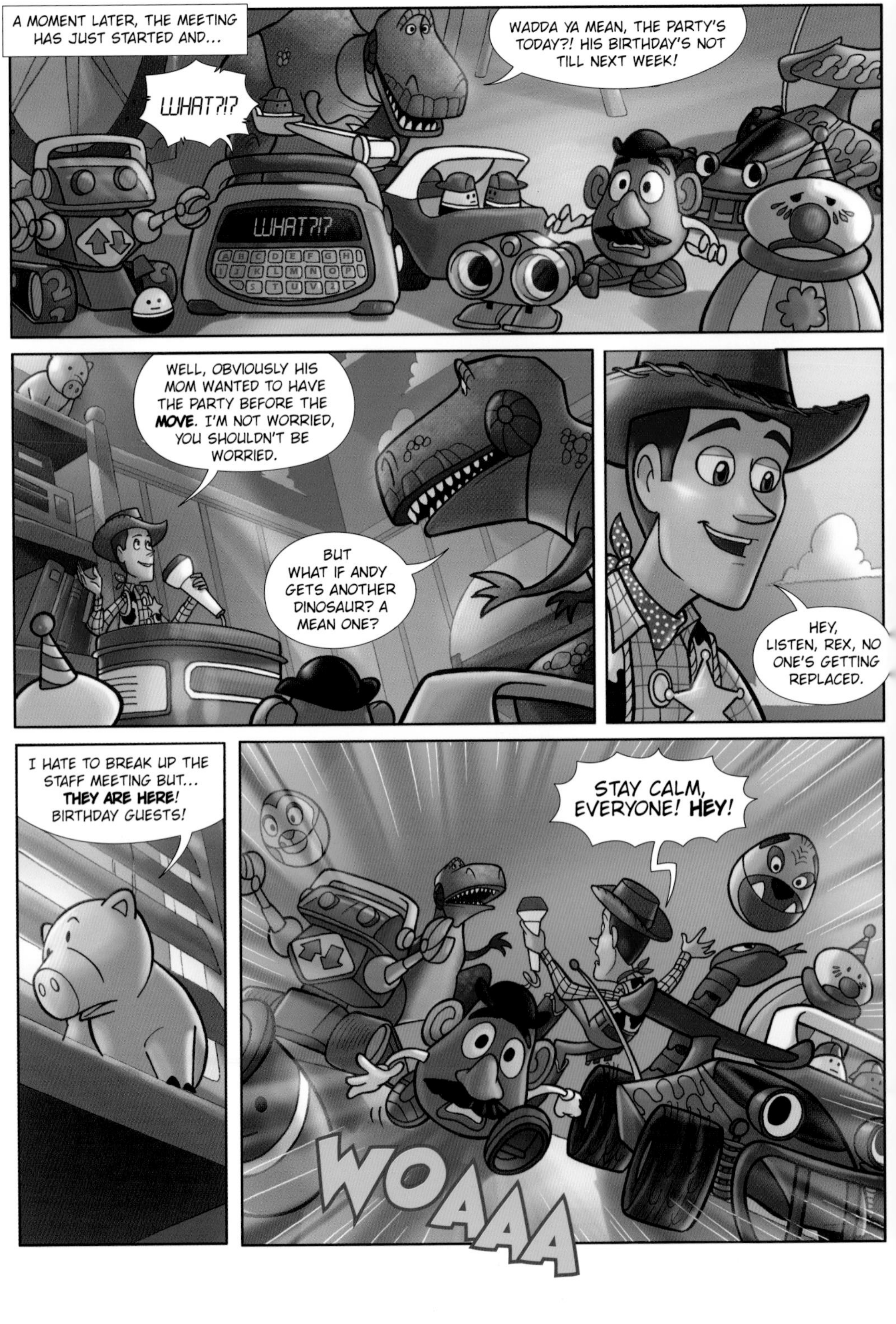
A MOMENT LATER, THE MEETING HAS JUST STARTED AND...
WHAT?!?
WHAT?!?
WADDA YA MEAN, THE PARTY'S TODAY?! HIS BIRTHDAY'S NOT TILL NEXT WEEK!
WELL, OBVIOUSLY HIS MOM WANTED TO HAVE THE PARTY BEFORE THE **MOVE**. I'M NOT WORRIED, YOU SHOULDN'T BE WORRIED.
BUT WHAT IF ANDY GETS ANOTHER DINOSAUR? A MEAN ONE?
HEY, LISTEN, REX, NO ONE'S GETTING REPLACED.
I HATE TO BREAK UP THE STAFF MEETING BUT... **THEY ARE HERE**! BIRTHDAY GUESTS!
STAY CALM, EVERYONE! **HEY**!
WOAAA

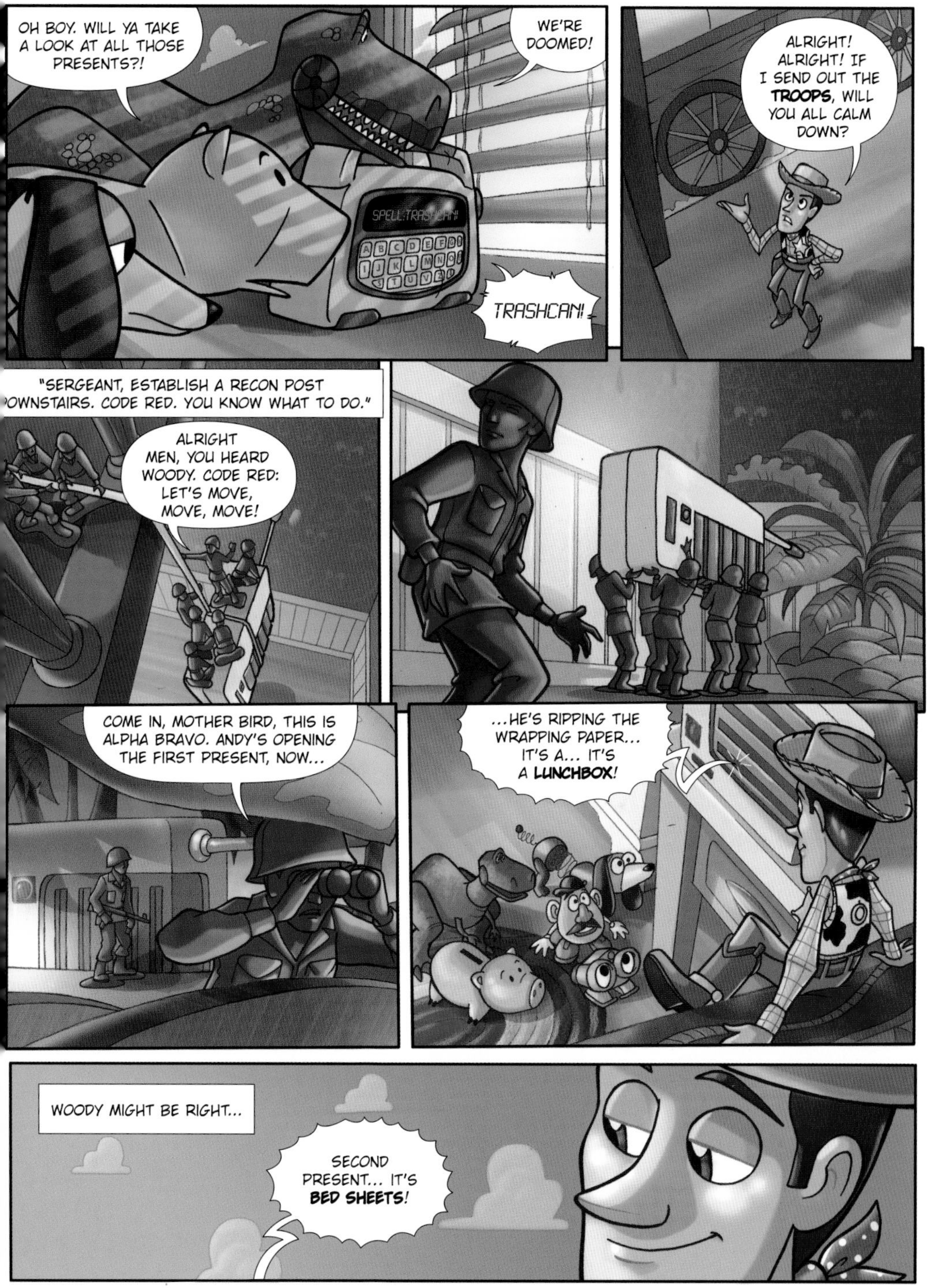
OH BOY. WILL YA TAKE A LOOK AT ALL THOSE PRESENTS?!
WE'RE DOOMED!
SPELL: TRASHCAN
TRASHCAN!
ALRIGHT! ALRIGHT! IF I SEND OUT THE **TROOPS**, WILL YOU ALL CALM DOWN?
"SERGEANT, ESTABLISH A RECON POST DOWNSTAIRS. CODE RED. YOU KNOW WHAT TO DO."
ALRIGHT MEN, YOU HEARD WOODY. CODE RED: LET'S MOVE, MOVE, MOVE!
COME IN, MOTHER BIRD, THIS IS ALPHA BRAVO. ANDY'S OPENING THE FIRST PRESENT, NOW...
...HE'S RIPPING THE WRAPPING PAPER... IT'S A... IT'S A **LUNCHBOX**!
WOODY MIGHT BE RIGHT...
SECOND PRESENT... IT'S **BED SHEETS**!

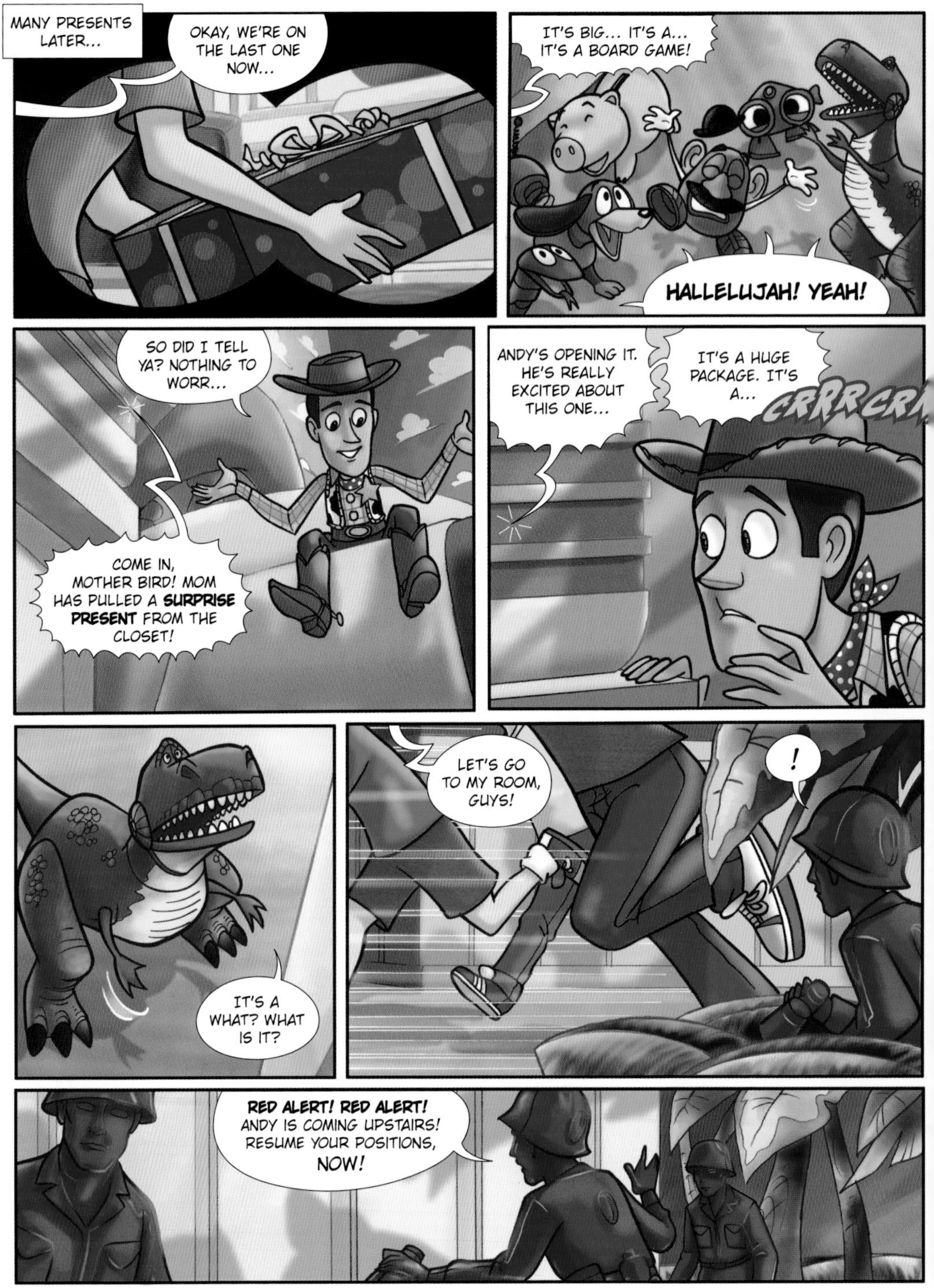
MANY PRESENTS LATER...
OKAY, WE'RE ON THE LAST ONE NOW...
IT'S BIG... IT'S A... IT'S A BOARD GAME!
HALLELUJAH! YEAH!
SO DID I TELL YA? NOTHING TO WORR...
COME IN, MOTHER BIRD! MOM HAS PULLED A **SURPRISE PRESENT** FROM THE CLOSET!
ANDY'S OPENING IT. HE'S REALLY EXCITED ABOUT THIS ONE...
IT'S A HUGE PACKAGE. IT'S A...
CRRRCRR
IT'S A WHAT? WHAT IS IT?
LET'S GO TO MY ROOM, GUYS!
!
RED ALERT! RED ALERT! ANDY IS COMING UPSTAIRS! RESUME YOUR POSITIONS, NOW!

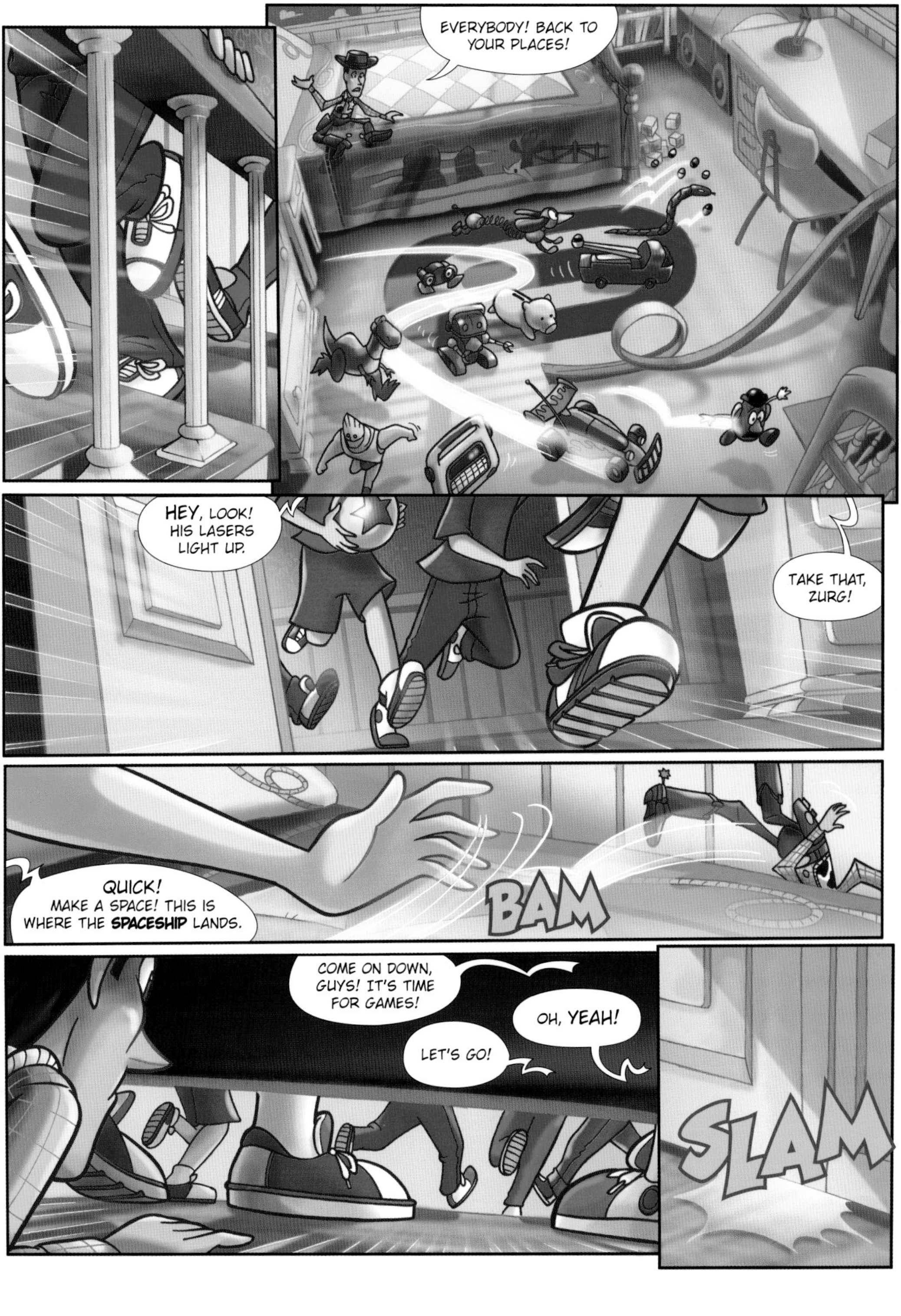
EVERYBODY! BACK TO YOUR PLACES!
HEY, LOOK! HIS LASERS LIGHT UP.
TAKE THAT, ZURG!
QUICK! MAKE A SPACE! THIS IS WHERE THE SPACESHIP LANDS.
BAM
COME ON DOWN, GUYS! IT'S TIME FOR GAMES!
OH, YEAH!
LET'S GO!
SLAM

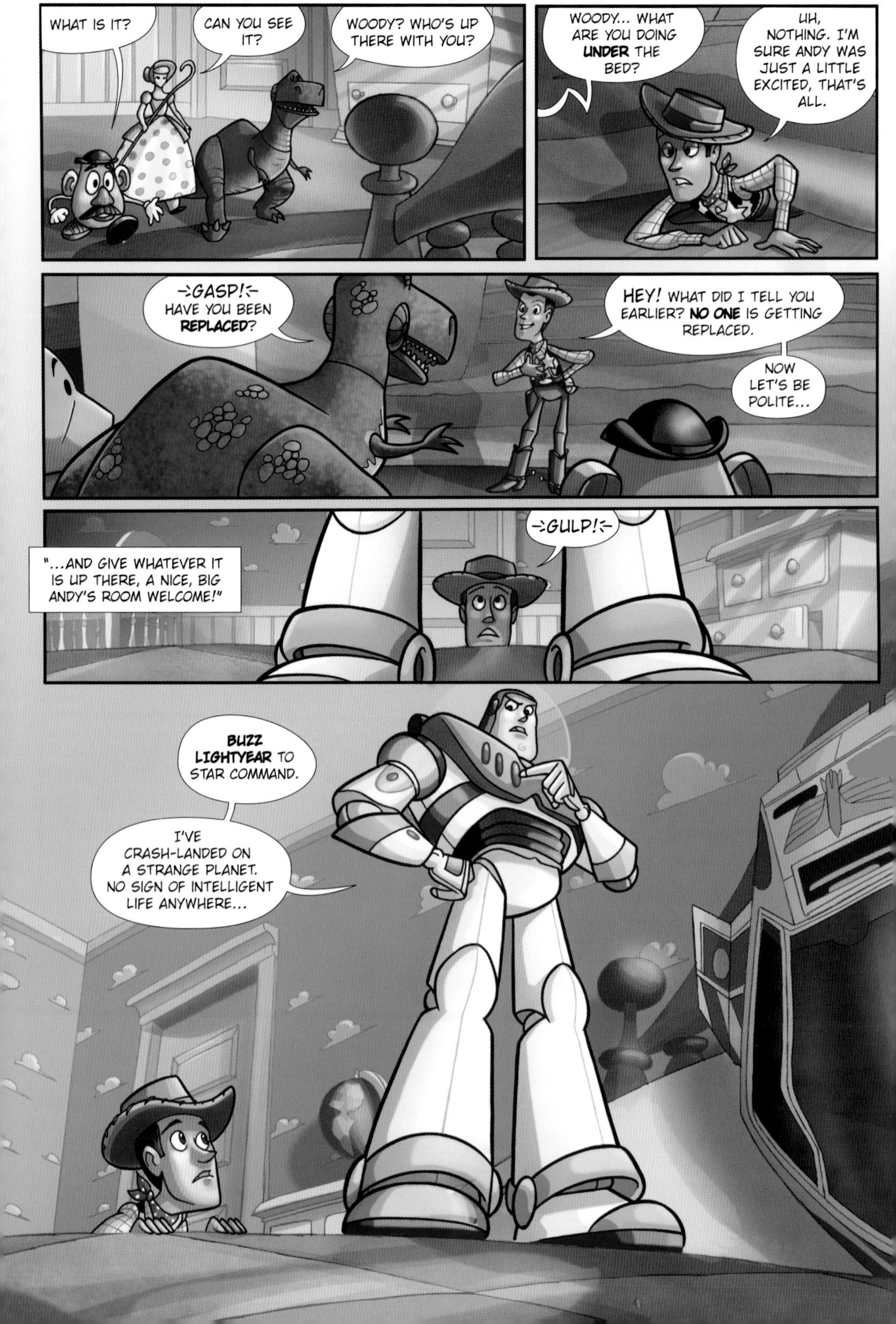
WHAT IS IT?
CAN YOU SEE IT?
WOODY? WHO'S UP THERE WITH YOU?
WOODY... WHAT ARE YOU DOING **UNDER** THE BED?
UH, NOTHING. I'M SURE ANDY WAS JUST A LITTLE EXCITED, THAT'S ALL.
-GASP!- HAVE YOU BEEN **REPLACED**?
HEY! WHAT DID I TELL YOU EARLIER? **NO ONE** IS GETTING REPLACED.
NOW LET'S BE POLITE...
"...AND GIVE WHATEVER IT IS UP THERE, A NICE, BIG ANDY'S ROOM WELCOME!"
-GULP!-
BUZZ LIGHTYEAR TO STAR COMMAND.
I'VE CRASH-LANDED ON A STRANGE PLANET. NO SIGN OF INTELLIGENT LIFE ANYWHERE...

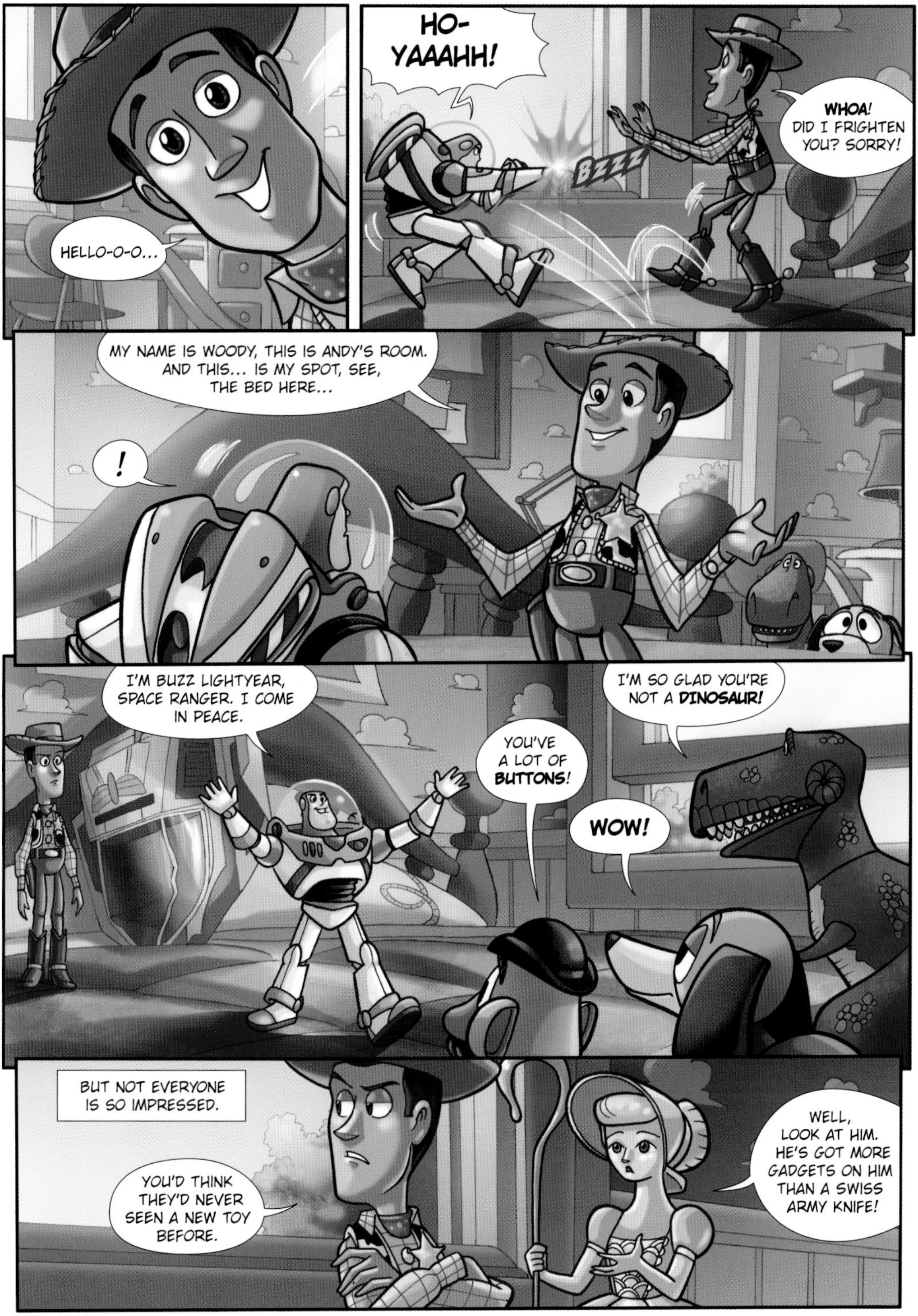
HELLO-O-O...
HO-YAAAHH!
BZZZ
WHOA! DID I FRIGHTEN YOU? SORRY!
MY NAME IS WOODY, THIS IS ANDY'S ROOM. AND THIS... IS MY SPOT, SEE, THE BED HERE...
!
I'M BUZZ LIGHTYEAR, SPACE RANGER. I COME IN PEACE.
YOU'VE A LOT OF BUTTONS!
I'M SO GLAD YOU'RE NOT A DINOSAUR!
WOW!
BUT NOT EVERYONE IS SO IMPRESSED.
YOU'D THINK THEY'D NEVER SEEN A NEW TOY BEFORE.
WELL, LOOK AT HIM. HE'S GOT MORE GADGETS ON HIM THAN A SWISS ARMY KNIFE!

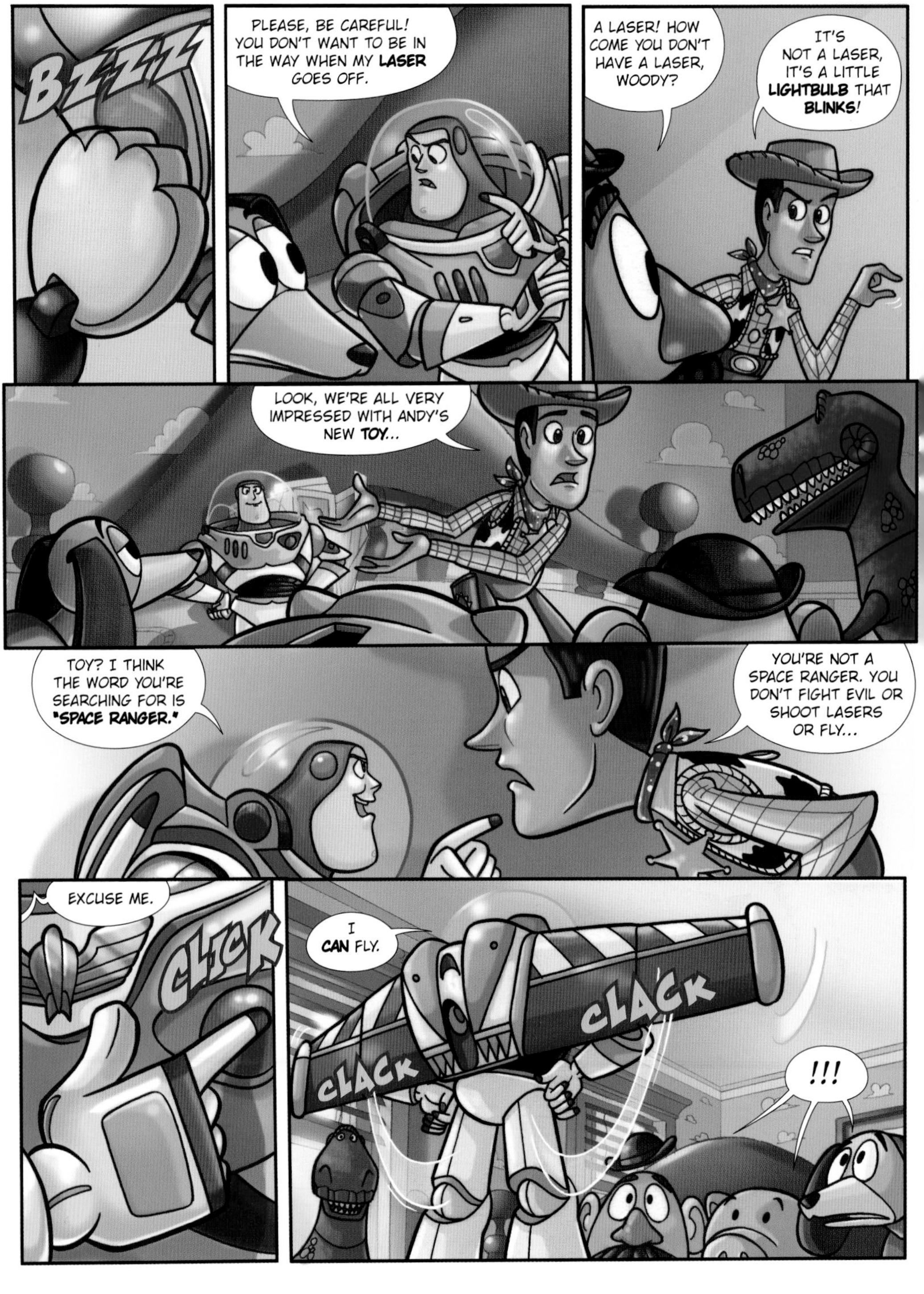
BZZZZ
PLEASE, BE CAREFUL! YOU DON'T WANT TO BE IN THE WAY WHEN MY LASER GOES OFF.
A LASER! HOW COME YOU DON'T HAVE A LASER, WOODY?
IT'S NOT A LASER, IT'S A LITTLE LIGHTBULB THAT BLINKS!
LOOK, WE'RE ALL VERY IMPRESSED WITH ANDY'S NEW TOY...
TOY? I THINK THE WORD YOU'RE SEARCHING FOR IS "SPACE RANGER."
YOU'RE NOT A SPACE RANGER. YOU DON'T FIGHT EVIL OR SHOOT LASERS OR FLY...
EXCUSE ME.
CLICK
I CAN FLY.
CLACK
CLACK
!!!

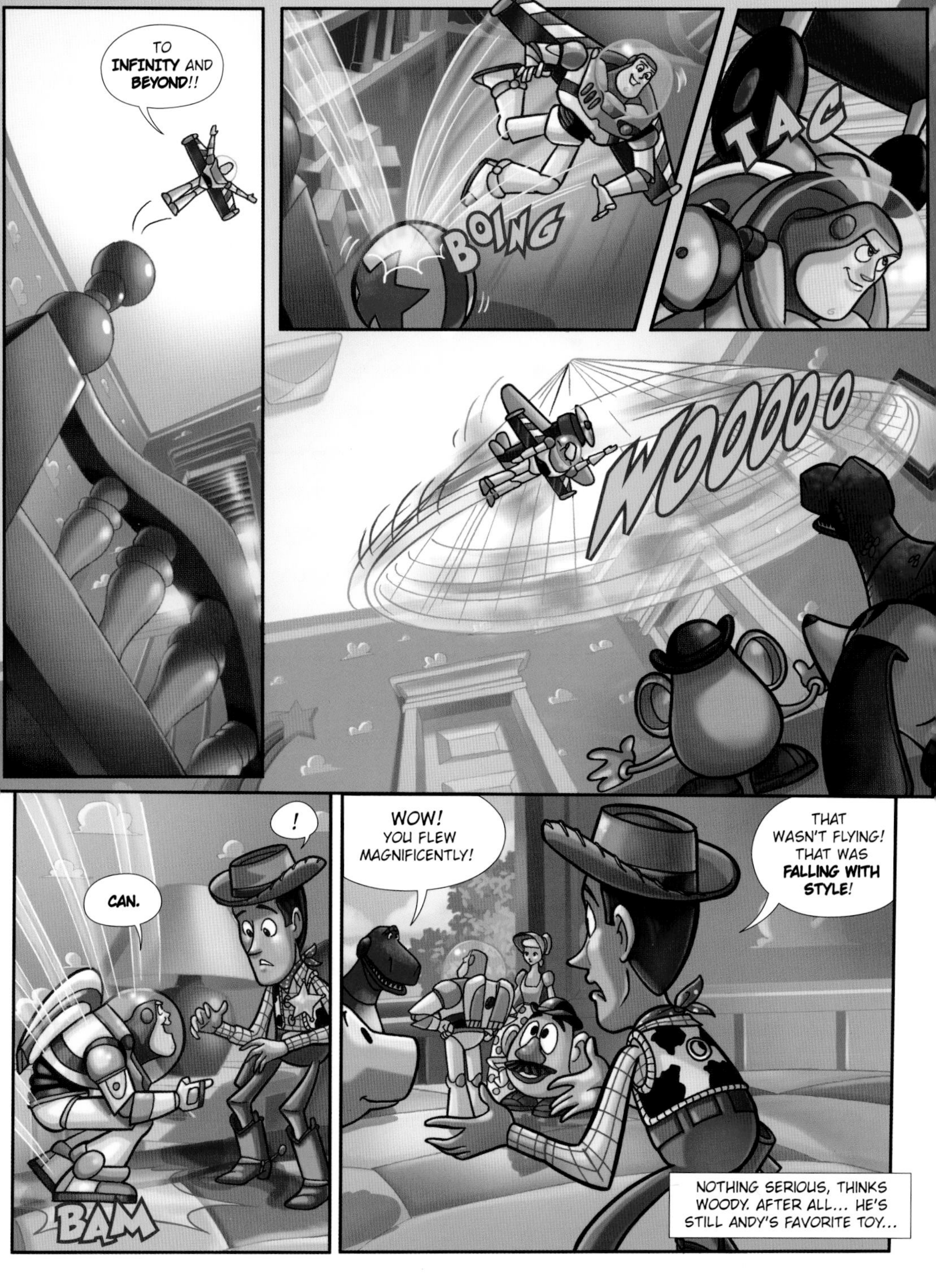
TO INFINITY AND BEYOND!!
BOING
TAC
WOOOOO
CAN.
!
BAM
WOW! YOU FLEW MAGNIFICENTLY!
THAT WASN'T FLYING! THAT WAS FALLING WITH STYLE!
NOTHING SERIOUS, THINKS WOODY. AFTER ALL... HE'S STILL ANDY'S FAVORITE TOY...

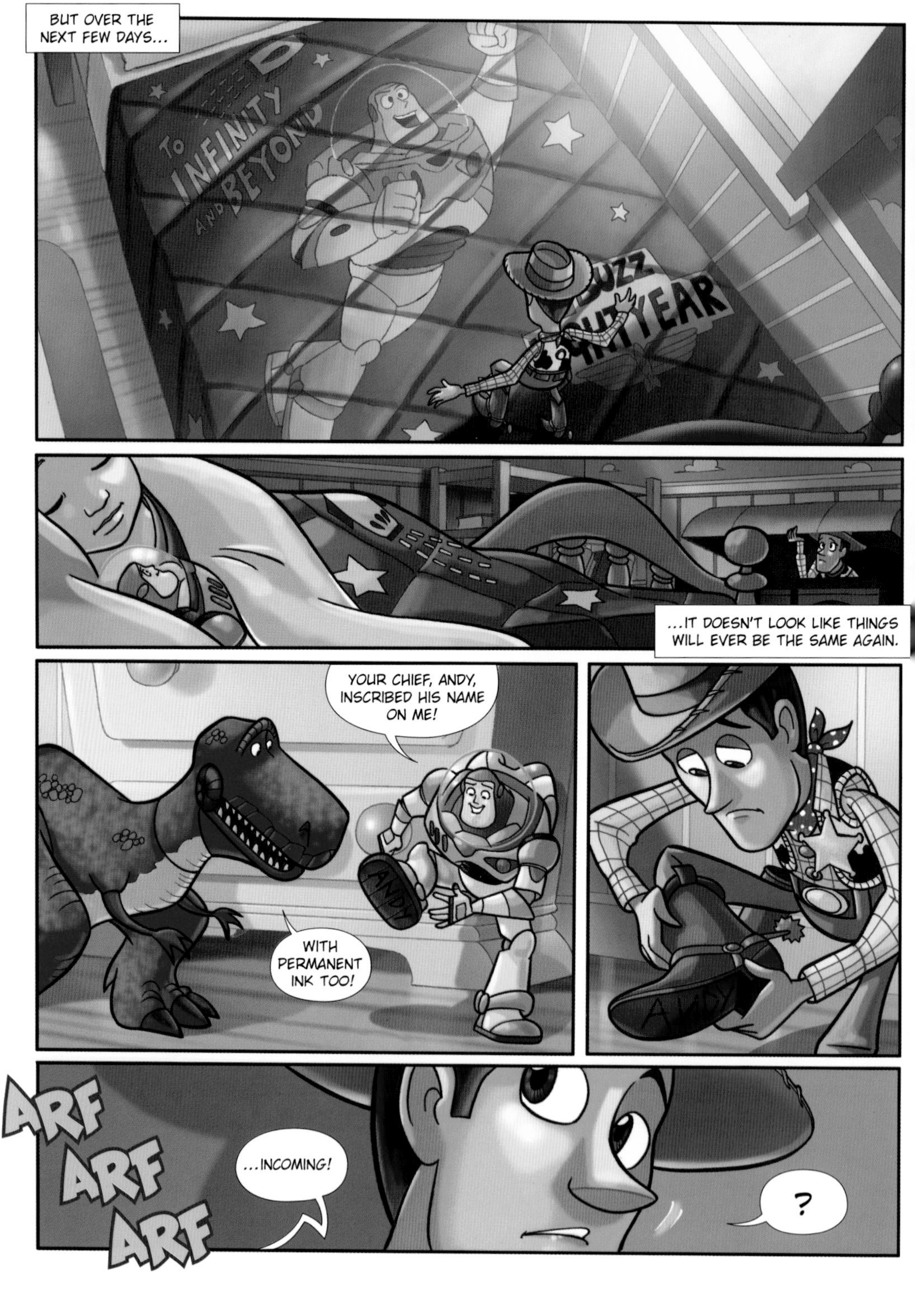
BUT OVER THE NEXT FEW DAYS...
TO INFINITY AND BEYOND
...IT DOESN'T LOOK LIKE THINGS WILL EVER BE THE SAME AGAIN.
YOUR CHIEF, ANDY, INSCRIBED HIS NAME ON ME!
WITH PERMANENT INK TOO!
ANDY
ARF ARF ARF
...INCOMING!
?

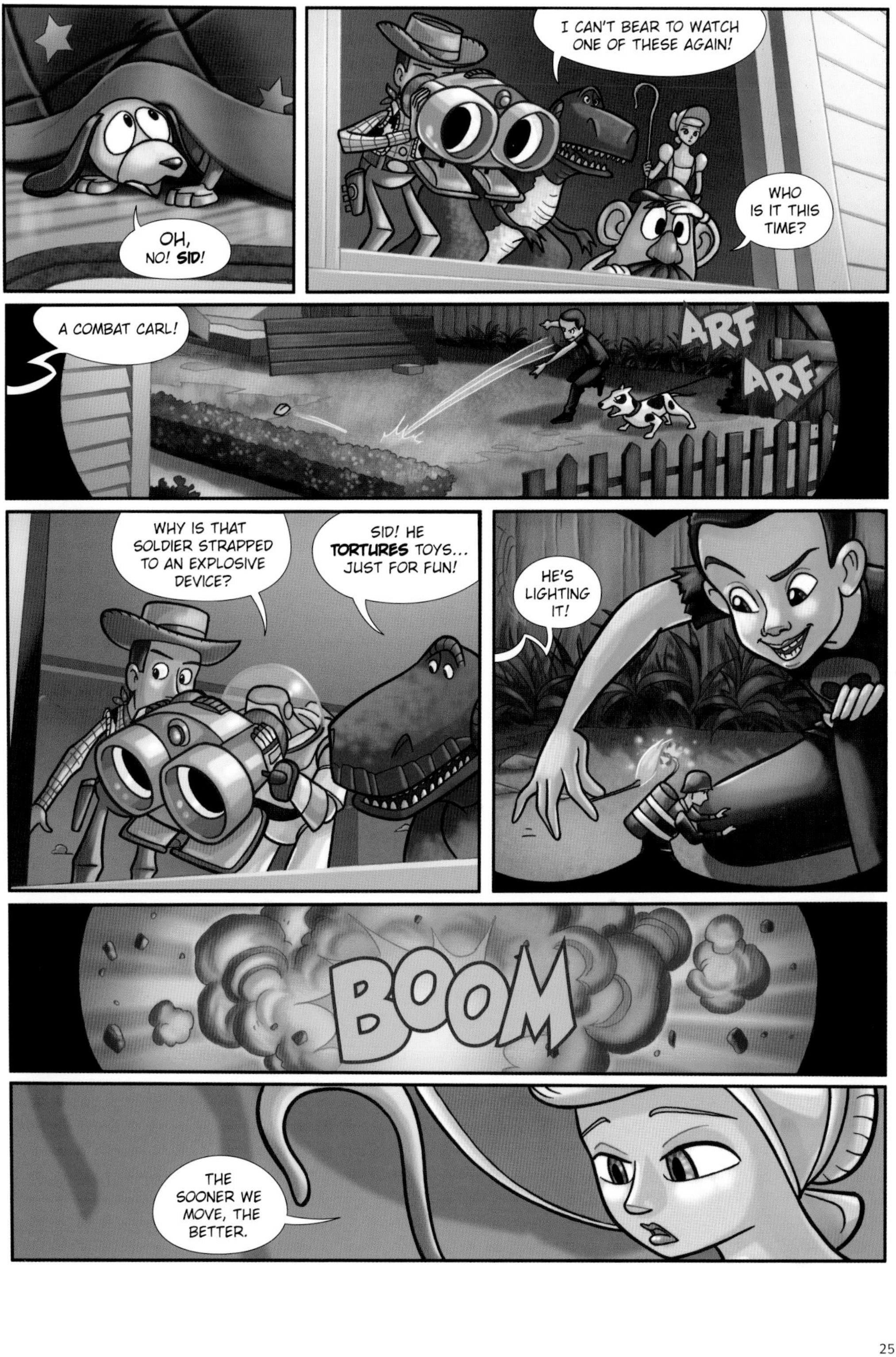
OH, NO! SID!
I CAN'T BEAR TO WATCH ONE OF THESE AGAIN!
WHO IS IT THIS TIME?
A COMBAT CARL!
ARF
ARF
WHY IS THAT SOLDIER STRAPPED TO AN EXPLOSIVE DEVICE?
SID! HE TORTURES TOYS... JUST FOR FUN!
HE'S LIGHTING IT!
BOOM
THE SOONER WE MOVE, THE BETTER.

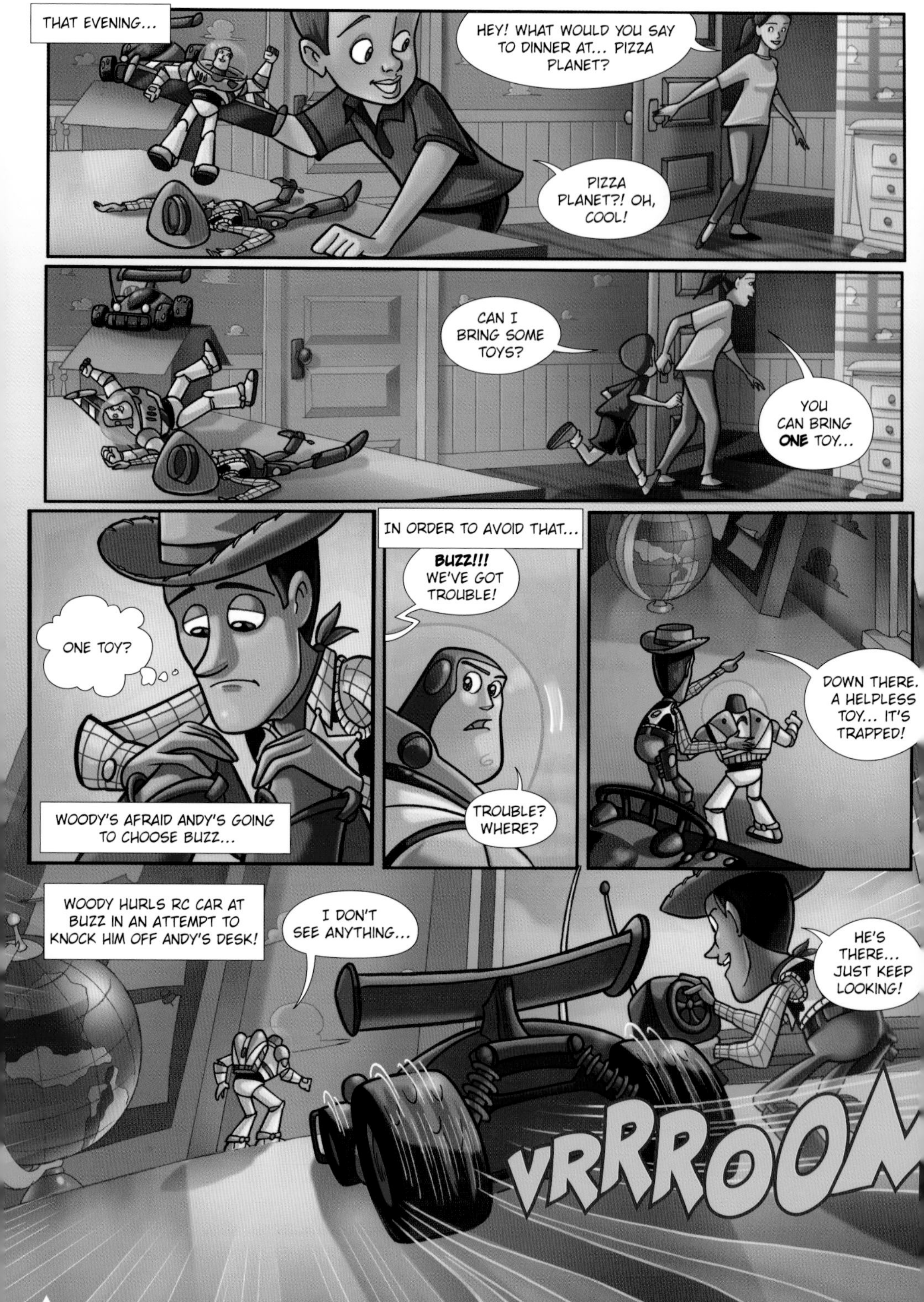
THAT EVENING...
HEY! WHAT WOULD YOU SAY TO DINNER AT... PIZZA PLANET?
PIZZA PLANET?! OH, COOL!
CAN I BRING SOME TOYS?
YOU CAN BRING **ONE** TOY...
ONE TOY?
WOODY'S AFRAID ANDY'S GOING TO CHOOSE BUZZ...
IN ORDER TO AVOID THAT...
BUZZ!!! WE'VE GOT TROUBLE!
TROUBLE? WHERE?
DOWN THERE. A HELPLESS TOY... IT'S TRAPPED!
WOODY HURLS RC CAR AT BUZZ IN AN ATTEMPT TO KNOCK HIM OFF ANDY'S DESK!
I DON'T SEE ANYTHING...
HE'S THERE... JUST KEEP LOOKING!
VRRROOM

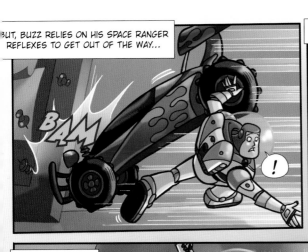

BUT, BUZZ RELIES ON HIS SPACE RANGER REFLEXES TO GET OUT OF THE WAY...

BAM

!

...AND CAUSES AN OUTRAGEOUS...

BUMP

WHOA!

...UNSTOPPABLE...

KRRR

KRRRR RR

TACK

...CHAIN REACTION!

POW

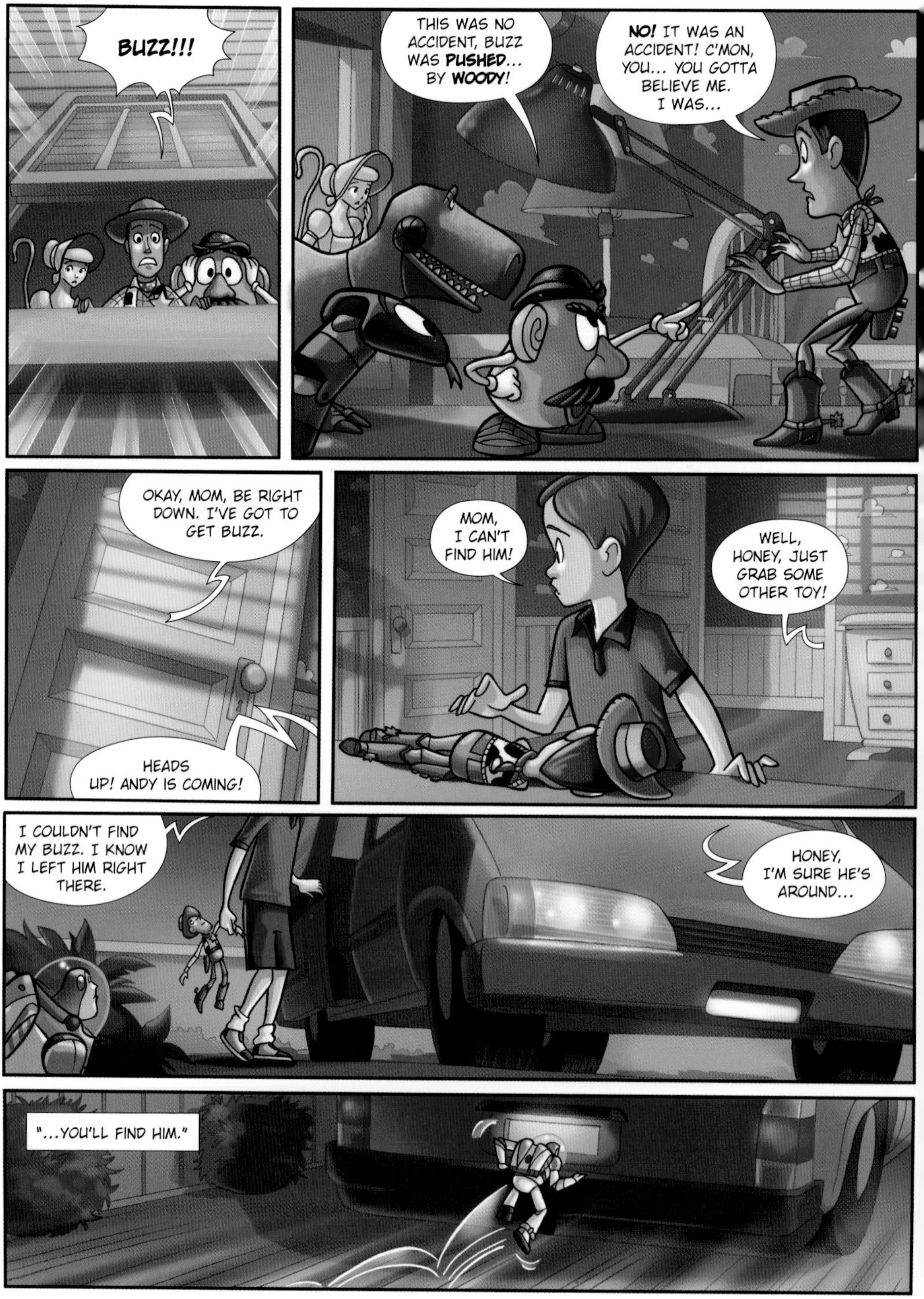
BUZZ!!!
THIS WAS NO ACCIDENT, BUZZ WAS PUSHED... BY WOODY!
NO! IT WAS AN ACCIDENT! C'MON, YOU... YOU GOTTA BELIEVE ME. I WAS...
OKAY, MOM, BE RIGHT DOWN. I'VE GOT TO GET BUZZ.
HEADS UP! ANDY IS COMING!
MOM, I CAN'T FIND HIM!
WELL, HONEY, JUST GRAB SOME OTHER TOY!
I COULDN'T FIND MY BUZZ. I KNOW I LEFT HIM RIGHT THERE.
HONEY, I'M SURE HE'S AROUND...
"...YOU'LL FIND HIM."

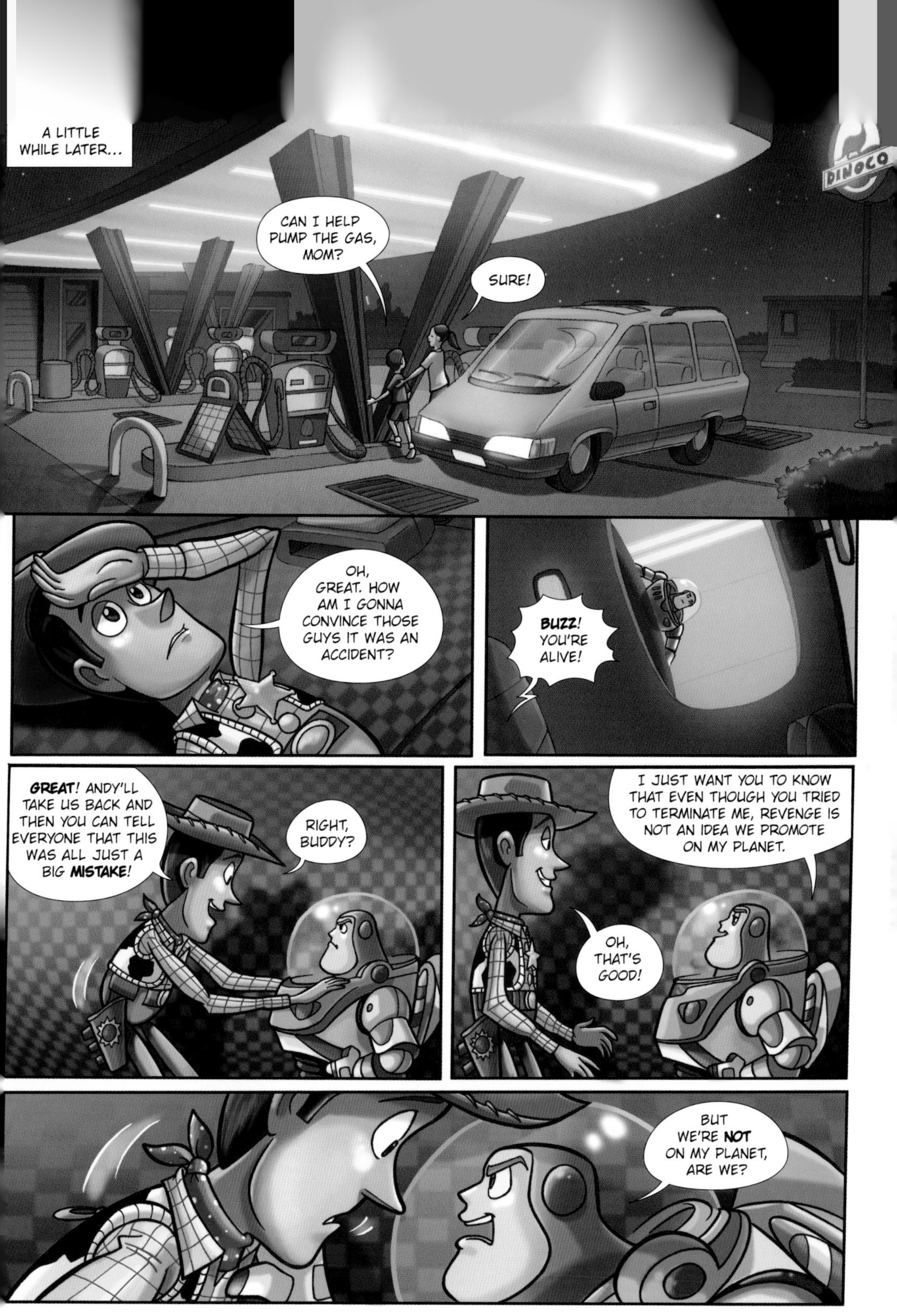
A LITTLE WHILE LATER...
DINOCO
CAN I HELP PUMP THE GAS, MOM?
SURE!
OH, GREAT. HOW AM I GONNA CONVINCE THOSE GUYS IT WAS AN ACCIDENT?
BUZZ! YOU'RE ALIVE!
GREAT! ANDY'LL TAKE US BACK AND THEN YOU CAN TELL EVERYONE THAT THIS WAS ALL JUST A BIG MISTAKE!
RIGHT, BUDDY?
I JUST WANT YOU TO KNOW THAT EVEN THOUGH YOU TRIED TO TERMINATE ME, REVENGE IS NOT AN IDEA WE PROMOTE ON MY PLANET.
OH, THAT'S GOOD!
BUT WE'RE NOT ON MY PLANET, ARE WE?

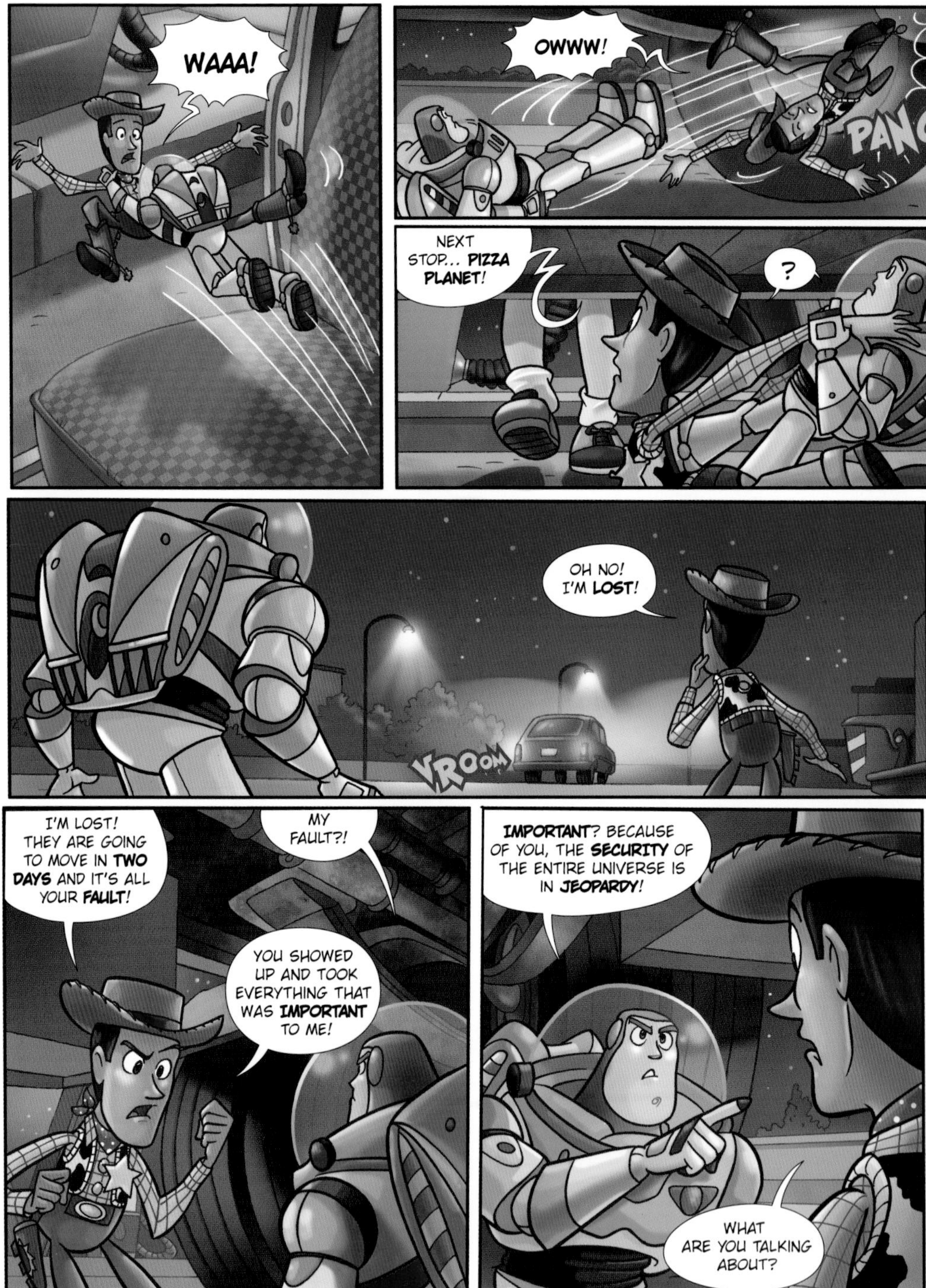
WAAA!
OWWW!
PANG
NEXT STOP... **PIZZA PLANET**!
?
OH NO! I'M **LOST**!
VROOM
I'M LOST! THEY ARE GOING TO MOVE IN **TWO DAYS** AND IT'S ALL YOUR **FAULT**!
MY FAULT?!
YOU SHOWED UP AND TOOK EVERYTHING THAT WAS **IMPORTANT** TO ME!
IMPORTANT? BECAUSE OF YOU, THE **SECURITY** OF THE ENTIRE UNIVERSE IS IN **JEOPARDY**!
WHAT ARE YOU TALKING ABOUT?

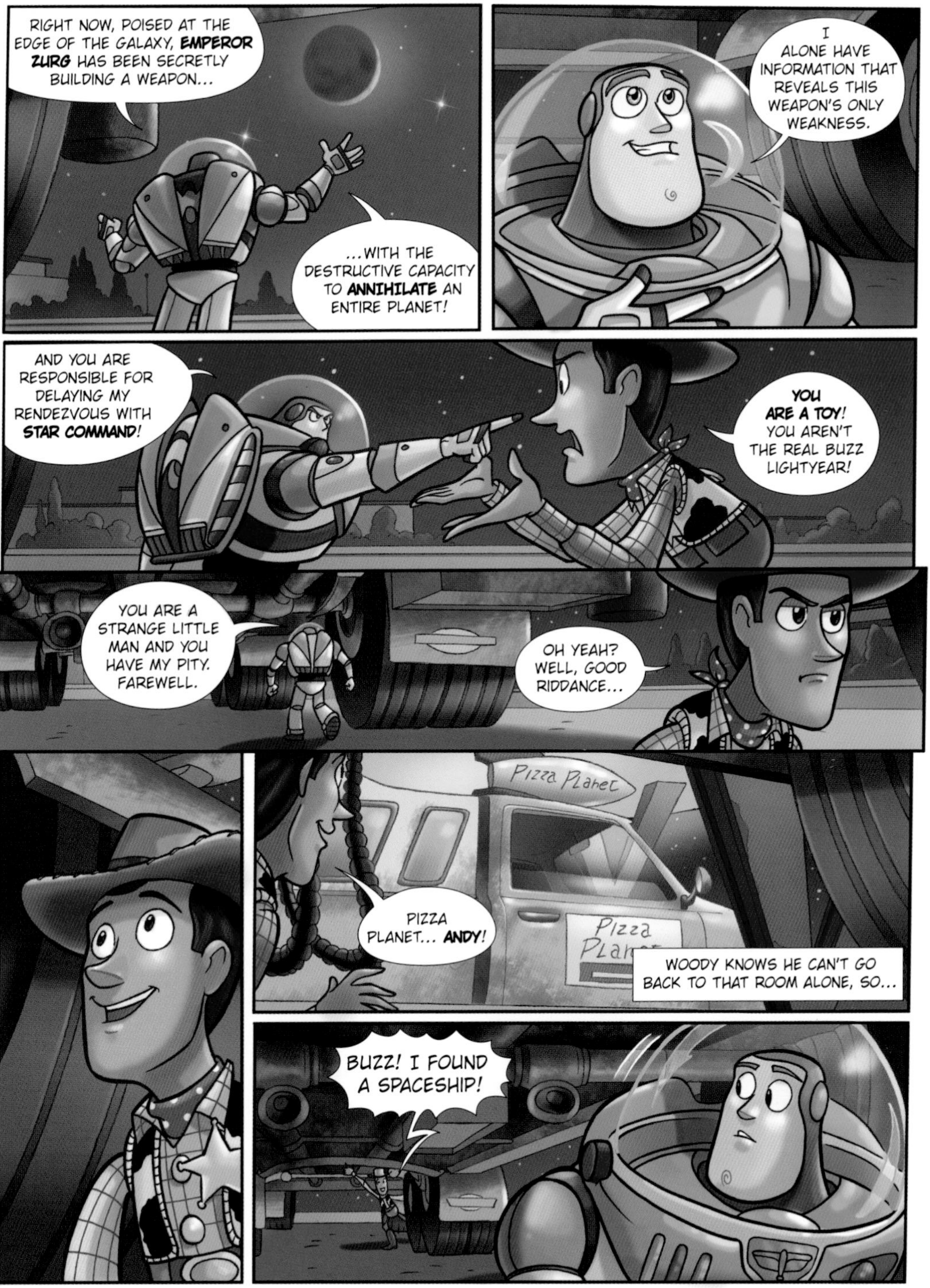
RIGHT NOW, POISED AT THE EDGE OF THE GALAXY, **EMPEROR ZURG** HAS BEEN SECRETLY BUILDING A WEAPON...
...WITH THE DESTRUCTIVE CAPACITY TO **ANNIHILATE** AN ENTIRE PLANET!
I ALONE HAVE INFORMATION THAT REVEALS THIS WEAPON'S ONLY WEAKNESS.
AND YOU ARE RESPONSIBLE FOR DELAYING MY RENDEZVOUS WITH **STAR COMMAND**!
YOU ARE A TOY! YOU AREN'T THE REAL BUZZ LIGHTYEAR!
YOU ARE A STRANGE LITTLE MAN AND YOU HAVE MY PITY. FAREWELL.
OH YEAH? WELL, GOOD RIDDANCE...
Pizza Planet
PIZZA PLANET... **ANDY**!
Pizza Planet
WOODY KNOWS HE CAN'T GO BACK TO THAT ROOM ALONE, SO...
BUZZ! I FOUND A SPACESHIP!

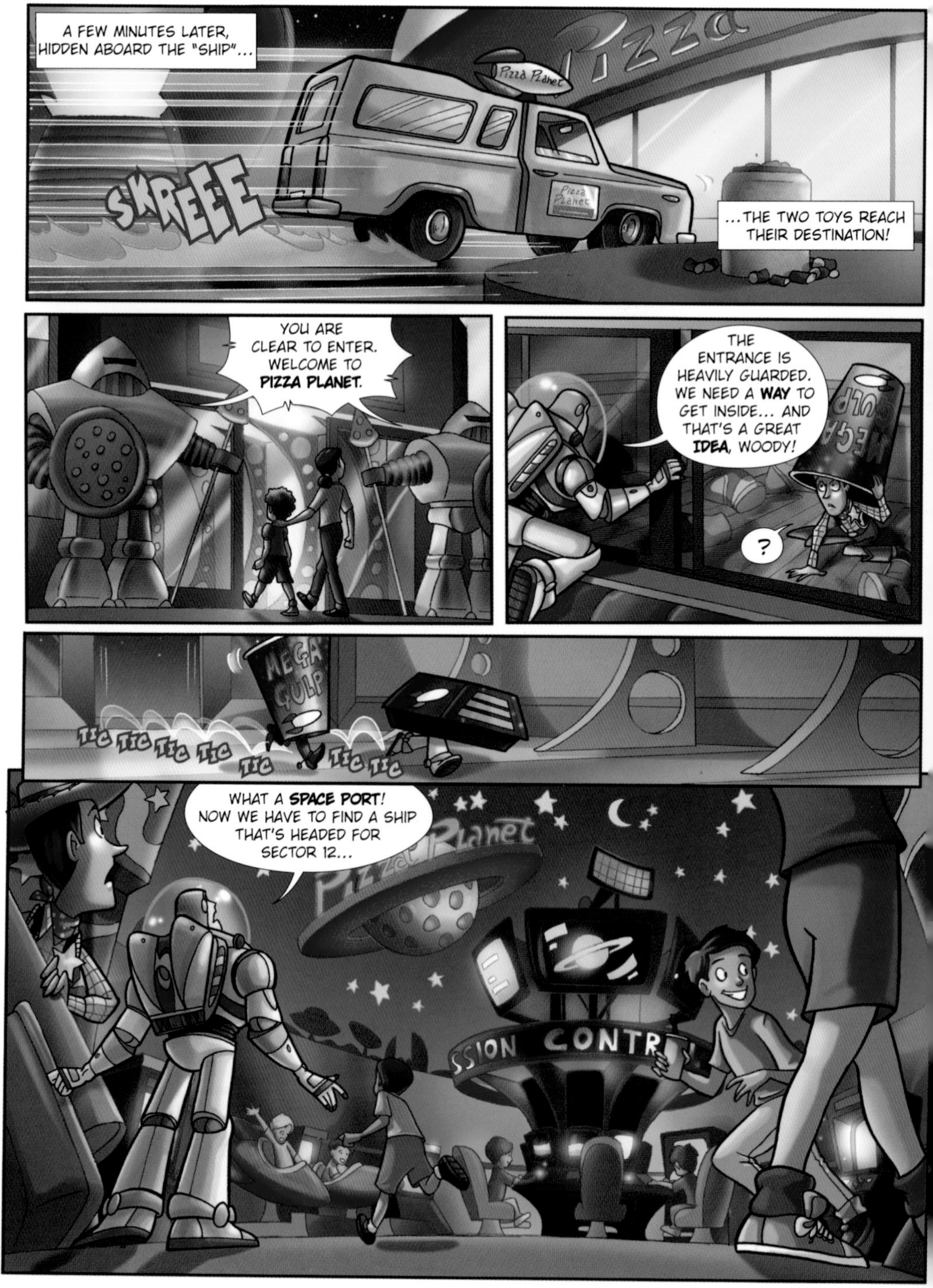
A FEW MINUTES LATER, HIDDEN ABOARD THE "SHIP"...
SKREEE
...THE TWO TOYS REACH THEIR DESTINATION!
YOU ARE CLEAR TO ENTER. WELCOME TO PIZZA PLANET.
THE ENTRANCE IS HEAVILY GUARDED. WE NEED A WAY TO GET INSIDE... AND THAT'S A GREAT IDEA, WOODY!
?
TIC TIC TIC TIC TIC TIC TIC
WHAT A SPACE PORT! NOW WE HAVE TO FIND A SHIP THAT'S HEADED FOR SECTOR 12...

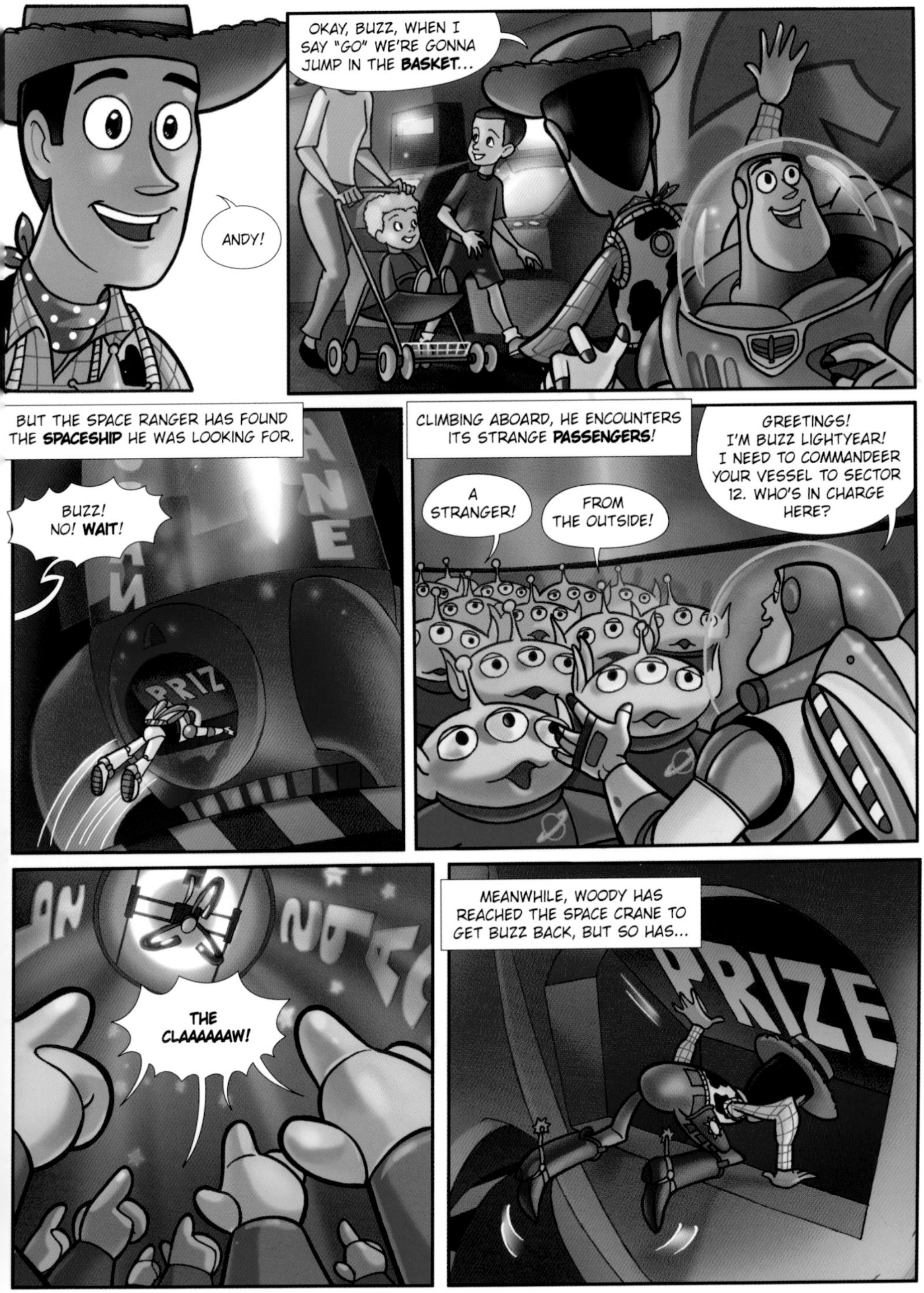
ANDY!
OKAY, BUZZ, WHEN I SAY "GO" WE'RE GONNA JUMP IN THE **BASKET**...
BUT THE SPACE RANGER HAS FOUND THE **SPACESHIP** HE WAS LOOKING FOR.
BUZZ! NO! **WAIT**!
PRIZ
CLIMBING ABOARD, HE ENCOUNTERS ITS STRANGE **PASSENGERS**!
A STRANGER!
FROM THE OUTSIDE!
GREETINGS! I'M BUZZ LIGHTYEAR! I NEED TO COMMANDEER YOUR VESSEL TO SECTOR 12. WHO'S IN CHARGE HERE?
THE CLAAAAAAW!
MEANWHILE, WOODY HAS REACHED THE SPACE CRANE TO GET BUZZ BACK, BUT SO HAS...
PRIZE

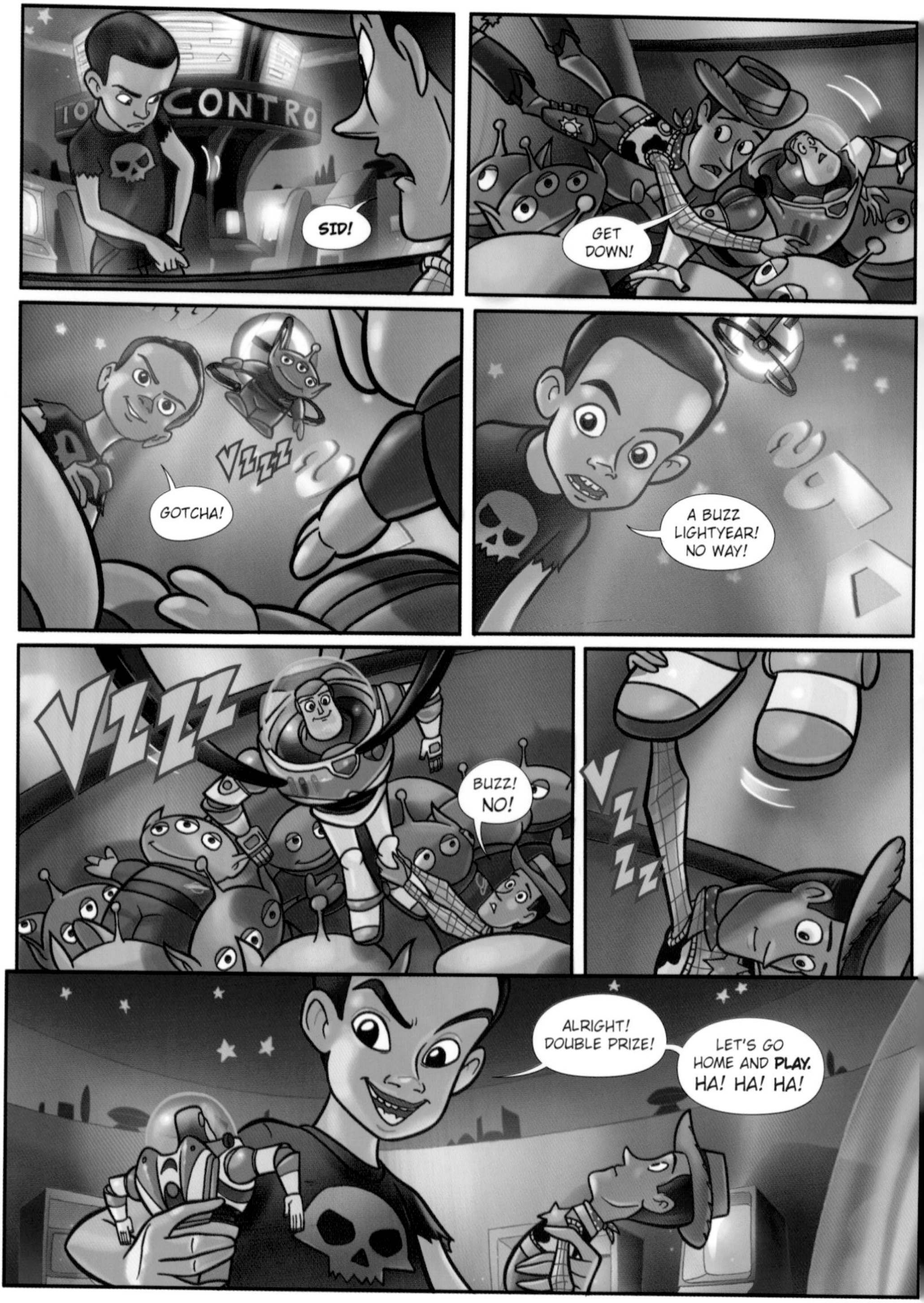
CONTRO
SID!
GET DOWN!
VZZZ
GOTCHA!
A BUZZ LIGHTYEAR! NO WAY!
VZZZ
BUZZ! NO!
VZZZ
ALRIGHT! DOUBLE PRIZE!
LET'S GO HOME AND **PLAY.** HA! HA! HA!

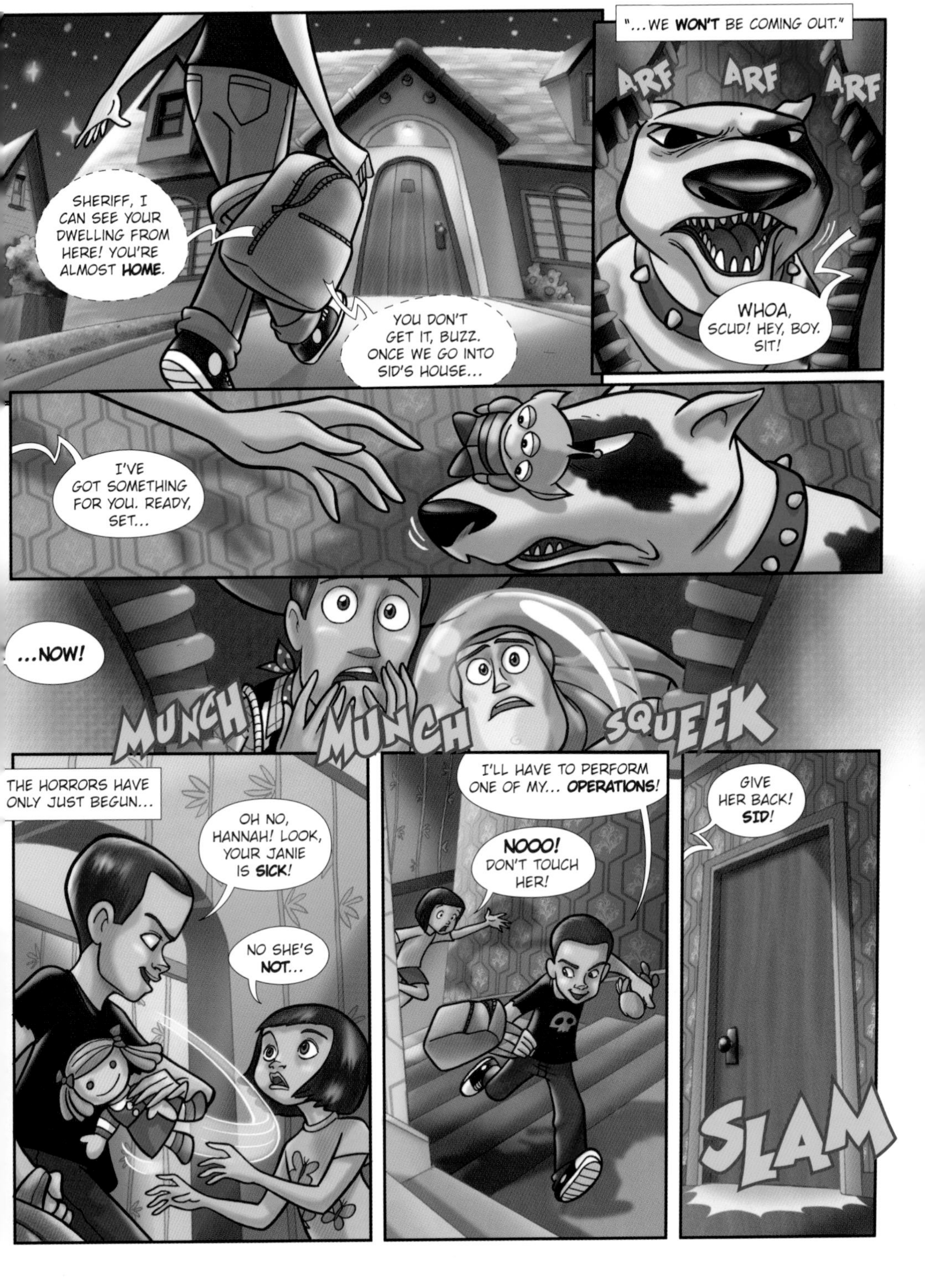
SHERIFF, I CAN SEE YOUR DWELLING FROM HERE! YOU'RE ALMOST **HOME**.
YOU DON'T GET IT, BUZZ. ONCE WE GO INTO SID'S HOUSE...
"...WE **WON'T** BE COMING OUT."
ARF ARF ARF
WHOA, SCUD! HEY, BOY. SIT!
I'VE GOT SOMETHING FOR YOU. READY, SET...
...NOW!
MUNCH MUNCH SQUEEK
THE HORRORS HAVE ONLY JUST BEGUN...
OH NO, HANNAH! LOOK, YOUR JANIE IS **SICK**!
NO SHE'S **NOT**...
I'LL HAVE TO PERFORM ONE OF MY... **OPERATIONS**!
NOOO! DON'T TOUCH HER!
GIVE HER BACK! **SID**!
SLAM

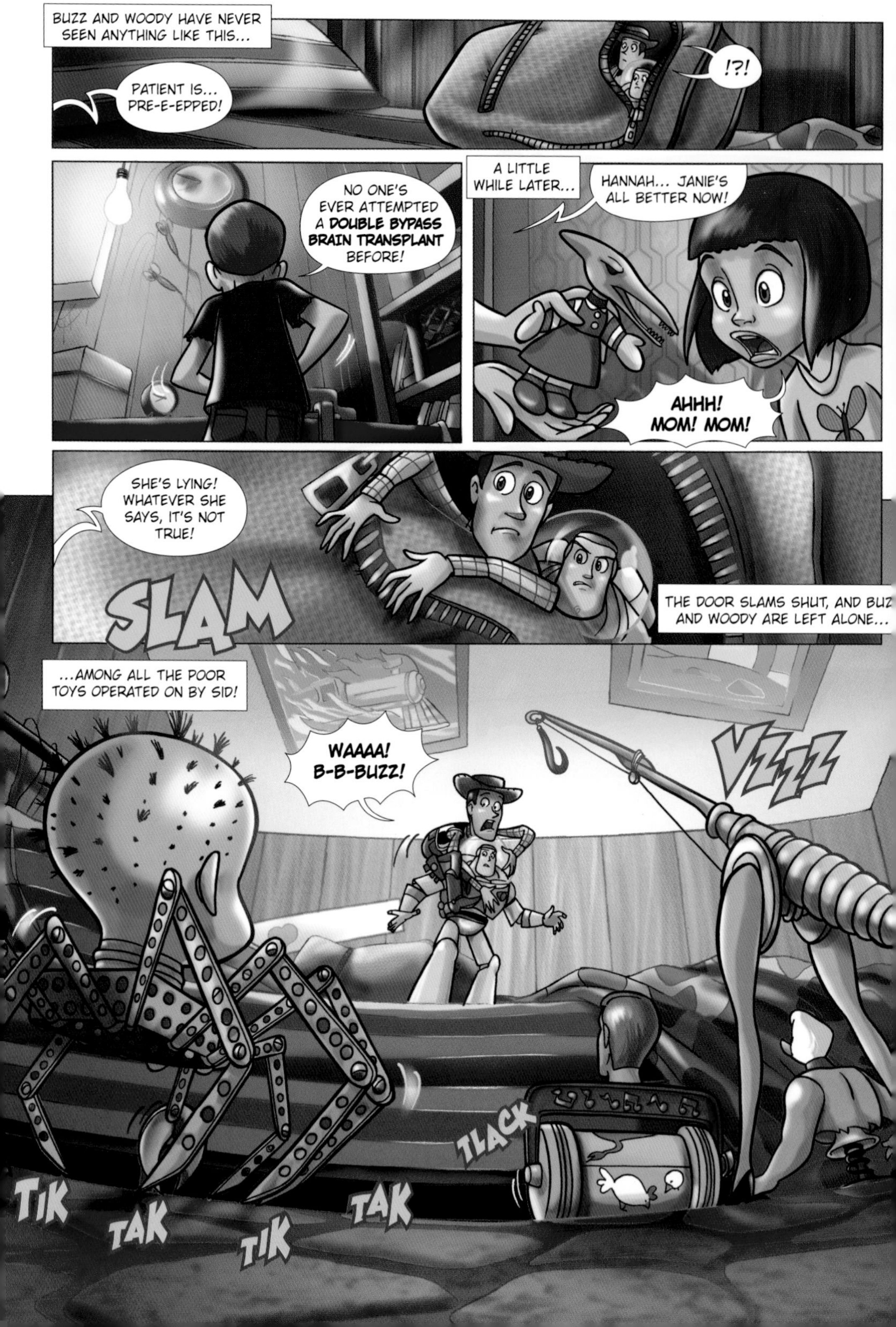
BUZZ AND WOODY HAVE NEVER SEEN ANYTHING LIKE THIS...
PATIENT IS... PRE-E-EPPED!
!?!
NO ONE'S EVER ATTEMPTED A DOUBLE BYPASS BRAIN TRANSPLANT BEFORE!
A LITTLE WHILE LATER...
HANNAH... JANIE'S ALL BETTER NOW!
AHHH! MOM! MOM!
SHE'S LYING! WHATEVER SHE SAYS, IT'S NOT TRUE!
SLAM
THE DOOR SLAMS SHUT, AND BUZ
AND WOODY ARE LEFT ALONE...
...AMONG ALL THE POOR TOYS OPERATED ON BY SID!
WAAAA! B-B-BUZZ!
VZZZ
TLACK
TIK
TAK
TIK
TAK

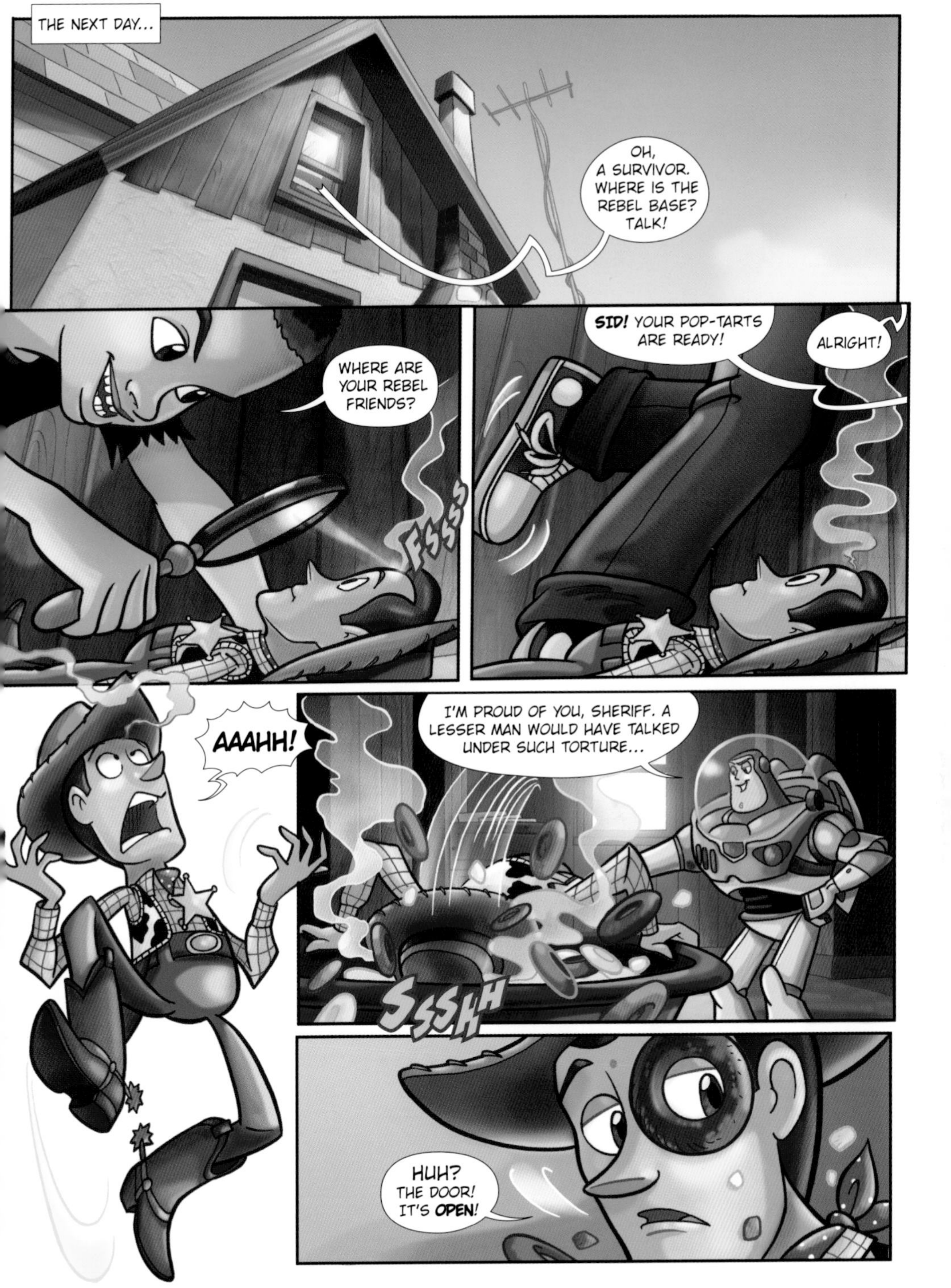
THE NEXT DAY...
OH, A SURVIVOR. WHERE IS THE REBEL BASE? TALK!
WHERE ARE YOUR REBEL FRIENDS?
FSSSS
SID! YOUR POP-TARTS ARE READY!
ALRIGHT!
AAAHH!
I'M PROUD OF YOU, SHERIFF. A LESSER MAN WOULD HAVE TALKED UNDER SUCH TORTURE...
SSSHH
HUH? THE DOOR! IT'S OPEN!

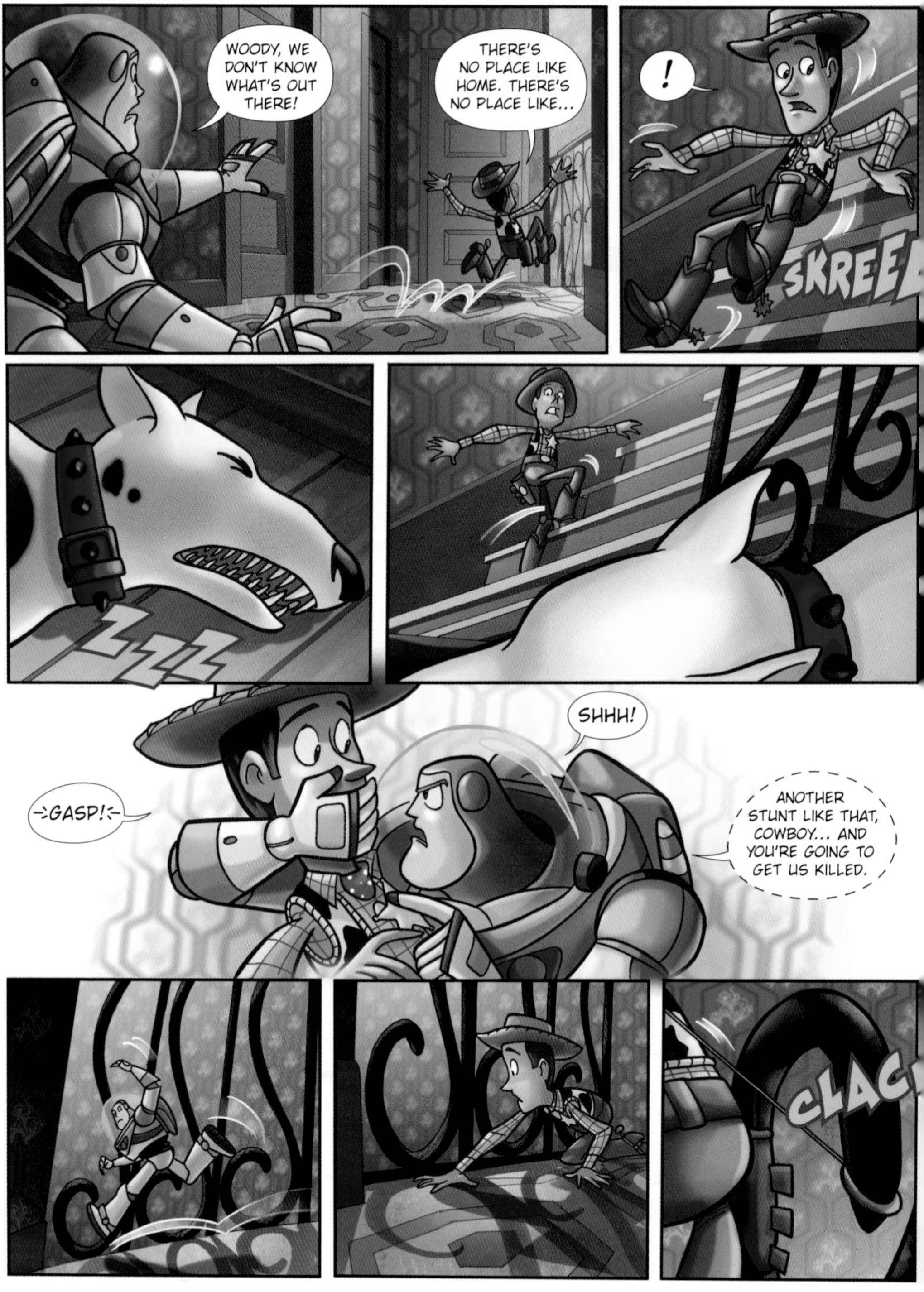
WOODY, WE DON'T KNOW WHAT'S OUT THERE!
THERE'S NO PLACE LIKE HOME. THERE'S NO PLACE LIKE...
!
SKREE
ZZZ
SHHH!
-GASP!-
ANOTHER STUNT LIKE THAT, COWBOY... AND YOU'RE GOING TO GET US KILLED.
CLAC

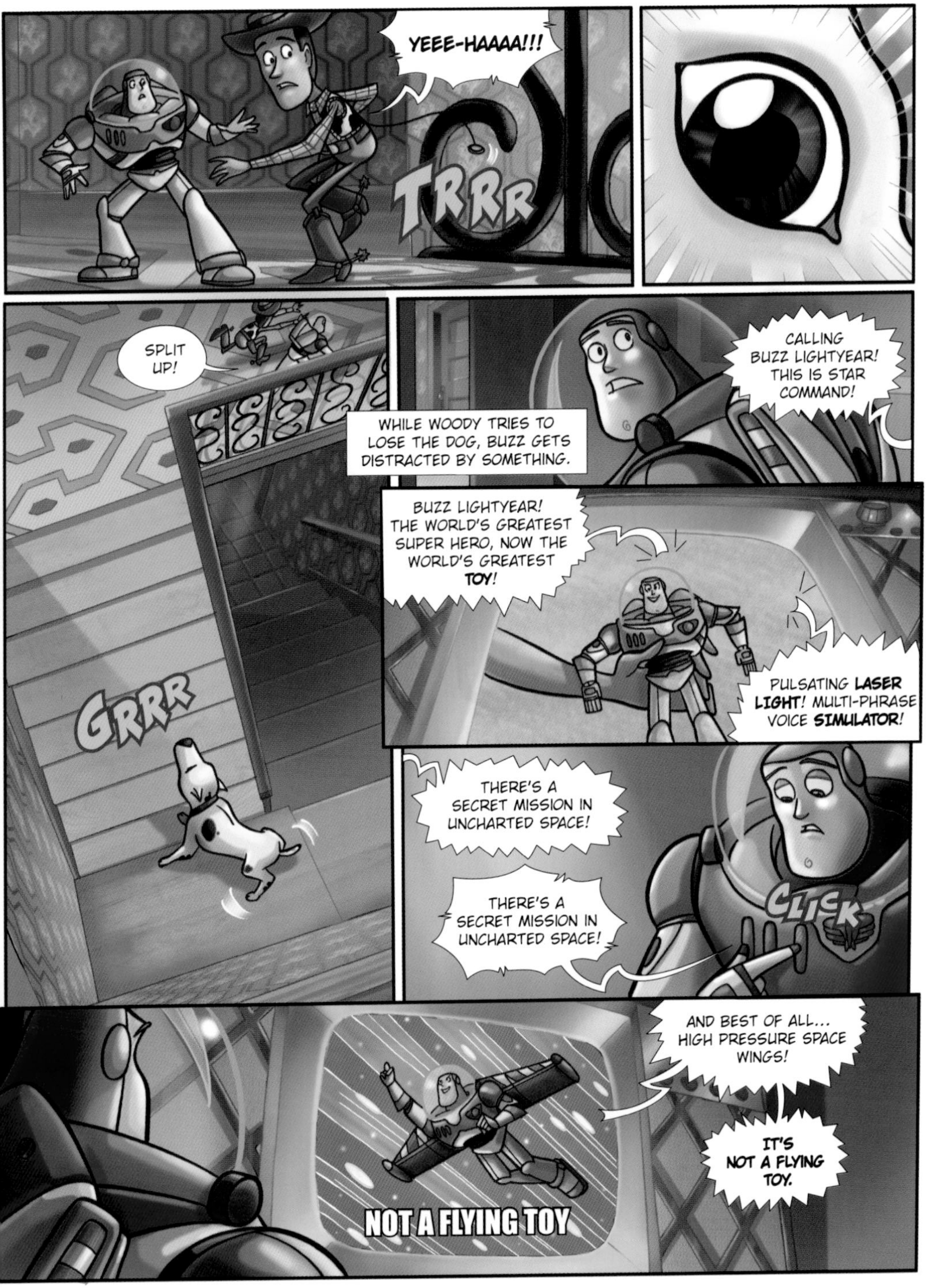
YEEE-HAAAA!!!
TRRR
SPLIT UP!
GRRR
WHILE WOODY TRIES TO LOSE THE DOG, BUZZ GETS DISTRACTED BY SOMETHING.
CALLING BUZZ LIGHTYEAR! THIS IS STAR COMMAND!
BUZZ LIGHTYEAR! THE WORLD'S GREATEST SUPER HERO, NOW THE WORLD'S GREATEST TOY!
PULSATING LASER LIGHT! MULTI-PHRASE VOICE SIMULATOR!
THERE'S A SECRET MISSION IN UNCHARTED SPACE!
THERE'S A SECRET MISSION IN UNCHARTED SPACE!
CLICK
AND BEST OF ALL... HIGH PRESSURE SPACE WINGS!
IT'S NOT A FLYING TOY.
NOT A FLYING TOY

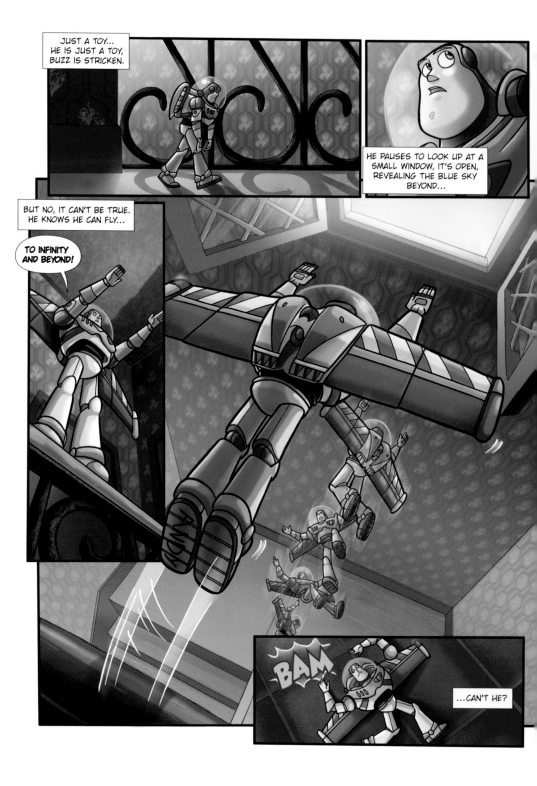

JUST A TOY...
HE IS JUST A TOY,
BUZZ IS STRICKEN.

HE PAUSES TO LOOK UP AT A
SMALL WINDOW, IT'S OPEN,
REVEALING THE BLUE SKY
BEYOND...

BUT NO, IT CAN'T BE TRUE.
HE KNOWS HE CAN FLY...

TO INFINITY
AND BEYOND!

BAM

...CAN'T HE?

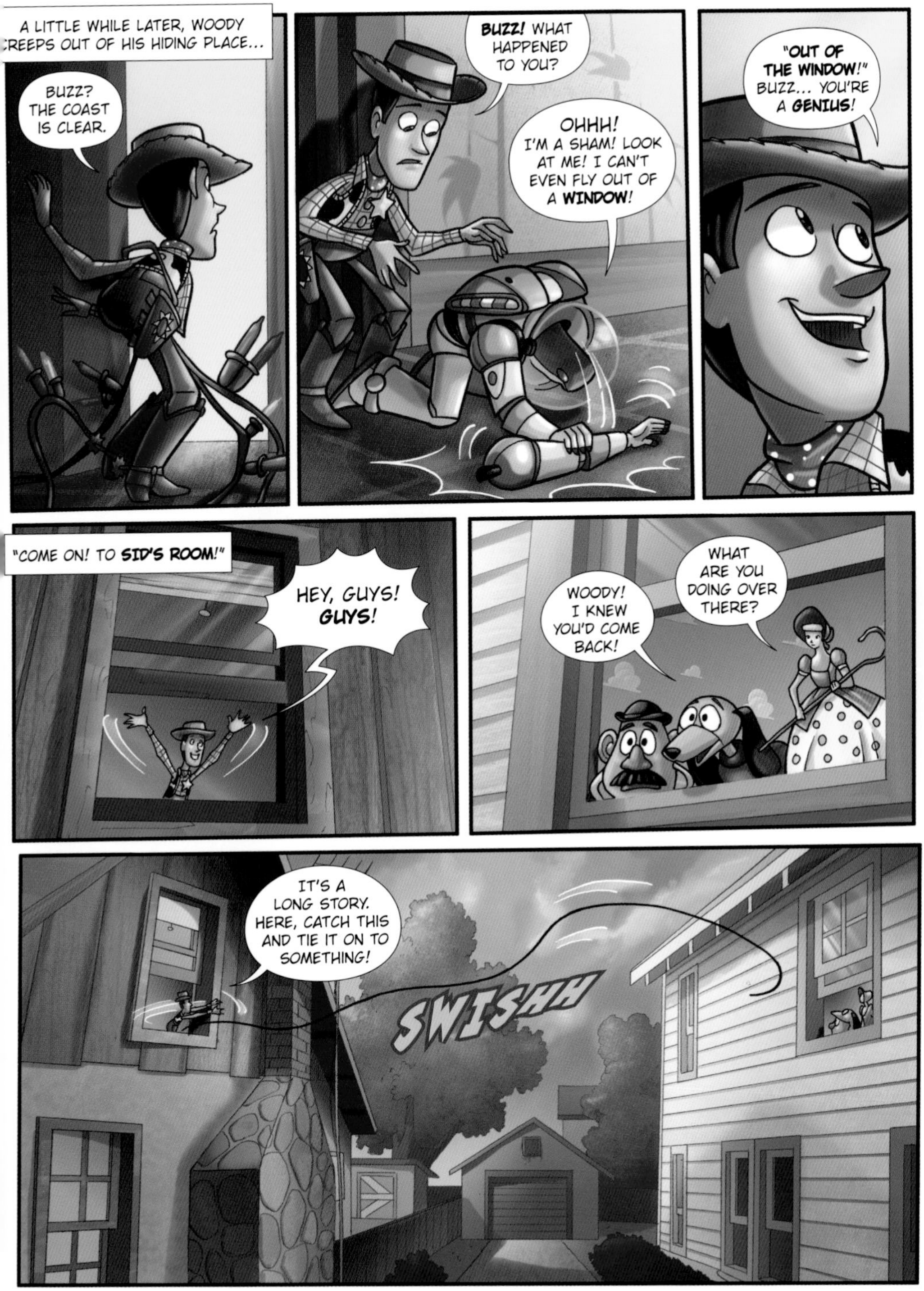
A LITTLE WHILE LATER, WOODY CREEPS OUT OF HIS HIDING PLACE...
BUZZ? THE COAST IS CLEAR.
BUZZ! WHAT HAPPENED TO YOU?
OHHH! I'M A SHAM! LOOK AT ME! I CAN'T EVEN FLY OUT OF A WINDOW!
"OUT OF THE WINDOW!" BUZZ... YOU'RE A GENIUS!
"COME ON! TO SID'S ROOM!"
HEY, GUYS! GUYS!
WOODY! I KNEW YOU'D COME BACK!
WHAT ARE YOU DOING OVER THERE?
IT'S A LONG STORY. HERE, CATCH THIS AND TIE IT ON TO SOMETHING!
SWISHH

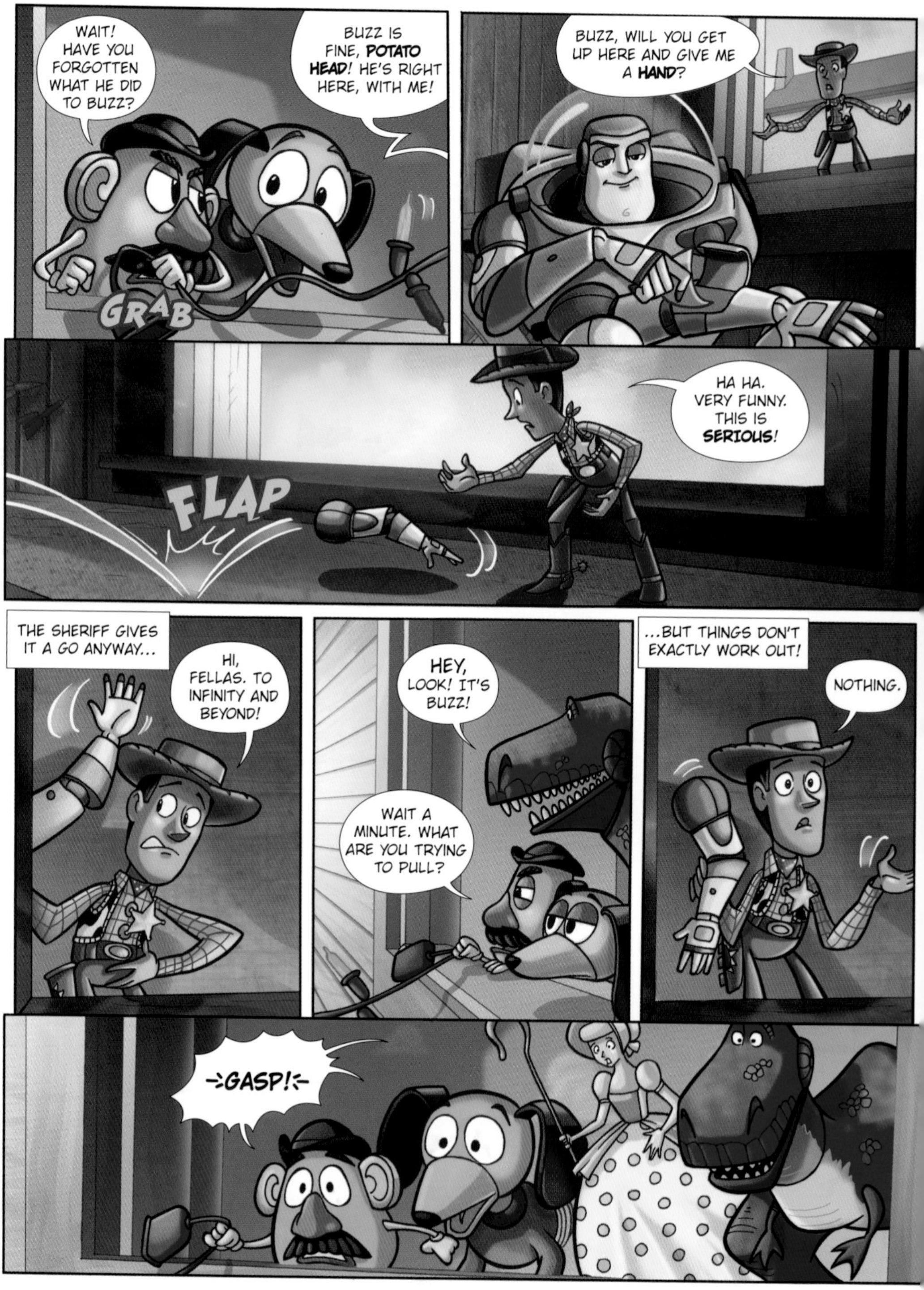
WAIT! HAVE YOU FORGOTTEN WHAT HE DID TO BUZZ?
GRAB
BUZZ IS FINE, POTATO HEAD! HE'S RIGHT HERE, WITH ME!
BUZZ, WILL YOU GET UP HERE AND GIVE ME A HAND?
HA HA. VERY FUNNY. THIS IS SERIOUS!
FLAP
THE SHERIFF GIVES IT A GO ANYWAY...
HI, FELLAS. TO INFINITY AND BEYOND!
HEY, LOOK! IT'S BUZZ!
WAIT A MINUTE. WHAT ARE YOU TRYING TO PULL?
...BUT THINGS DON'T EXACTLY WORK OUT!
NOTHING.
GASP!

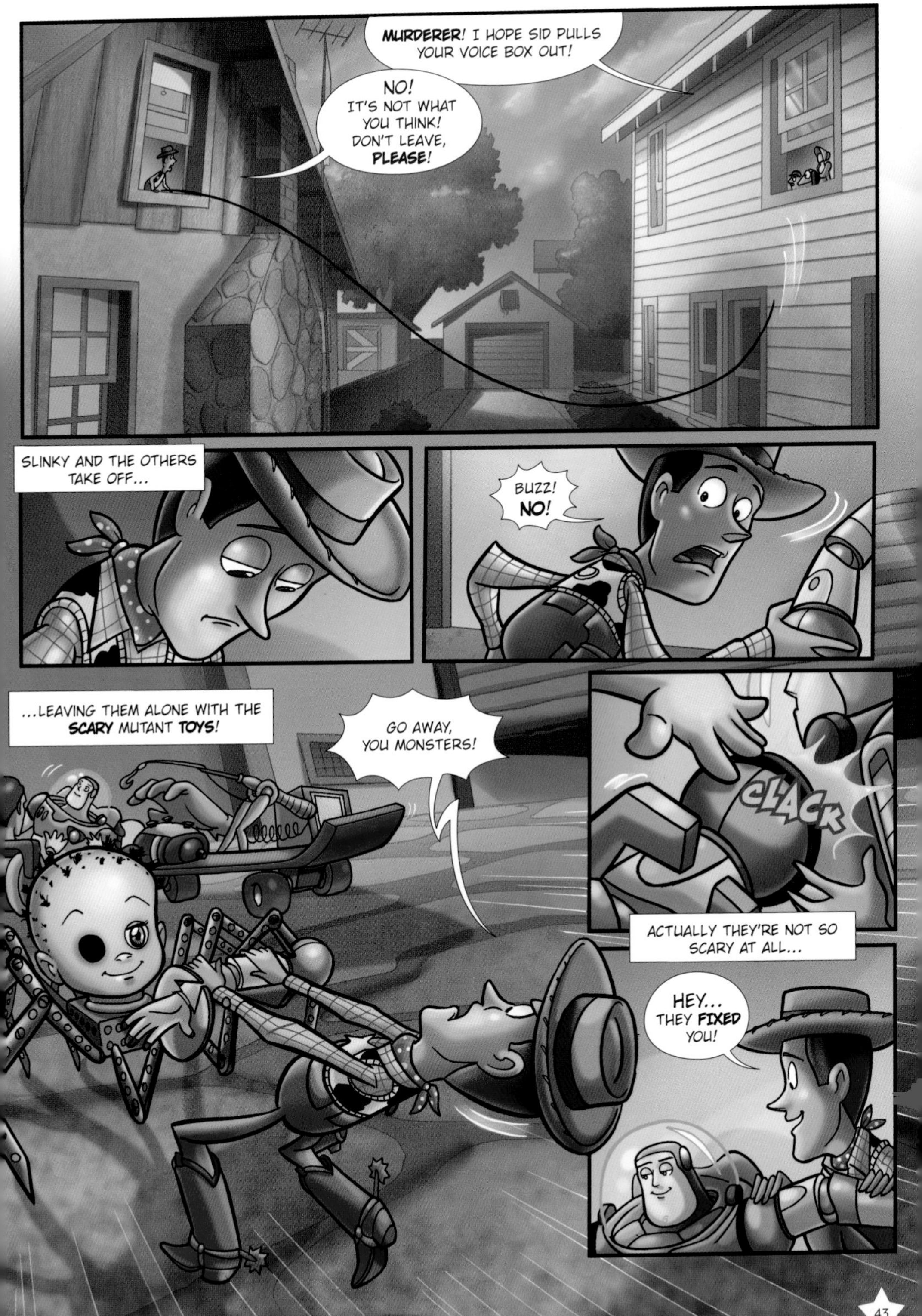

MURDERER! I HOPE SID PULLS YOUR VOICE BOX OUT!
NO! IT'S NOT WHAT YOU THINK! DON'T LEAVE, PLEASE!
SLINKY AND THE OTHERS TAKE OFF...
BUZZ! NO!
...LEAVING THEM ALONE WITH THE SCARY MUTANT TOYS!
GO AWAY, YOU MONSTERS!
CLACK
ACTUALLY THEY'RE NOT SO SCARY AT ALL...
HEY... THEY FIXED YOU!

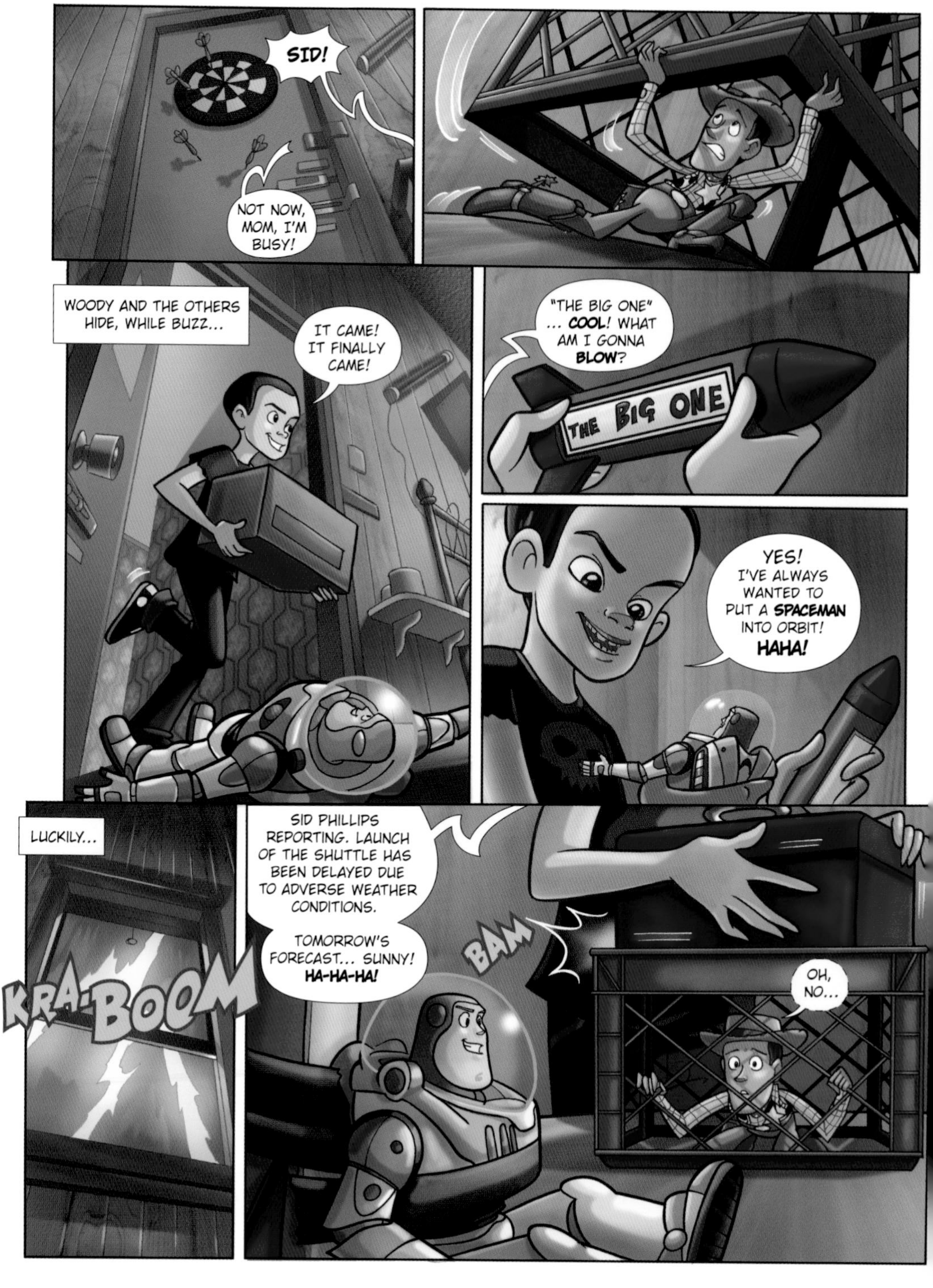
SID!
NOT NOW, MOM, I'M BUSY!
WOODY AND THE OTHERS HIDE, WHILE BUZZ...
IT CAME! IT FINALLY CAME!
"THE BIG ONE" ... COOL! WHAT AM I GONNA BLOW?
THE BIG ONE
YES! I'VE ALWAYS WANTED TO PUT A SPACEMAN INTO ORBIT! HAHA!
LUCKILY...
KRA-BOOM
SID PHILLIPS REPORTING. LAUNCH OF THE SHUTTLE HAS BEEN DELAYED DUE TO ADVERSE WEATHER CONDITIONS.
TOMORROW'S FORECAST... SUNNY! HA-HA-HA!
BAM
OH, NO...

MUCH LATER...

ZZZ

PSSST! HEY, BUZZ! GET OVER HERE AND SEE IF YOU CAN GET THIS **TOOLBOX** OFF ME!

COME ON, BUZZ. I... I NEED YOUR HELP.

I CAN'T HELP ANYONE...

YOU WERE RIGHT, I'M NOT A SPACE RANGER. I'M JUST A **STUPID INSIGNIFICANT** TOY.

HEY... BEING A TOY IS A LOT BETTER THAN BEING A SPACE RANGER!

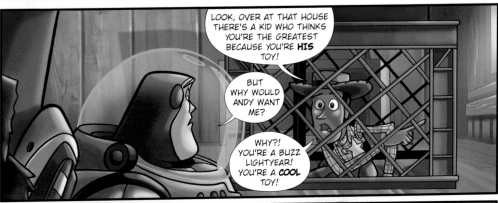

LOOK, OVER AT THAT HOUSE THERE'S A KID WHO THINKS YOU'RE THE GREATEST BECAUSE YOU'RE **HIS** TOY!

BUT WHY WOULD ANDY WANT ME?

WHY?! YOU'RE A BUZZ LIGHTYEAR! YOU'RE A **COOL** TOY!

AS A MATTER OF FACT, YOU'RE TOO COOL. WHY WOULD ANDY EVER WANT TO PLAY WITH **ME** WHEN HE'S GOT **YOU**?

45

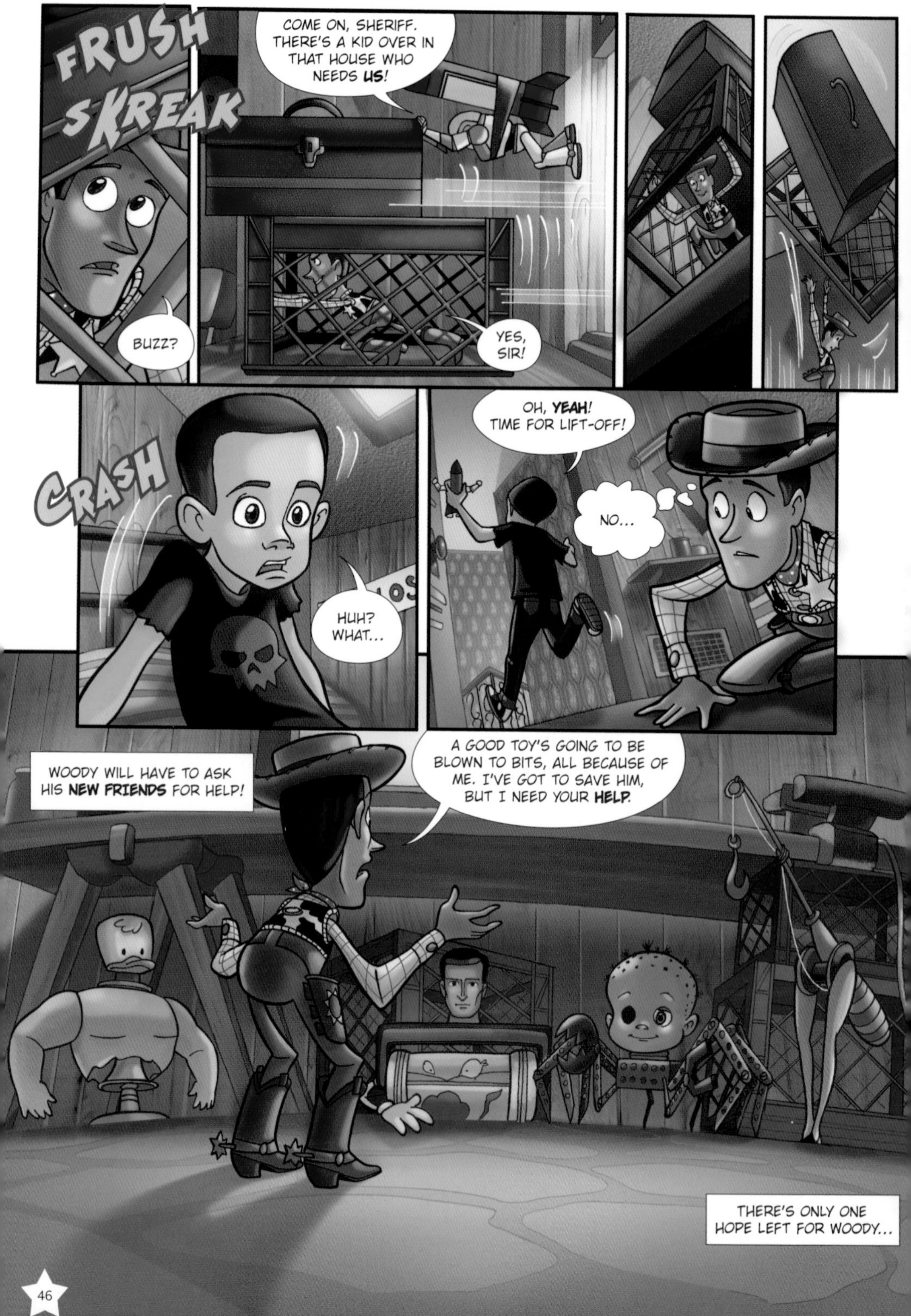
FRUSH
SKREAK
BUZZ?
COME ON, SHERIFF. THERE'S A KID OVER IN THAT HOUSE WHO NEEDS **US**!
YES, SIR!
CRASH
HUH? WHAT...
OH, **YEAH**! TIME FOR LIFT-OFF!
NO...
WOODY WILL HAVE TO ASK HIS **NEW FRIENDS** FOR HELP!
A GOOD TOY'S GOING TO BE BLOWN TO BITS, ALL BECAUSE OF ME. I'VE GOT TO SAVE HIM, BUT I NEED YOUR **HELP**.
THERE'S ONLY ONE HOPE LEFT FOR WOODY...

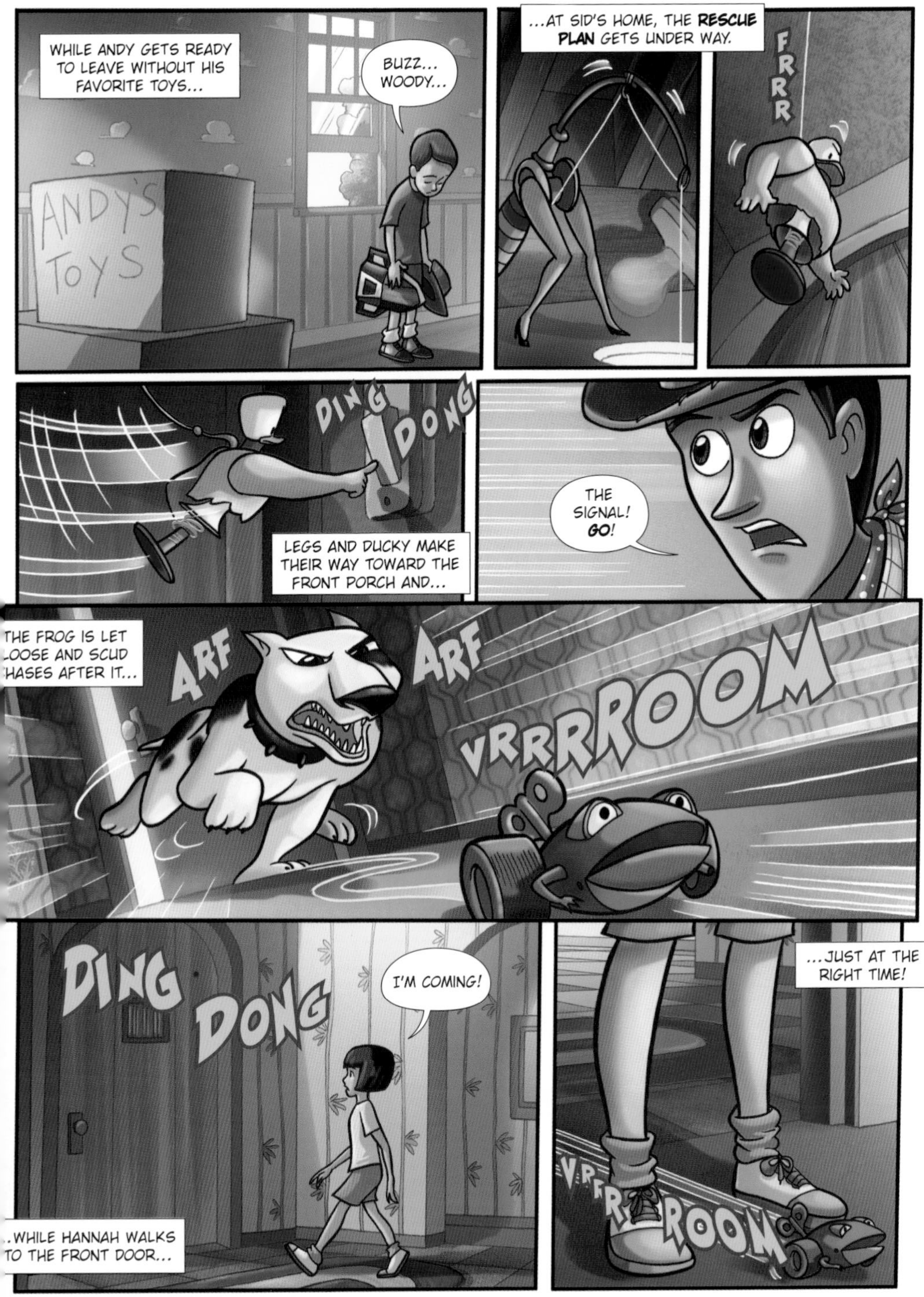

WHILE ANDY GETS READY TO LEAVE WITHOUT HIS FAVORITE TOYS...
BUZZ... WOODY...
ANDY'S TOYS
...AT SID'S HOME, THE **RESCUE PLAN** GETS UNDER WAY.
FRRR
DING DONG
LEGS AND DUCKY MAKE THEIR WAY TOWARD THE FRONT PORCH AND...
THE SIGNAL! **GO**!
THE FROG IS LET LOOSE AND SCUD CHASES AFTER IT...
ARF ARF
VRRRROOM
DING DONG
I'M COMING!
...WHILE HANNAH WALKS TO THE FRONT DOOR...
...JUST AT THE RIGHT TIME!
VRRRROOM

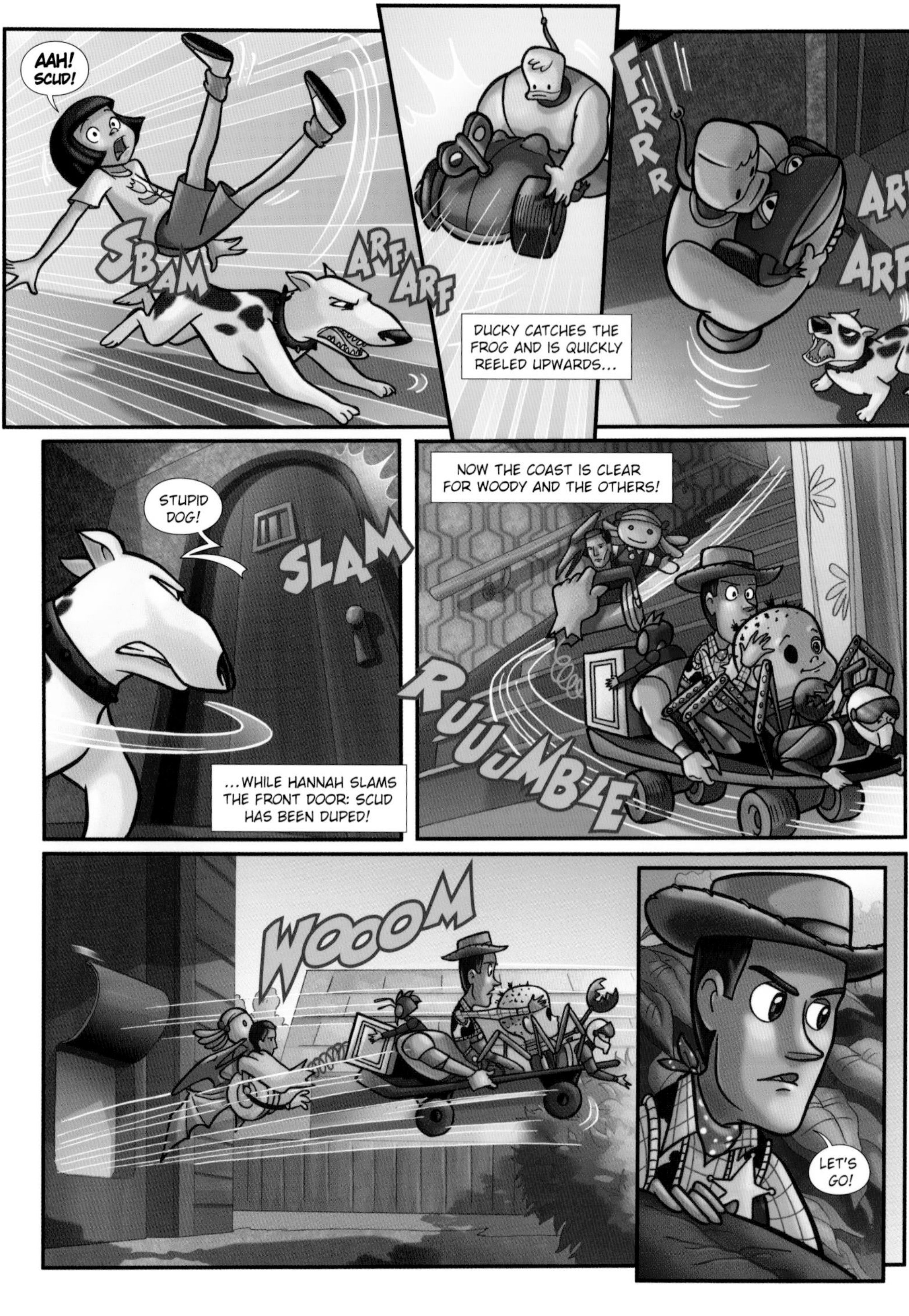
AAH! SCUD!
SBAM
ARF ARF
DUCKY CATCHES THE FROG AND IS QUICKLY REELED UPWARDS...
FRRRR
ARF
ARF
STUPID DOG!
SLAM
...WHILE HANNAH SLAMS THE FRONT DOOR: SCUD HAS BEEN DUPED!
NOW THE COAST IS CLEAR FOR WOODY AND THE OTHERS!
RUUUMBLE
WOOOM
LET'S GO!

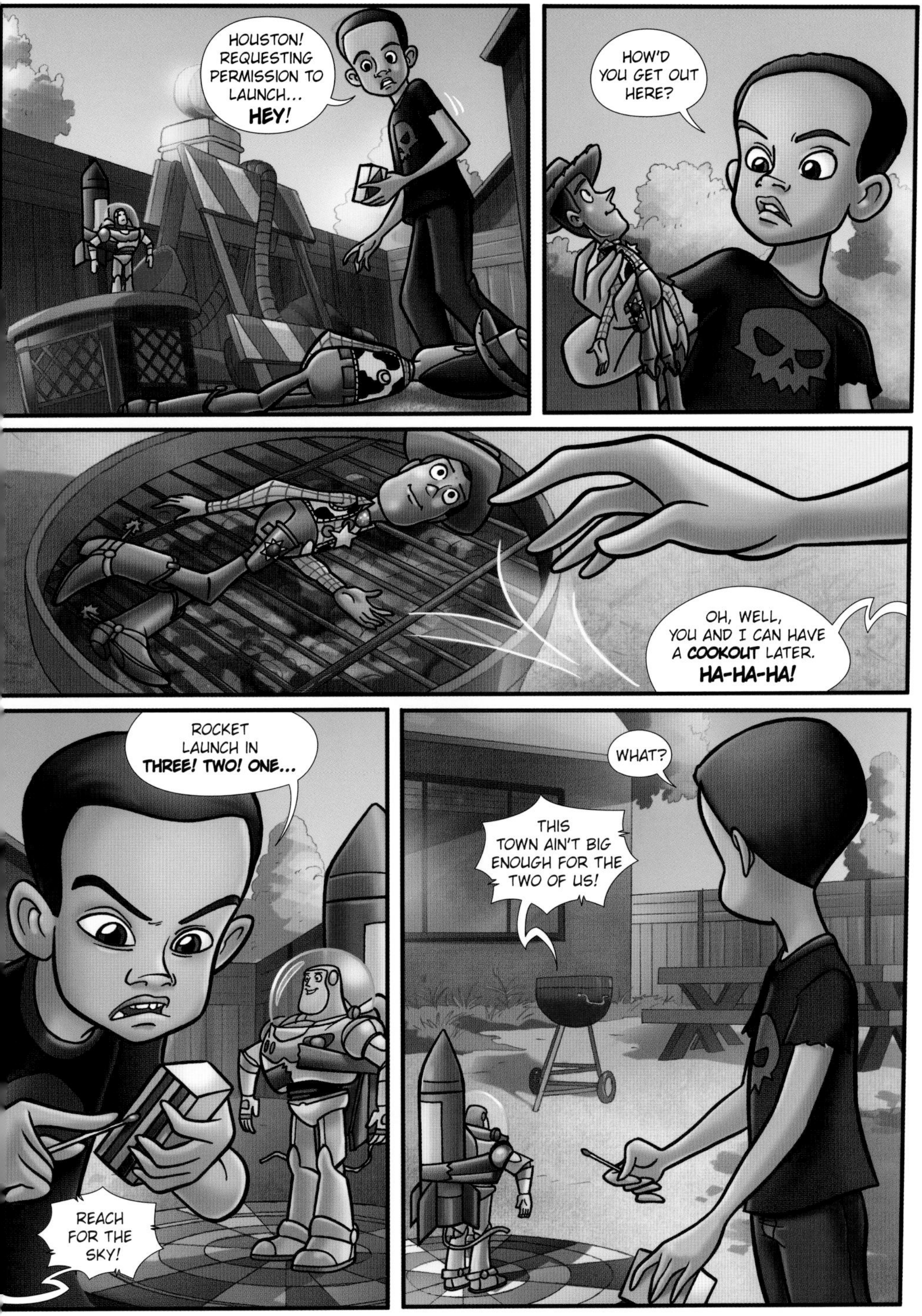
HOUSTON! REQUESTING PERMISSION TO LAUNCH... HEY!
HOW'D YOU GET OUT HERE?
OH, WELL, YOU AND I CAN HAVE A COOKOUT LATER. HA-HA-HA!
ROCKET LAUNCH IN THREE! TWO! ONE...
REACH FOR THE SKY!
WHAT?
THIS TOWN AIN'T BIG ENOUGH FOR THE TWO OF US!

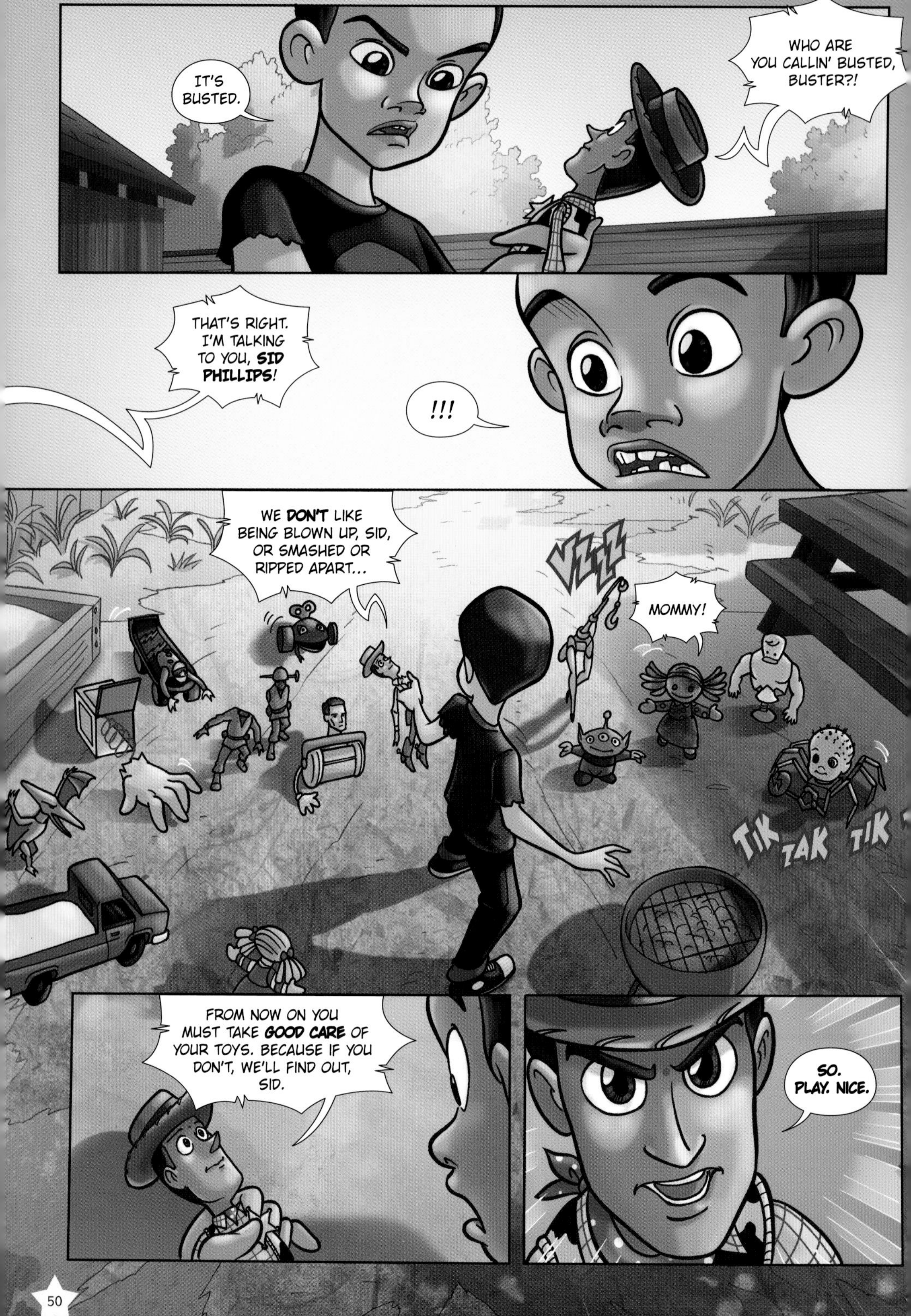
IT'S BUSTED.
WHO ARE YOU CALLIN' BUSTED, BUSTER?!
THAT'S RIGHT. I'M TALKING TO YOU, **SID PHILLIPS**!
!!!
WE **DON'T** LIKE BEING BLOWN UP, SID, OR SMASHED OR RIPPED APART...
MOMMY!
TIK TAK TIK
FROM NOW ON YOU MUST TAKE **GOOD CARE** OF YOUR TOYS. BECAUSE IF YOU DON'T, WE'LL FIND OUT, SID.
SO. PLAY. NICE.

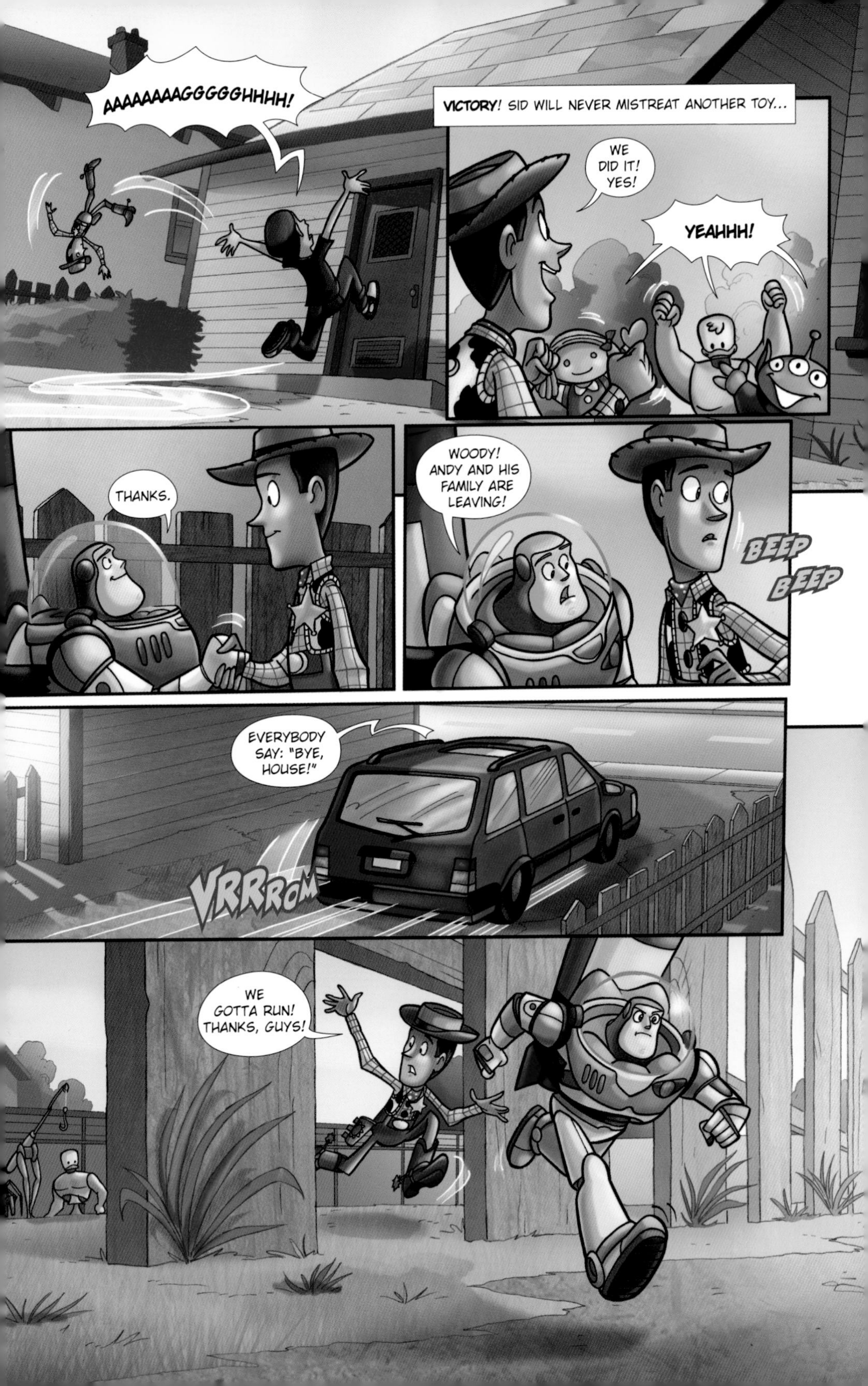
AAAAAAAAGGGGGHHHH!
VICTORY! SID WILL NEVER MISTREAT ANOTHER TOY...
WE DID IT! YES!
YEAHHH!
THANKS.
WOODY! ANDY AND HIS FAMILY ARE LEAVING!
BEEP
BEEP
EVERYBODY SAY: "BYE, HOUSE!"
VRRROM
WE GOTTA RUN! THANKS, GUYS!

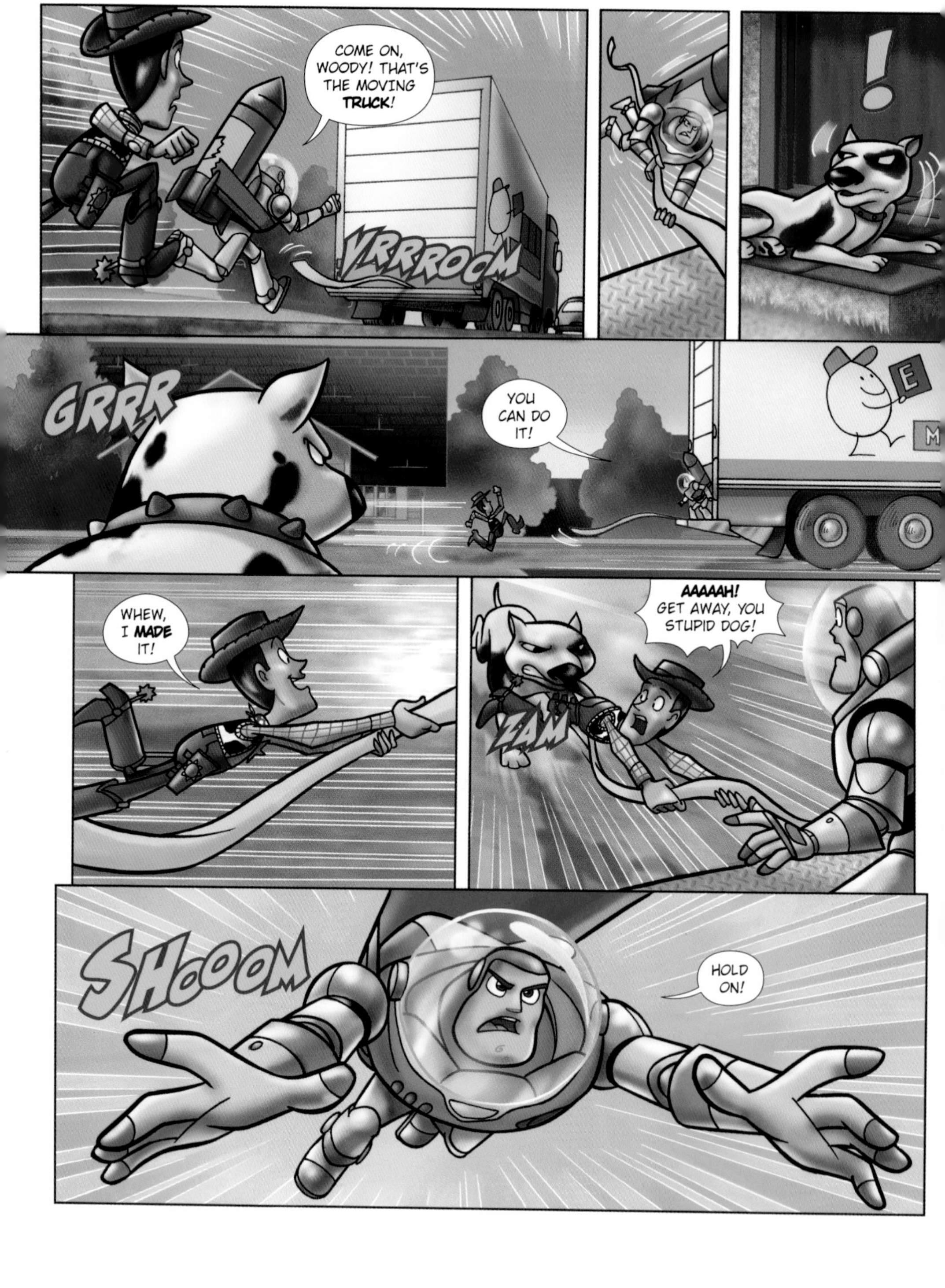
COME ON, WOODY! THAT'S THE MOVING **TRUCK**!
VRRROOM
!
GRRR
YOU CAN DO IT!
WHEW, I **MADE** IT!
AAAAAH! GET AWAY, YOU STUPID DOG!
ZAM
SHOOOM
HOLD ON!

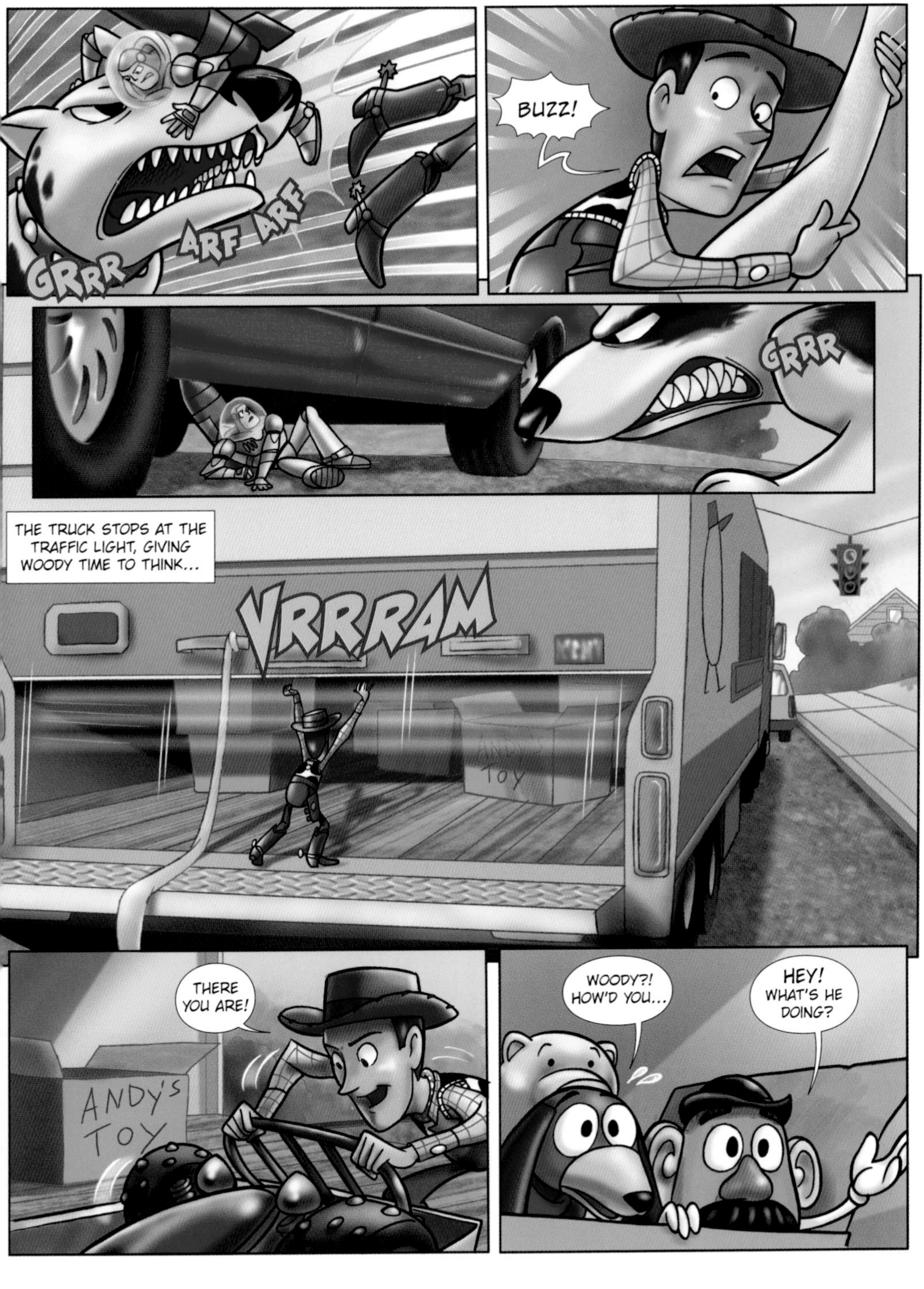
GRRR
ARF ARF
BUZZ!
GRRR
THE TRUCK STOPS AT THE TRAFFIC LIGHT, GIVING WOODY TIME TO THINK...
VRRRAM
ANDY'S TOY
ANDY'S TOY
THERE YOU ARE!
WOODY?! HOW'D YOU...
HEY! WHAT'S HE DOING?

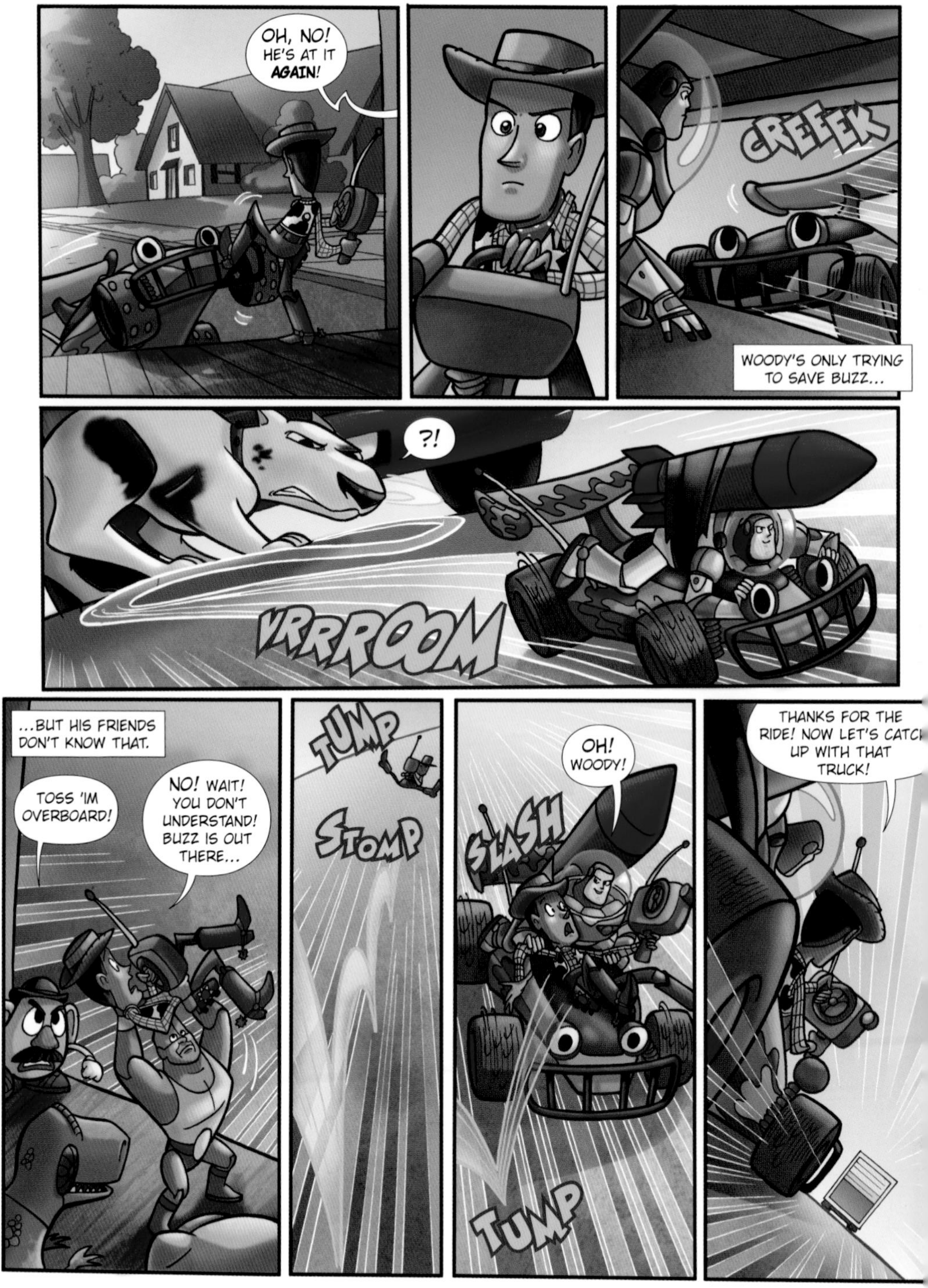
OH, NO! HE'S AT IT **AGAIN**!
CREEEK
WOODY'S ONLY TRYING TO SAVE BUZZ...
?!
VRRROOM
...BUT HIS FRIENDS DON'T KNOW THAT.
TOSS 'IM OVERBOARD!
NO! WAIT! YOU DON'T UNDERSTAND! BUZZ IS OUT THERE...
TUMP
STOMP
OH! WOODY!
SLASH
TUMP
THANKS FOR THE RIDE! NOW LET'S CATC UP WITH THAT TRUCK!

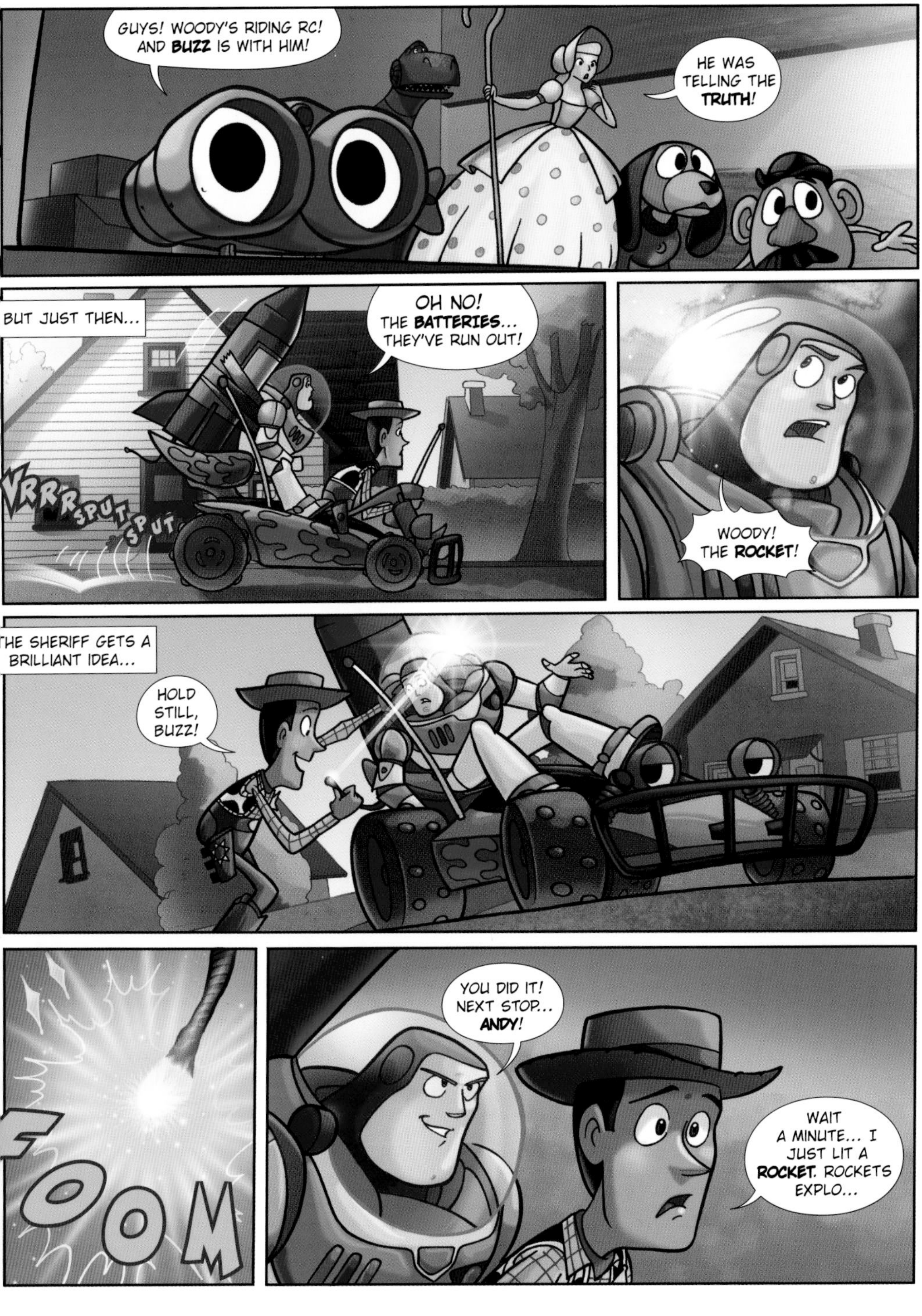
GUYS! WOODY'S RIDING RC! AND BUZZ IS WITH HIM!
HE WAS TELLING THE TRUTH!
BUT JUST THEN...
OH NO! THE BATTERIES... THEY'VE RUN OUT!
VRRR SPUT SPUT
WOODY! THE ROCKET!
THE SHERIFF GETS A BRILLIANT IDEA...
HOLD STILL, BUZZ!
FOOM
YOU DID IT! NEXT STOP... ANDY!
WAIT A MINUTE... I JUST LIT A ROCKET. ROCKETS EXPLO...

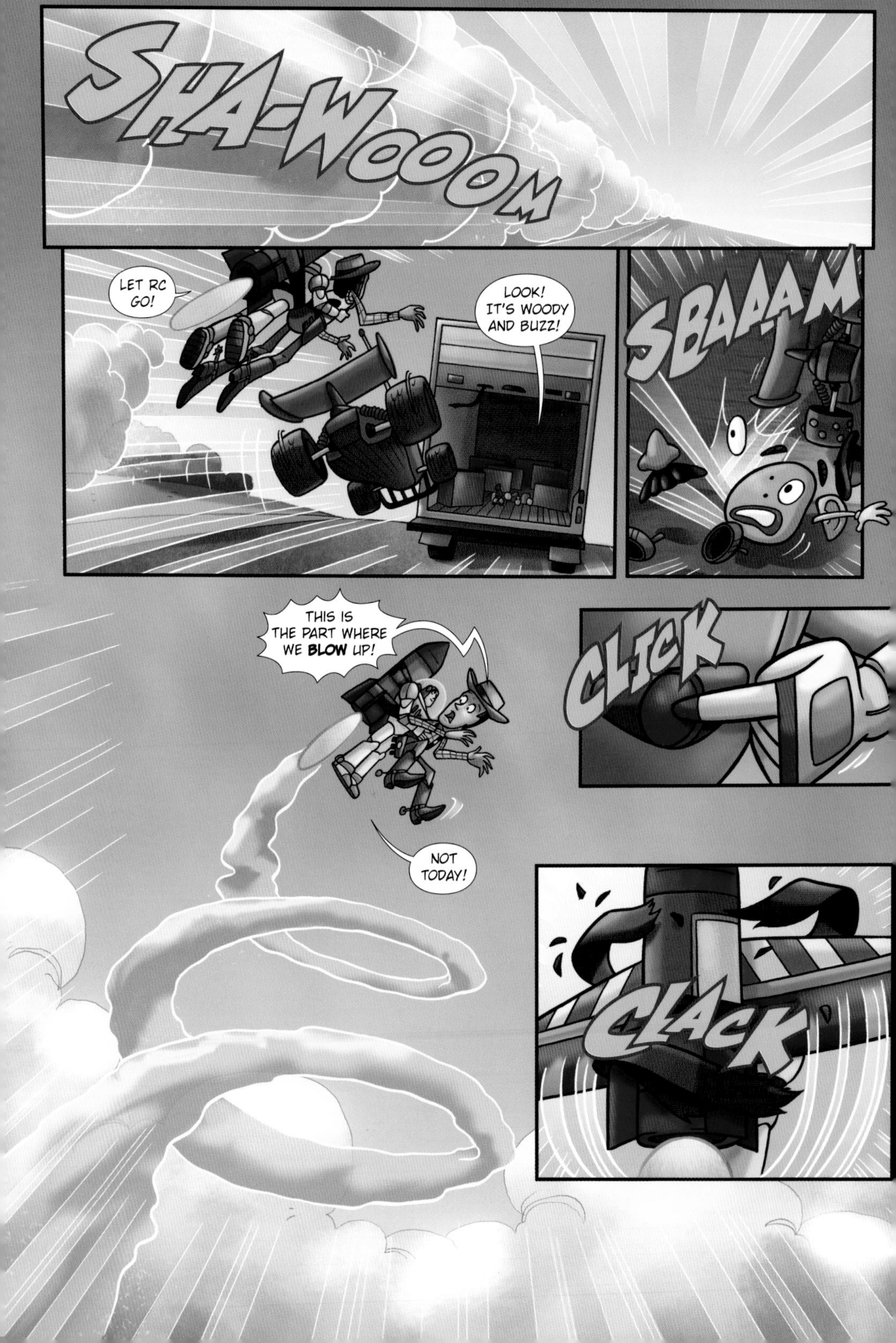
SHA-WOOOM
LET RC GO!
LOOK! IT'S WOODY AND BUZZ!
SBAAAM
THIS IS THE PART WHERE WE **BLOW** UP!
CLICK
NOT TODAY!
CLACK

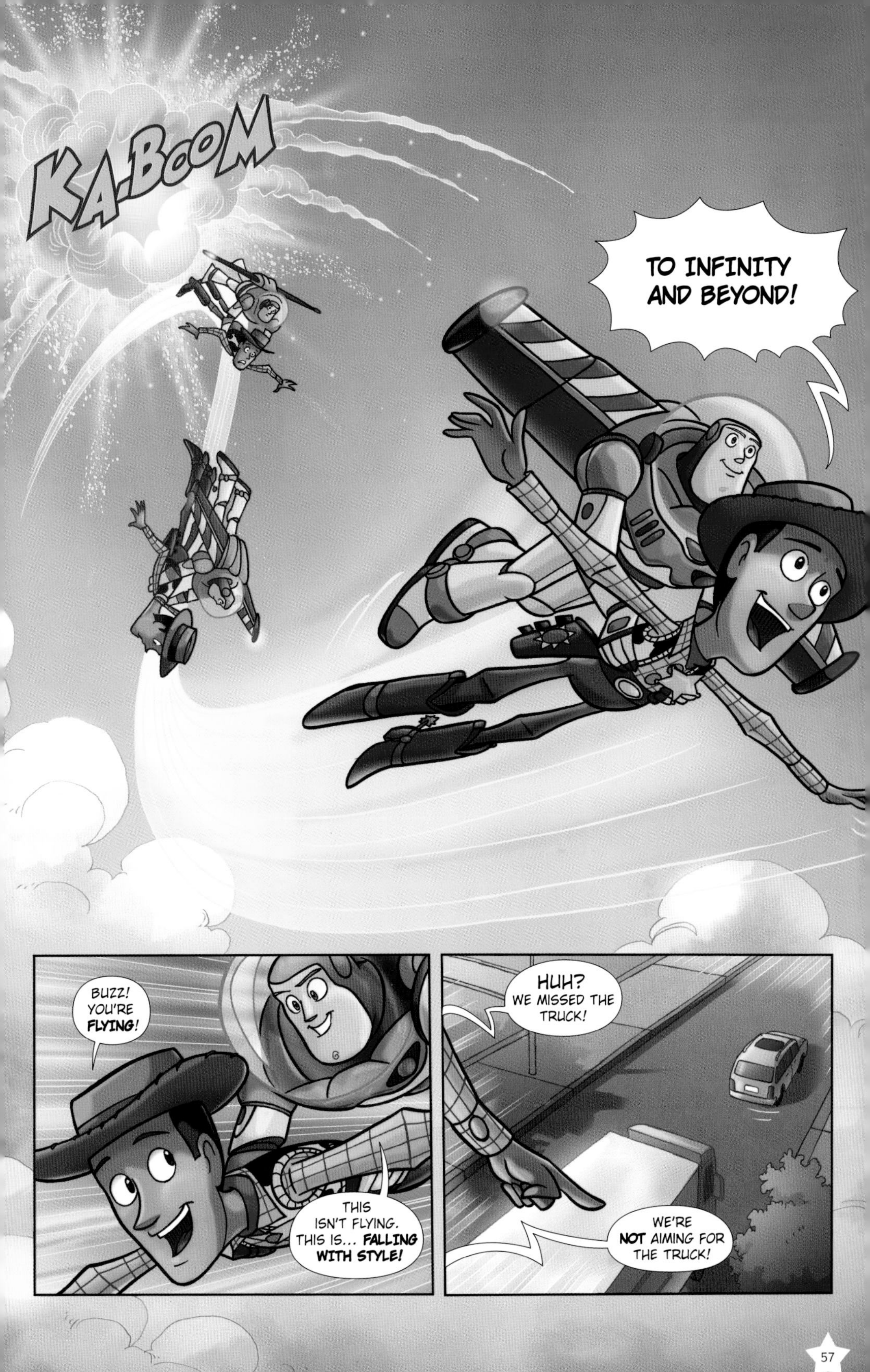
KA-BOOM
TO INFINITY AND BEYOND!
BUZZ! YOU'RE **FLYING**!
THIS ISN'T FLYING. THIS IS... **FALLING WITH STYLE!**
HUH? WE MISSED THE TRUCK!
WE'RE **NOT** AIMING FOR THE TRUCK!

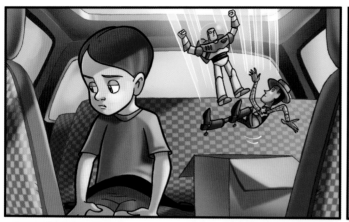

!

WHUMP

WOODY! BUZZ!

OH, GREAT, YOU FOUND THEM. WHERE WERE THEY?

HERE! IN THE CAR!

SEE? NOW, WHAT DID I TELL YOU?

RIGHT WHERE YOU LEFT THEM...

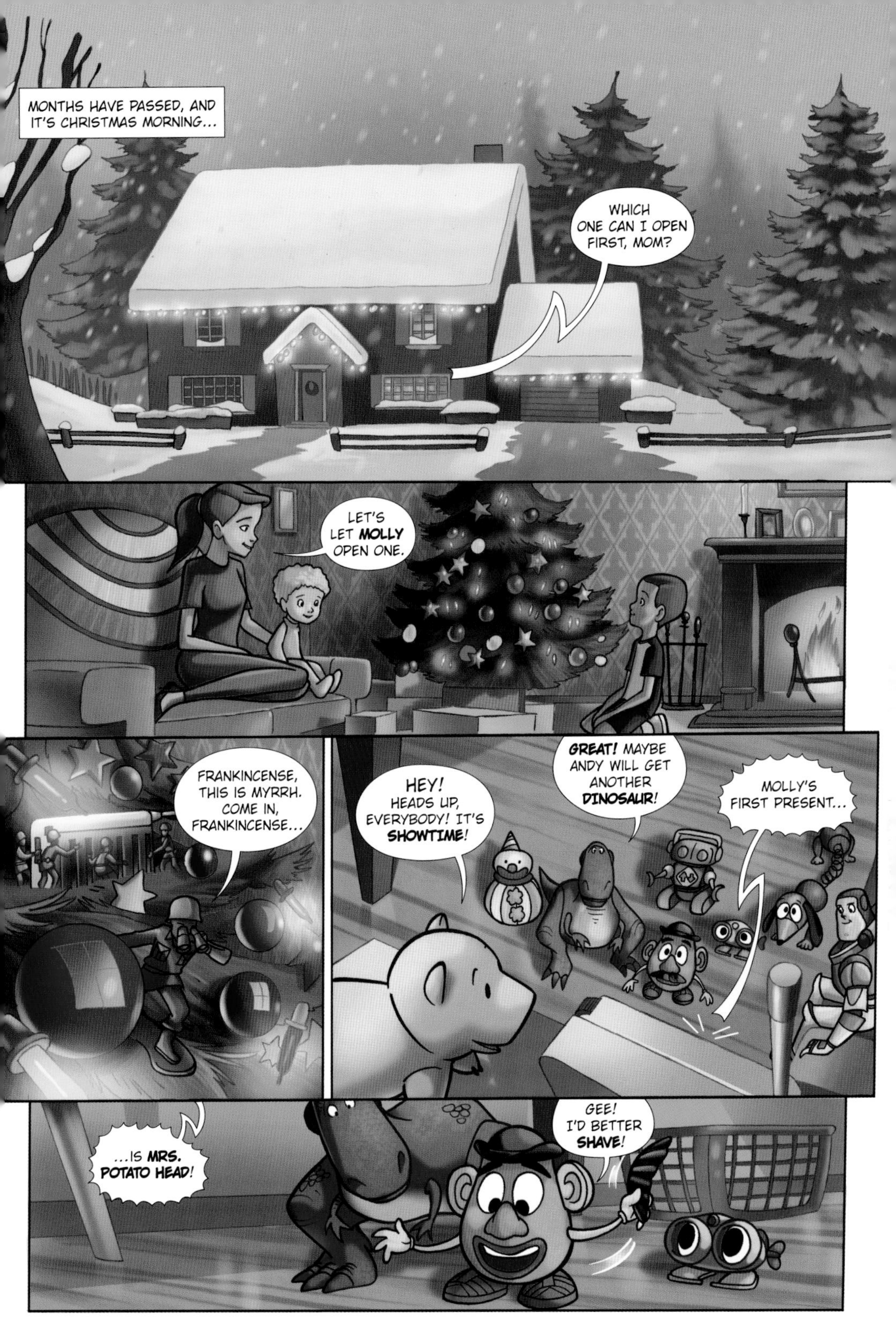
MONTHS HAVE PASSED, AND IT'S CHRISTMAS MORNING...
WHICH ONE CAN I OPEN FIRST, MOM?
LET'S LET **MOLLY** OPEN ONE.
FRANKINCENSE, THIS IS MYRRH. COME IN, FRANKINCENSE...
HEY! HEADS UP, EVERYBODY! IT'S **SHOWTIME**!
GREAT! MAYBE ANDY WILL GET ANOTHER **DINOSAUR**!
MOLLY'S FIRST PRESENT...
...IS **MRS. POTATO HEAD**!
GEE! I'D BETTER **SHAVE**!

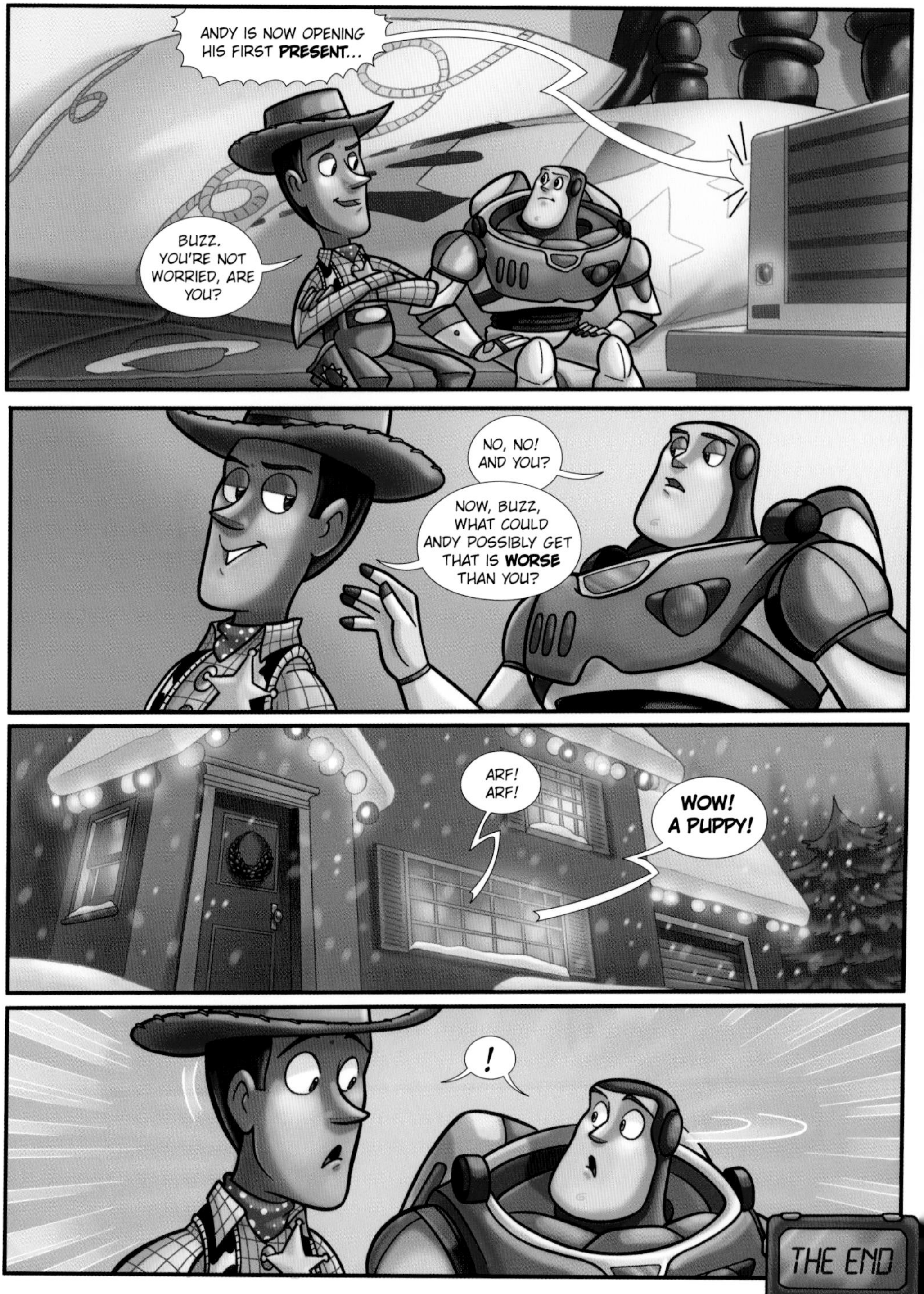
ANDY IS NOW OPENING HIS FIRST **PRESENT**...
BUZZ. YOU'RE NOT WORRIED, ARE YOU?
NO, NO! AND YOU?
NOW, BUZZ, WHAT COULD ANDY POSSIBLY GET THAT IS **WORSE** THAN YOU?
ARF! ARF!
WOW! A PUPPY!
!
THE END

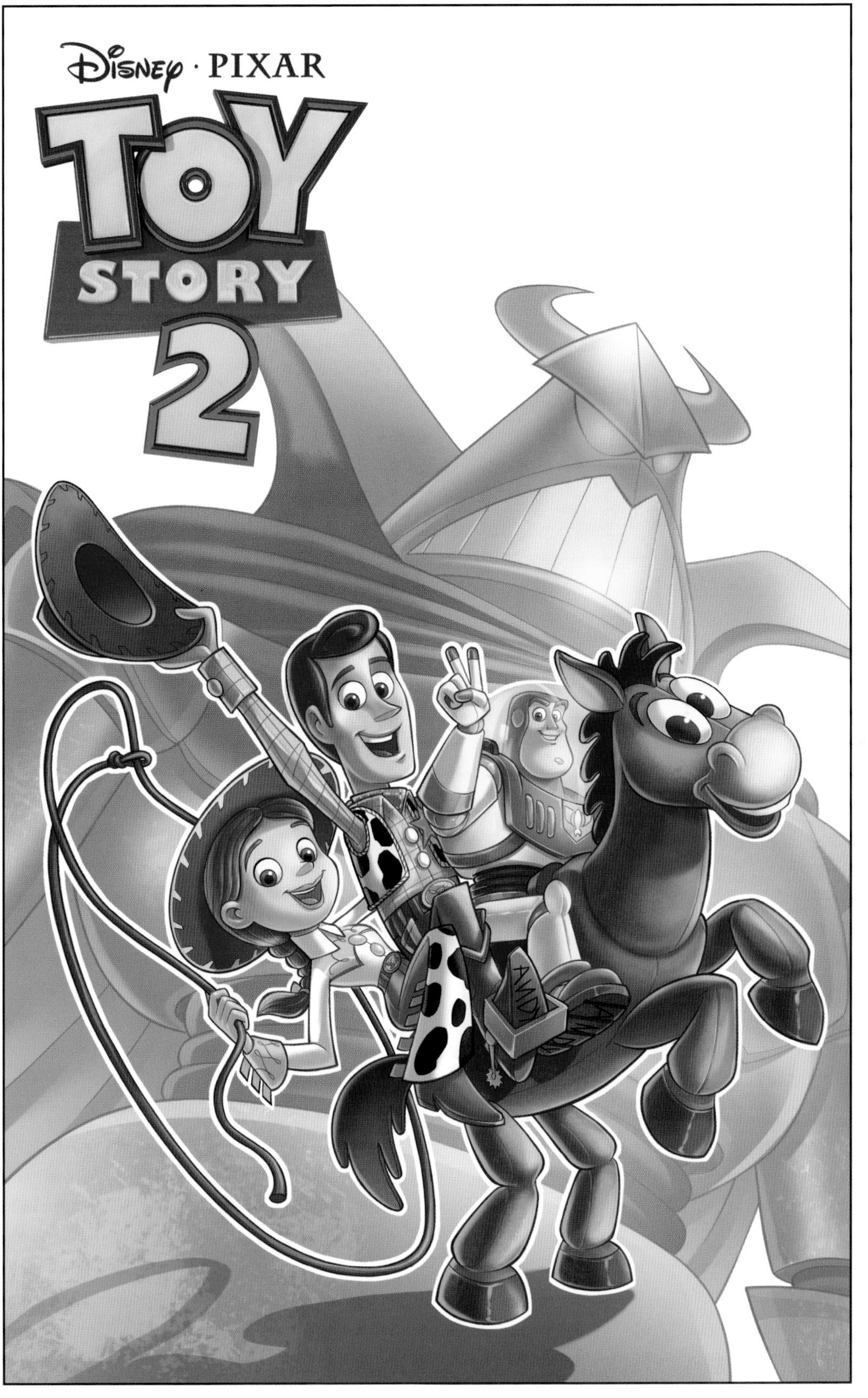
Disney · PIXAR
TOY STORY 2
ANDY

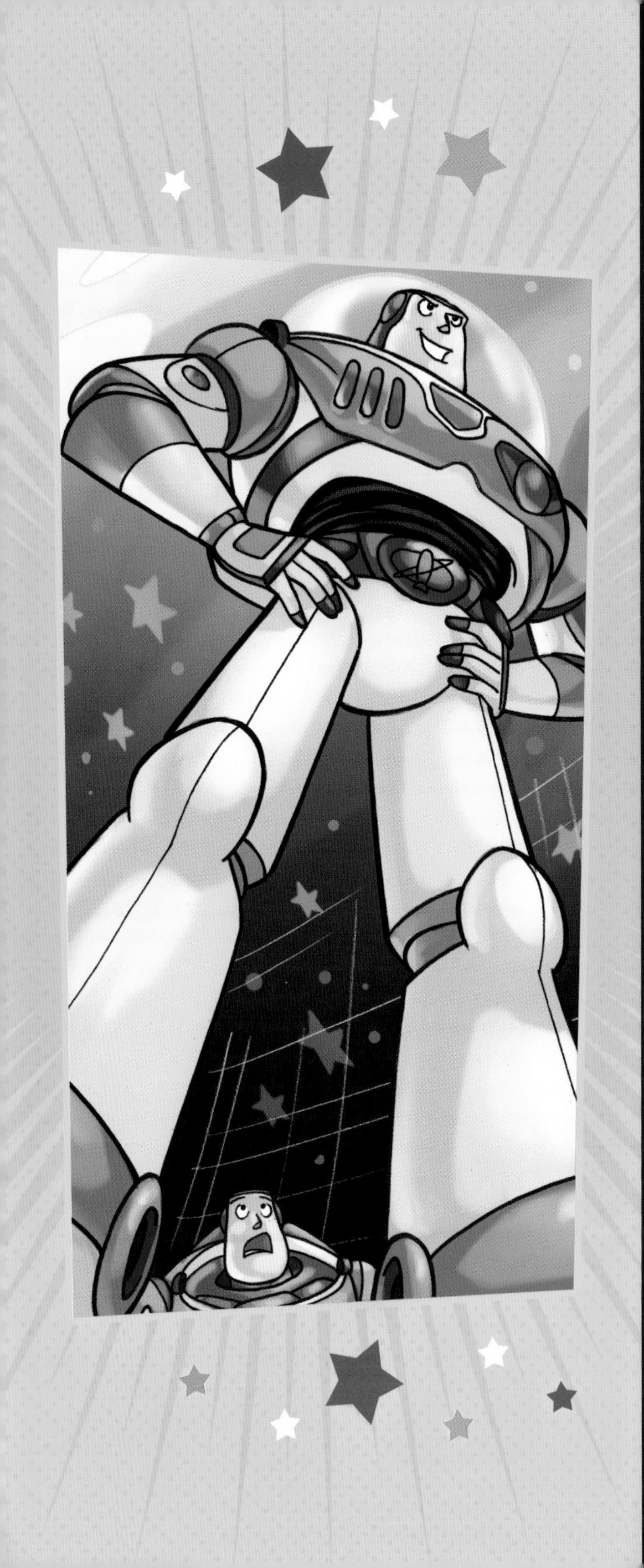

script adaptation
Alessandro Ferrari

art
Ettore Gula

paint
Kawaii Creative Studio

art optimization
Stefano Attardi

editing
Kawaii Creative Studio

contributor
Elisabetta Sedda

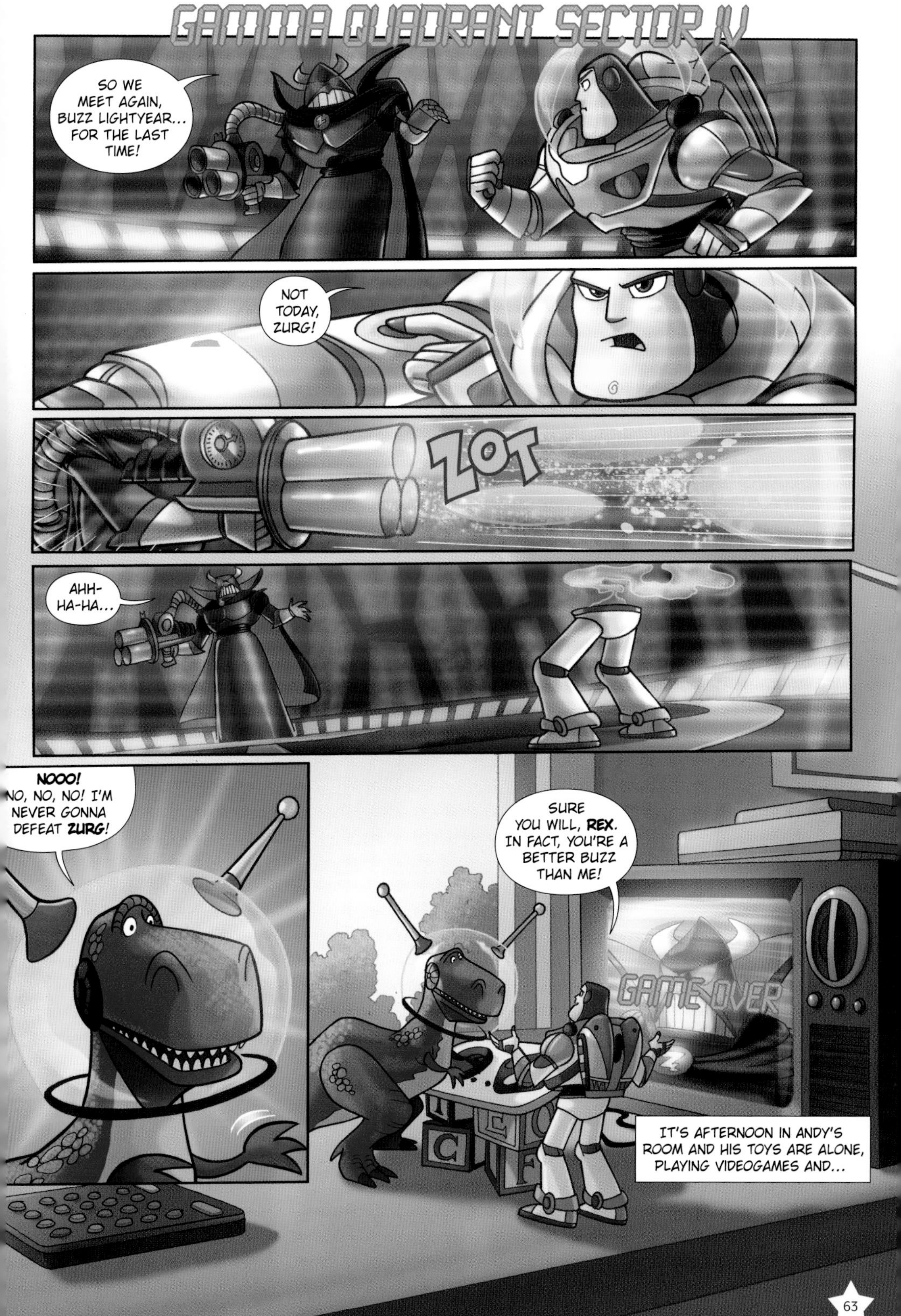
GAMMA QUADRANT SECTOR IV
SO WE MEET AGAIN, BUZZ LIGHTYEAR... FOR THE LAST TIME!
NOT TODAY, ZURG!
ZOT
AHH-HA-HA...
NOOO! NO, NO, NO! I'M NEVER GONNA DEFEAT ZURG!
SURE YOU WILL, REX. IN FACT, YOU'RE A BETTER BUZZ THAN ME!
GAME OVER
IT'S AFTERNOON IN ANDY'S ROOM AND HIS TOYS ARE ALONE, PLAYING VIDEOGAMES AND...

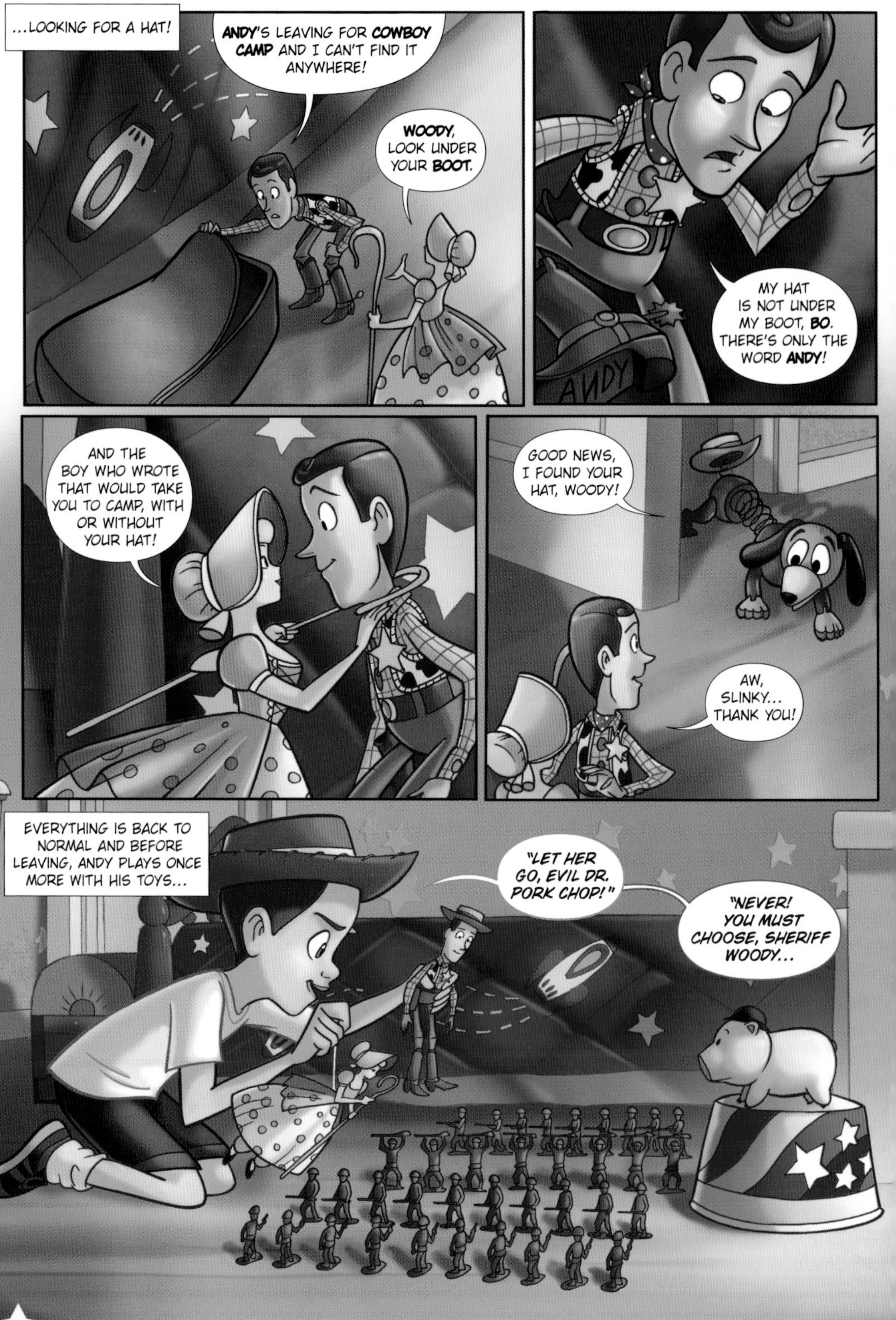
...LOOKING FOR A HAT!
ANDY'S LEAVING FOR COWBOY CAMP AND I CAN'T FIND IT ANYWHERE!
WOODY, LOOK UNDER YOUR BOOT.
MY HAT IS NOT UNDER MY BOOT, BO. THERE'S ONLY THE WORD ANDY!
ANDY
AND THE BOY WHO WROTE THAT WOULD TAKE YOU TO CAMP, WITH OR WITHOUT YOUR HAT!
GOOD NEWS, I FOUND YOUR HAT, WOODY!
AW, SLINKY... THANK YOU!
EVERYTHING IS BACK TO NORMAL AND BEFORE LEAVING, ANDY PLAYS ONCE MORE WITH HIS TOYS...
"LET HER GO, EVIL DR. PORK CHOP!"
"NEVER! YOU MUST CHOOSE, SHERIFF WOODY...

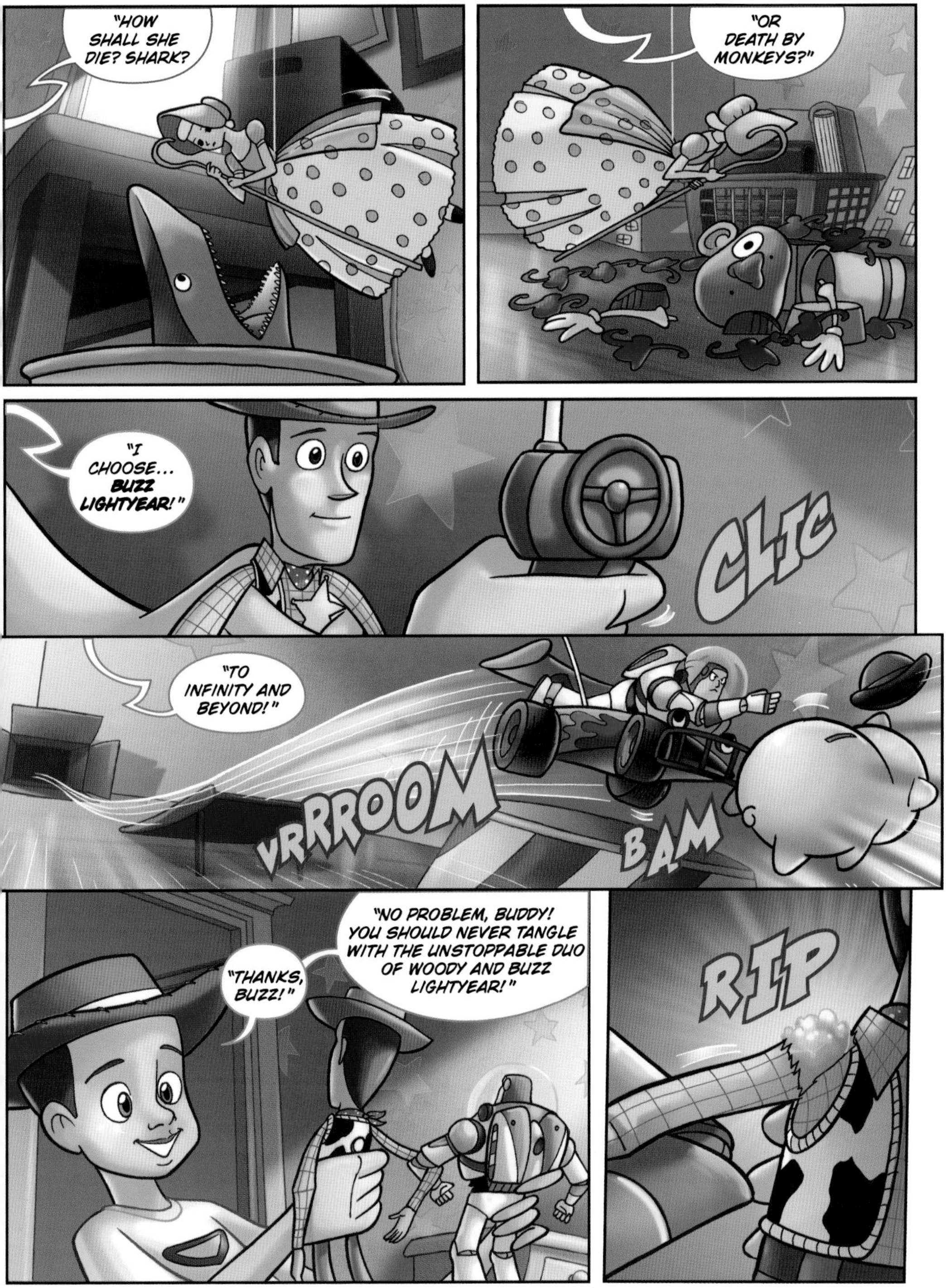
"HOW SHALL SHE DIE? SHARK?
"OR DEATH BY MONKEYS?"
"I CHOOSE... BUZZ LIGHTYEAR!"
CLIC
"TO INFINITY AND BEYOND!"
VRRROOM
BAM
"THANKS, BUZZ!"
"NO PROBLEM, BUDDY! YOU SHOULD NEVER TANGLE WITH THE UNSTOPPABLE DUO OF WOODY AND BUZZ LIGHTYEAR!"
RIP

OH,
NO...

ANDY, LET'S GO.
THE CAMP IS
WAITING.

BUT, MOM,
WOODY'S ARM
RIPPED.

I'M SORRY, HONEY, BUT
YOU KNOW, **TOYS DON'T
LAST FOREVER**.

FOR THE FIRST TIME ANDY
GOES TO COWBOY CAMP
WITHOUT HIS FAVORITE TOY.

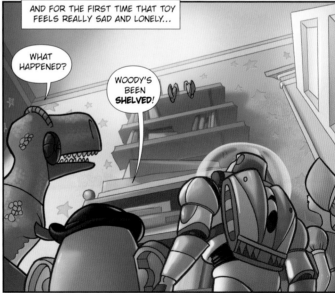

AND FOR THE FIRST TIME THAT TOY
FEELS REALLY SAD AND LONELY...

WHAT
HAPPENED?

WOODY'S
BEEN
SHELVED!

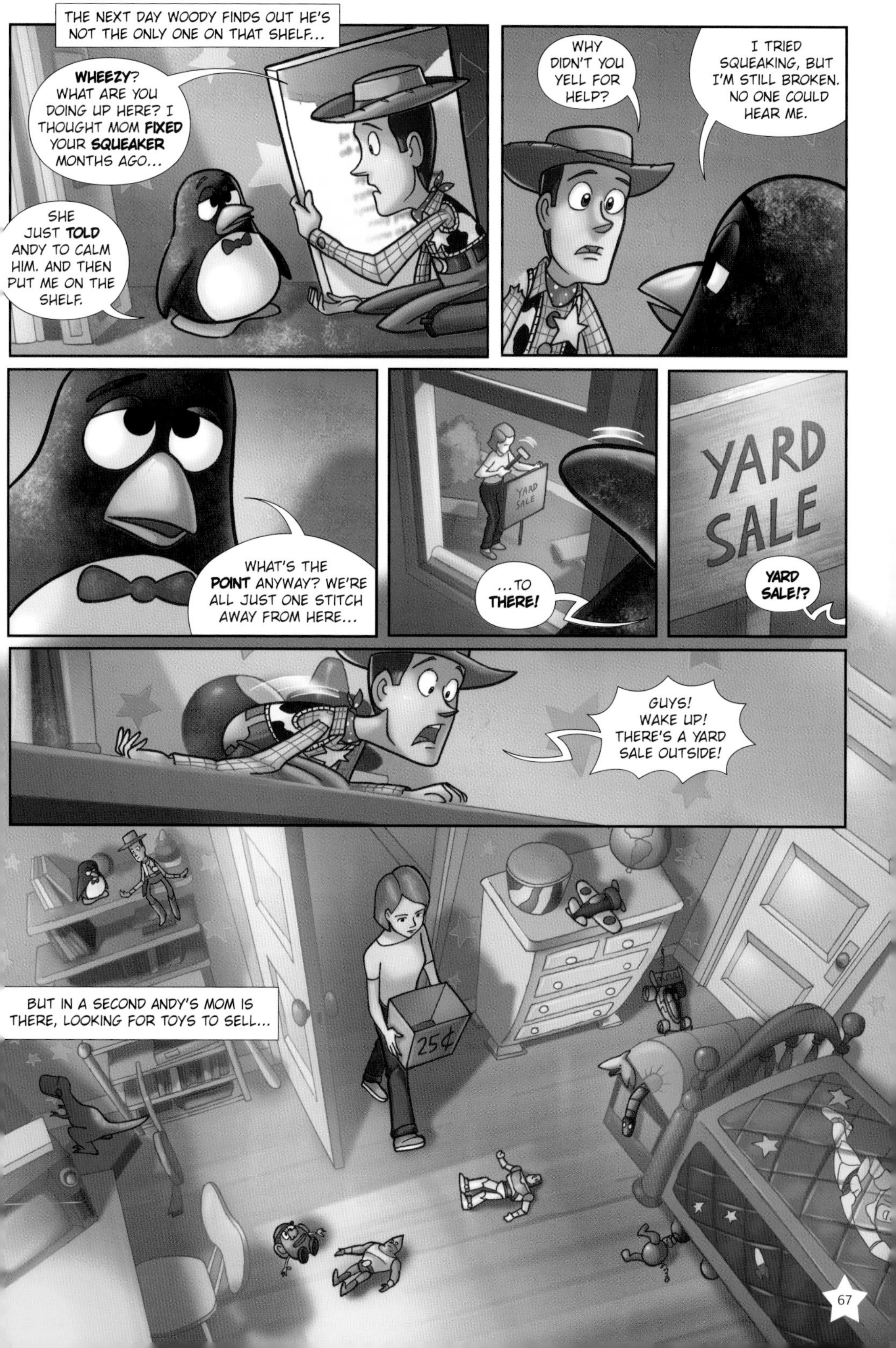

THE NEXT DAY WOODY FINDS OUT HE'S NOT THE ONLY ONE ON THAT SHELF...
WHEEZY? WHAT ARE YOU DOING UP HERE? I THOUGHT MOM FIXED YOUR SQUEAKER MONTHS AGO...
SHE JUST TOLD ANDY TO CALM HIM. AND THEN PUT ME ON THE SHELF.
WHY DIDN'T YOU YELL FOR HELP?
I TRIED SQUEAKING, BUT I'M STILL BROKEN. NO ONE COULD HEAR ME.
WHAT'S THE POINT ANYWAY? WE'RE ALL JUST ONE STITCH AWAY FROM HERE...
YARD SALE
...TO THERE!
YARD SALE
YARD SALE!?
GUYS! WAKE UP! THERE'S A YARD SALE OUTSIDE!
BUT IN A SECOND ANDY'S MOM IS THERE, LOOKING FOR TOYS TO SELL...
25¢

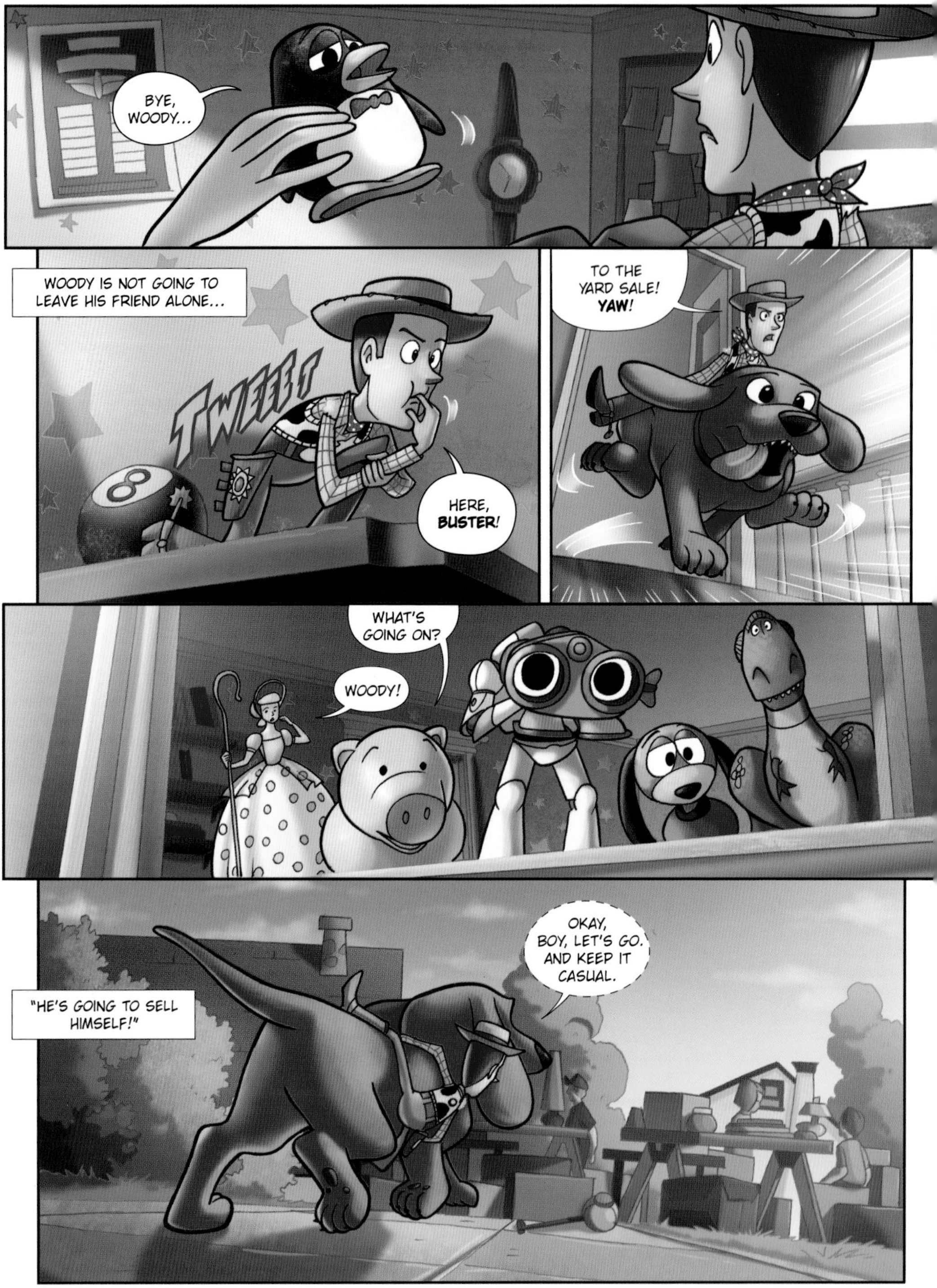
BYE, WOODY...
WOODY IS NOT GOING TO LEAVE HIS FRIEND ALONE...
TWEEET
HERE, **BUSTER**!
TO THE YARD SALE! **YAW**!
WHAT'S GOING ON?
WOODY!
OKAY, BOY, LET'S GO. AND KEEP IT CASUAL.
"HE'S GOING TO SELL HIMSELF!"

"HE'S SELLING HIMSELF FOR 25 CENTS!"

"HOLD ON, HOLD ON, HE'S GOT SOMETHING... IT'S **WHEEZY!**"

"IT'S NOT **SUICIDE,** IT'S A **RESCUE!**"

BUT EVERY RESCUE HAS ITS INCONVENIENCES...

NOW... BACK TO ANDY'S **ROO-OOF!**

NO, NO, NO...

MOMMY! LOOK AT THIS! IT'S A COWBOY DOLLY...

TRRR

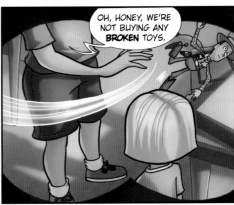

OH, HONEY, WE'RE NOT BUYING ANY **BROKEN** TOYS.

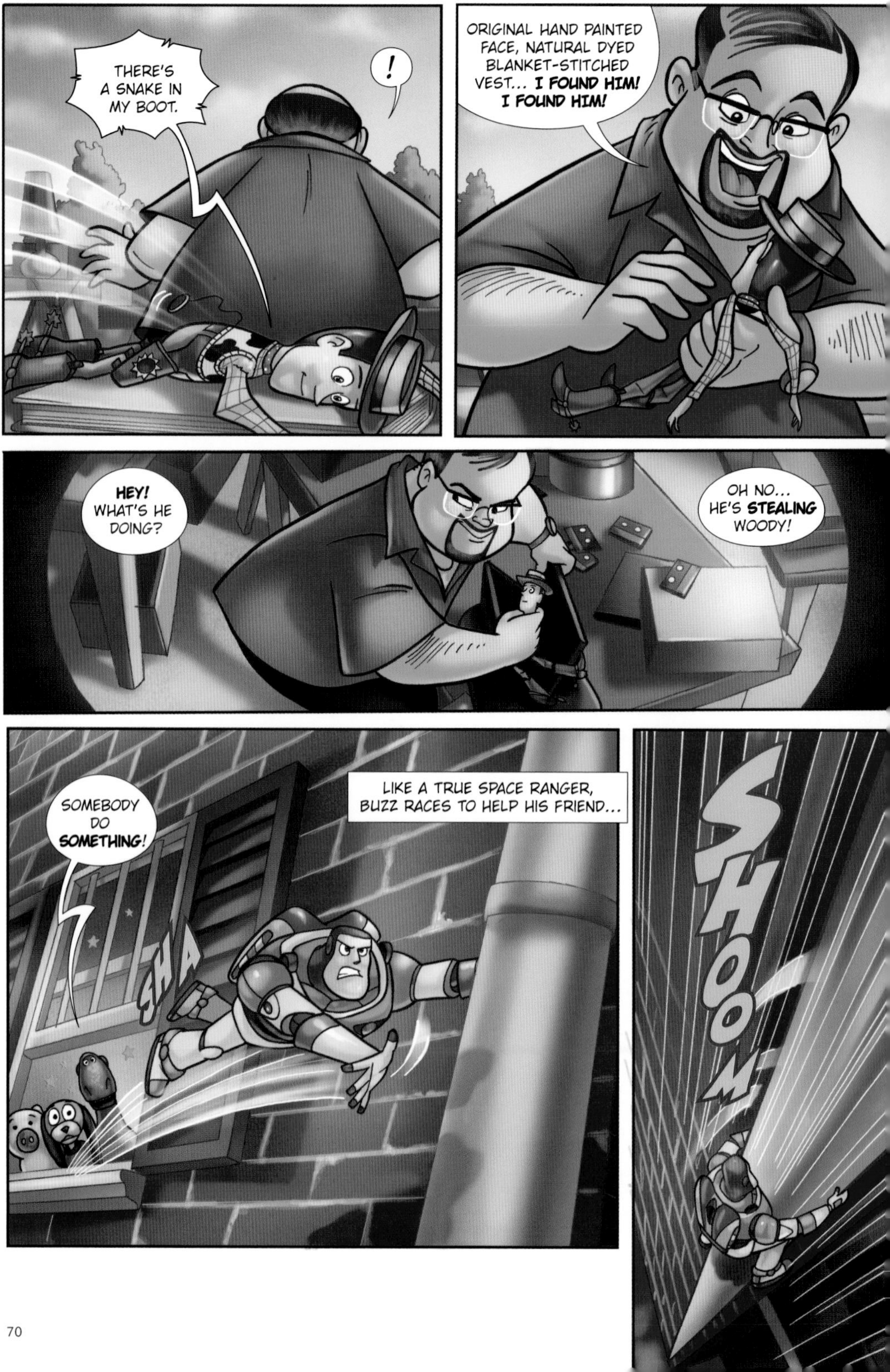
THERE'S A SNAKE IN MY BOOT.
!
ORIGINAL HAND PAINTED FACE, NATURAL DYED BLANKET-STITCHED VEST... I FOUND HIM! I FOUND HIM!
HEY! WHAT'S HE DOING?
OH NO... HE'S STEALING WOODY!
LIKE A TRUE SPACE RANGER, BUZZ RACES TO HELP HIS FRIEND...
SOMEBODY DO SOMETHING!
SHA
SHOOOM

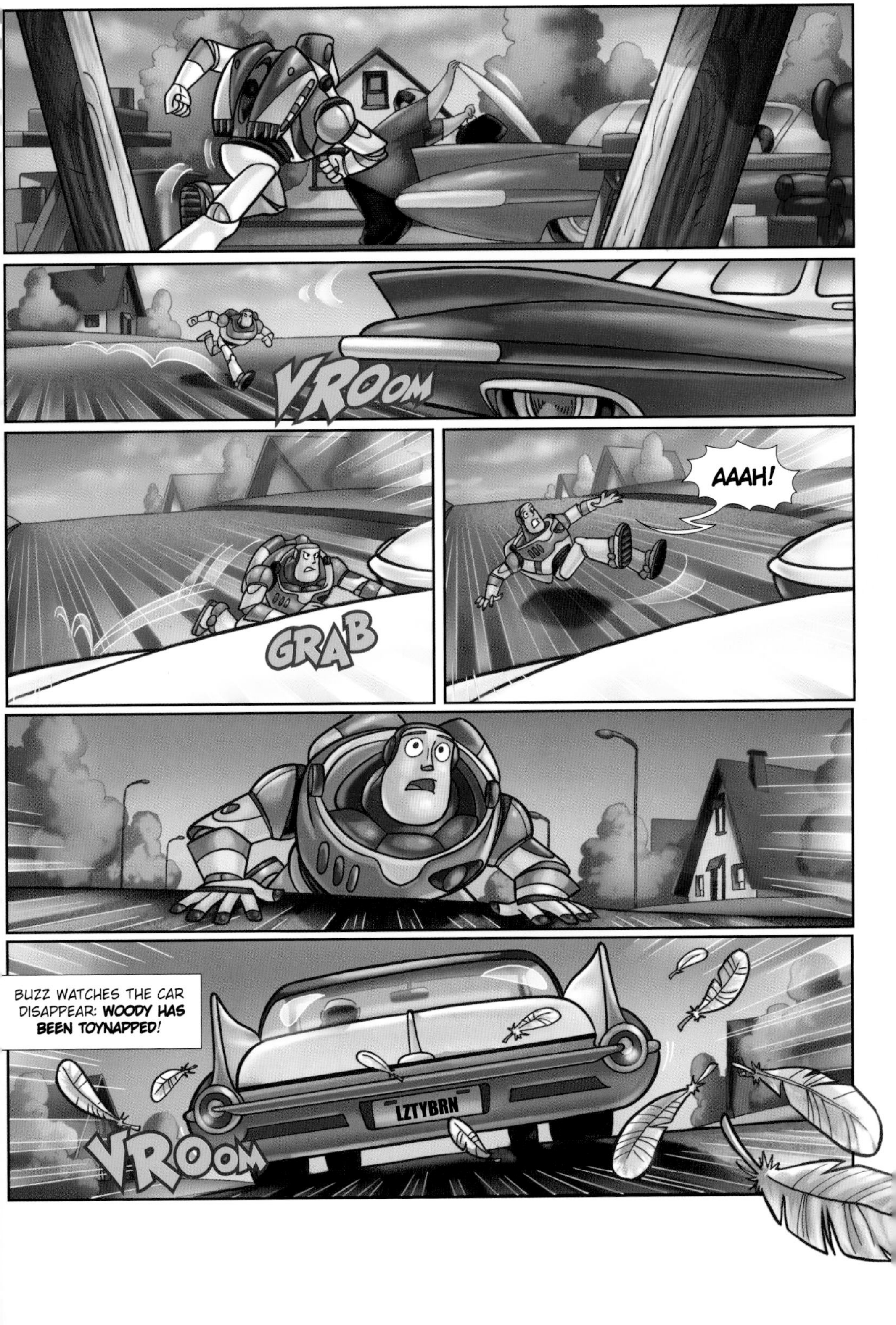
VROOM
GRAB
AAAH!
BUZZ WATCHES THE CAR DISAPPEAR: WOODY HAS BEEN TOYNAPPED!
LZTYBRN
VROOM

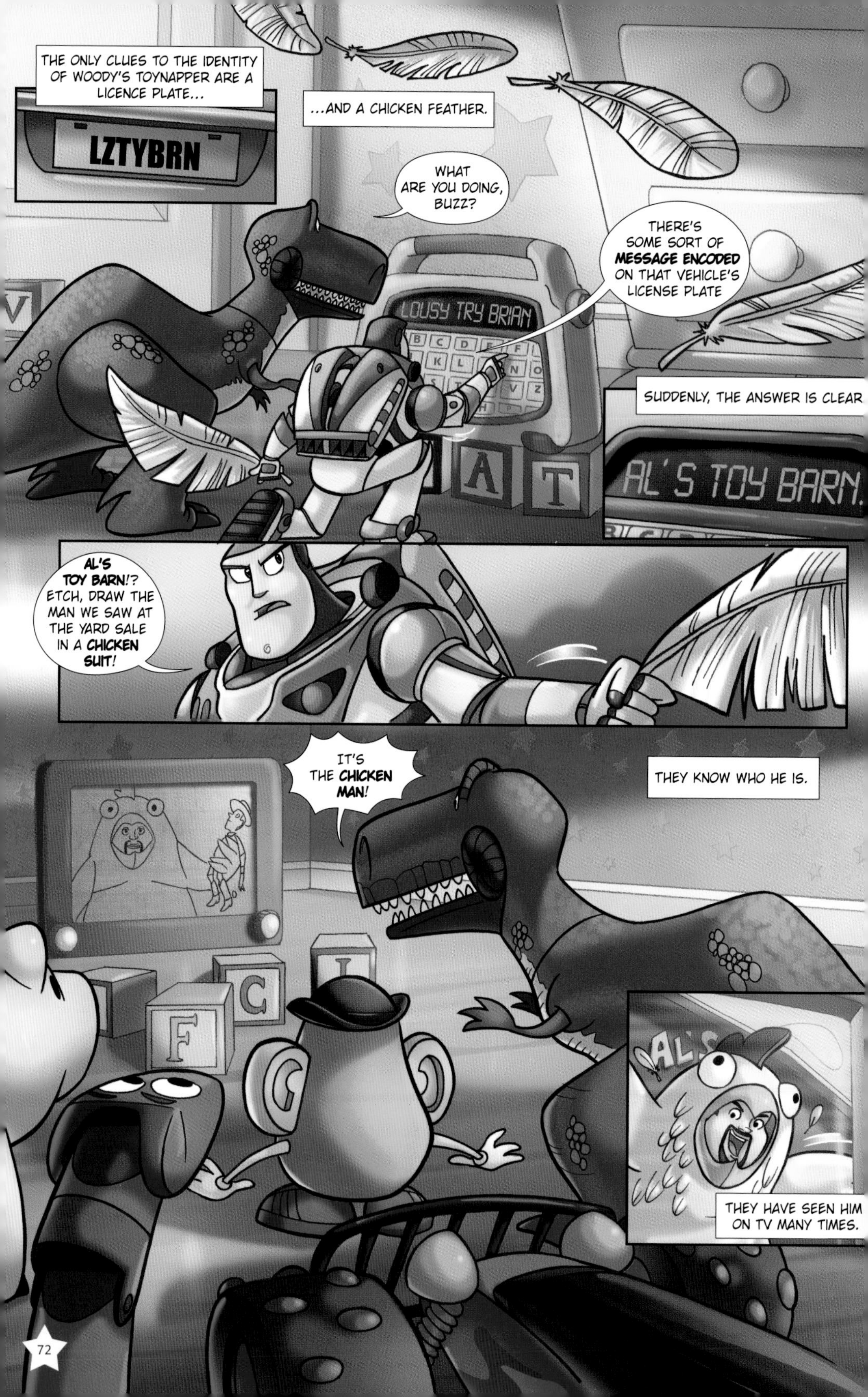
THE ONLY CLUES TO THE IDENTITY OF WOODY'S TOYNAPPER ARE A LICENCE PLATE...
LZTYBRN
...AND A CHICKEN FEATHER.
WHAT ARE YOU DOING, BUZZ?
THERE'S SOME SORT OF **MESSAGE ENCODED** ON THAT VEHICLE'S LICENSE PLATE
LOUSY TRY BRIAN
SUDDENLY, THE ANSWER IS CLEAR
AL'S TOY BARN.
AL'S TOY BARN!? ETCH, DRAW THE MAN WE SAW AT THE YARD SALE IN A **CHICKEN SUIT**!
IT'S THE **CHICKEN MAN**!
THEY KNOW WHO HE IS.
THEY HAVE SEEN HIM ON TV MANY TIMES.

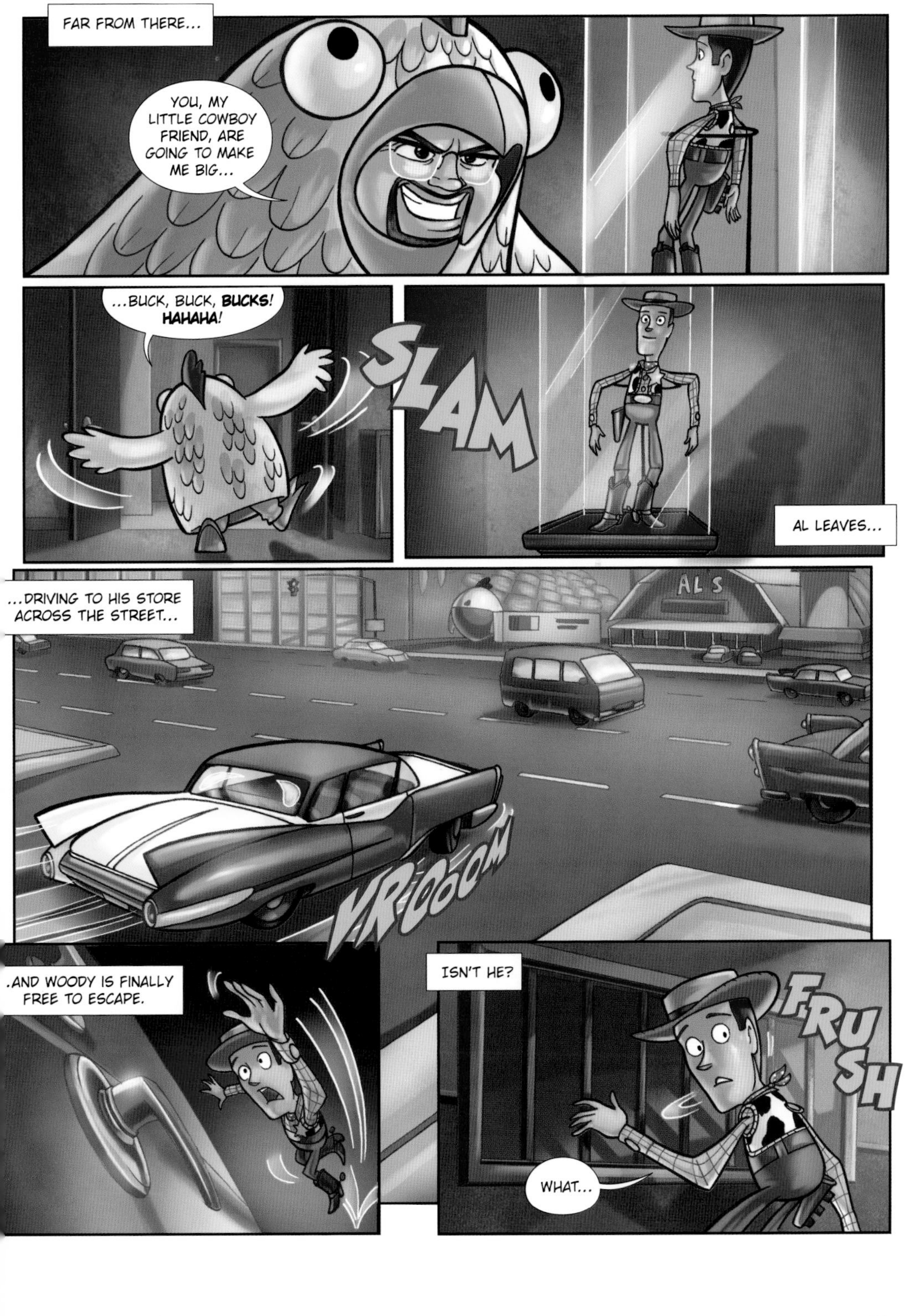
FAR FROM THERE...
YOU, MY LITTLE COWBOY FRIEND, ARE GOING TO MAKE ME BIG...
...BUCK, BUCK, BUCKS! HAHAHA!
SLAM
AL LEAVES...
...DRIVING TO HIS STORE ACROSS THE STREET...
AL S
VROOOM
.AND WOODY IS FINALLY FREE TO ESCAPE.
ISN'T HE?
FRUSH
WHAT...

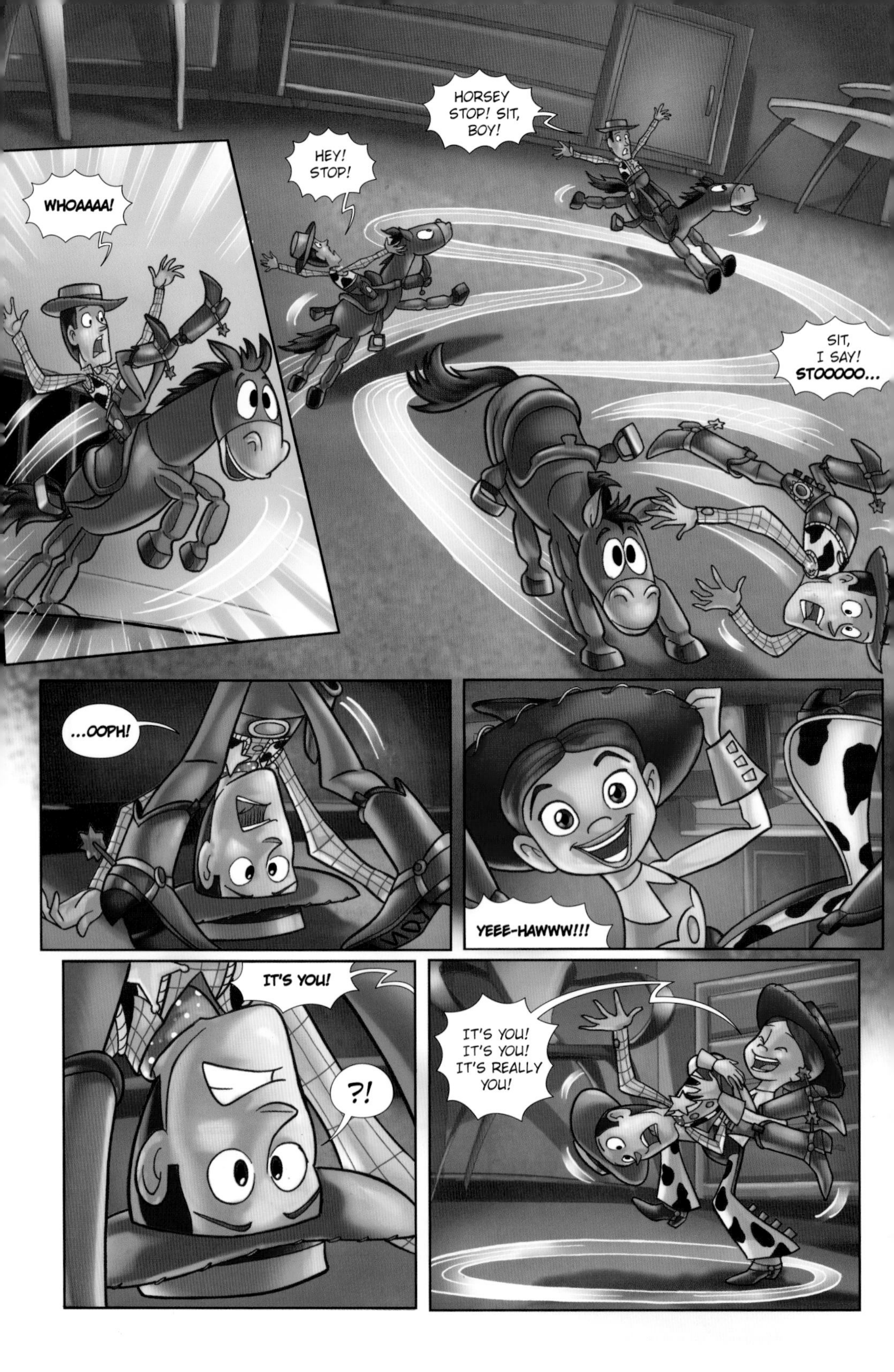
WHOAAAA!
HEY! STOP!
HORSEY STOP! SIT, BOY!
SIT, I SAY! STOOOOO...
...OOPH!
YEEE-HAWWW!!!
IT'S YOU!
?!
IT'S YOU! IT'S YOU! IT'S REALLY YOU!

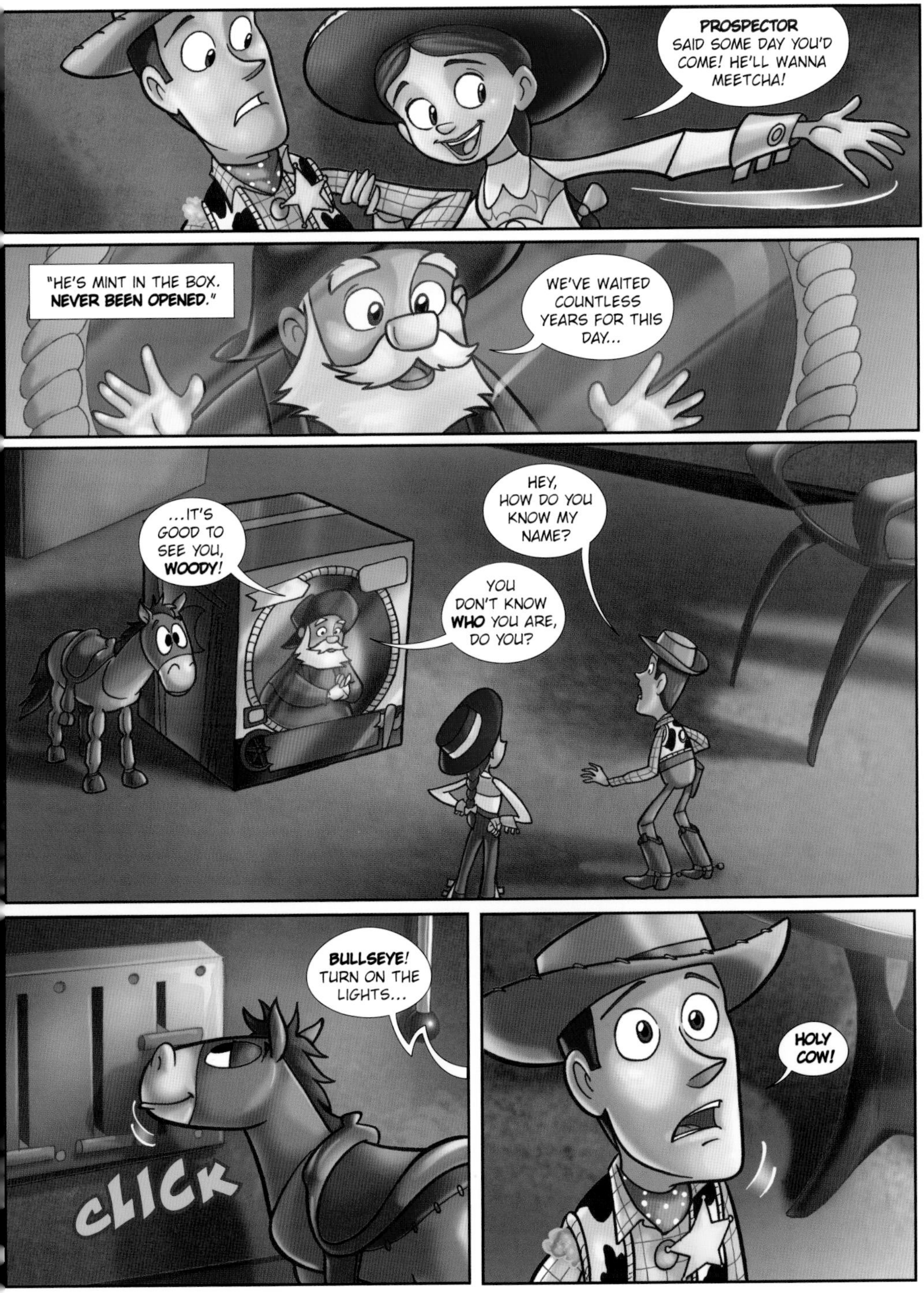
PROSPECTOR SAID SOME DAY YOU'D COME! HE'LL WANNA MEETCHA!
"HE'S MINT IN THE BOX. NEVER BEEN OPENED."
WE'VE WAITED COUNTLESS YEARS FOR THIS DAY...
...IT'S GOOD TO SEE YOU, WOODY!
HEY, HOW DO YOU KNOW MY NAME?
YOU DON'T KNOW WHO YOU ARE, DO YOU?
BULLSEYE! TURN ON THE LIGHTS...
CLICK
HOLY COW!

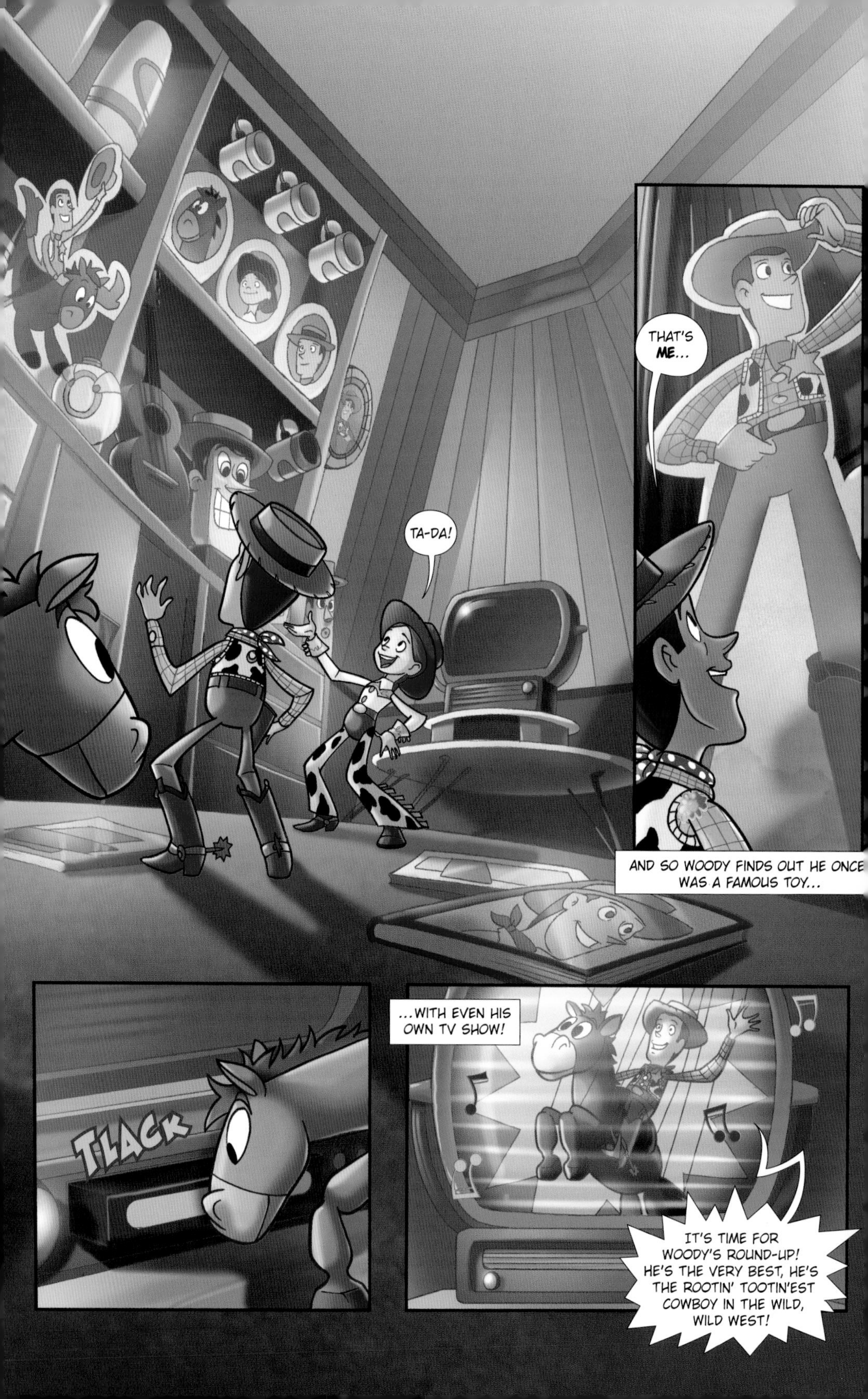
TA-DA!
THAT'S **ME**...
AND SO WOODY FINDS OUT HE ONCE WAS A FAMOUS TOY...
TLACK
...WITH EVEN HIS OWN TV SHOW!
IT'S TIME FOR WOODY'S ROUND-UP! HE'S THE VERY BEST, HE'S THE ROOTIN' TOOTIN'EST COWBOY IN THE WILD, WILD WEST!

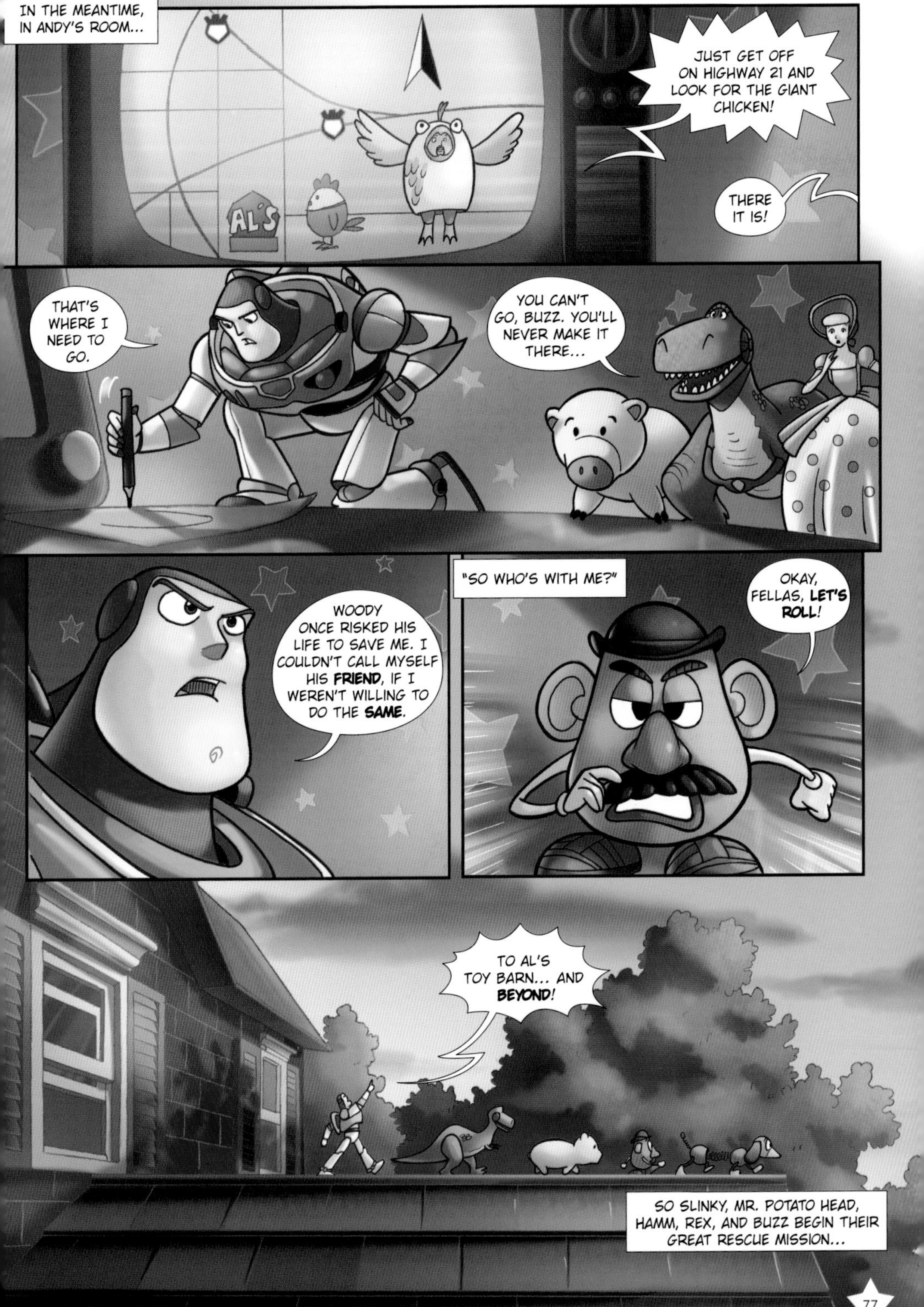
IN THE MEANTIME, IN ANDY'S ROOM...
AL'S
JUST GET OFF ON HIGHWAY 21 AND LOOK FOR THE GIANT CHICKEN!
THERE IT IS!
THAT'S WHERE I NEED TO GO.
YOU CAN'T GO, BUZZ. YOU'LL NEVER MAKE IT THERE...
WOODY ONCE RISKED HIS LIFE TO SAVE ME. I COULDN'T CALL MYSELF HIS FRIEND, IF I WEREN'T WILLING TO DO THE SAME.
"SO WHO'S WITH ME?"
OKAY, FELLAS, LET'S ROLL!
TO AL'S TOY BARN... AND BEYOND!
SO SLINKY, MR. POTATO HEAD, HAMM, REX, AND BUZZ BEGIN THEIR GREAT RESCUE MISSION...

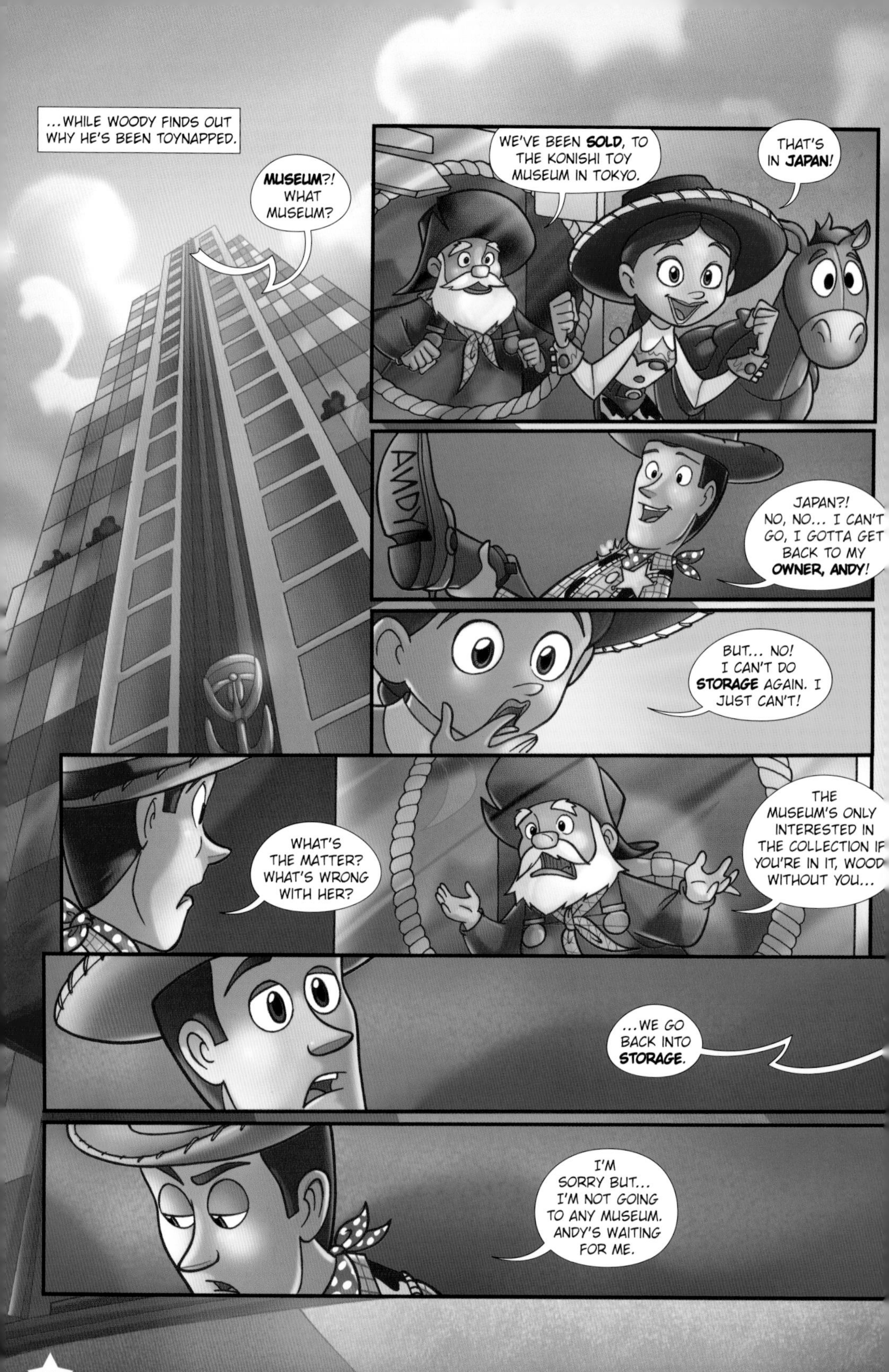
...WHILE WOODY FINDS OUT WHY HE'S BEEN TOYNAPPED.
MUSEUM?! WHAT MUSEUM?
WE'VE BEEN SOLD, TO THE KONISHI TOY MUSEUM IN TOKYO.
THAT'S IN JAPAN!
ANDY
JAPAN?! NO, NO... I CAN'T GO, I GOTTA GET BACK TO MY OWNER, ANDY!
BUT... NO! I CAN'T DO STORAGE AGAIN. I JUST CAN'T!
WHAT'S THE MATTER? WHAT'S WRONG WITH HER?
THE MUSEUM'S ONLY INTERESTED IN THE COLLECTION IF YOU'RE IN IT, WOOD
WITHOUT YOU...
...WE GO BACK INTO STORAGE.
I'M SORRY BUT... I'M NOT GOING TO ANY MUSEUM. ANDY'S WAITING FOR ME.

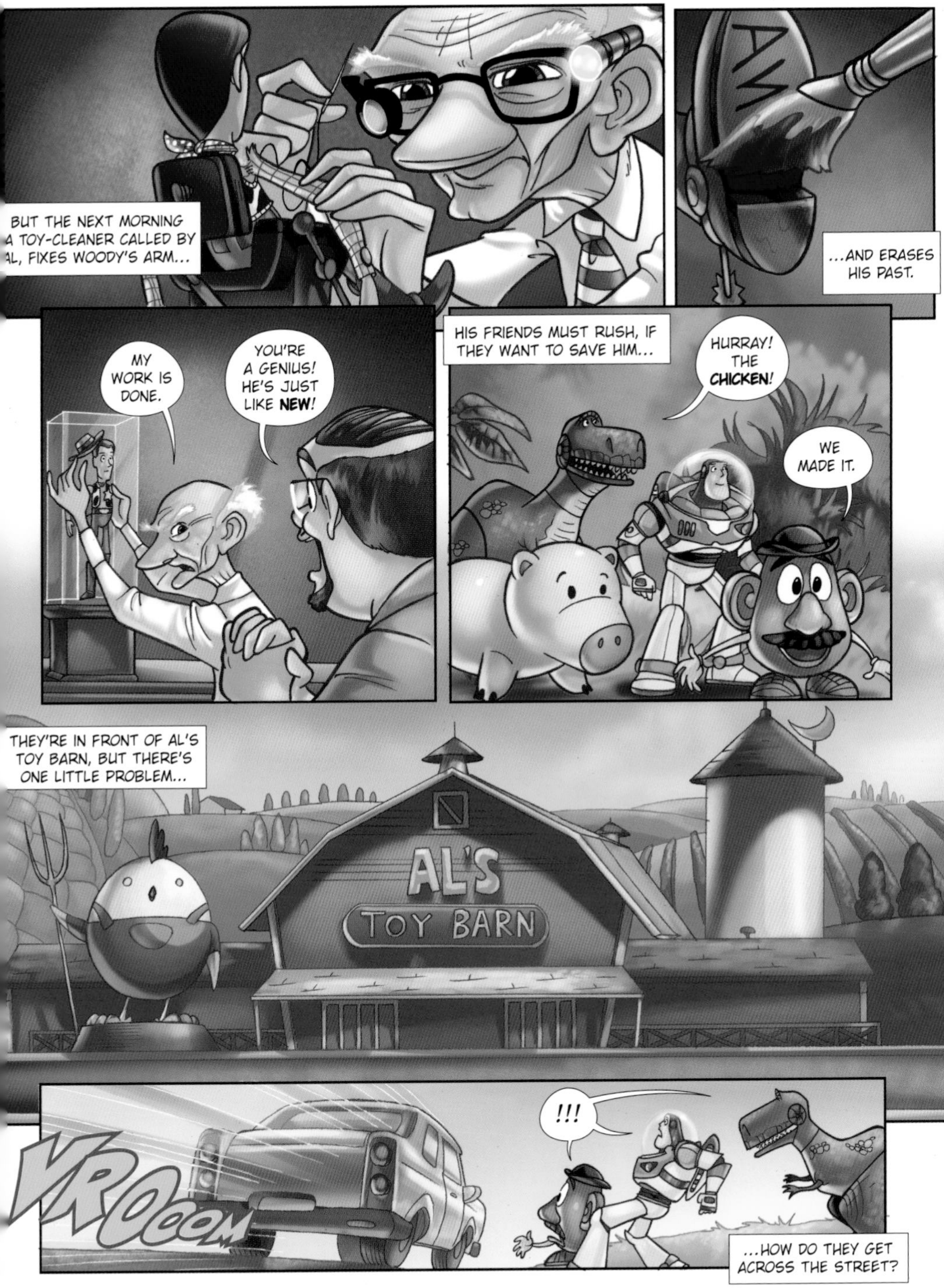

BUT THE NEXT MORNING A TOY-CLEANER CALLED BY AL, FIXES WOODY'S ARM...
...AND ERASES HIS PAST.
MY WORK IS DONE.
YOU'RE A GENIUS! HE'S JUST LIKE NEW!
HIS FRIENDS MUST RUSH, IF THEY WANT TO SAVE HIM...
HURRAY! THE CHICKEN!
WE MADE IT.
THEY'RE IN FRONT OF AL'S TOY BARN, BUT THERE'S ONE LITTLE PROBLEM...
AL'S
TOY BARN
VROOOOM
!!!
...HOW DO THEY GET ACROSS THE STREET?

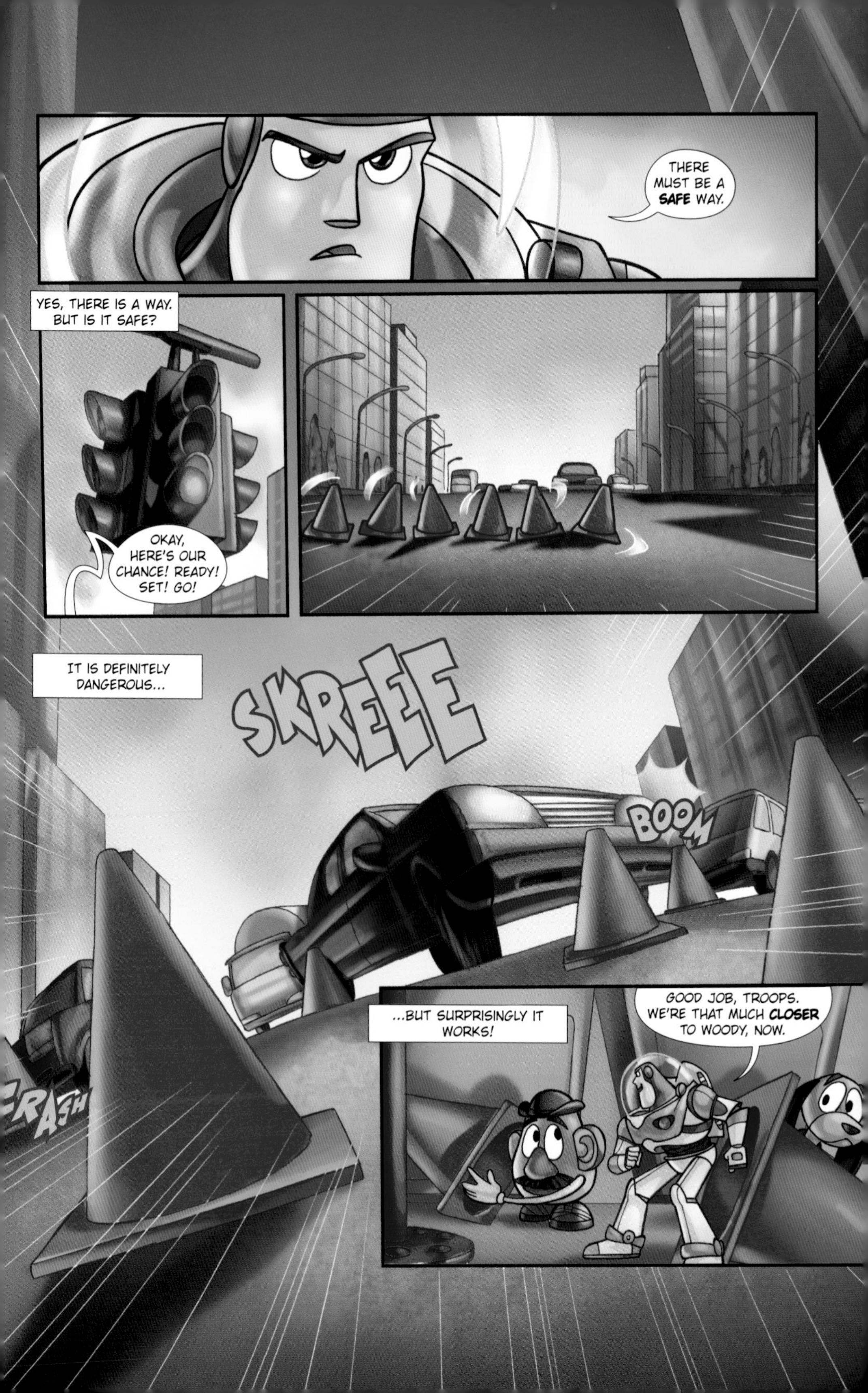

THERE MUST BE A SAFE WAY.
YES, THERE IS A WAY. BUT IS IT SAFE?
OKAY, HERE'S OUR CHANCE! READY! SET! GO!
IT IS DEFINITELY DANGEROUS...
SKREEE
BOOM
CRASH
...BUT SURPRISINGLY IT WORKS!
GOOD JOB, TROOPS. WE'RE THAT MUCH CLOSER TO WOODY, NOW.

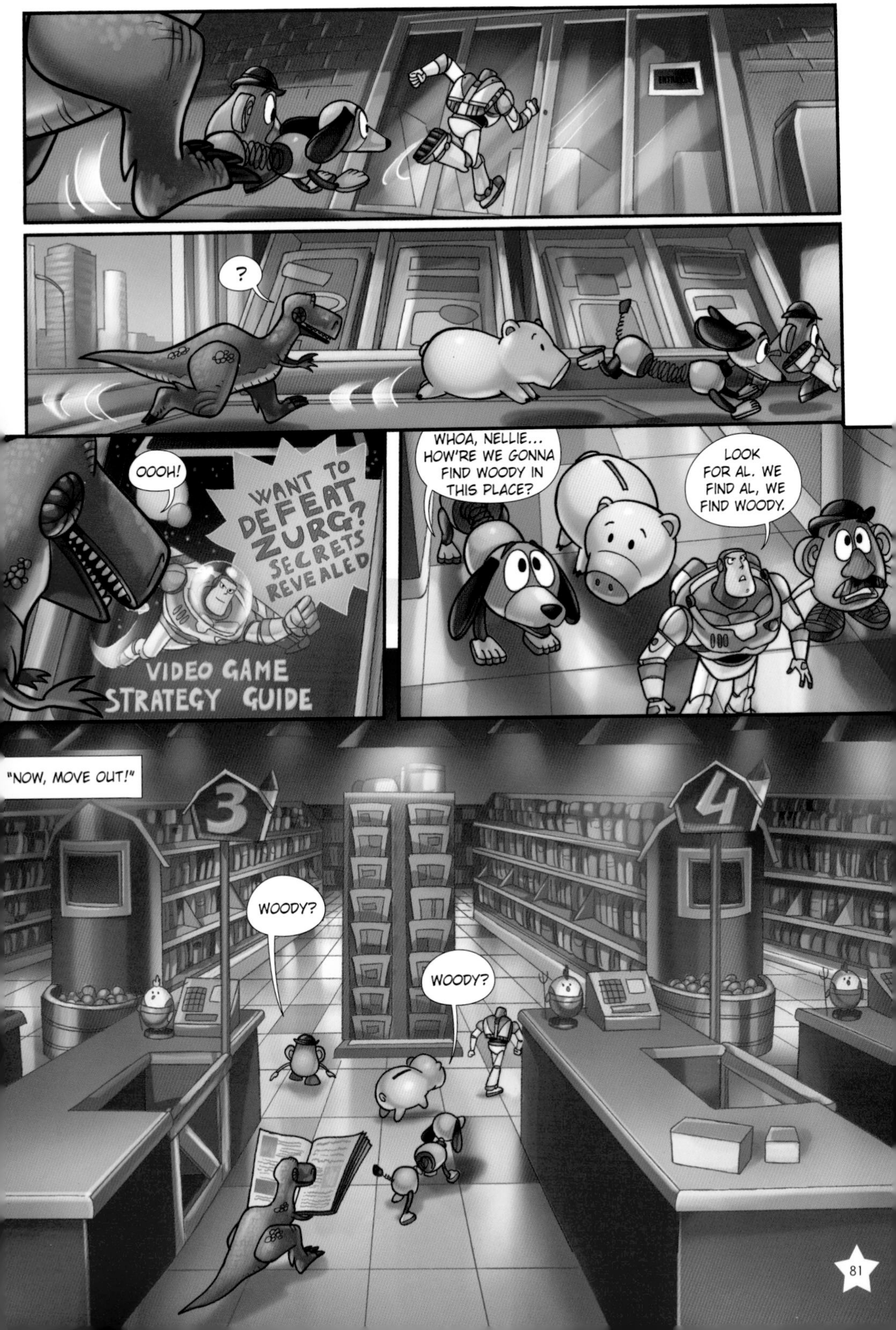
?
OOOH!
WANT TO DEFEAT ZURG? SECRETS REVEALED
VIDEO GAME STRATEGY GUIDE
WHOA, NELLIE... HOW'RE WE GONNA FIND WOODY IN THIS PLACE?
LOOK FOR AL. WE FIND AL, WE FIND WOODY.
"NOW, MOVE OUT!"
3
4
WOODY?
WOODY?

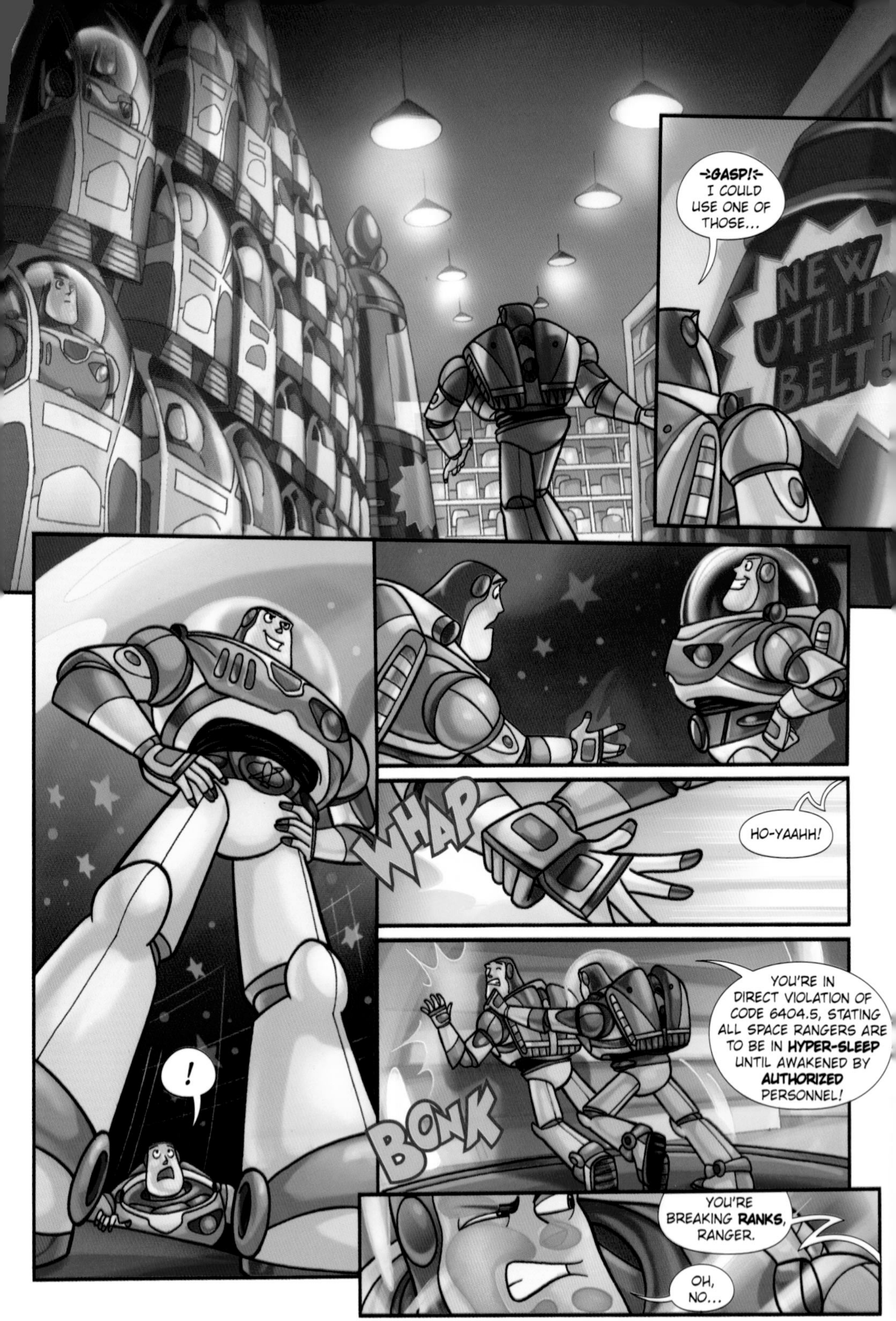
-GASP!- I COULD USE ONE OF THOSE...
NEW UTILITY BELT!
WHAP
HO-YAAHH!
!
BONK
YOU'RE IN DIRECT VIOLATION OF CODE 6404.5, STATING ALL SPACE RANGERS ARE TO BE IN **HYPER-SLEEP** UNTIL AWAKENED BY **AUTHORIZED** PERSONNEL!
YOU'RE BREAKING **RANKS**, RANGER.
OH, NO...

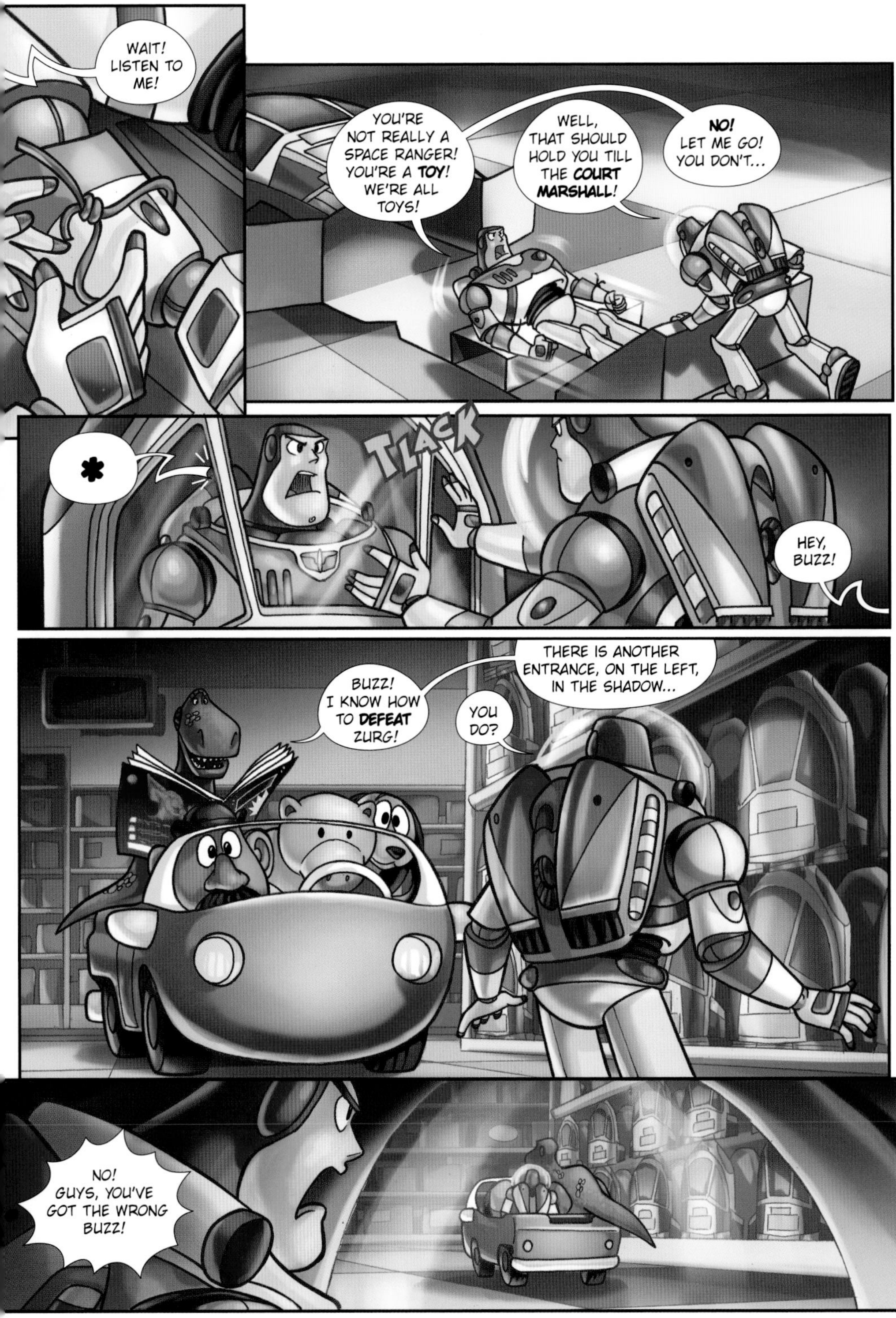
WAIT! LISTEN TO ME!
YOU'RE NOT REALLY A SPACE RANGER! YOU'RE A TOY! WE'RE ALL TOYS!
WELL, THAT SHOULD HOLD YOU TILL THE COURT MARSHALL!
NO! LET ME GO! YOU DON'T...
*
TLACK
HEY, BUZZ!
BUZZ! I KNOW HOW TO DEFEAT ZURG!
YOU DO?
THERE IS ANOTHER ENTRANCE, ON THE LEFT, IN THE SHADOW...
NO! GUYS, YOU'VE GOT THE WRONG BUZZ!

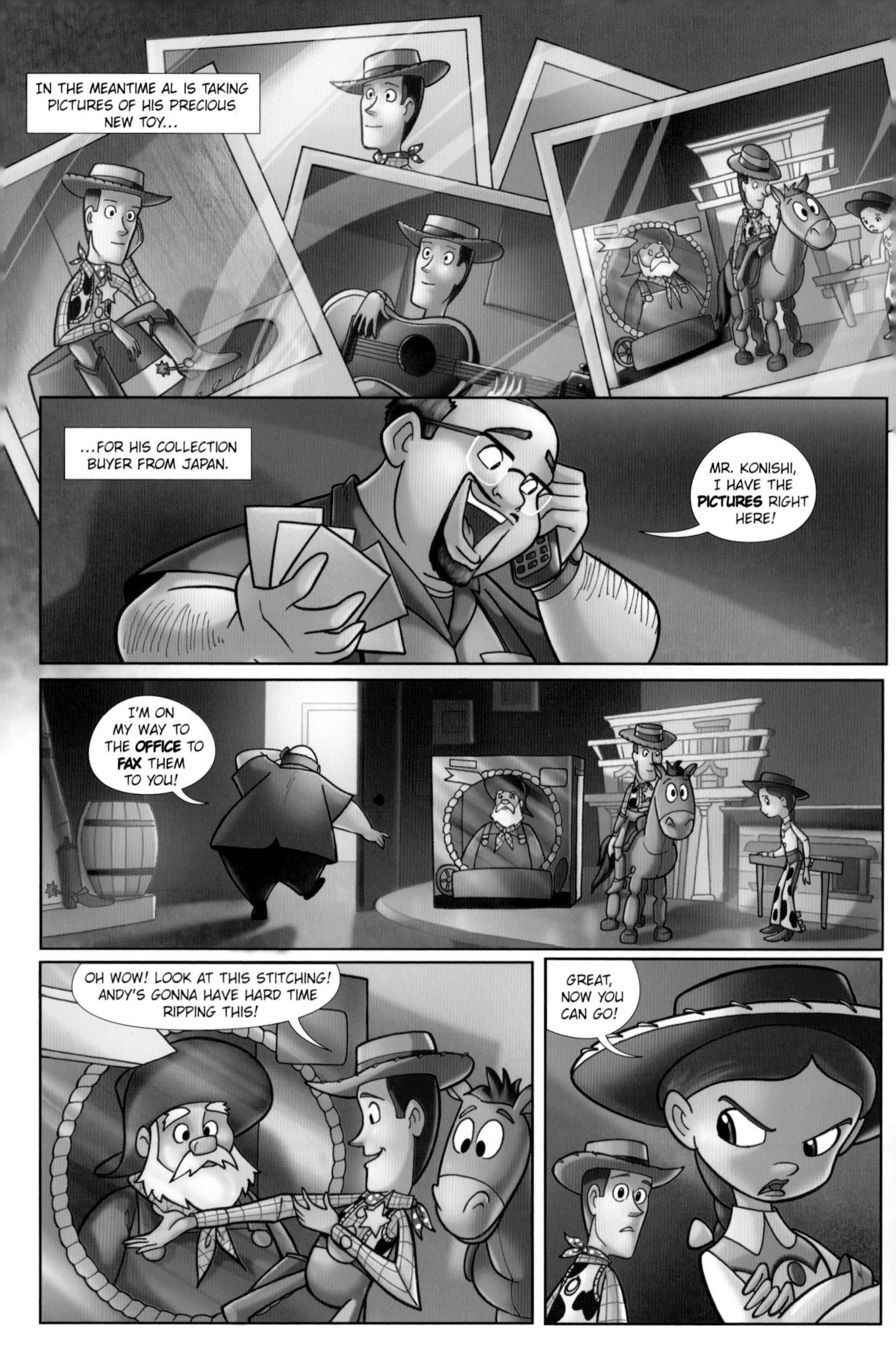
IN THE MEANTIME AL IS TAKING PICTURES OF HIS PRECIOUS NEW TOY...
...FOR HIS COLLECTION BUYER FROM JAPAN.
MR. KONISHI, I HAVE THE **PICTURES** RIGHT HERE!
I'M ON MY WAY TO THE **OFFICE** TO **FAX** THEM TO YOU!
OH WOW! LOOK AT THIS STITCHING! ANDY'S GONNA HAVE HARD TIME RIPPING THIS!
GREAT, NOW YOU CAN GO!

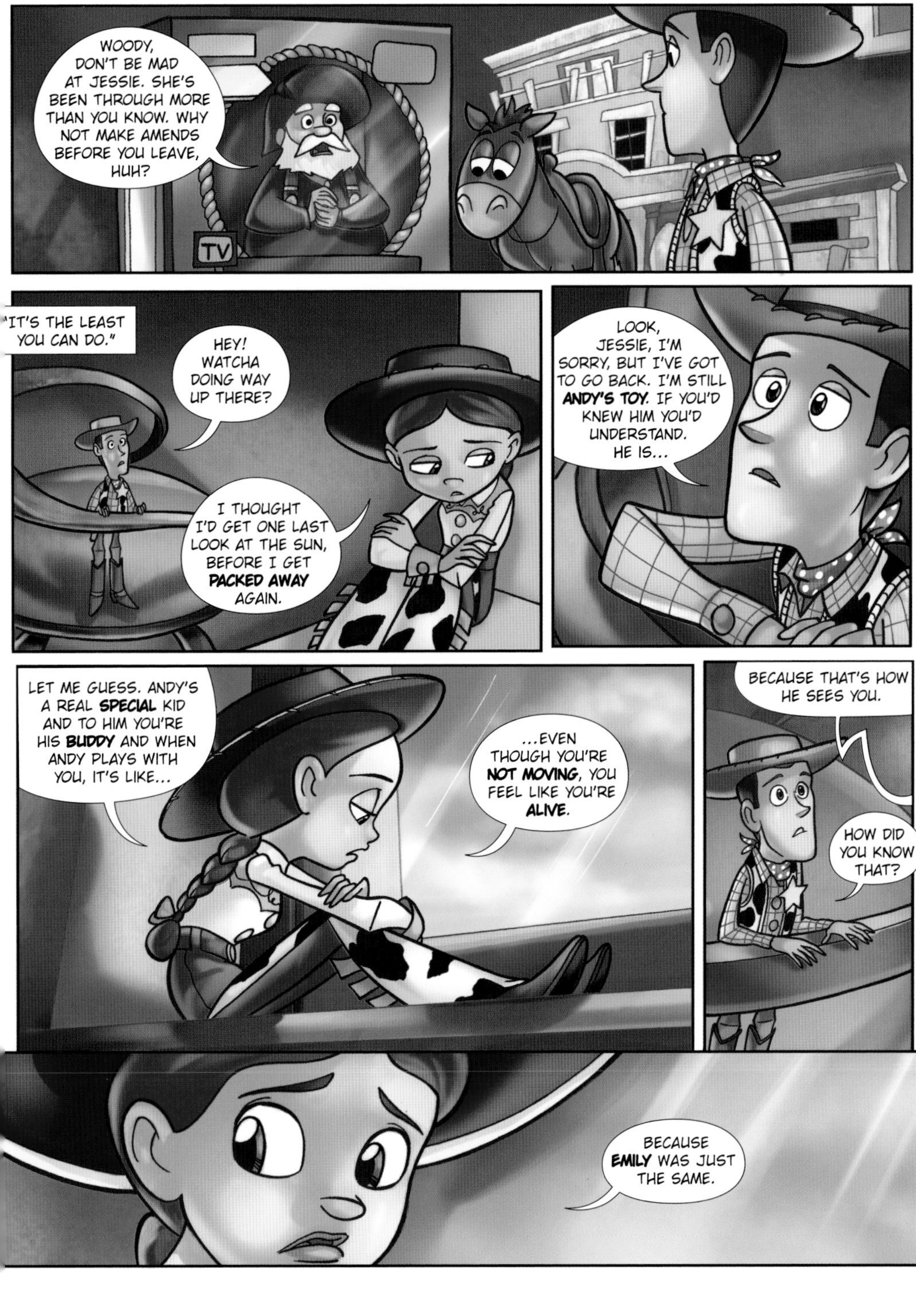
WOODY, DON'T BE MAD AT JESSIE. SHE'S BEEN THROUGH MORE THAN YOU KNOW. WHY NOT MAKE AMENDS BEFORE YOU LEAVE, HUH?
TV
"IT'S THE LEAST YOU CAN DO."
HEY! WATCHA DOING WAY UP THERE?
I THOUGHT I'D GET ONE LAST LOOK AT THE SUN, BEFORE I GET **PACKED AWAY** AGAIN.
LOOK, JESSIE, I'M SORRY, BUT I'VE GOT TO GO BACK. I'M STILL **ANDY'S TOY**. IF YOU'D KNEW HIM YOU'D UNDERSTAND. HE IS...
LET ME GUESS. ANDY'S A REAL **SPECIAL** KID AND TO HIM YOU'RE HIS **BUDDY** AND WHEN ANDY PLAYS WITH YOU, IT'S LIKE...
...EVEN THOUGH YOU'RE **NOT MOVING**, YOU FEEL LIKE YOU'RE **ALIVE**.
BECAUSE THAT'S HOW HE SEES YOU.
HOW DID YOU KNOW THAT?
BECAUSE **EMILY** WAS JUST THE SAME.

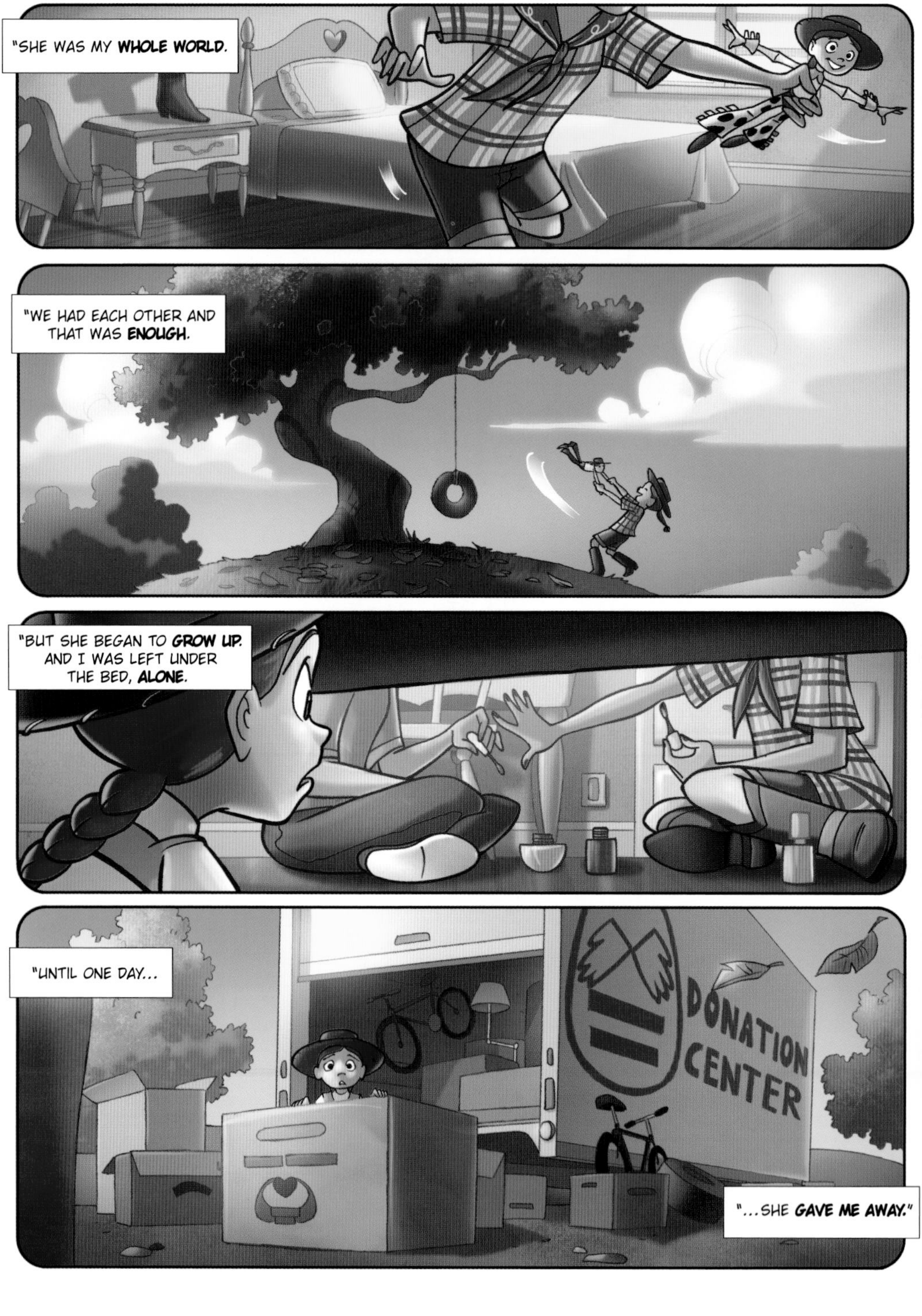

"SHE WAS MY **WHOLE WORLD**.
"WE HAD EACH OTHER AND THAT WAS **ENOUGH**.
"BUT SHE BEGAN TO **GROW UP**. AND I WAS LEFT UNDER THE BED, **ALONE**.
"UNTIL ONE DAY...
DONATION CENTER
"...SHE **GAVE ME AWAY**."

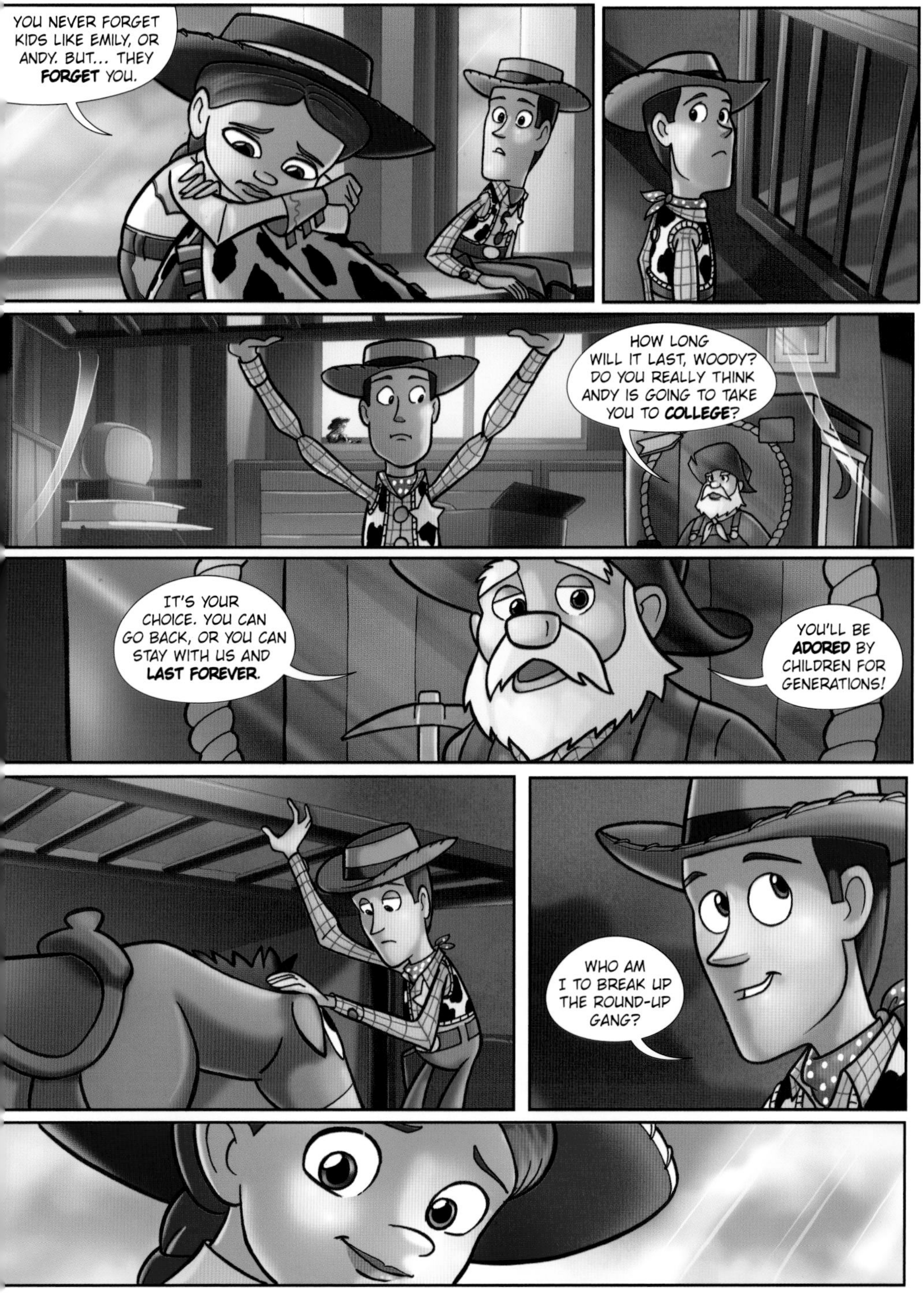
YOU NEVER FORGET KIDS LIKE EMILY, OR ANDY. BUT... THEY FORGET YOU.
HOW LONG WILL IT LAST, WOODY? DO YOU REALLY THINK ANDY IS GOING TO TAKE YOU TO COLLEGE?
IT'S YOUR CHOICE. YOU CAN GO BACK, OR YOU CAN STAY WITH US AND LAST FOREVER.
YOU'LL BE ADORED BY CHILDREN FOR GENERATIONS!
WHO AM I TO BREAK UP THE ROUND-UP GANG?

WOODY MADE HIS DECISION... BUT SOMEONE WOULD NOT BE HAPPY TO HEAR THAT!

WOODY? ARE YOU HERE?

YOU SEE, THE SECRET ENTRANCE TO ZURG'S FORTRESS IS TO THE LEFT, IN THE SHADOWS!

LEFT. SHADOWS. GOT IT.

CLACK

SHH... SOMEONE'S COMING!

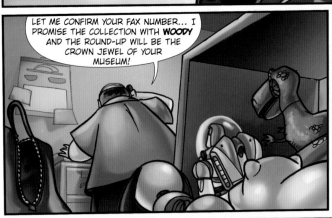

LET ME CONFIRM YOUR FAX NUMBER... I PROMISE THE COLLECTION WITH **WOODY** AND THE ROUND-UP WILL BE THE CROWN JEWEL OF YOUR MUSEUM!

THAT'S THE **KIDNAPPER!**

AN AGENT OF ZURG!

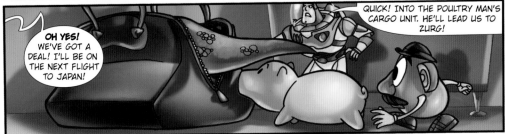

OH YES! WE'VE GOT A DEAL! I'LL BE ON THE NEXT FLIGHT TO JAPAN!

QUICK! INTO THE POULTRY MAN'S CARGO UNIT. HE'LL LEAD US TO ZURG!

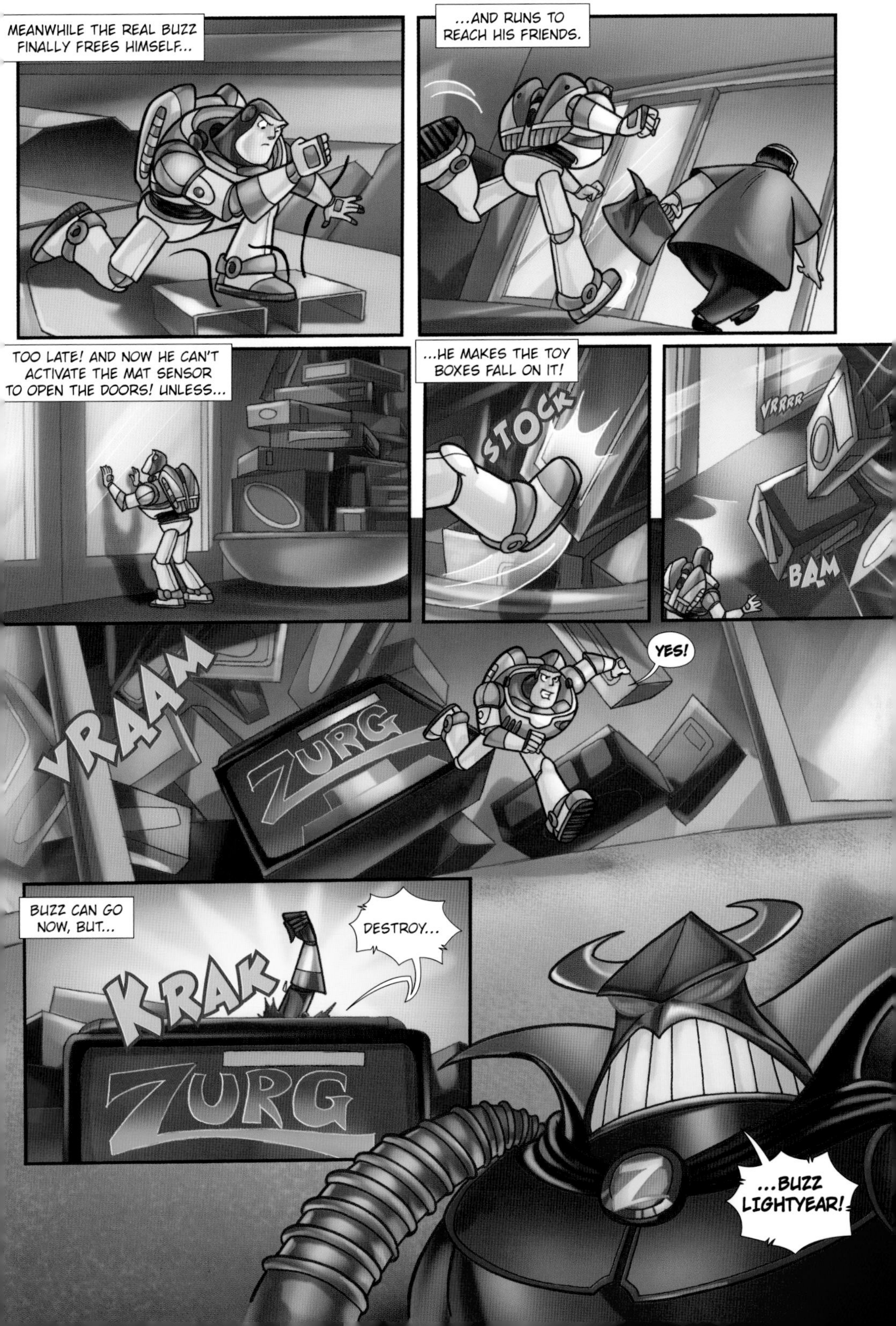
MEANWHILE THE REAL BUZZ FINALLY FREES HIMSELF...
...AND RUNS TO REACH HIS FRIENDS.
TOO LATE! AND NOW HE CAN'T ACTIVATE THE MAT SENSOR TO OPEN THE DOORS! UNLESS...
...HE MAKES THE TOY BOXES FALL ON IT!
STOCK
VRRRR
BAM
VRAAM
ZURG
YES!
BUZZ CAN GO NOW, BUT...
DESTROY...
KRAK
ZURG
...BUZZ LIGHTYEAR!

ON THE OTHER SIDE OF THE STREET, AL WALKS TOWARDS HIS APARTMENT...

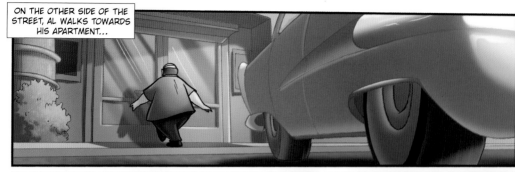

...LEAVING HIS BAG BEHIND!

LET'S GO!

HE'S ASCENDING IN THE **VERTICAL TRANSPORTER!**

OH NO! HOW ARE WE GONNA GET UP THERE?

TROOPS! **OVER HERE!**

JUST LIKE YOU SAID, LIZARD MAN. IN THE **SHADOWS**, TO THE **LEFT!** LET'S MOVE!

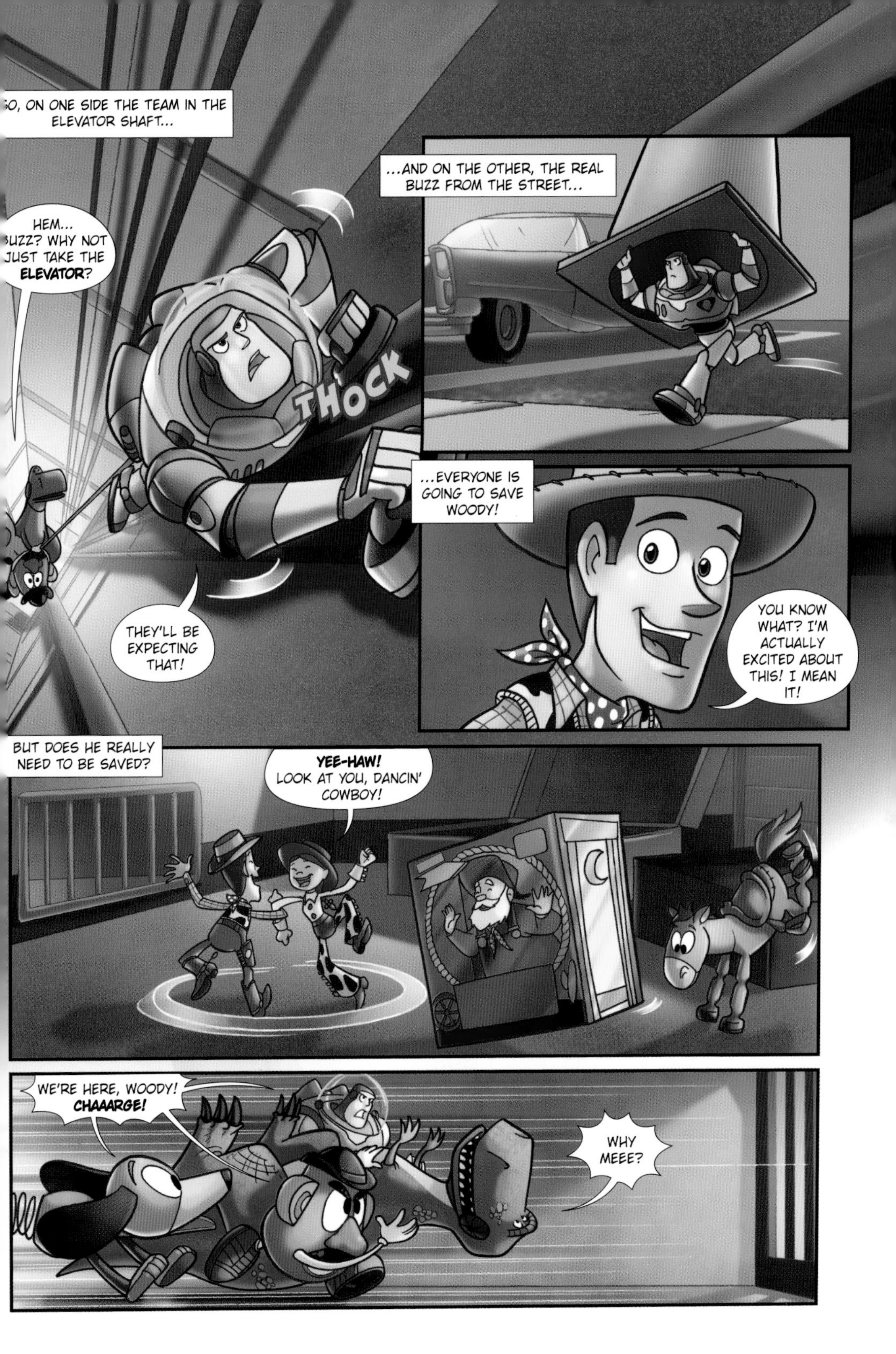

SO, ON ONE SIDE THE TEAM IN THE ELEVATOR SHAFT...
HEM... BUZZ? WHY NOT JUST TAKE THE **ELEVATOR**?
THOCK
THEY'LL BE EXPECTING THAT!
...AND ON THE OTHER, THE REAL BUZZ FROM THE STREET...
...EVERYONE IS GOING TO SAVE WOODY!
YOU KNOW WHAT? I'M ACTUALLY EXCITED ABOUT THIS! I MEAN IT!
BUT DOES HE REALLY NEED TO BE SAVED?
YEE-HAW! LOOK AT YOU, DANCIN' COWBOY!
WE'RE HERE, WOODY! **CHAAARGE!**
WHY MEEE?

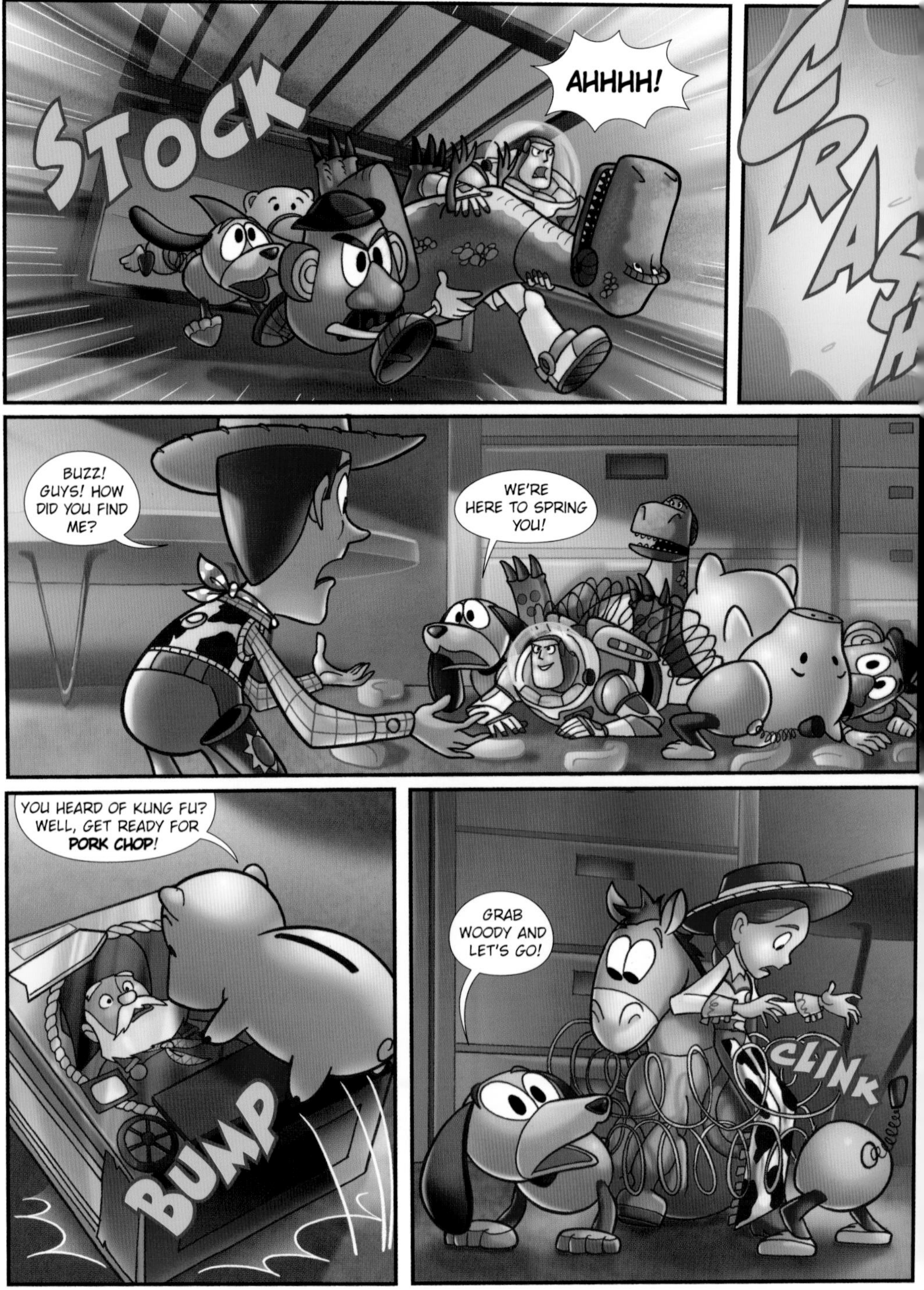
STOCK
AHHHH!
CRASH
BUZZ! GUYS! HOW DID YOU FIND ME?
WE'RE HERE TO SPRING YOU!
YOU HEARD OF KUNG FU? WELL, GET READY FOR PORK CHOP!
BUMP
GRAB WOODY AND LET'S GO!
CLINK

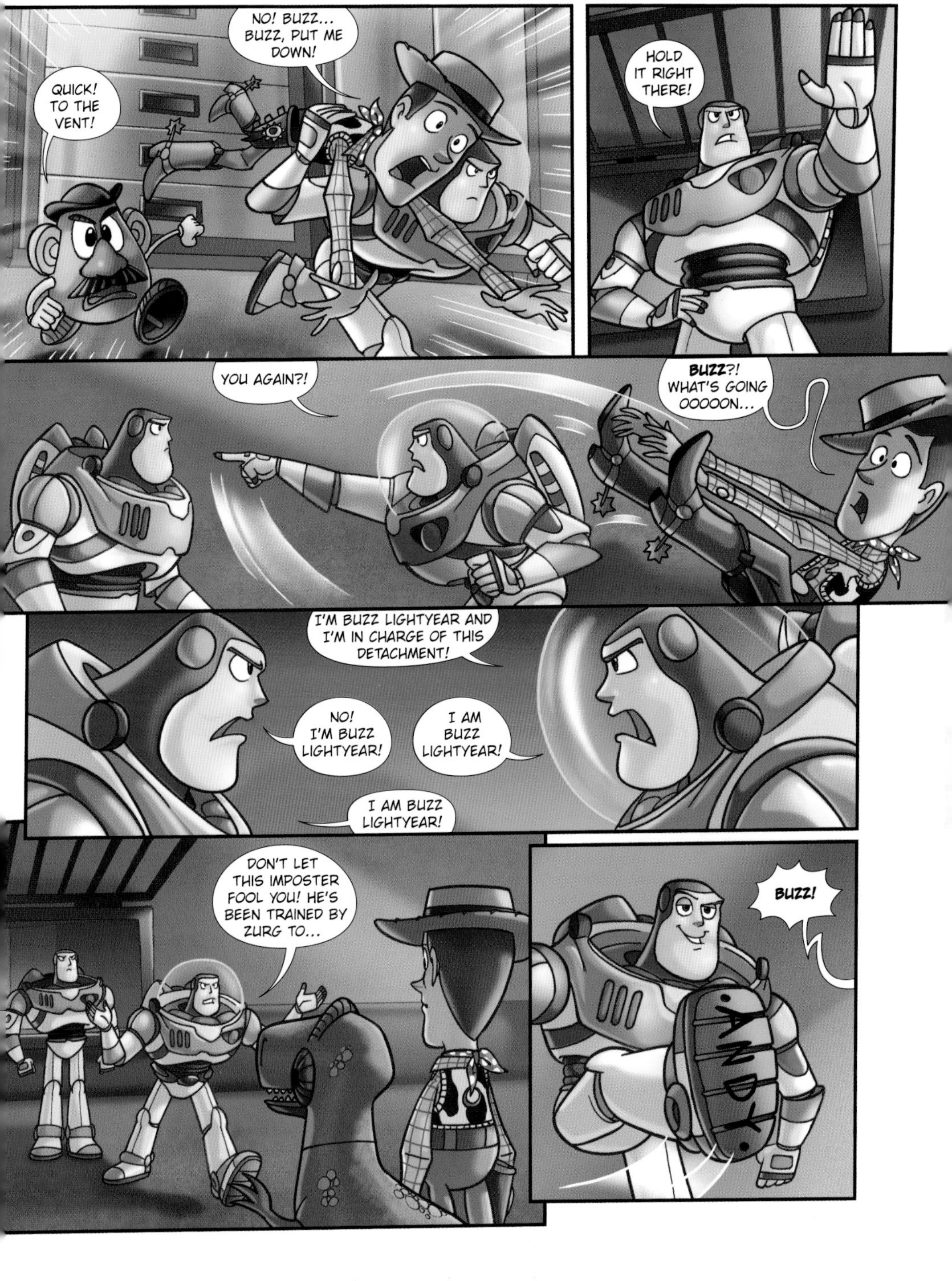
QUICK! TO THE VENT!
NO! BUZZ... BUZZ, PUT ME DOWN!
HOLD IT RIGHT THERE!
YOU AGAIN?!
BUZZ?! WHAT'S GOING OOOOON...
I'M BUZZ LIGHTYEAR AND I'M IN CHARGE OF THIS DETACHMENT!
NO! I'M BUZZ LIGHTYEAR!
I AM BUZZ LIGHTYEAR!
I AM BUZZ LIGHTYEAR!
DON'T LET THIS IMPOSTER FOOL YOU! HE'S BEEN TRAINED BY ZURG TO...
BUZZ!
ANDY

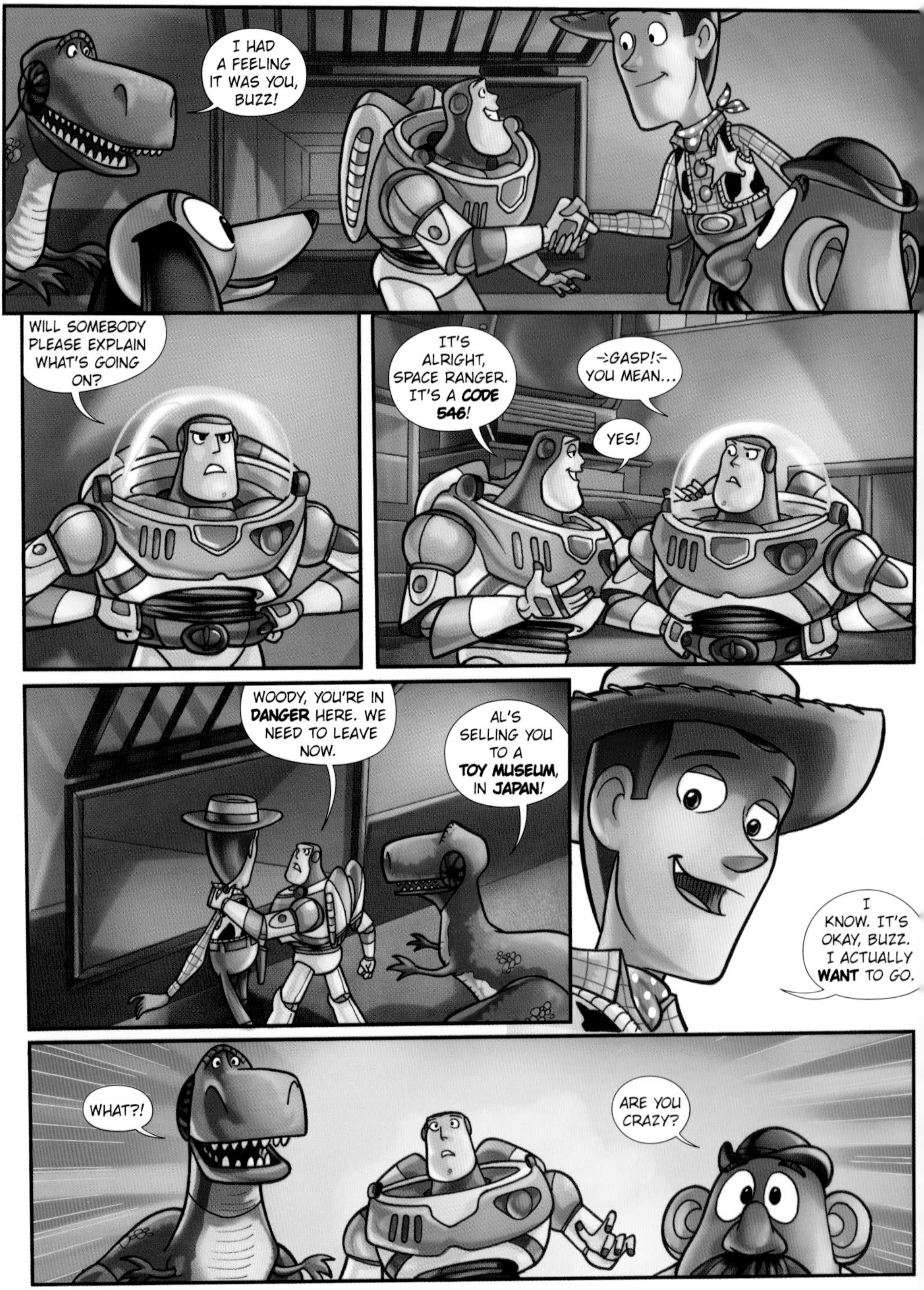
I HAD A FEELING IT WAS YOU, BUZZ!
WILL SOMEBODY PLEASE EXPLAIN WHAT'S GOING ON?
IT'S ALRIGHT, SPACE RANGER. IT'S A **CODE 546**!
GASP! YOU MEAN...
YES!
WOODY, YOU'RE IN **DANGER** HERE. WE NEED TO LEAVE NOW.
AL'S SELLING YOU TO A **TOY MUSEUM**, IN **JAPAN**!
I KNOW. IT'S OKAY, BUZZ. I ACTUALLY **WANT** TO GO.
WHAT?!
ARE YOU CRAZY?

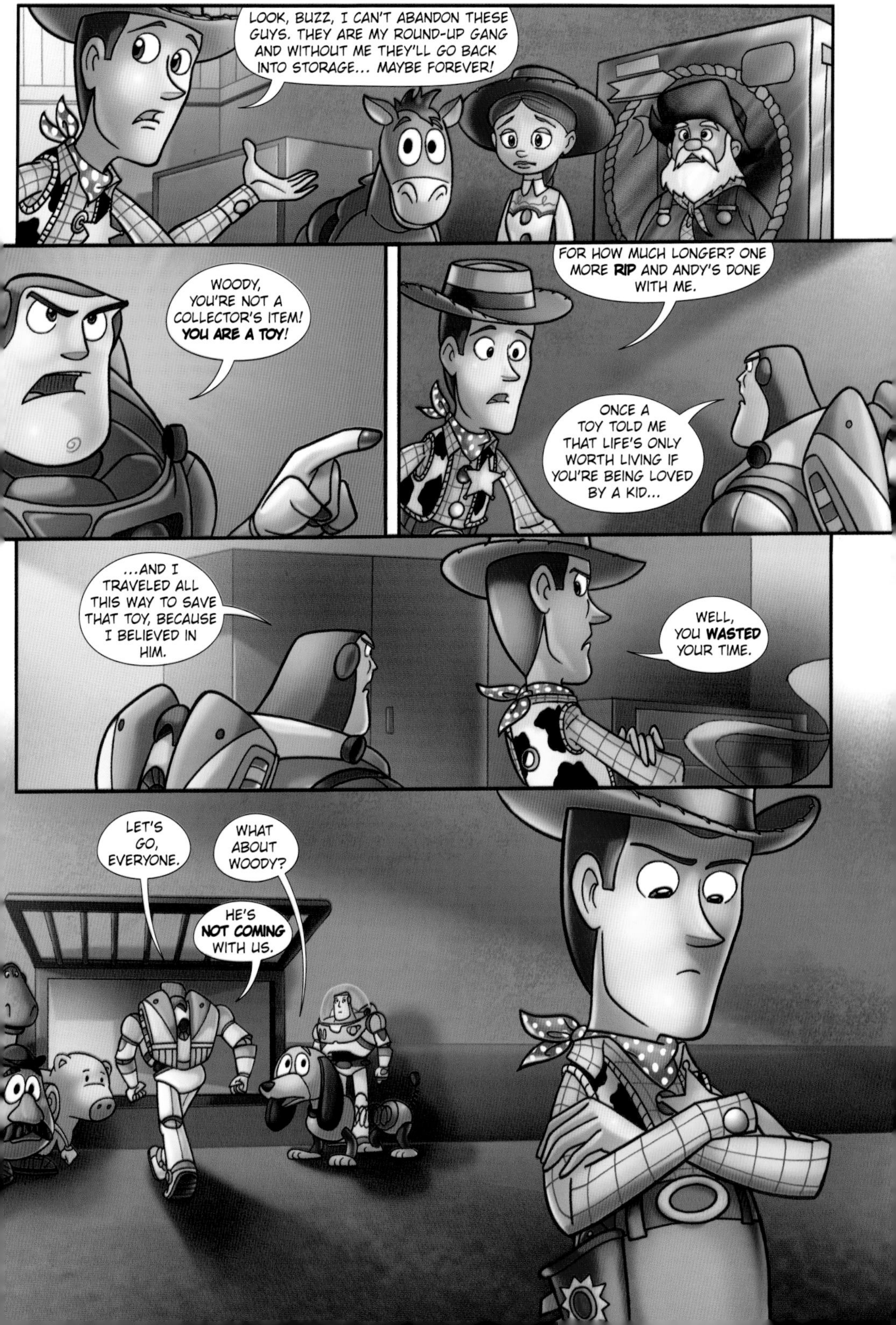

LOOK, BUZZ, I CAN'T ABANDON THESE GUYS. THEY ARE MY ROUND-UP GANG AND WITHOUT ME THEY'LL GO BACK INTO STORAGE... MAYBE FOREVER!
WOODY, YOU'RE NOT A COLLECTOR'S ITEM! **YOU ARE A TOY**!
FOR HOW MUCH LONGER? ONE MORE **RIP** AND ANDY'S DONE WITH ME.
ONCE A TOY TOLD ME THAT LIFE'S ONLY WORTH LIVING IF YOU'RE BEING LOVED BY A KID...
...AND I TRAVELED ALL THIS WAY TO SAVE THAT TOY, BECAUSE I BELIEVED IN HIM.
WELL, YOU **WASTED** YOUR TIME.
LET'S GO, EVERYONE.
WHAT ABOUT WOODY?
HE'S **NOT COMING** WITH US.

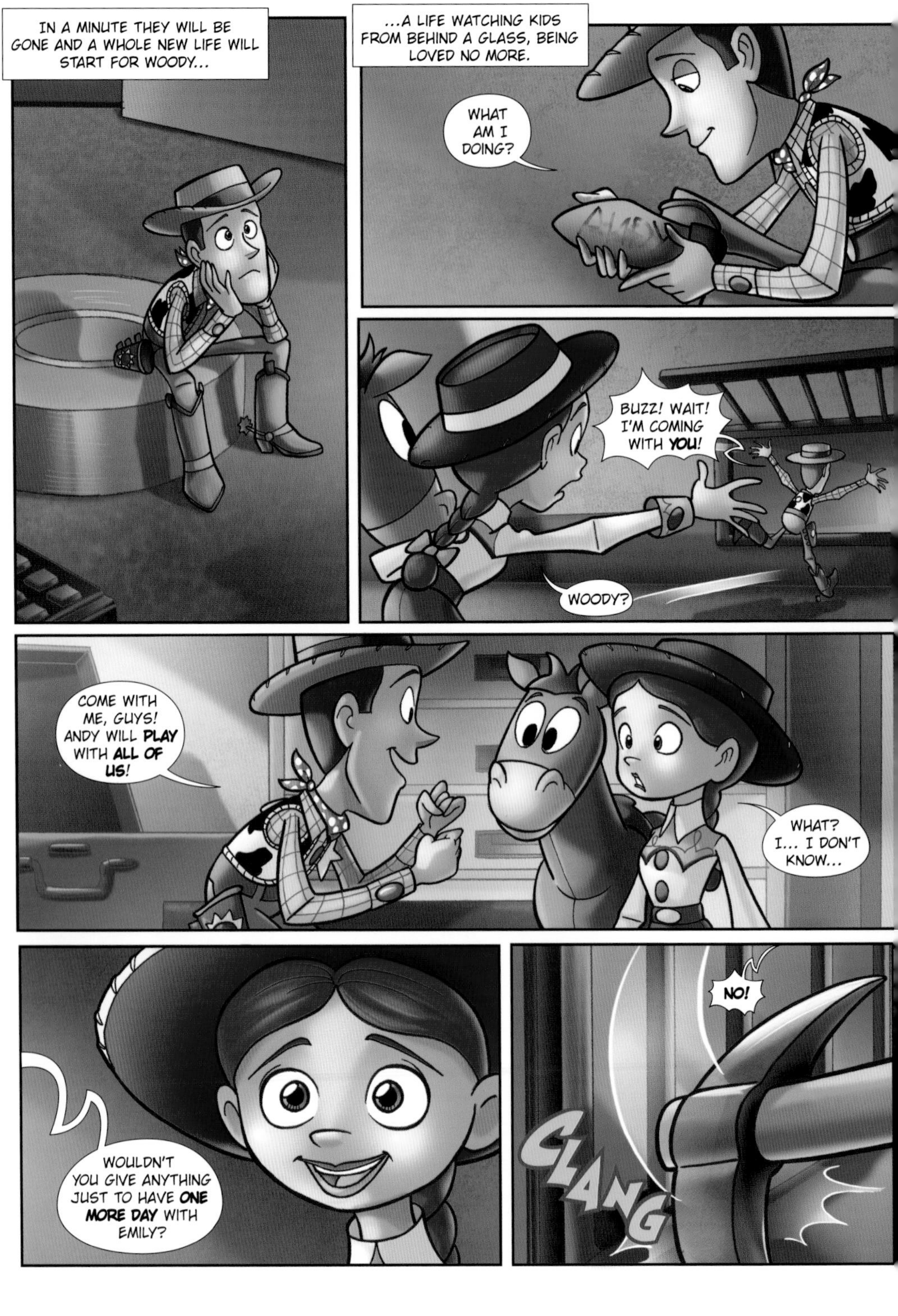
IN A MINUTE THEY WILL BE GONE AND A WHOLE NEW LIFE WILL START FOR WOODY...
...A LIFE WATCHING KIDS FROM BEHIND A GLASS, BEING LOVED NO MORE.
WHAT AM I DOING?
BUZZ! WAIT! I'M COMING WITH **YOU**!
WOODY?
COME WITH ME, GUYS! ANDY WILL **PLAY** WITH **ALL OF US**!
WHAT? I... I DON'T KNOW...
WOULDN'T YOU GIVE ANYTHING JUST TO HAVE **ONE MORE DAY** WITH EMILY?
NO!
CLANG

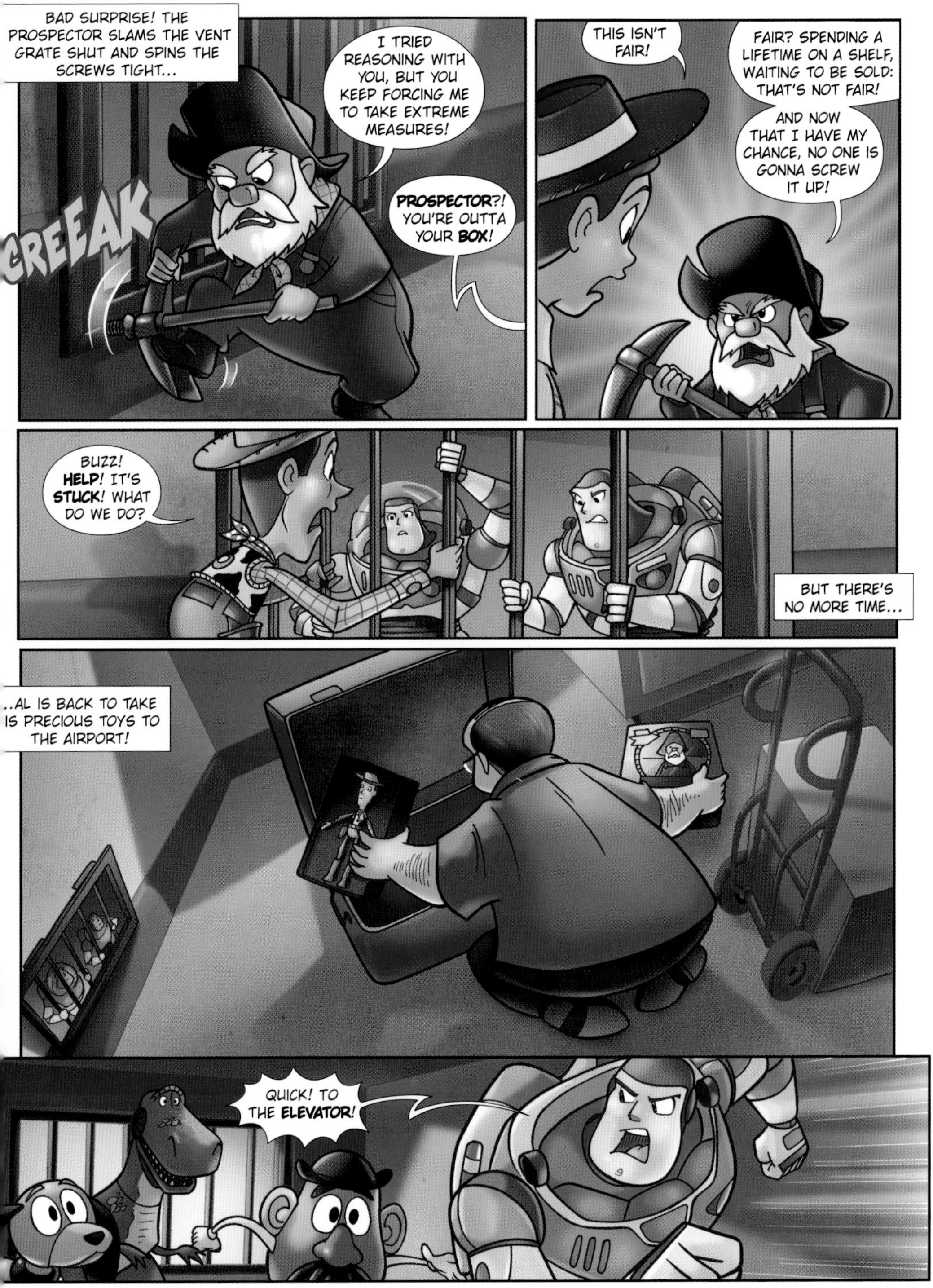
BAD SURPRISE! THE PROSPECTOR SLAMS THE VENT GRATE SHUT AND SPINS THE SCREWS TIGHT...
I TRIED REASONING WITH YOU, BUT YOU KEEP FORCING ME TO TAKE EXTREME MEASURES!
CREEAK
PROSPECTOR?! YOU'RE OUTTA YOUR BOX!
THIS ISN'T FAIR!
FAIR? SPENDING A LIFETIME ON A SHELF, WAITING TO BE SOLD: THAT'S NOT FAIR!
AND NOW THAT I HAVE MY CHANCE, NO ONE IS GONNA SCREW IT UP!
BUZZ! HELP! IT'S STUCK! WHAT DO WE DO?
BUT THERE'S NO MORE TIME...
..AL IS BACK TO TAKE IS PRECIOUS TOYS TO THE AIRPORT!
QUICK! TO THE ELEVATOR!

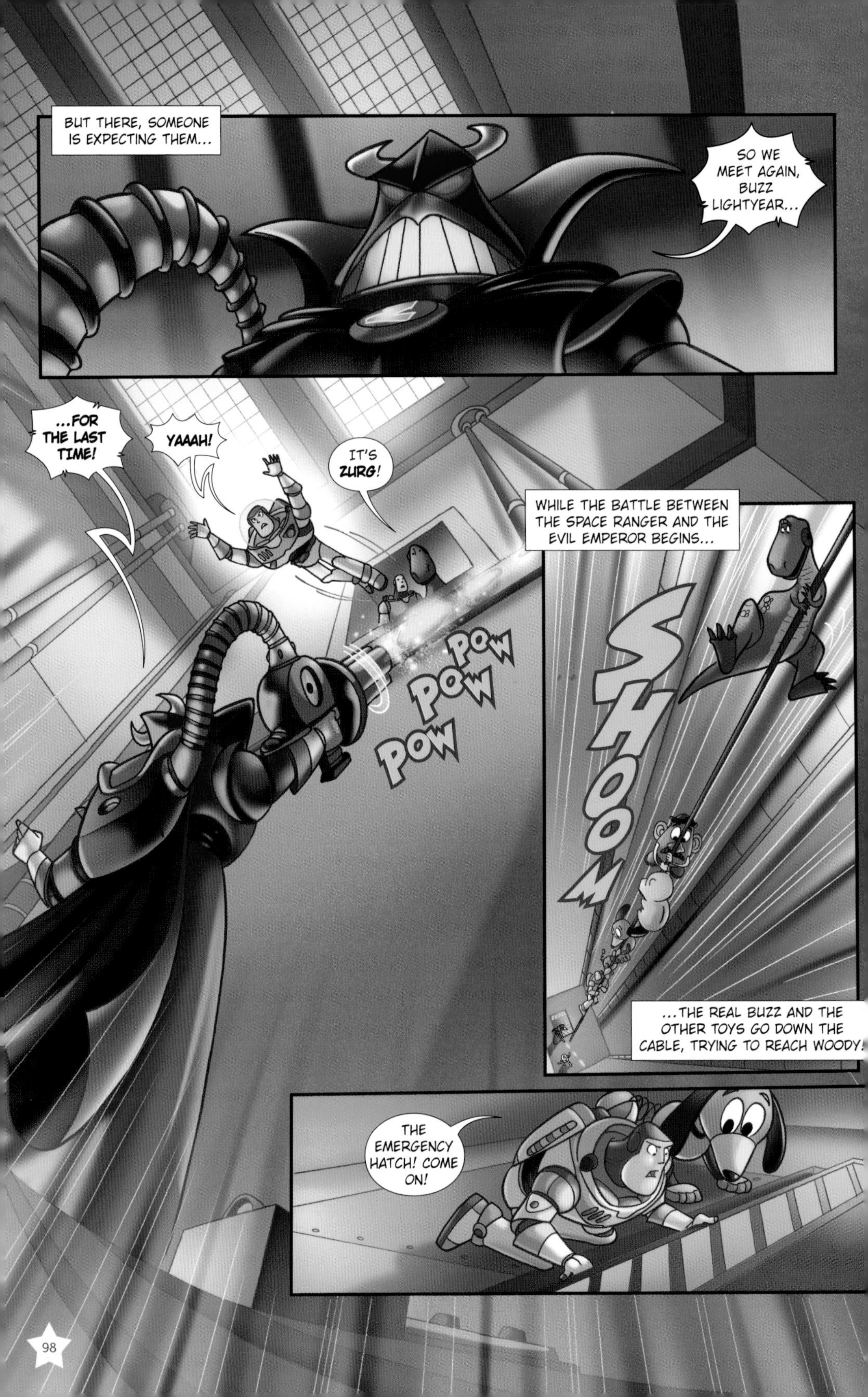

BUT THERE, SOMEONE IS EXPECTING THEM...
SO WE MEET AGAIN, BUZZ LIGHTYEAR...
...FOR THE LAST TIME!
YAAAH!
IT'S ZURG!
POW POW POW
WHILE THE BATTLE BETWEEN THE SPACE RANGER AND THE EVIL EMPEROR BEGINS...
SHOOOM
...THE REAL BUZZ AND THE OTHER TOYS GO DOWN THE CABLE, TRYING TO REACH WOODY!
THE EMERGENCY HATCH! COME ON!

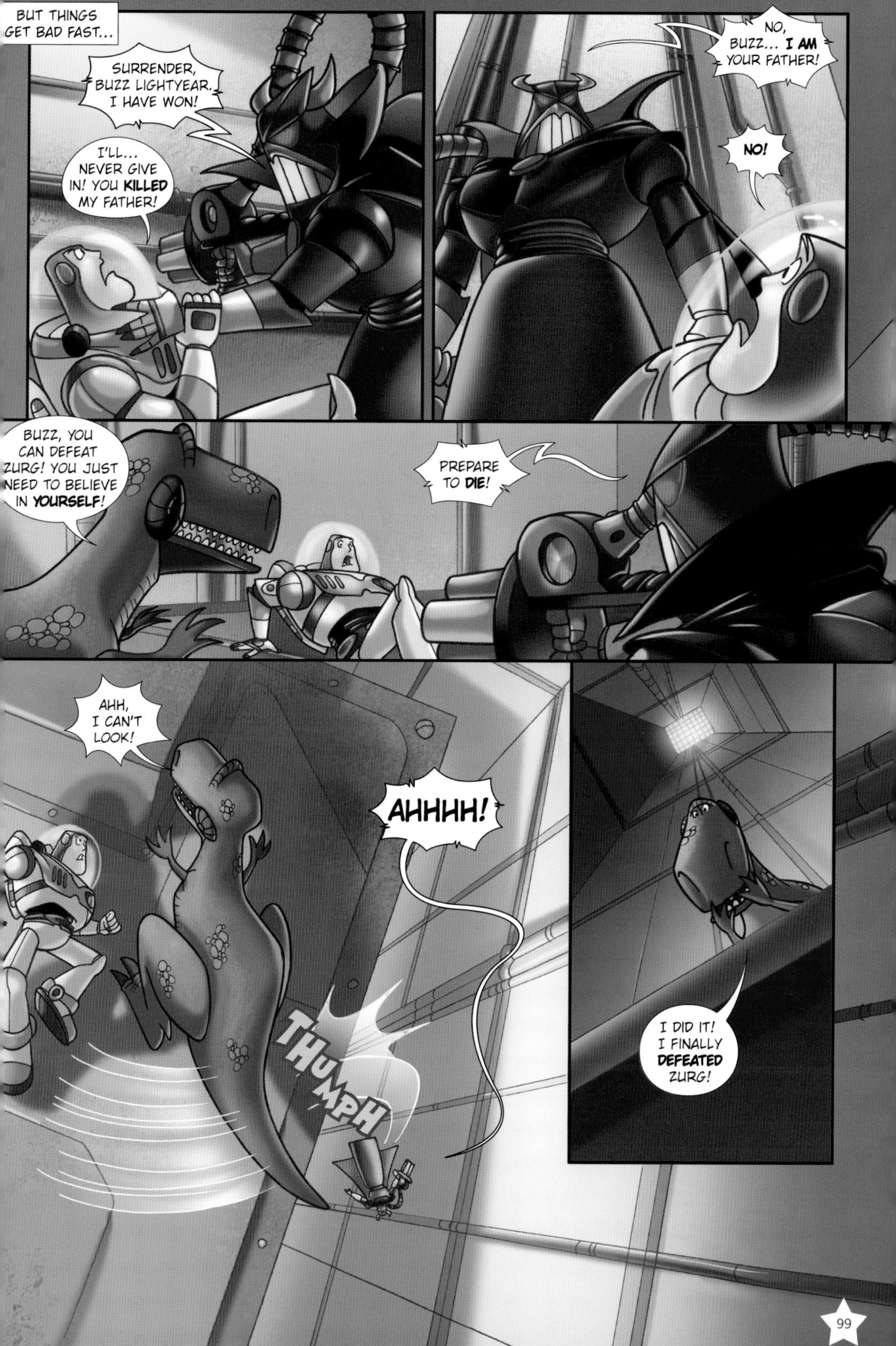
BUT THINGS GET BAD FAST...
SURRENDER, BUZZ LIGHTYEAR. I HAVE WON!
I'LL... NEVER GIVE IN! YOU **KILLED** MY FATHER!
NO, BUZZ... **I AM** YOUR FATHER!
NO!
BUZZ, YOU CAN DEFEAT ZURG! YOU JUST NEED TO BELIEVE IN **YOURSELF**!
PREPARE TO **DIE**!
AHH, I CAN'T LOOK!
AHHHH!
THUMPH
I DID IT! I FINALLY **DEFEATED** ZURG!

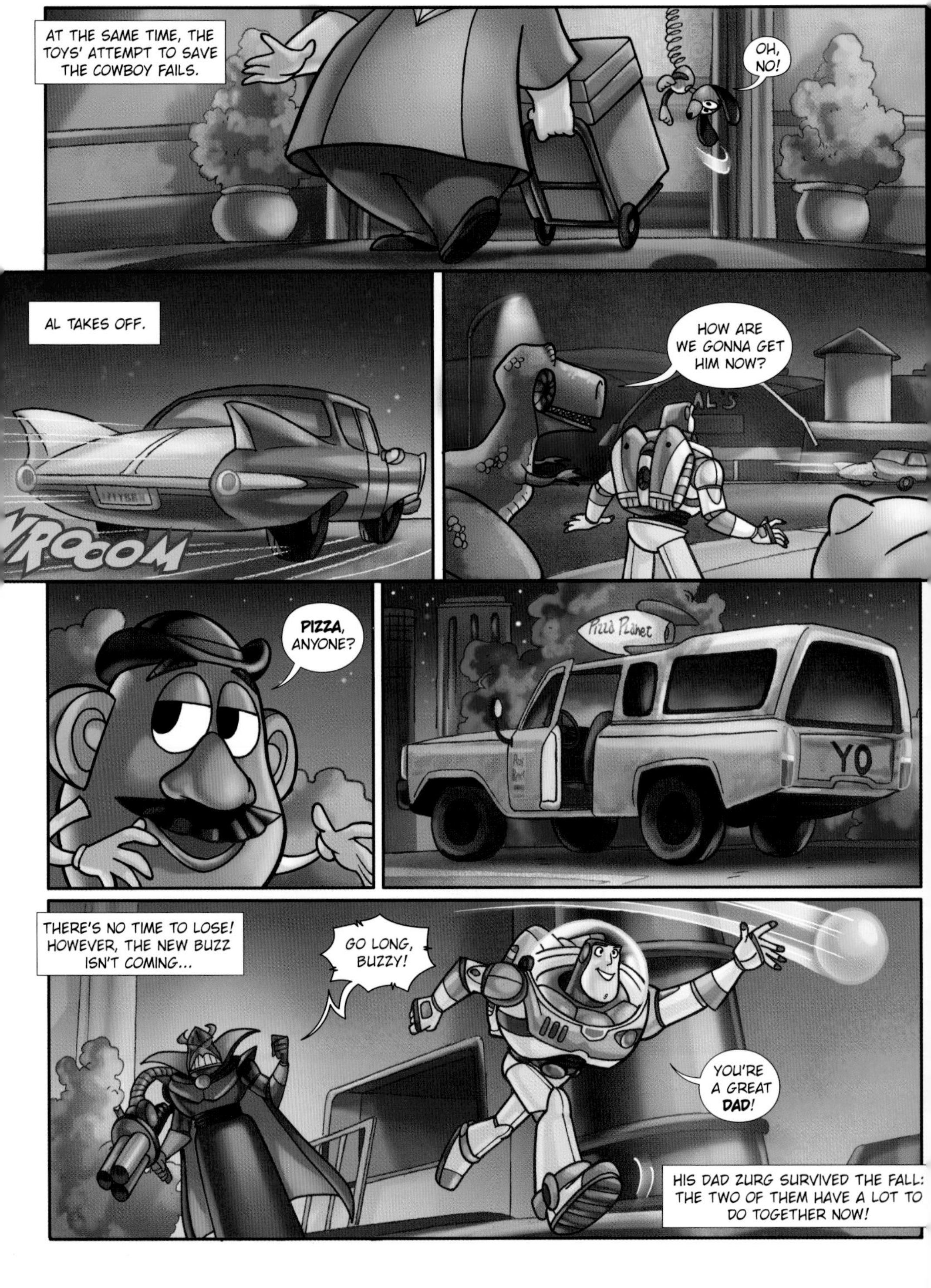
AT THE SAME TIME, THE TOYS' ATTEMPT TO SAVE THE COWBOY FAILS.
OH, NO!
AL TAKES OFF.
HOW ARE WE GONNA GET HIM NOW?
AL'S
PIZZA, ANYONE?
YO
THERE'S NO TIME TO LOSE! HOWEVER, THE NEW BUZZ ISN'T COMING...
GO LONG, BUZZY!
YOU'RE A GREAT **DAD**!
HIS DAD ZURG SURVIVED THE FALL: THE TWO OF THEM HAVE A LOT TO DO TOGETHER NOW!

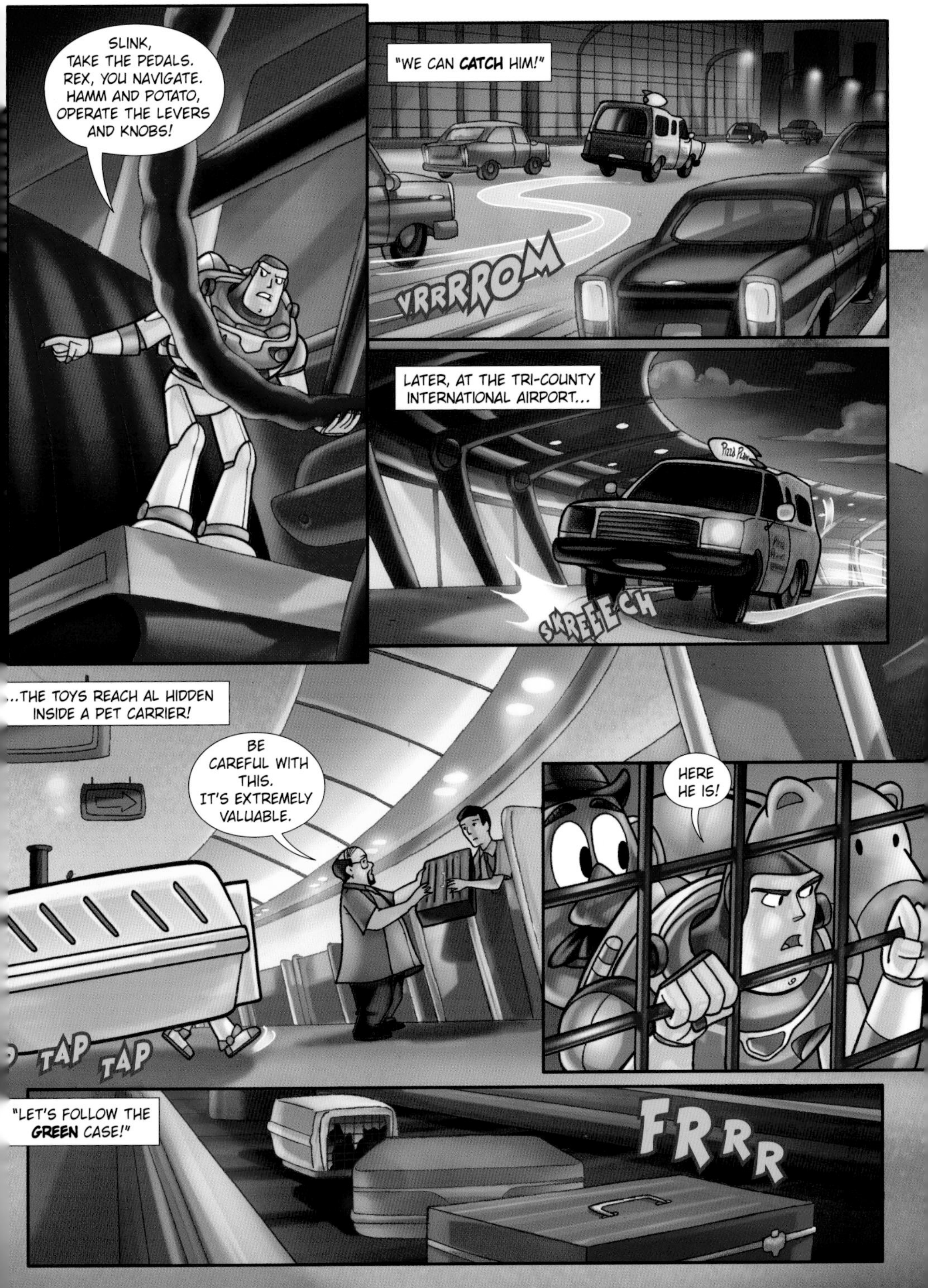
SLINK, TAKE THE PEDALS. REX, YOU NAVIGATE. HAMM AND POTATO, OPERATE THE LEVERS AND KNOBS!
"WE CAN **CATCH** HIM!"
VRRRROM
LATER, AT THE TRI-COUNTY INTERNATIONAL AIRPORT...
SKREEECH
...THE TOYS REACH AL HIDDEN INSIDE A PET CARRIER!
BE CAREFUL WITH THIS. IT'S EXTREMELY VALUABLE.
TAP TAP
HERE HE IS!
"LET'S FOLLOW THE **GREEN** CASE!"
FRRR

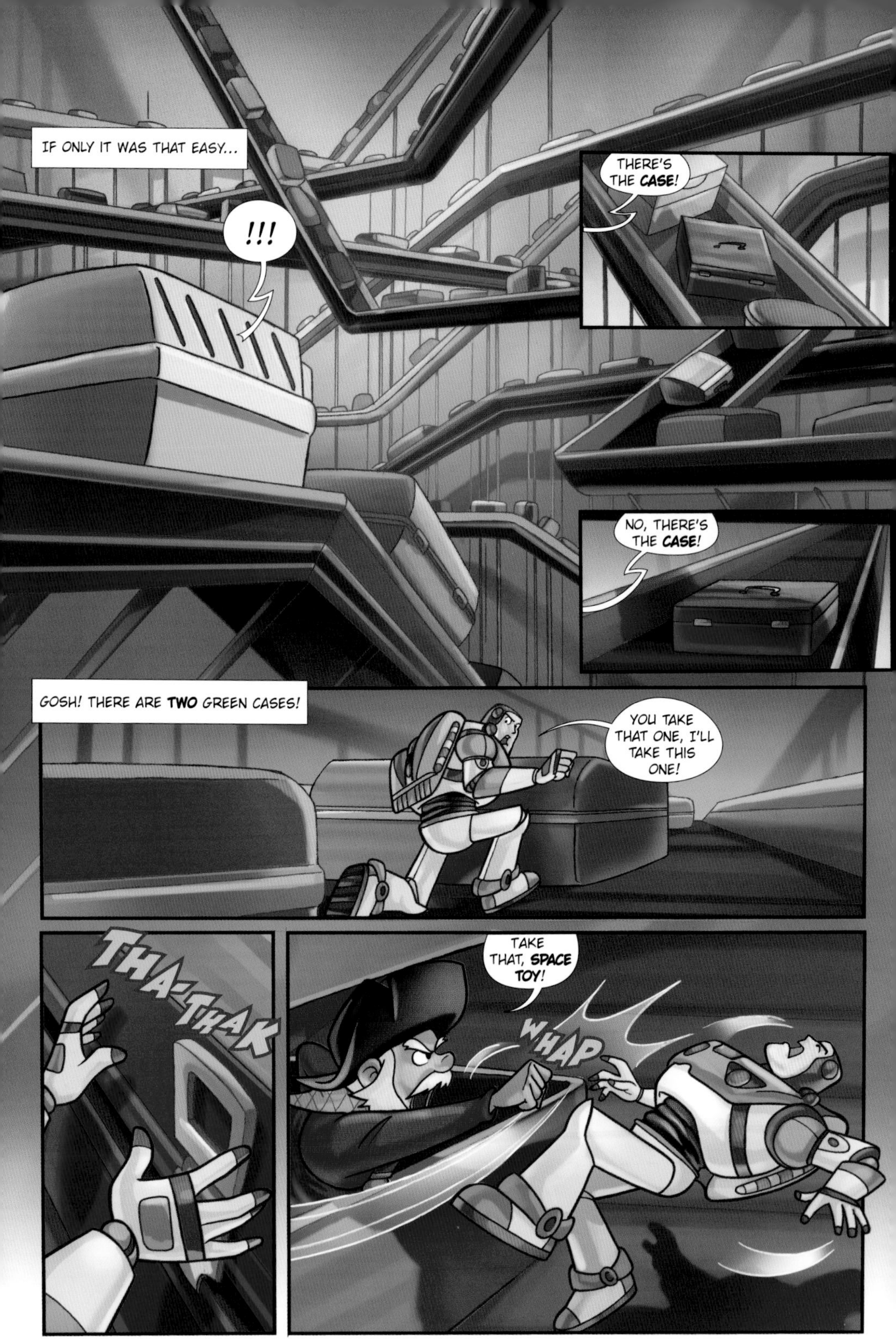
IF ONLY IT WAS THAT EASY...
!!!
THERE'S THE CASE!
NO, THERE'S THE CASE!
GOSH! THERE ARE TWO GREEN CASES!
YOU TAKE THAT ONE, I'LL TAKE THIS ONE!
THA-THAK
TAKE THAT, SPACE TOY!
WHAP

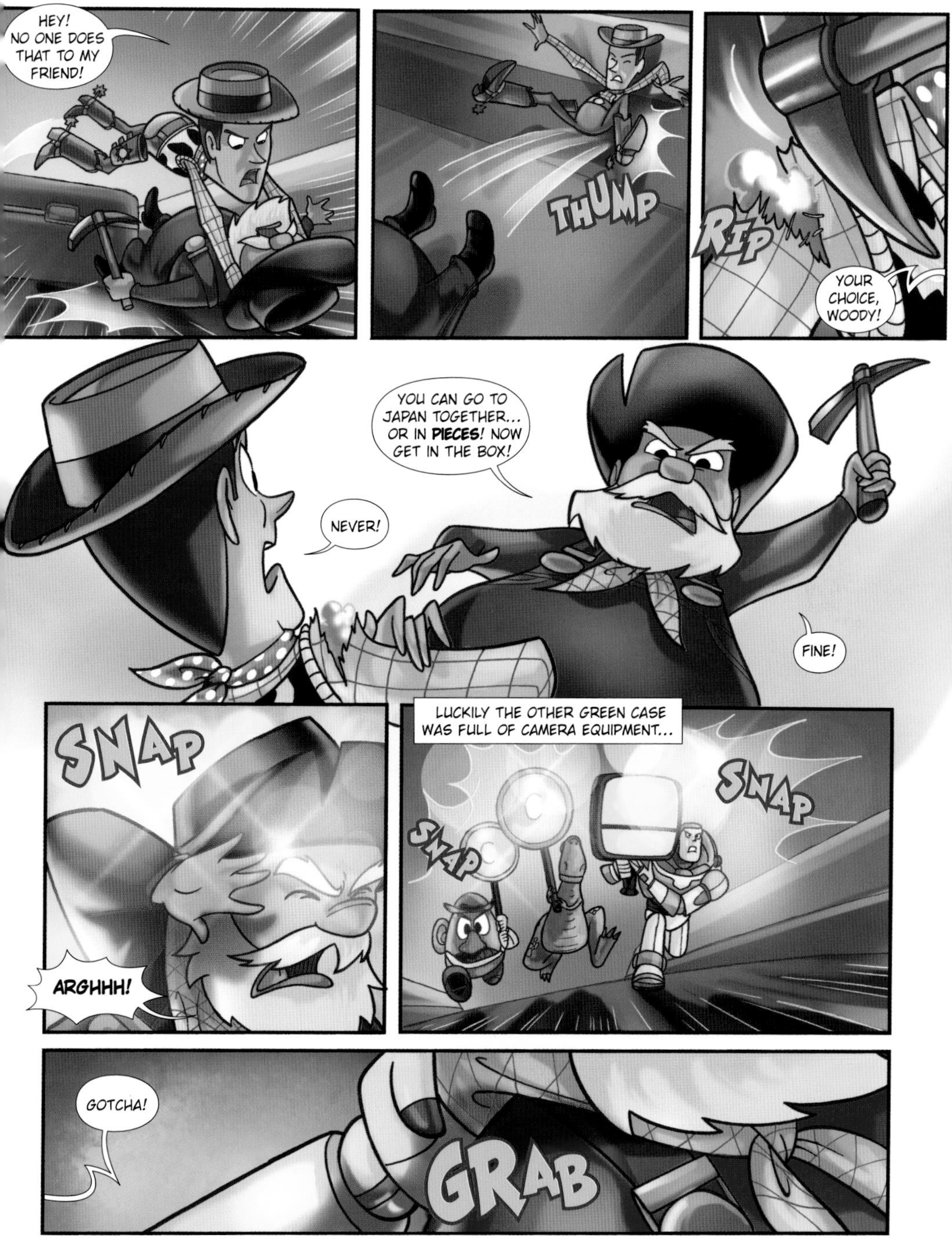
HEY! NO ONE DOES THAT TO MY FRIEND!
THUMP
RIP
YOUR CHOICE, WOODY!
YOU CAN GO TO JAPAN TOGETHER... OR IN **PIECES**! NOW GET IN THE BOX!
NEVER!
FINE!
SNAP
ARGHHH!
LUCKILY THE OTHER GREEN CASE WAS FULL OF CAMERA EQUIPMENT...
SNAP
SNAP
GOTCHA!
GRAB

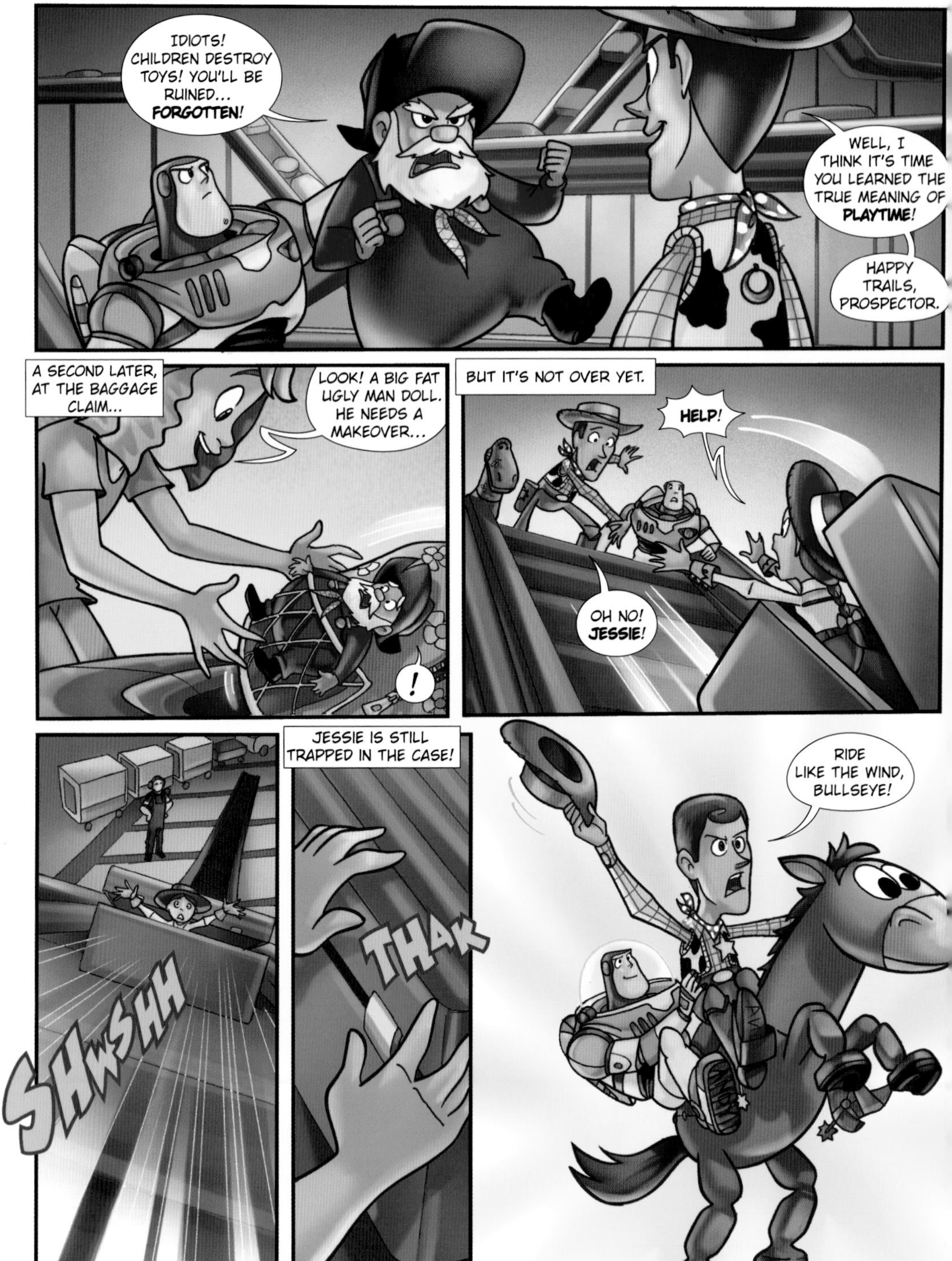
IDIOTS! CHILDREN DESTROY TOYS! YOU'LL BE RUINED... FORGOTTEN!
WELL, I THINK IT'S TIME YOU LEARNED THE TRUE MEANING OF PLAYTIME!
HAPPY TRAILS, PROSPECTOR.
A SECOND LATER, AT THE BAGGAGE CLAIM...
LOOK! A BIG FAT UGLY MAN DOLL. HE NEEDS A MAKEOVER...
!
BUT IT'S NOT OVER YET.
HELP!
OH NO! JESSIE!
SHWSHH
JESSIE IS STILL TRAPPED IN THE CASE!
THAK
RIDE LIKE THE WIND, BULLSEYE!

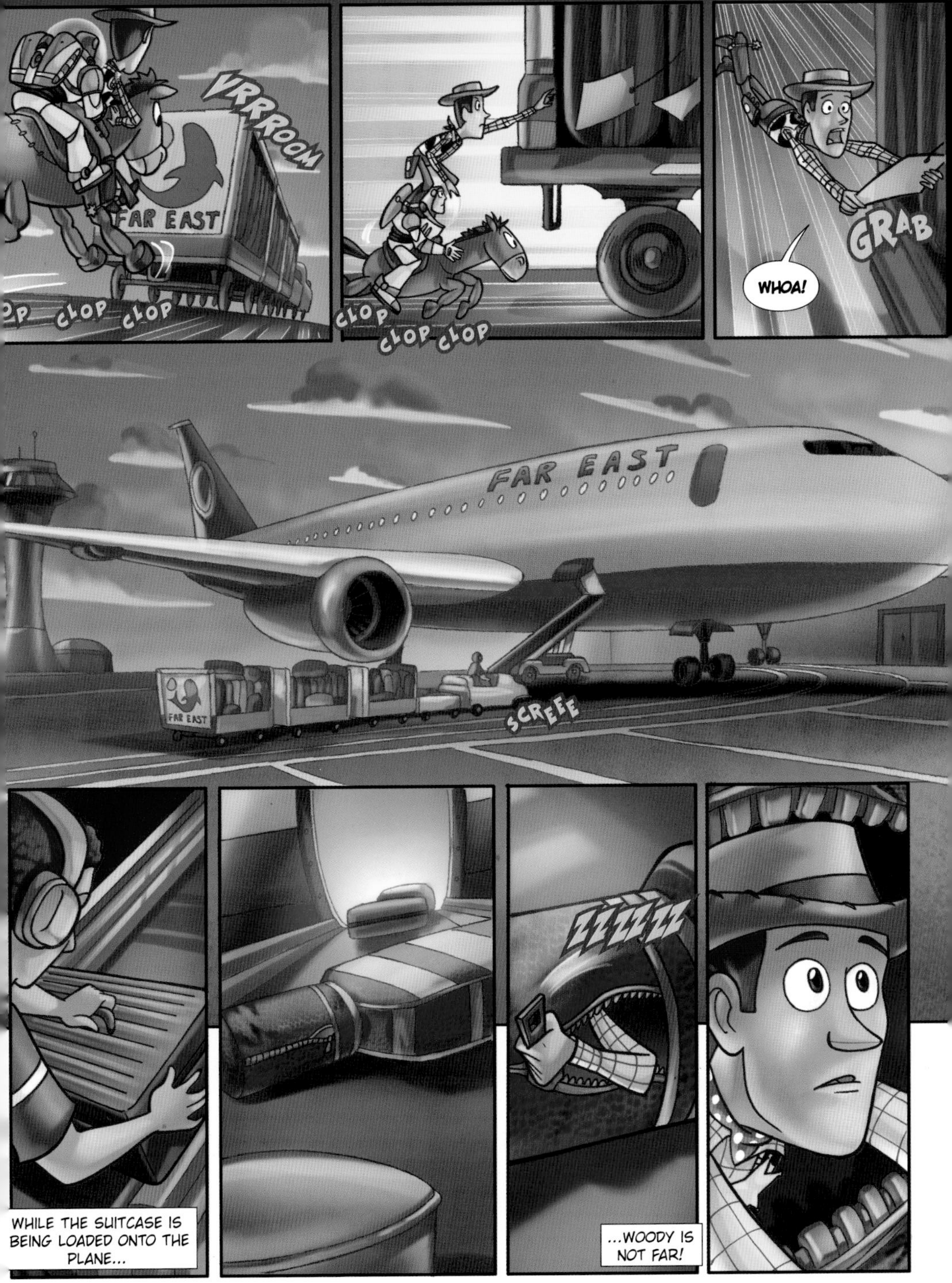
VRRROOM
FAR EAST
CLOP CLOP CLOP
CLOP CLOP CLOP
WHOA!
GRAB
FAR EAST
FAR EAST
SCREEE
WHILE THE SUITCASE IS BEING LOADED ONTO THE PLANE...
ZZZZZZ
...WOODY IS NOT FAR!

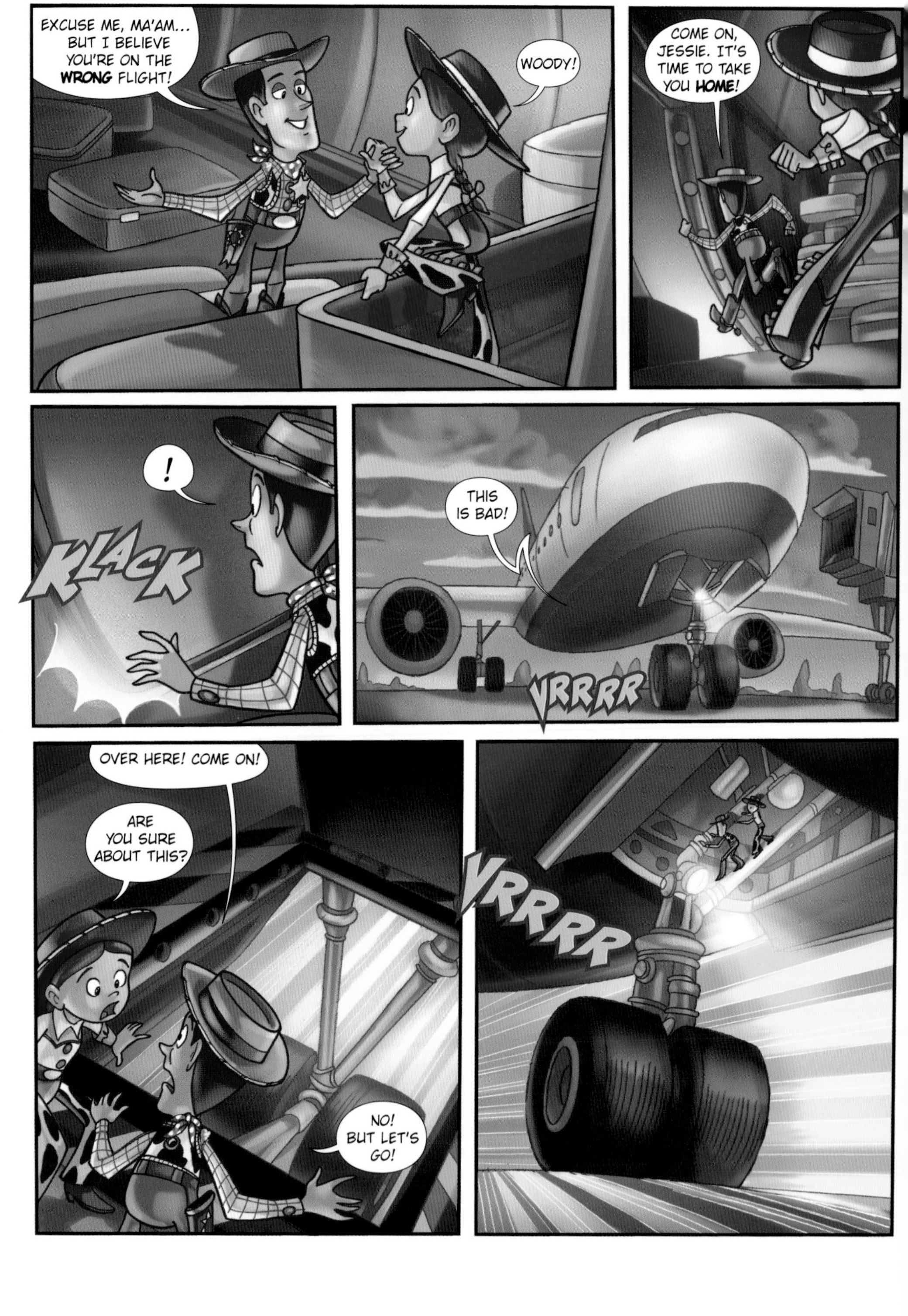
EXCUSE ME, MA'AM... BUT I BELIEVE YOU'RE ON THE **WRONG** FLIGHT!
WOODY!
COME ON, JESSIE. IT'S TIME TO TAKE YOU **HOME**!
!
KLACK
THIS IS BAD!
VRRRR
OVER HERE! COME ON!
ARE YOU SURE ABOUT THIS?
NO! BUT LET'S GO!
VRRRR

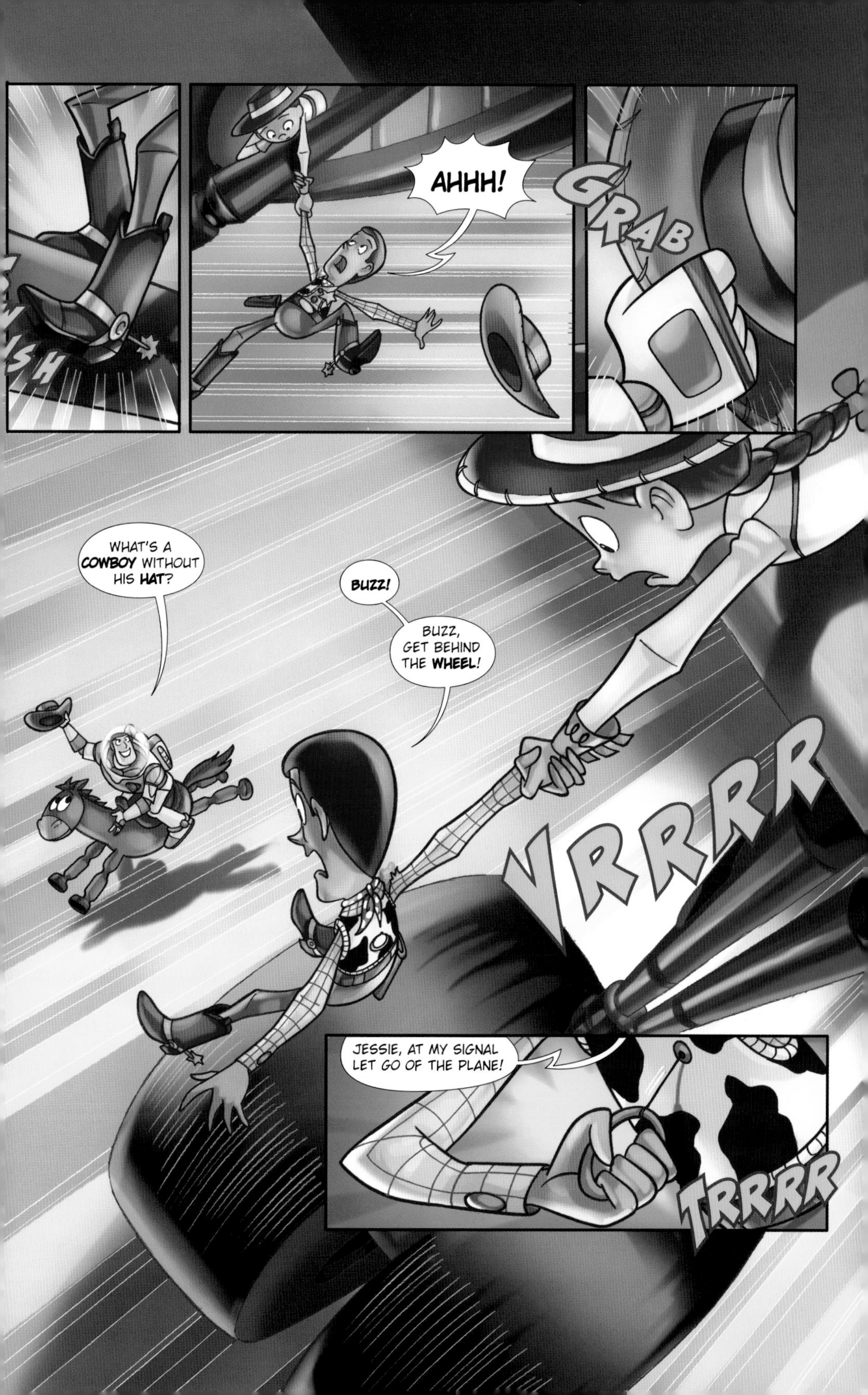

SWISH
AHHH!
GRAB
WHAT'S A **COWBOY** WITHOUT HIS **HAT**?
BUZZ!
BUZZ, GET BEHIND THE **WHEEL**!
VRRRR
JESSIE, AT MY SIGNAL LET GO OF THE PLANE!
TRRRR

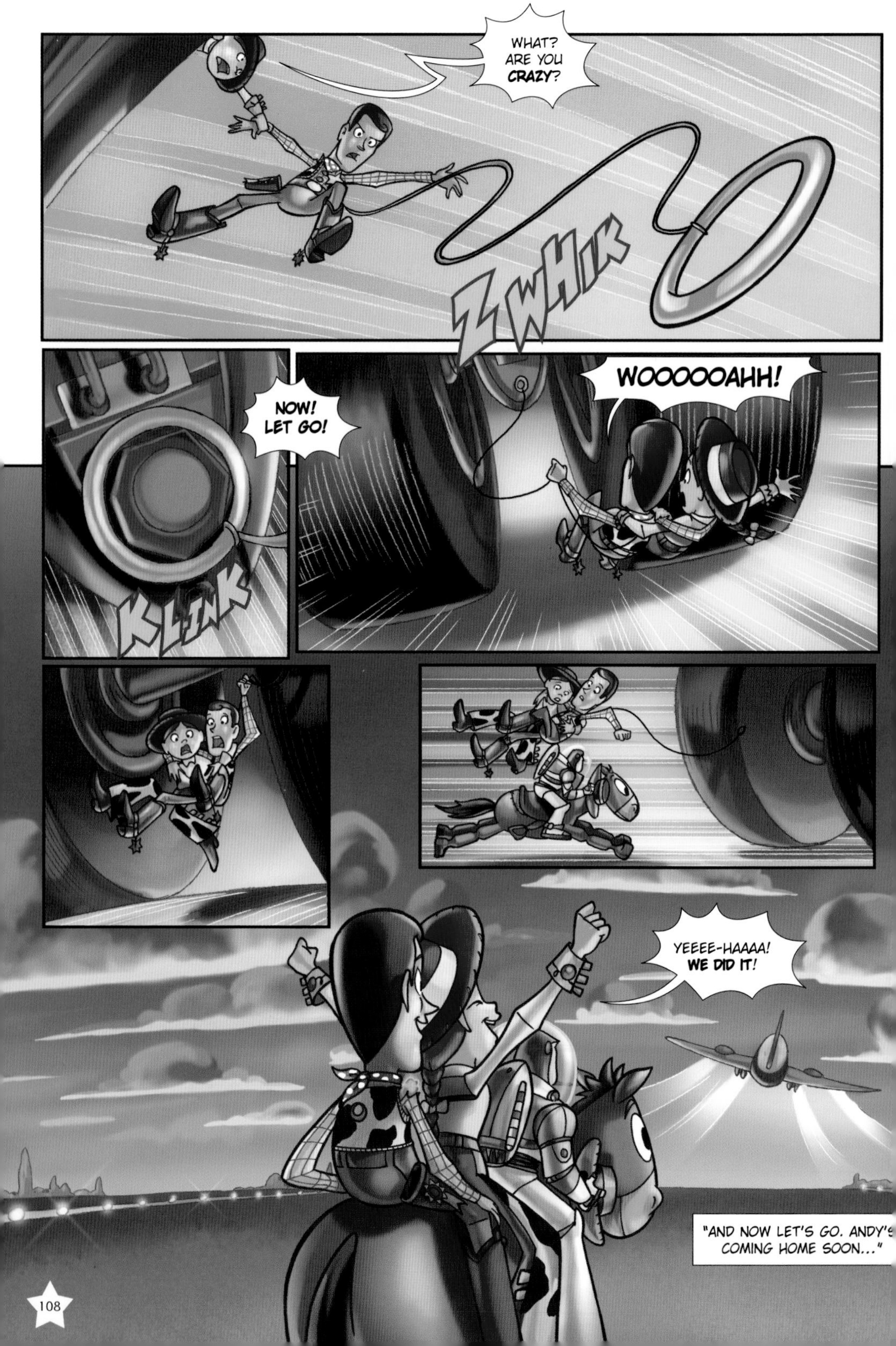
WHAT? ARE YOU CRAZY?
ZWHIK
NOW! LET GO!
KLINK
WOOOOOAHH!
YEEEE-HAAAA! WE DID IT!
"AND NOW LET'S GO. ANDY'S COMING HOME SOON..."

HEY, WOO...!

OH, WOW!
NEW TOYS.
COOL!

WELCOME
Home
ANDY

AND THE NEXT DAY...

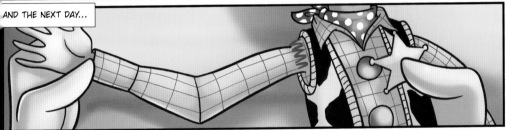

COME ON,
HON. TIME TO GO.
HEY, YOU **FIXED**
WOODY!

YEAH. GOOD THING I DIDN'T BRING
HIM TO COWBOY CAMP. HIS WHOLE
ARM MIGHT'VE COME OFF.

SLAM

WELL,
WHAT DO
YOU KNOW?

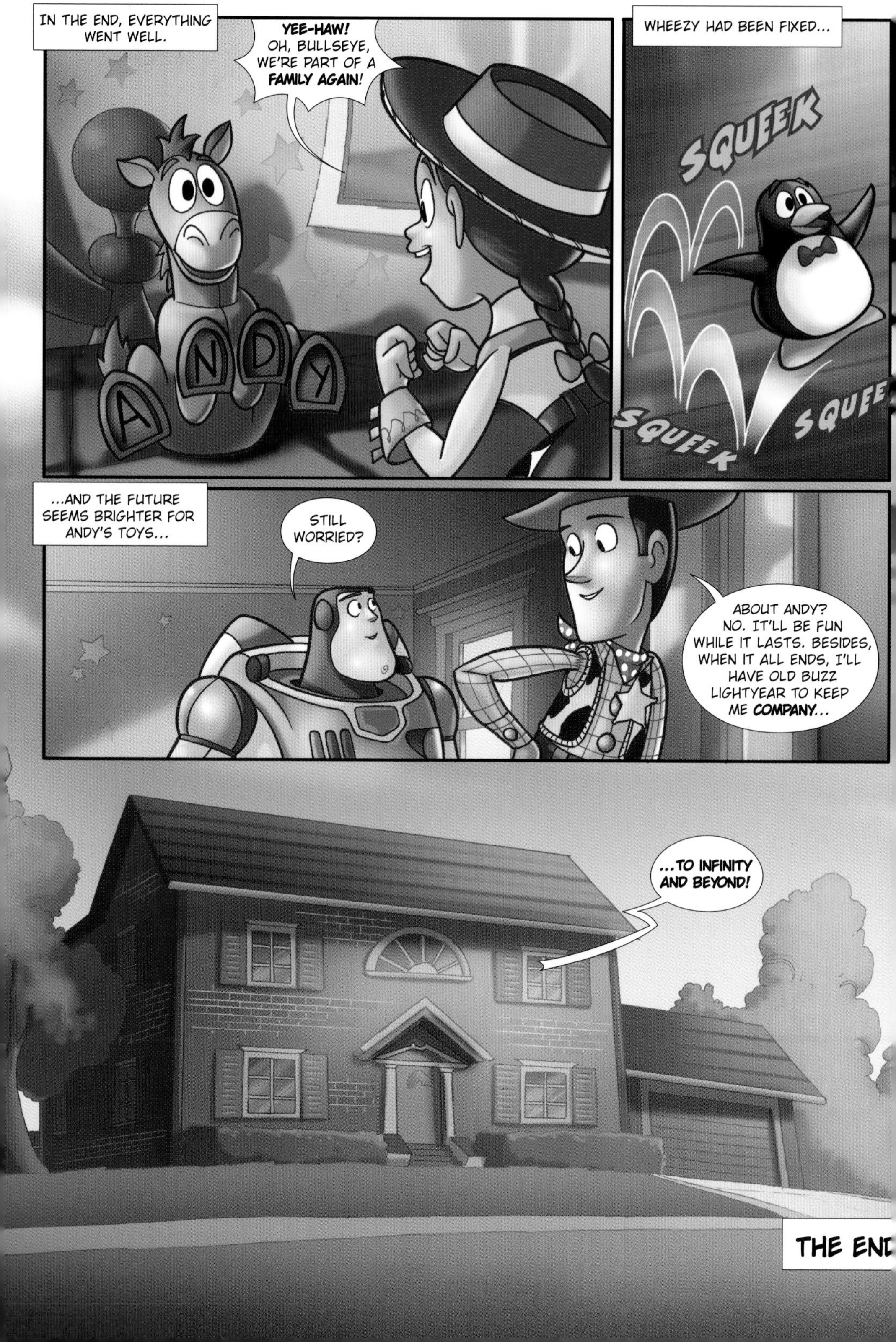
IN THE END, EVERYTHING WENT WELL.
YEE-HAW! OH, BULLSEYE, WE'RE PART OF A FAMILY AGAIN!
WHEEZY HAD BEEN FIXED...
SQUEEK
SQUEEK
SQUEE
...AND THE FUTURE SEEMS BRIGHTER FOR ANDY'S TOYS...
STILL WORRIED?
ABOUT ANDY? NO. IT'LL BE FUN WHILE IT LASTS. BESIDES, WHEN IT ALL ENDS, I'LL HAVE OLD BUZZ LIGHTYEAR TO KEEP ME COMPANY...
...TO INFINITY AND BEYOND!
THE END

Disney · PIXAR

TOY STORY 3

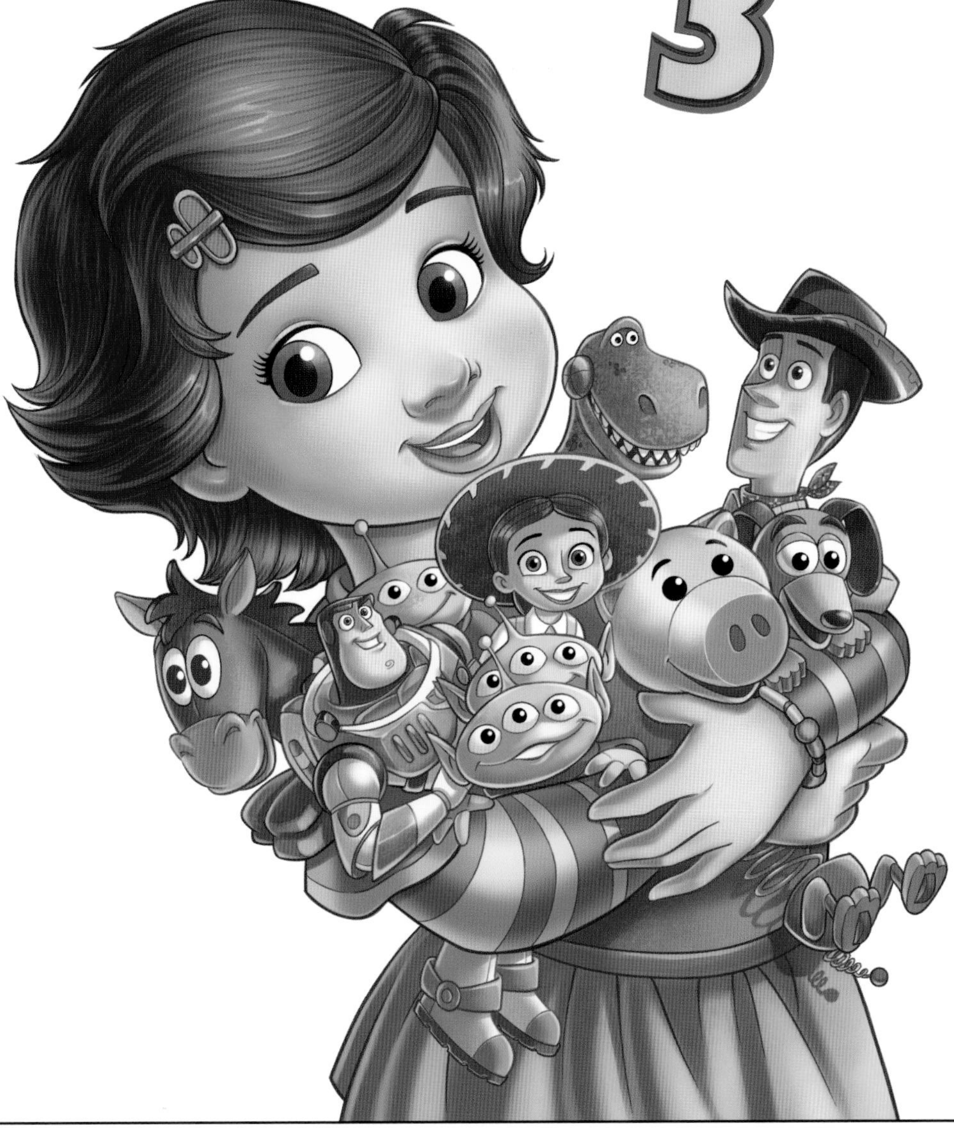

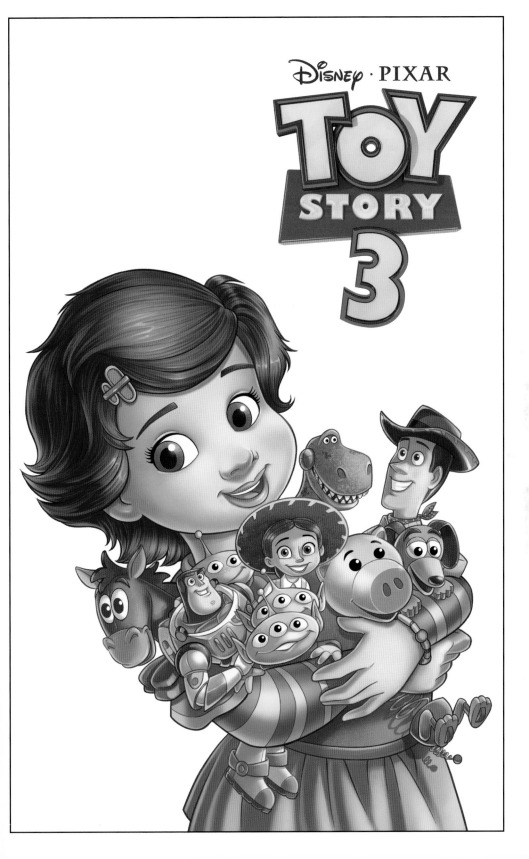

script adaptation
Alessandro Ferrari

art
Ettore Gula

paint
Kawaii Creative Studio

art optimization
Stefano Attardi
Guiseppe Fontana

editing
Kawaii Creative Studio

contributors
Paola Beretta
Elisabetta Sedda
Luca Usai

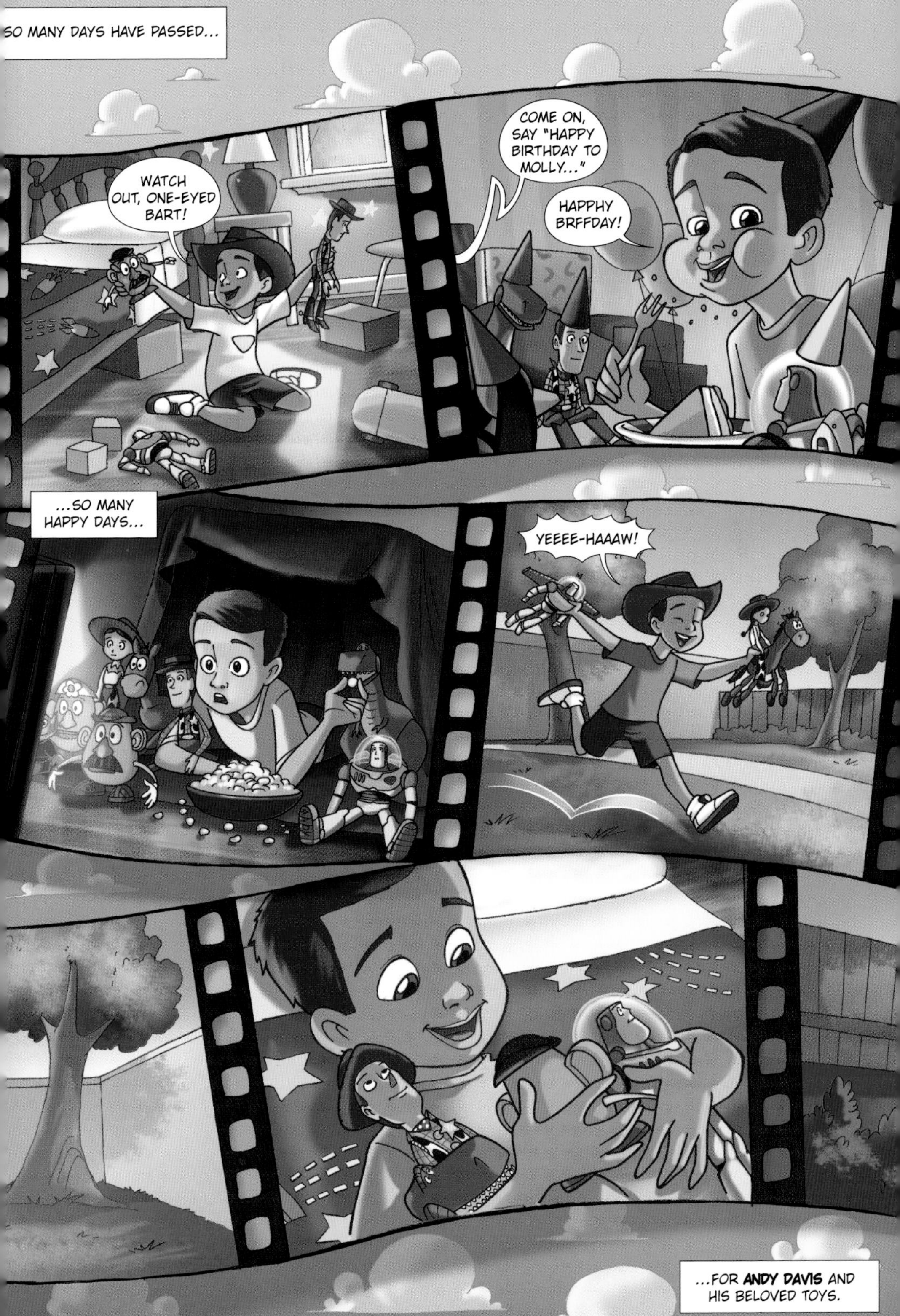
SO MANY DAYS HAVE PASSED...
WATCH OUT, ONE-EYED BART!
COME ON, SAY "HAPPY BIRTHDAY TO MOLLY..."
HAPPHY BRFFDAY!
...SO MANY HAPPY DAYS...
YEEEE-HAAAW!
...FOR **ANDY DAVIS** AND HIS BELOVED TOYS.

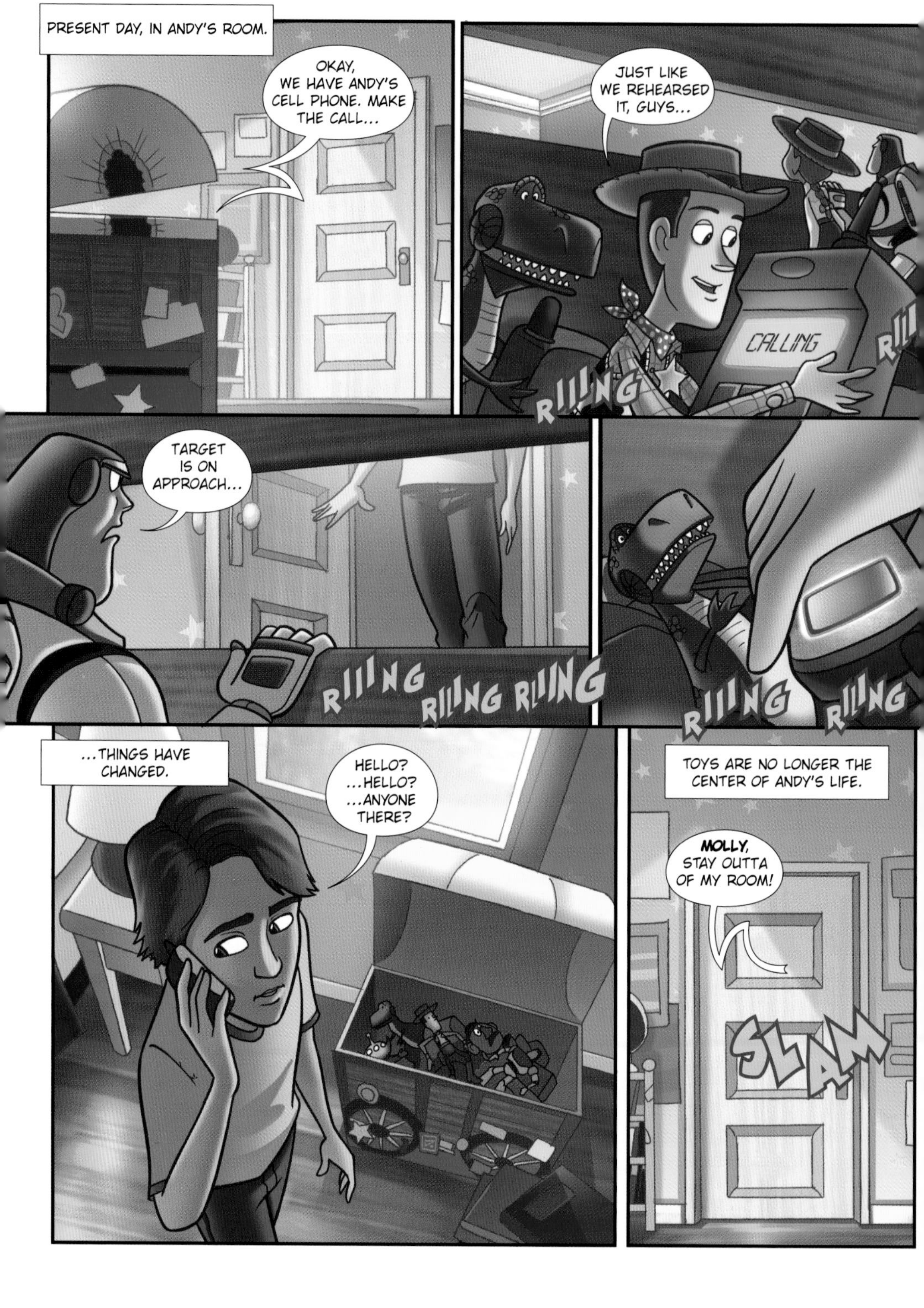
PRESENT DAY, IN ANDY'S ROOM.
OKAY, WE HAVE ANDY'S CELL PHONE. MAKE THE CALL...
JUST LIKE WE REHEARSED IT, GUYS...
CALLING
RIIING
RIII
TARGET IS ON APPROACH...
RIIING
RIIING RIIING
RIIING
RIIING
...THINGS HAVE CHANGED.
HELLO? ...HELLO? ...ANYONE THERE?
TOYS ARE NO LONGER THE CENTER OF ANDY'S LIFE.
MOLLY, STAY OUTTA OF MY ROOM!
SLAM

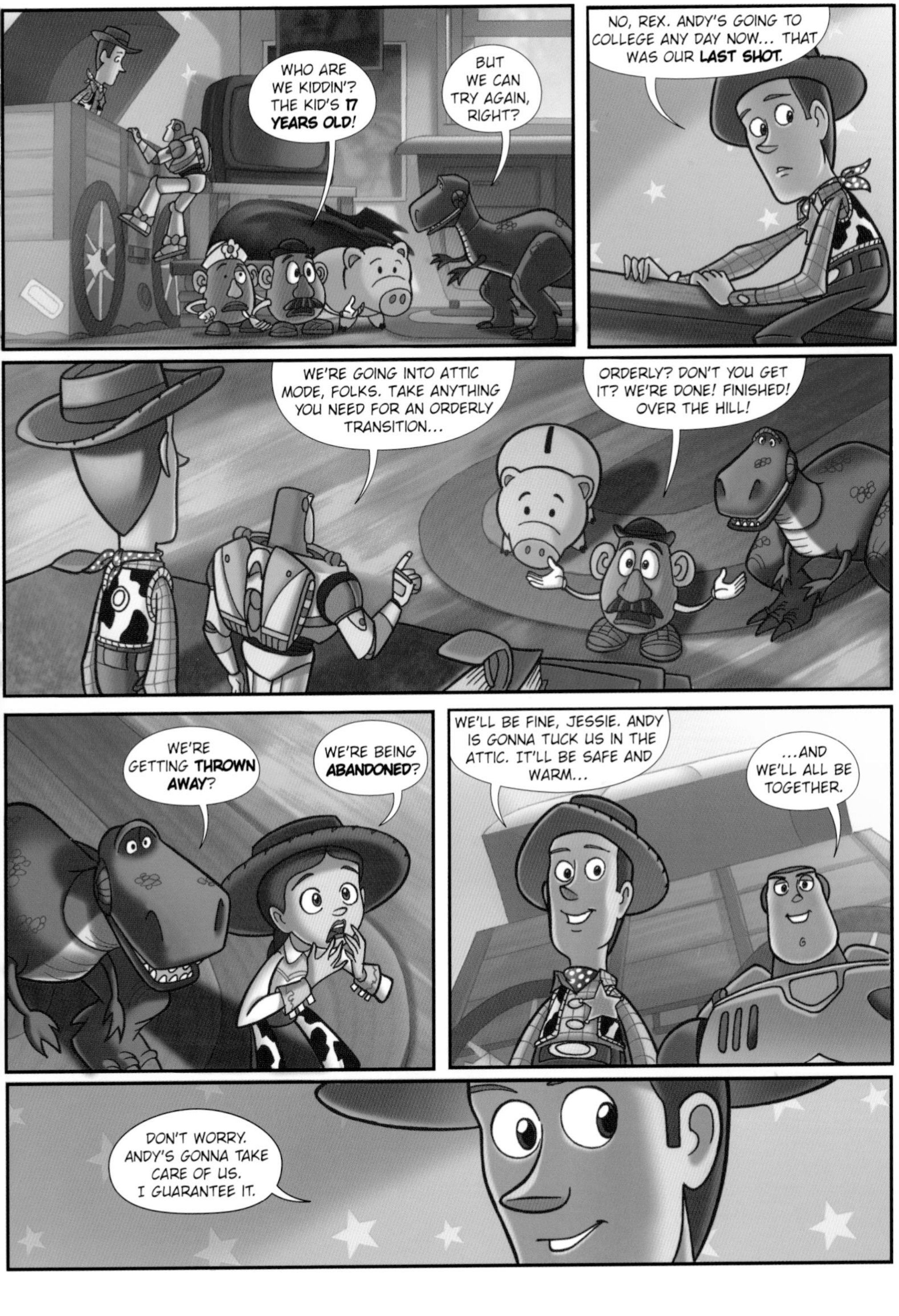

WHO ARE WE KIDDIN'? THE KID'S **17 YEARS OLD**!
BUT WE CAN TRY AGAIN, RIGHT?
NO, REX. ANDY'S GOING TO COLLEGE ANY DAY NOW... THAT WAS OUR **LAST SHOT**.
WE'RE GOING INTO ATTIC MODE, FOLKS. TAKE ANYTHING YOU NEED FOR AN ORDERLY TRANSITION...
ORDERLY? DON'T YOU GET IT? WE'RE DONE! FINISHED! OVER THE HILL!
WE'RE GETTING **THROWN AWAY**?
WE'RE BEING **ABANDONED**?
WE'LL BE FINE, JESSIE. ANDY IS GONNA TUCK US IN THE ATTIC. IT'LL BE SAFE AND WARM...
...AND WE'LL ALL BE TOGETHER.
DON'T WORRY. ANDY'S GONNA TAKE CARE OF US. I GUARANTEE IT.

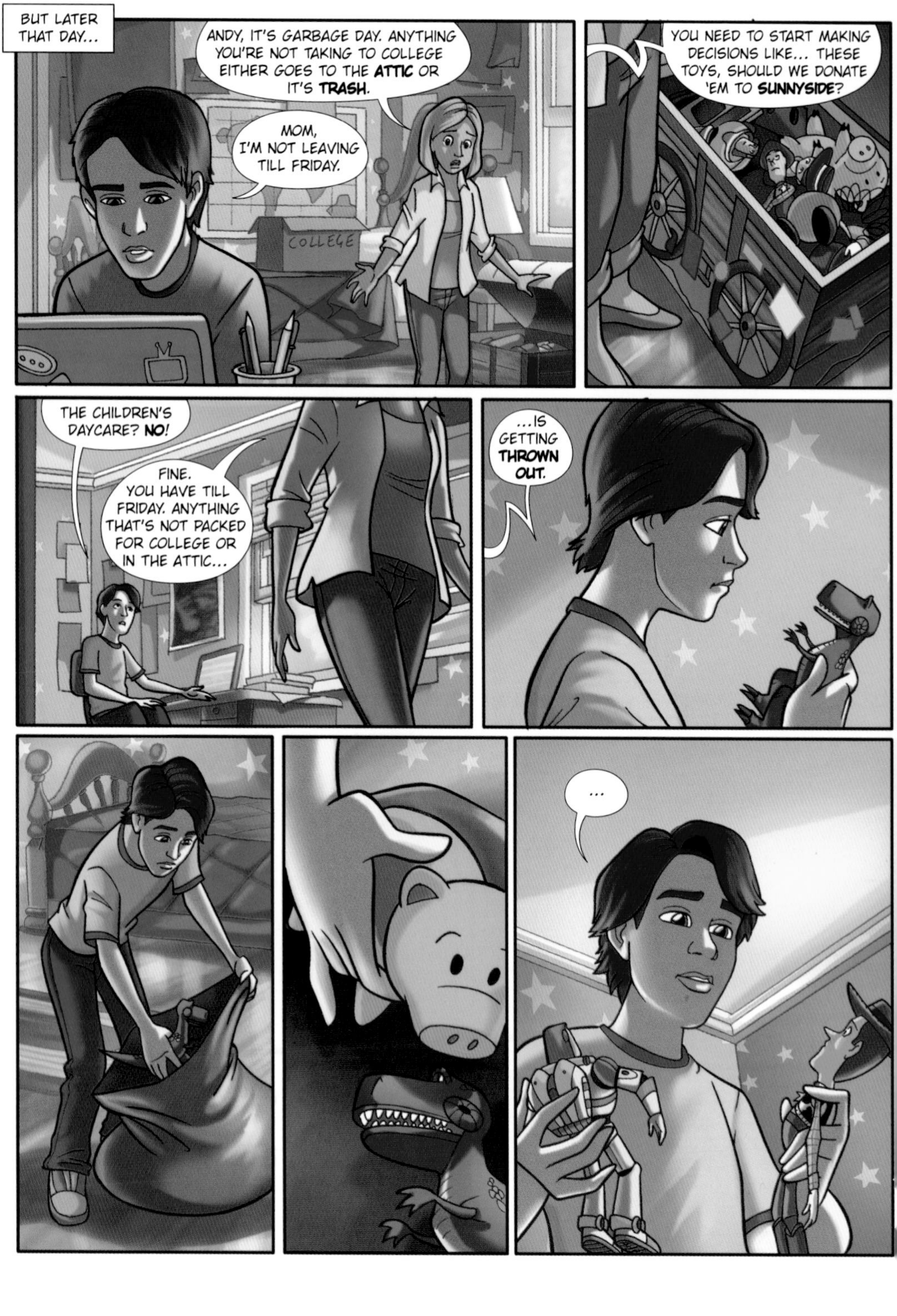
BUT LATER THAT DAY...
ANDY, IT'S GARBAGE DAY. ANYTHING YOU'RE NOT TAKING TO COLLEGE EITHER GOES TO THE ATTIC OR IT'S TRASH.
MOM, I'M NOT LEAVING TILL FRIDAY.
COLLEGE
YOU NEED TO START MAKING DECISIONS LIKE... THESE TOYS, SHOULD WE DONATE 'EM TO SUNNYSIDE?
THE CHILDREN'S DAYCARE? NO!
FINE. YOU HAVE TILL FRIDAY. ANYTHING THAT'S NOT PACKED FOR COLLEGE OR IN THE ATTIC...
...IS GETTING THROWN OUT.
...

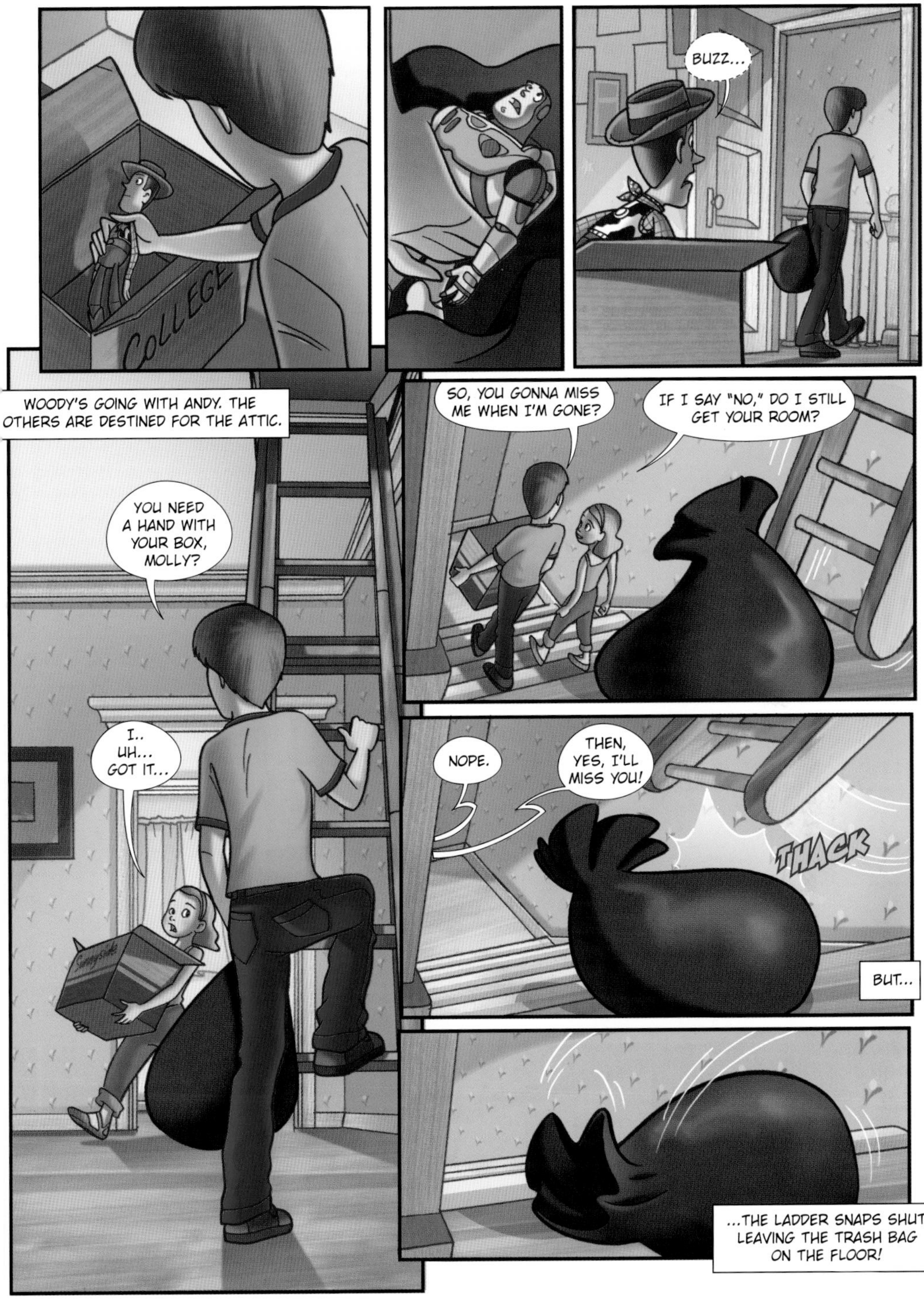
BUZZ...
WOODY'S GOING WITH ANDY. THE OTHERS ARE DESTINED FOR THE ATTIC.
YOU NEED A HAND WITH YOUR BOX, MOLLY?
I.. UH... GOT IT...
SO, YOU GONNA MISS ME WHEN I'M GONE?
IF I SAY "NO," DO I STILL GET YOUR ROOM?
NOPE.
THEN, YES, I'LL MISS YOU!
THACK
BUT...
...THE LADDER SNAPS SHUT, LEAVING THE TRASH BAG ON THE FLOOR!

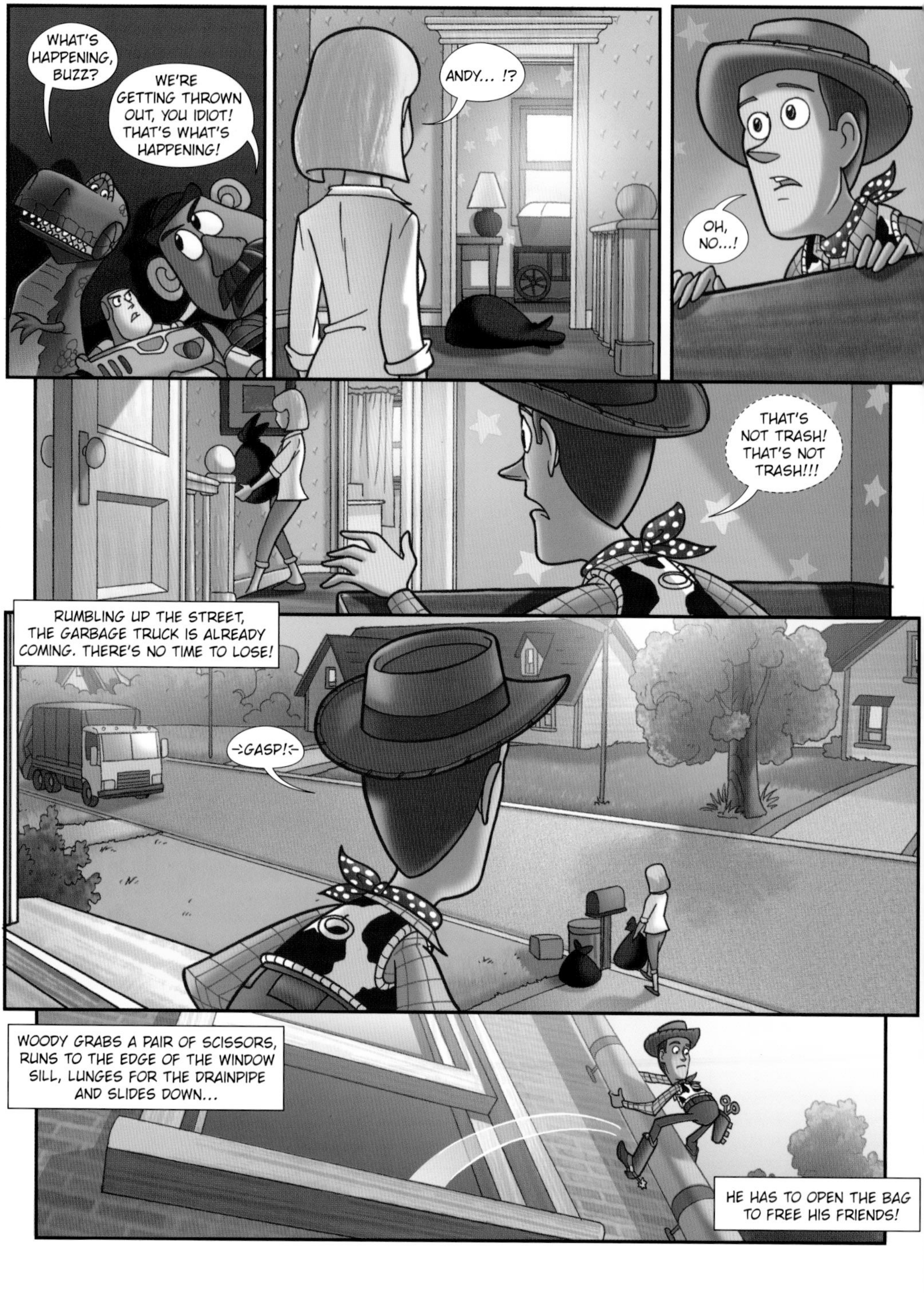
WHAT'S HAPPENING, BUZZ?
WE'RE GETTING THROWN OUT, YOU IDIOT! THAT'S WHAT'S HAPPENING!
ANDY... !?
OH, NO...!
THAT'S NOT TRASH! THAT'S NOT TRASH!!!
RUMBLING UP THE STREET, THE GARBAGE TRUCK IS ALREADY COMING. THERE'S NO TIME TO LOSE!
GASP!
WOODY GRABS A PAIR OF SCISSORS, RUNS TO THE EDGE OF THE WINDOW SILL, LUNGES FOR THE DRAINPIPE AND SLIDES DOWN...
HE HAS TO OPEN THE BAG TO FREE HIS FRIENDS!

WE'RE ON THE CURB!

I KNEW IT WOULD COME TO THIS!

PULL, EVERYONE! **PULL!**

IT WON'T RIP!

ANDY DOESN'T WANT US! WHAT'S THE POINT?

POINT... POINT... **POINT!**

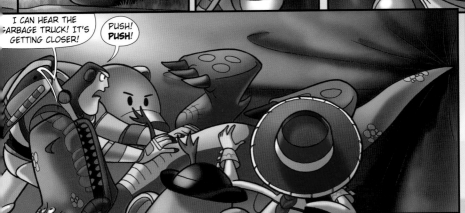

I CAN HEAR THE GARBAGE TRUCK! IT'S GETTING CLOSER!

PUSH! **PUSH!**

RIIIP

AND THE GARBAGE TRUCK IS THERE!

OH, NO! BUZZ... JESSIE...

THEY ALREADY SET THEMSELVES FREE!

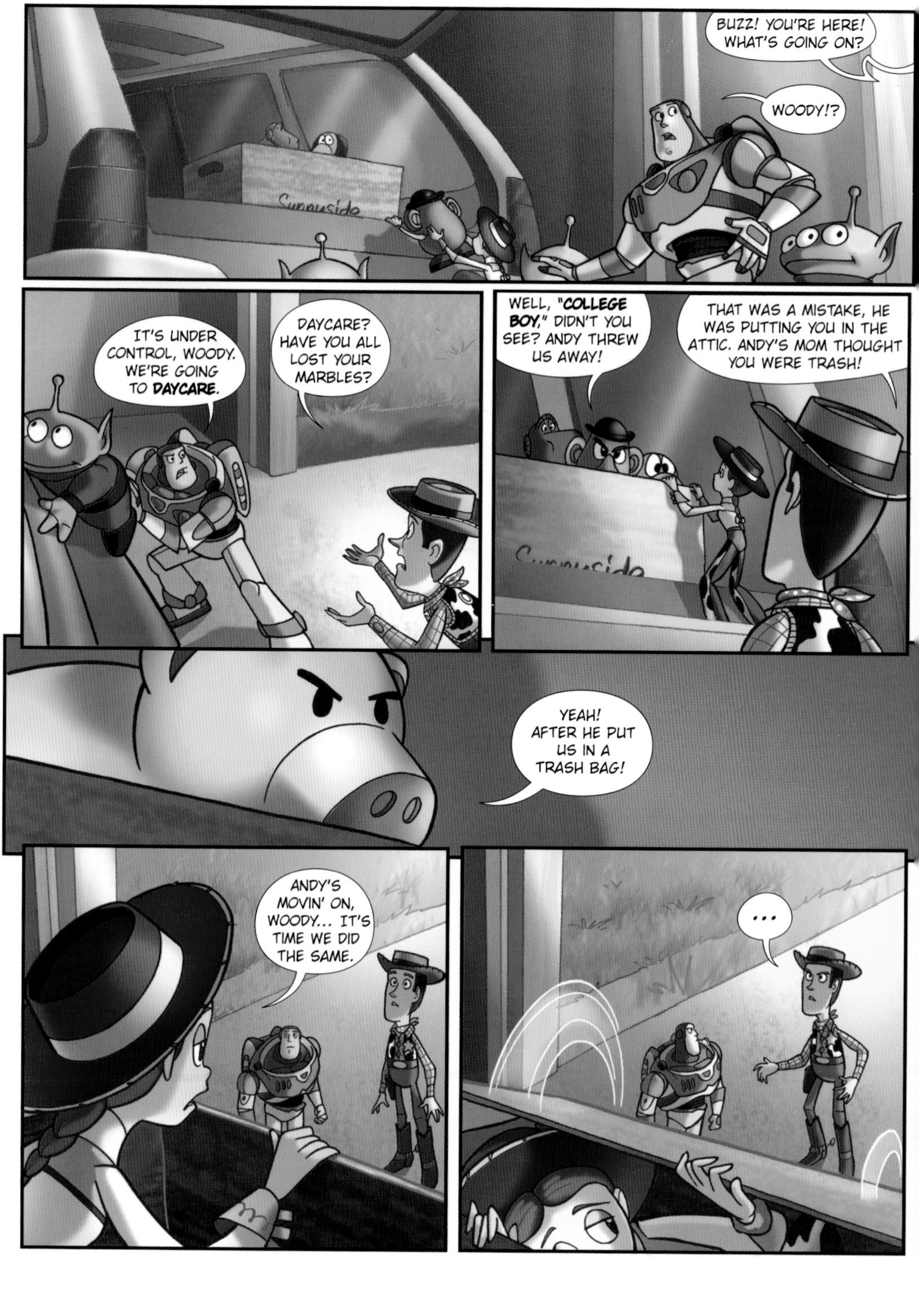
BUZZ! YOU'RE HERE! WHAT'S GOING ON?
WOODY!?
IT'S UNDER CONTROL, WOODY. WE'RE GOING TO DAYCARE.
DAYCARE? HAVE YOU ALL LOST YOUR MARBLES?
WELL, "COLLEGE BOY," DIDN'T YOU SEE? ANDY THREW US AWAY!
THAT WAS A MISTAKE, HE WAS PUTTING YOU IN THE ATTIC. ANDY'S MOM THOUGHT YOU WERE TRASH!
YEAH! AFTER HE PUT US IN A TRASH BAG!
ANDY'S MOVIN' ON, WOODY... IT'S TIME WE DID THE SAME.
...

OKAY, OUT OF THE BOX! EVERYONE!

WOODY, WAIT! WE NEED TO...

SLAM

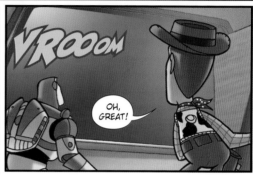

VROOOM

OH, GREAT!

IT'S GONNA TAKE US FOREVER TO GET BACK HERE!

CUT IT, WOODY! ANDY DOESN'T WANT US ANYMORE!

HE WAS PUTTING YOU... **IN THE ATTIC!**

HE LEFT US... **ON THE CURB!**

ALRIGHT, CALM DOWN! BOTH OF YOU!

OKAY, FINE! JUST WAIT'LL YOU SEE WHAT DAY-CARE IS!

WHY? WHAT'S IT LIKE?

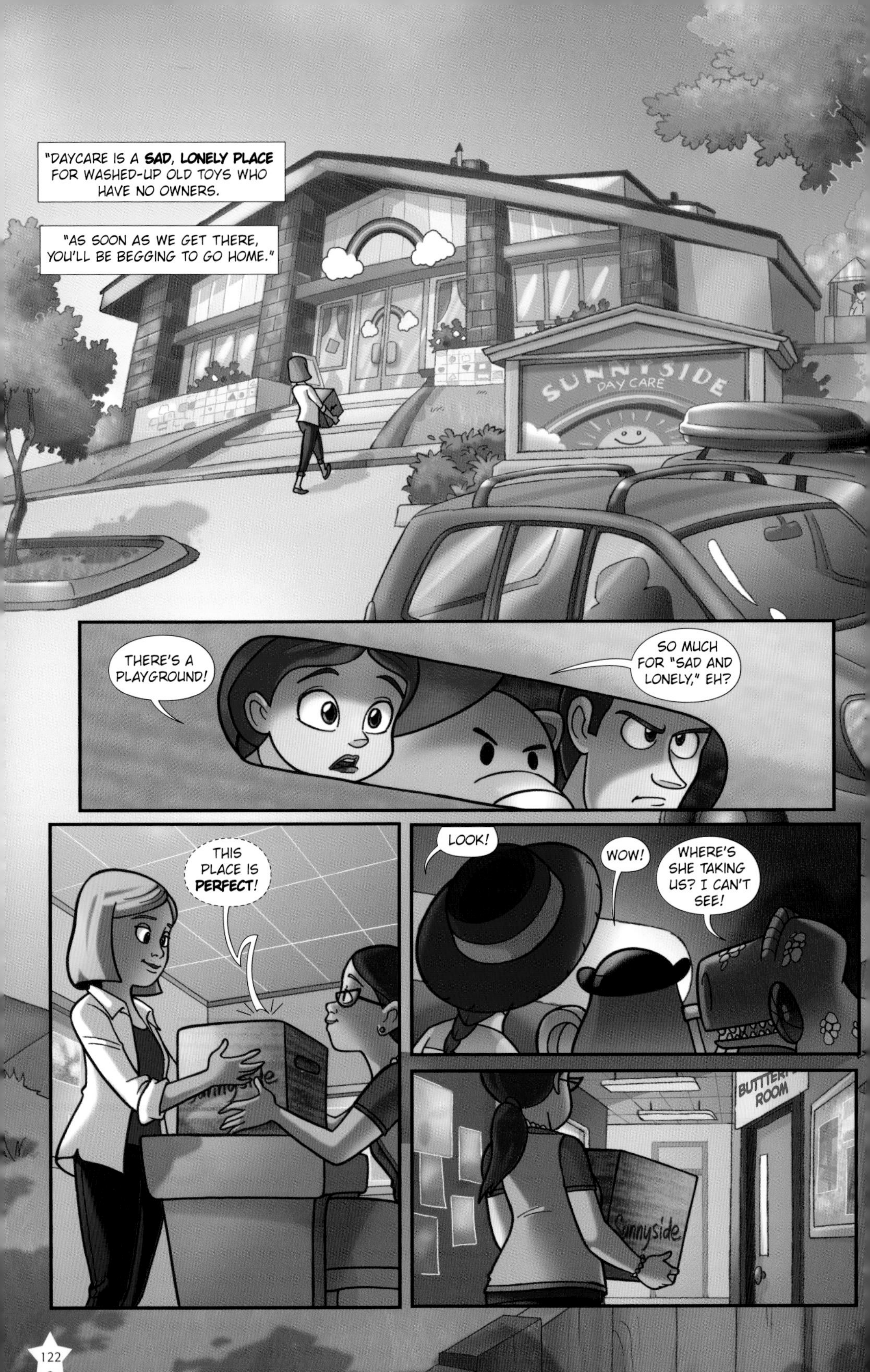
"DAYCARE IS A **SAD, LONELY PLACE** FOR WASHED-UP OLD TOYS WHO HAVE NO OWNERS.
"AS SOON AS WE GET THERE, YOU'LL BE BEGGING TO GO HOME."
SUNNYSIDE DAY CARE
THERE'S A PLAYGROUND!
SO MUCH FOR "SAD AND LONELY," EH?
THIS PLACE IS **PERFECT**!
Sunnyside
LOOK!
WOW!
WHERE'S SHE TAKING US? I CAN'T SEE!
BUTTERF ROOM
Sunnyside

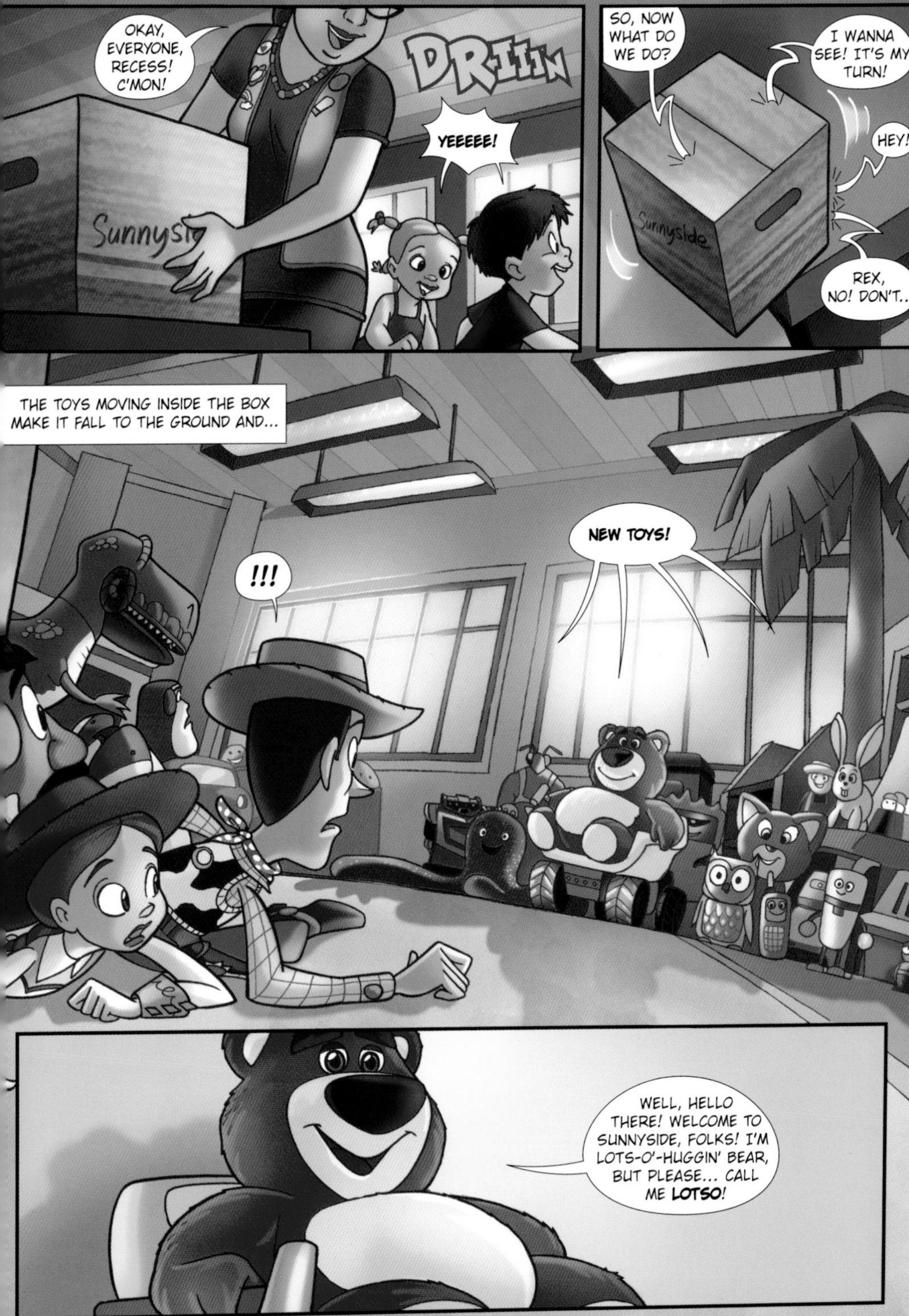

OKAY, EVERYONE, RECESS! C'MON!
DRIIIN
YEEEEE!
Sunnyside
SO, NOW WHAT DO WE DO?
I WANNA SEE! IT'S MY TURN!
HEY!
Sunnyside
REX, NO! DON'T...
THE TOYS MOVING INSIDE THE BOX MAKE IT FALL TO THE GROUND AND...
!!!
NEW TOYS!
WELL, HELLO THERE! WELCOME TO SUNNYSIDE, FOLKS! I'M LOTS-O'-HUGGIN' BEAR, BUT PLEASE... CALL ME **LOTSO**!

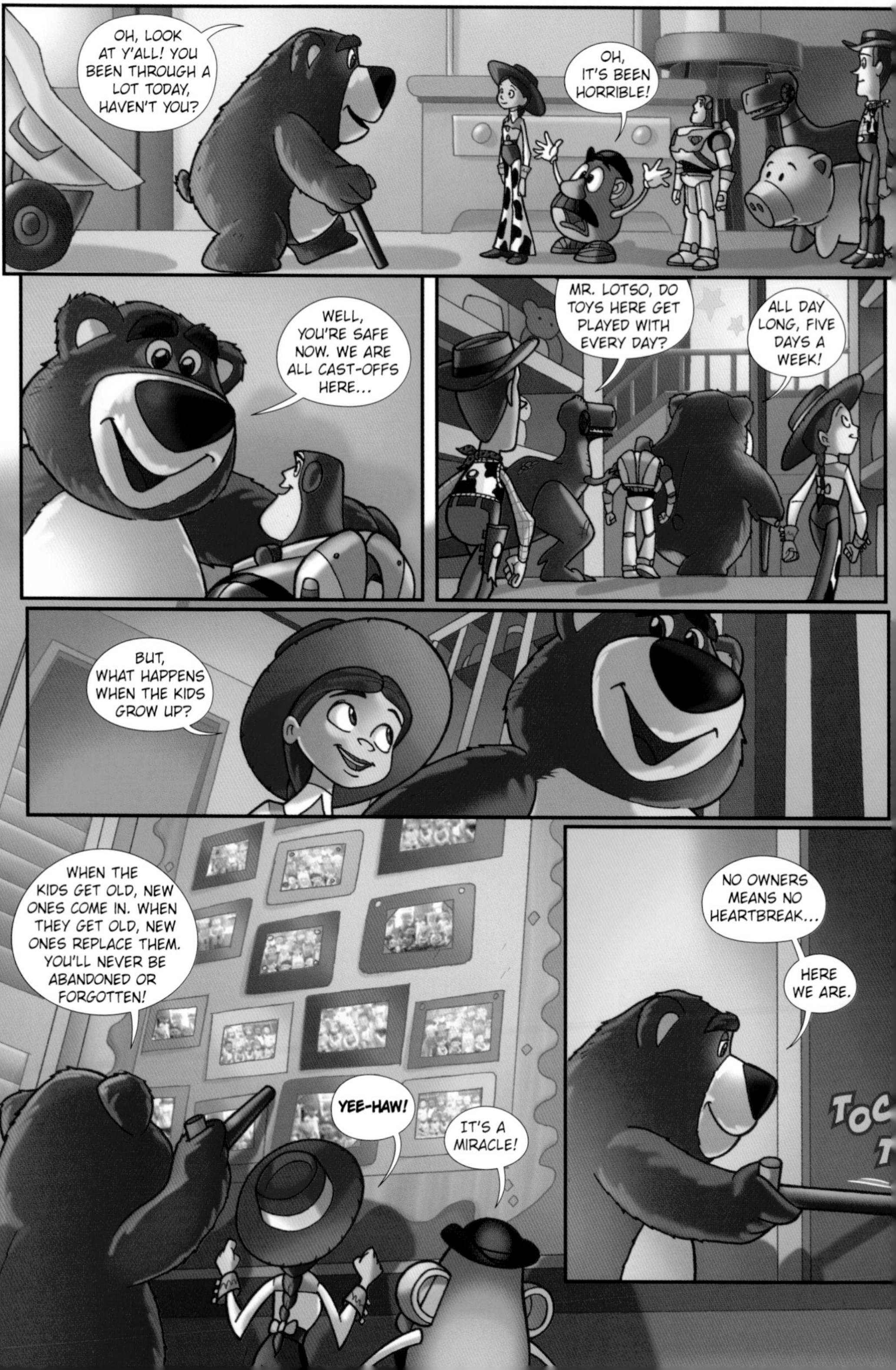
OH, LOOK AT Y'ALL! YOU BEEN THROUGH A LOT TODAY, HAVEN'T YOU?
OH, IT'S BEEN HORRIBLE!
WELL, YOU'RE SAFE NOW. WE ARE ALL CAST-OFFS HERE...
MR. LOTSO, DO TOYS HERE GET PLAYED WITH EVERY DAY?
ALL DAY LONG, FIVE DAYS A WEEK!
BUT, WHAT HAPPENS WHEN THE KIDS GROW UP?
WHEN THE KIDS GET OLD, NEW ONES COME IN. WHEN THEY GET OLD, NEW ONES REPLACE THEM. YOU'LL NEVER BE ABANDONED OR FORGOTTEN!
YEE-HAW!
IT'S A MIRACLE!
NO OWNERS MEANS NO HEARTBREAK...
HERE WE ARE.

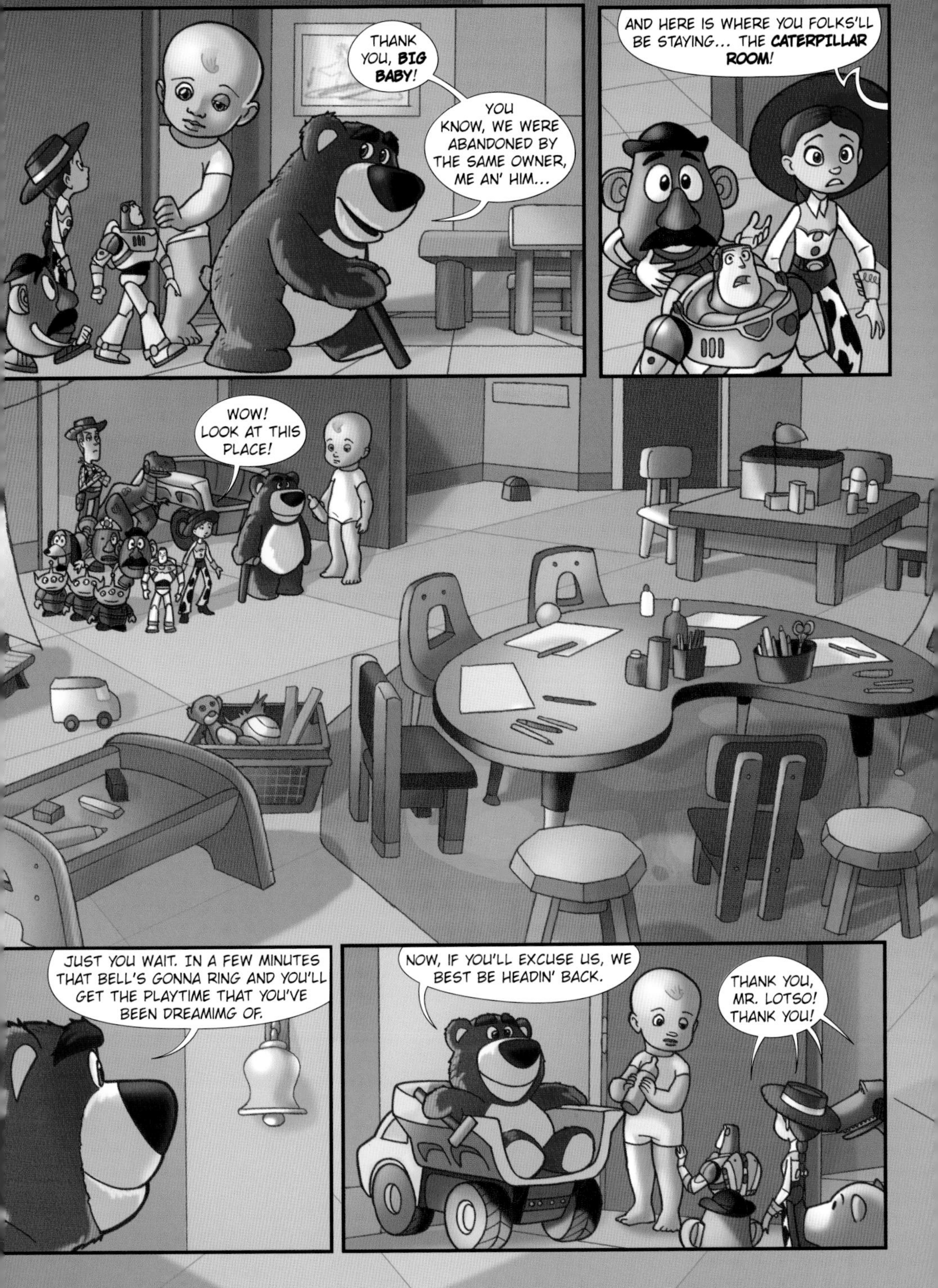
THANK YOU, **BIG BABY**!
YOU KNOW, WE WERE ABANDONED BY THE SAME OWNER, ME AN' HIM...
AND HERE IS WHERE YOU FOLKS'LL BE STAYING... THE **CATERPILLAR ROOM**!
WOW! LOOK AT THIS PLACE!
JUST YOU WAIT. IN A FEW MINUTES THAT BELL'S GONNA RING AND YOU'LL GET THE PLAYTIME THAT YOU'VE BEEN DREAMIMG OF.
NOW, IF YOU'LL EXCUSE US, WE BEST BE HEADIN' BACK.
THANK YOU, MR. LOTSO! THANK YOU!

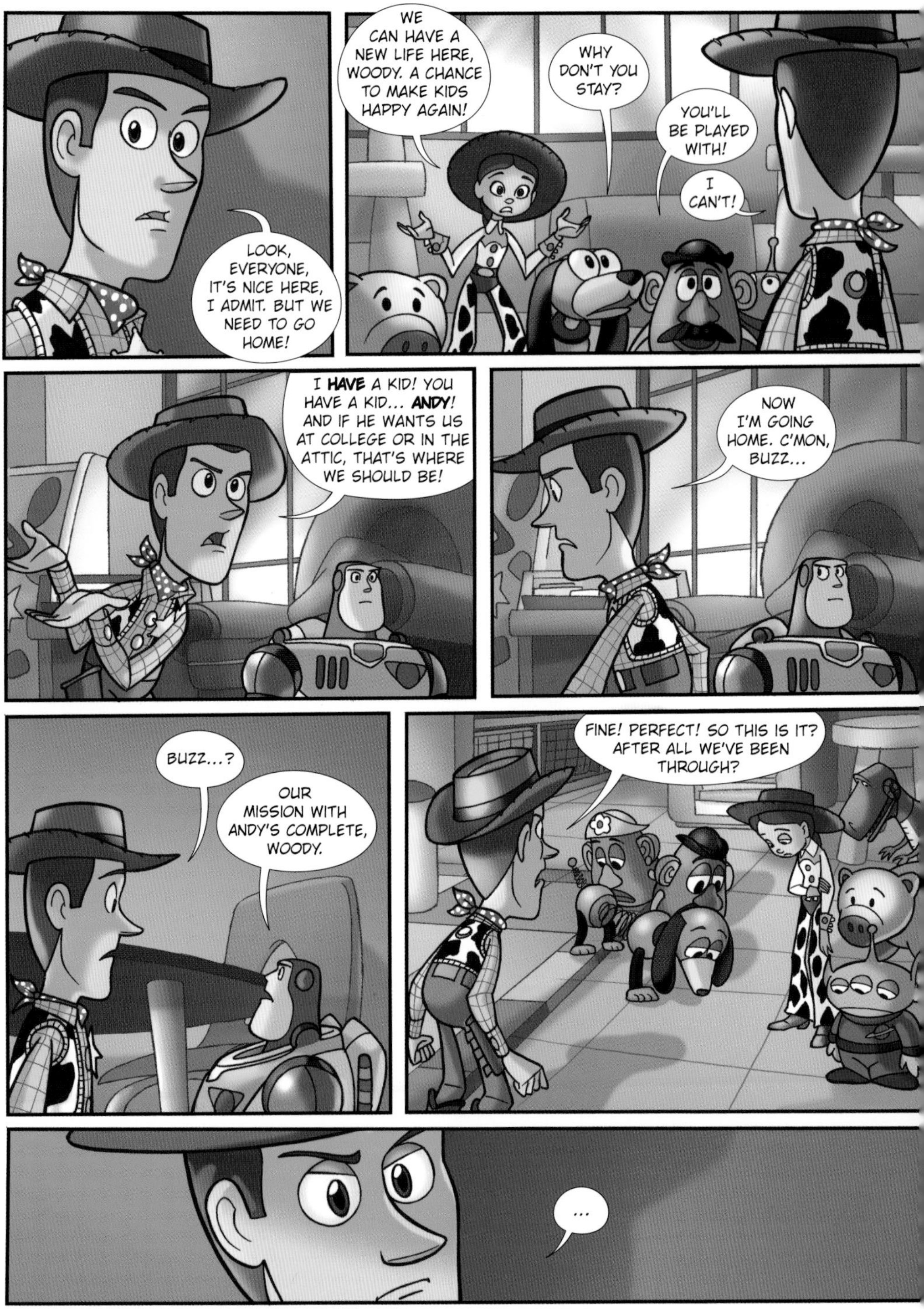
LOOK, EVERYONE, IT'S NICE HERE, I ADMIT. BUT WE NEED TO GO HOME!
WE CAN HAVE A NEW LIFE HERE, WOODY. A CHANCE TO MAKE KIDS HAPPY AGAIN!
WHY DON'T YOU STAY?
YOU'LL BE PLAYED WITH!
I CAN'T!
I **HAVE** A KID! YOU HAVE A KID... **ANDY**! AND IF HE WANTS US AT COLLEGE OR IN THE ATTIC, THAT'S WHERE WE SHOULD BE!
NOW I'M GOING HOME. C'MON, BUZZ...
BUZZ...?
OUR MISSION WITH ANDY'S COMPLETE, WOODY.
FINE! PERFECT! SO THIS IS IT? AFTER ALL WE'VE BEEN THROUGH?
...

SO WOODY LEAVES, ALONE.

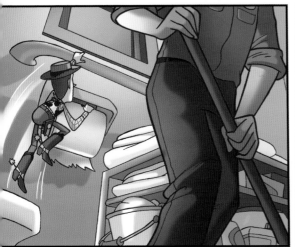

GASP! PRETTY HIGH!

FWOoo

OH, NO!

A KITE?!

127

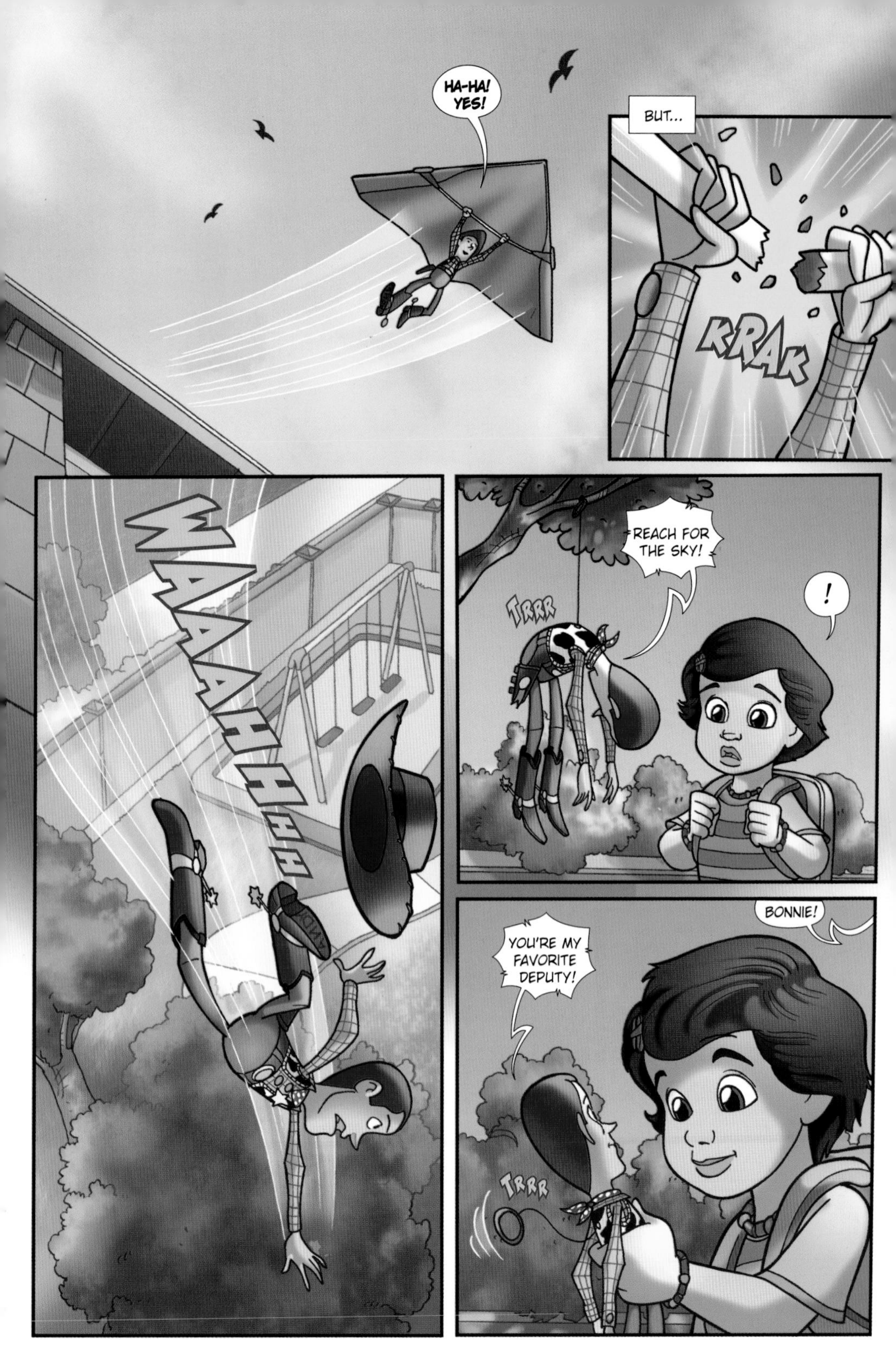
HA-HA! YES!
BUT...
KRAK
WAAAHHHHH!
REACH FOR THE SKY!
TRRR
!
BONNIE!
YOU'RE MY FAVORITE DEPUTY!
TRRR

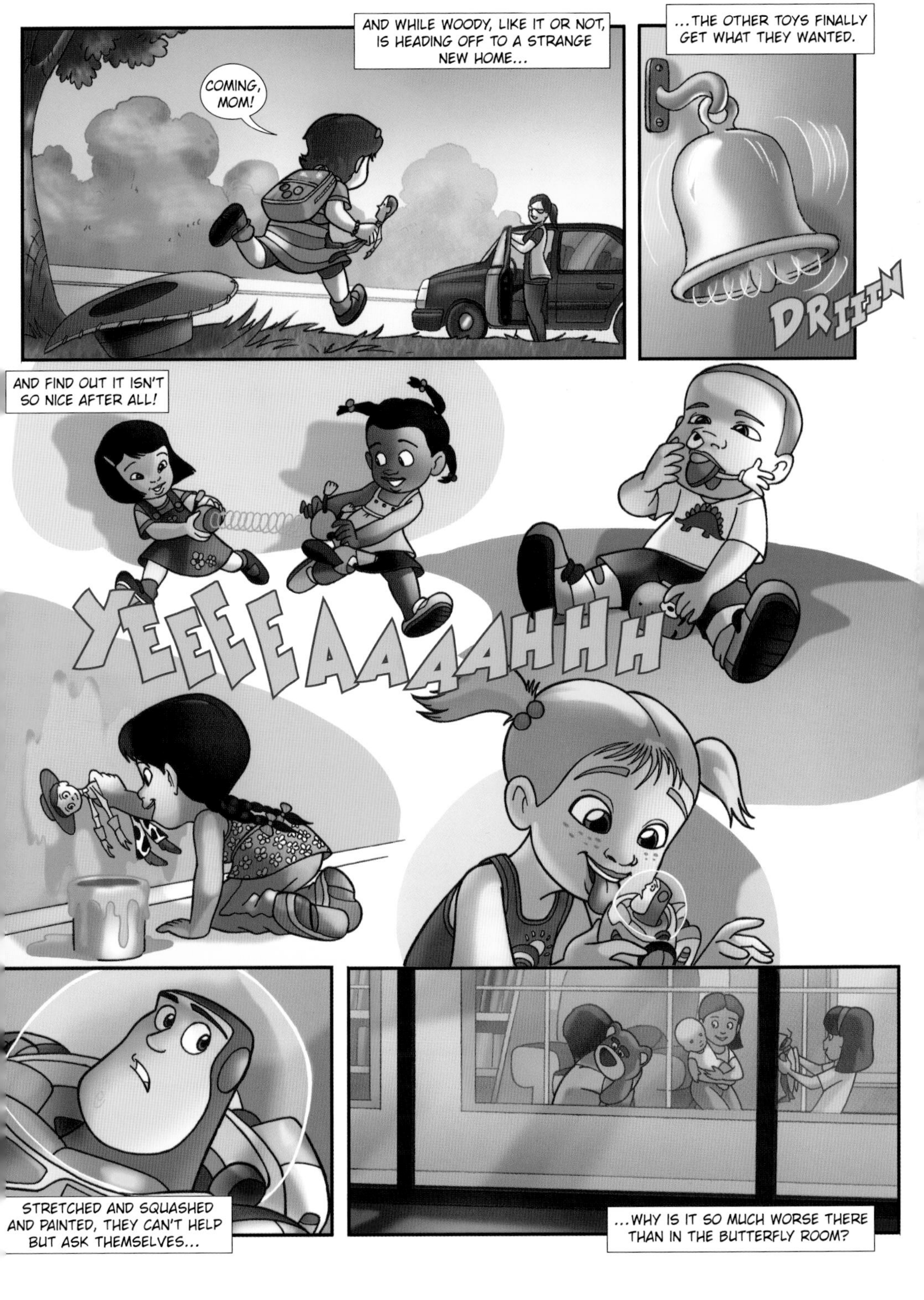
AND WHILE WOODY, LIKE IT OR NOT, IS HEADING OFF TO A STRANGE NEW HOME...
COMING, MOM!
...THE OTHER TOYS FINALLY GET WHAT THEY WANTED.
DRIIIN
AND FIND OUT IT ISN'T SO NICE AFTER ALL!
YEEEEAAAAHHH
STRETCHED AND SQUASHED AND PAINTED, THEY CAN'T HELP BUT ASK THEMSELVES...
...WHY IS IT SO MUCH WORSE THERE THAN IN THE BUTTERFLY ROOM?

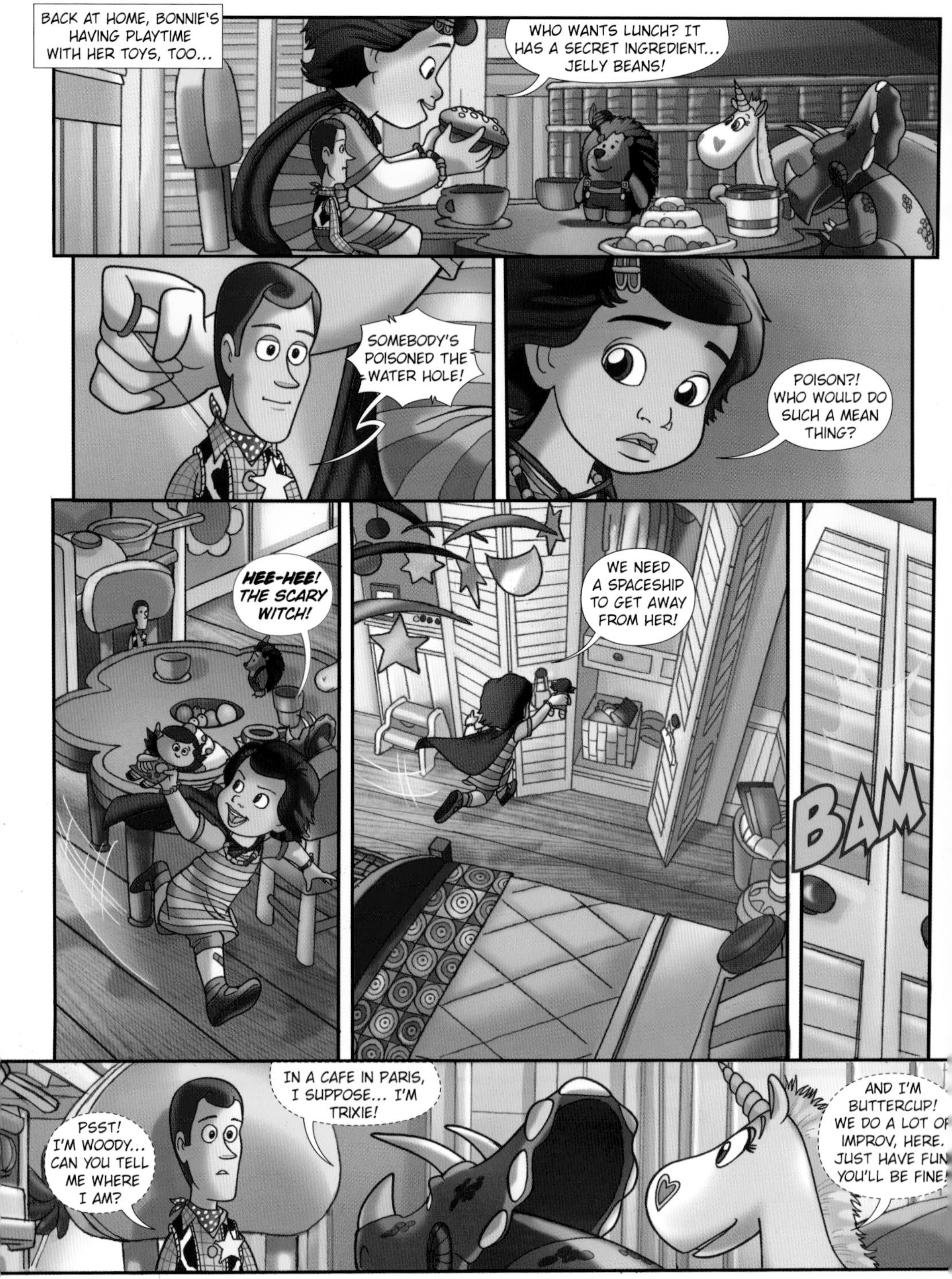
BACK AT HOME, BONNIE'S HAVING PLAYTIME WITH HER TOYS, TOO...
WHO WANTS LUNCH? IT HAS A SECRET INGREDIENT... JELLY BEANS!
SOMEBODY'S POISONED THE WATER HOLE!
POISON?! WHO WOULD DO SUCH A MEAN THING?
HEE-HEE! THE SCARY WITCH!
WE NEED A SPACESHIP TO GET AWAY FROM HER!
BAM
PSST! I'M WOODY... CAN YOU TELL ME WHERE I AM?
IN A CAFE IN PARIS, I SUPPOSE... I'M TRIXIE!
AND I'M BUTTERCUP! WE DO A LOT OF IMPROV, HERE. JUST HAVE FUN. YOU'LL BE FINE!

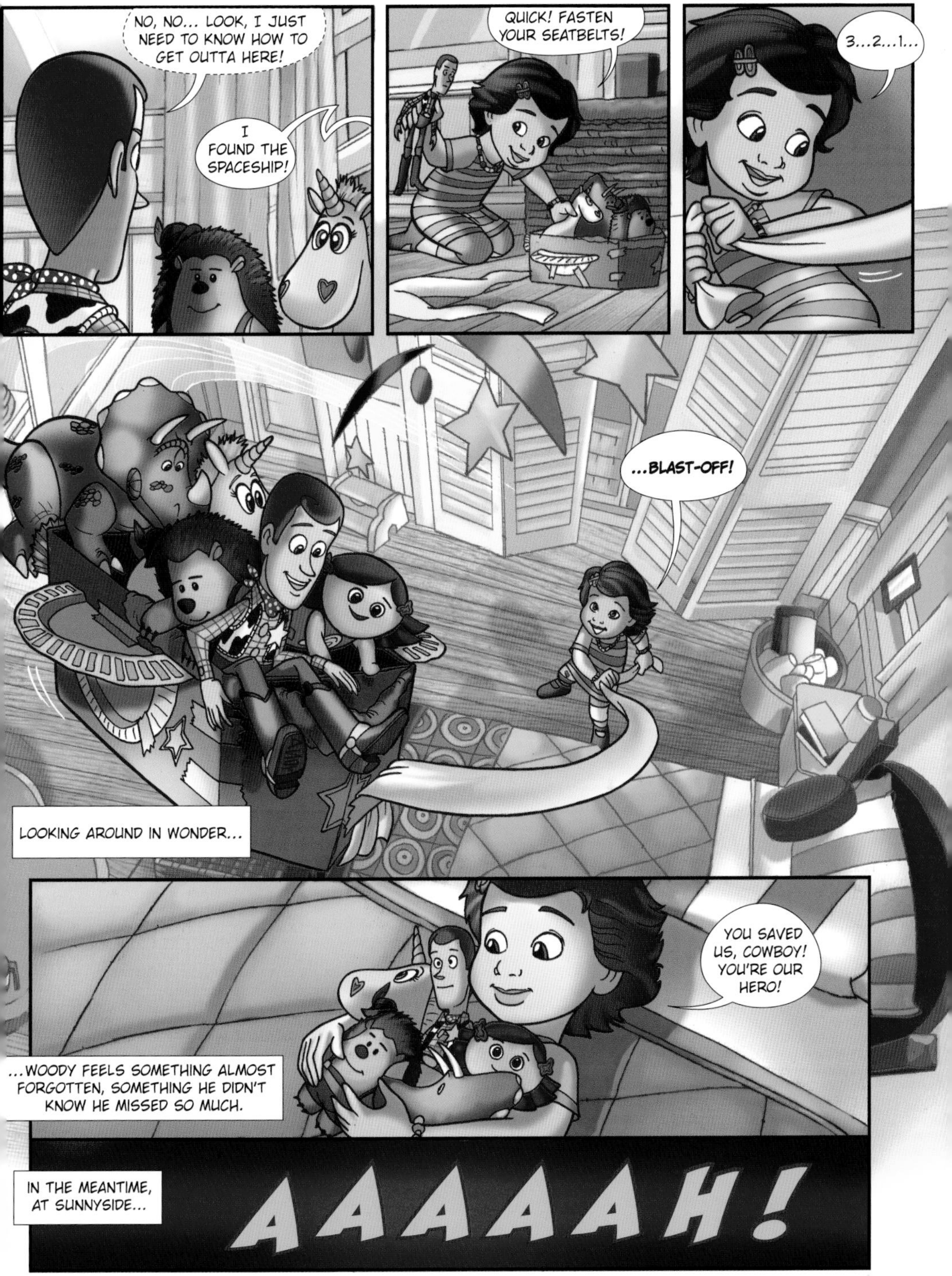
NO, NO... LOOK, I JUST NEED TO KNOW HOW TO GET OUTTA HERE!
I FOUND THE SPACESHIP!
QUICK! FASTEN YOUR SEATBELTS!
3...2...1...
...BLAST-OFF!
LOOKING AROUND IN WONDER...
...WOODY FEELS SOMETHING ALMOST FORGOTTEN, SOMETHING HE DIDN'T KNOW HE MISSED SO MUCH.
YOU SAVED US, COWBOY! YOU'RE OUR HERO!
IN THE MEANTIME, AT SUNNYSIDE...
AAAAAH!

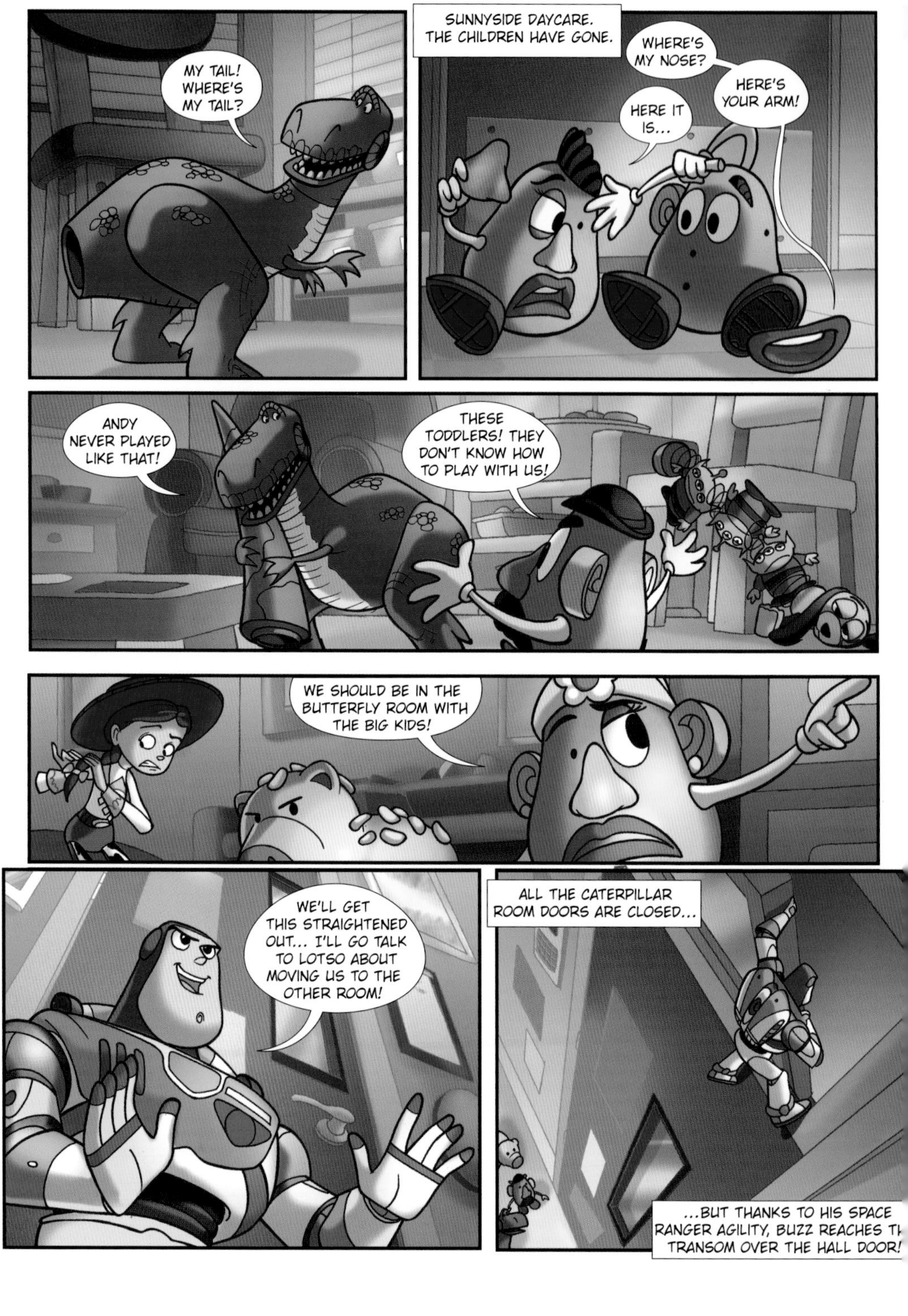
MY TAIL! WHERE'S MY TAIL?
SUNNYSIDE DAYCARE. THE CHILDREN HAVE GONE.
WHERE'S MY NOSE?
HERE IT IS...
HERE'S YOUR ARM!
ANDY NEVER PLAYED LIKE THAT!
THESE TODDLERS! THEY DON'T KNOW HOW TO PLAY WITH US!
WE SHOULD BE IN THE BUTTERFLY ROOM WITH THE BIG KIDS!
WE'LL GET THIS STRAIGHTENED OUT... I'LL GO TALK TO LOTSO ABOUT MOVING US TO THE OTHER ROOM!
ALL THE CATERPILLAR ROOM DOORS ARE CLOSED...
...BUT THANKS TO HIS SPACE RANGER AGILITY, BUZZ REACHES TH TRANSOM OVER THE HALL DOOR!

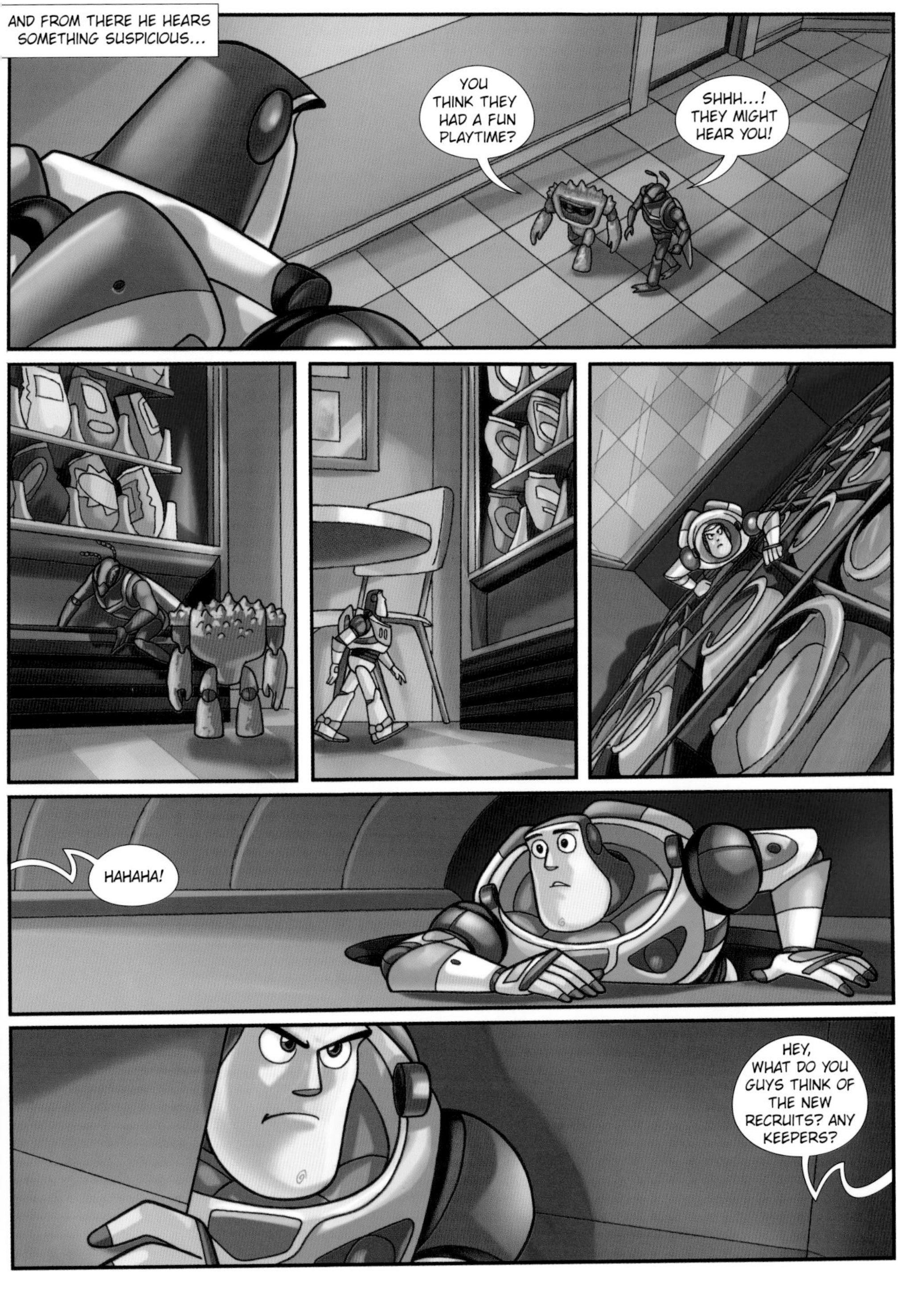
AND FROM THERE HE HEARS SOMETHING SUSPICIOUS...
YOU THINK THEY HAD A FUN PLAYTIME?
SHHH...! THEY MIGHT HEAR YOU!
HAHAHA!
HEY, WHAT DO YOU GUYS THINK OF THE NEW RECRUITS? ANY KEEPERS?

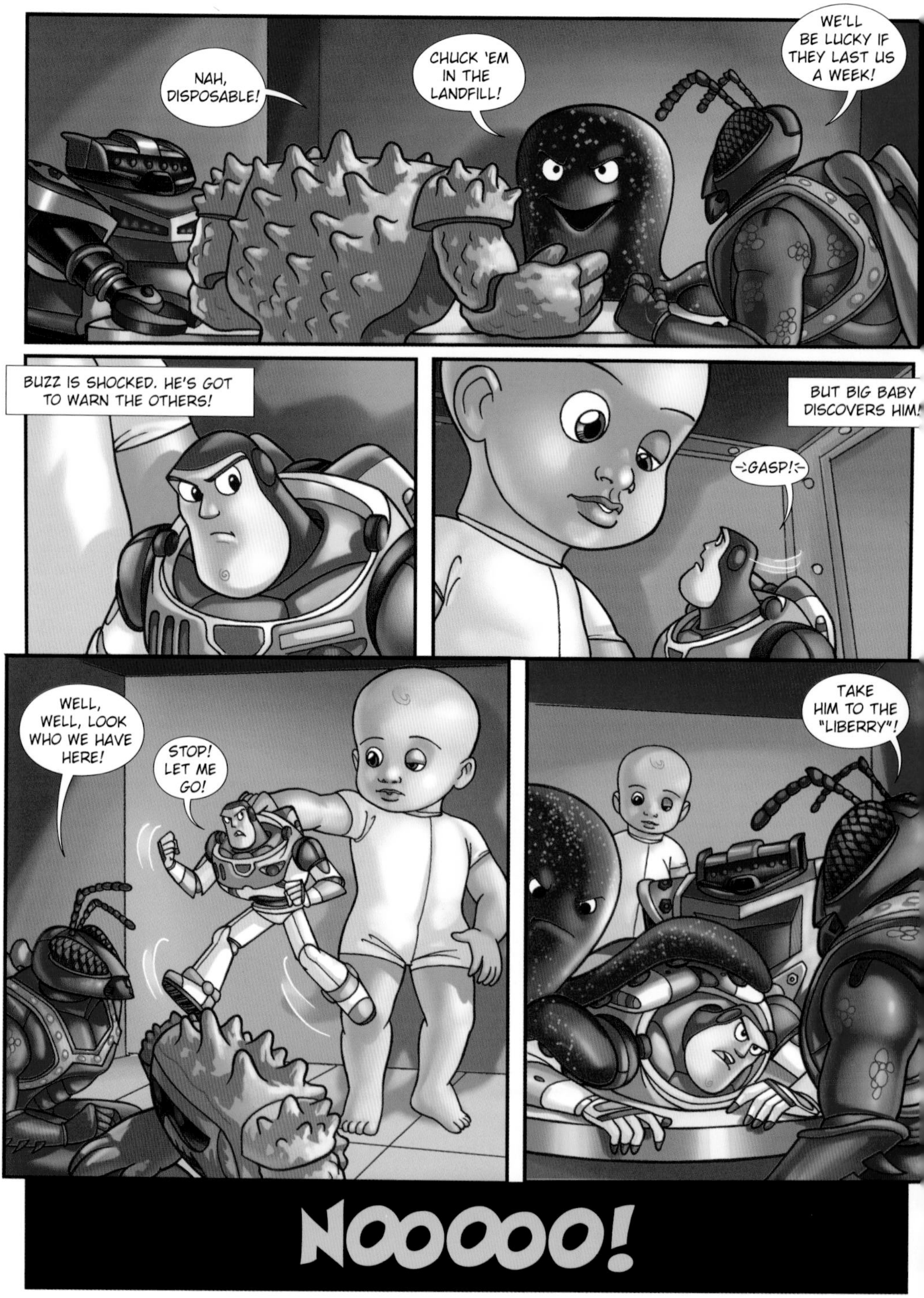
NAH, DISPOSABLE!
CHUCK 'EM IN THE LANDFILL!
WE'LL BE LUCKY IF THEY LAST US A WEEK!
BUZZ IS SHOCKED. HE'S GOT TO WARN THE OTHERS!
BUT BIG BABY DISCOVERS HIM!
GASP!
WELL, WELL, LOOK WHO WE HAVE HERE!
STOP! LET ME GO!
TAKE HIM TO THE "LIBERRY"!
NOOOOO!

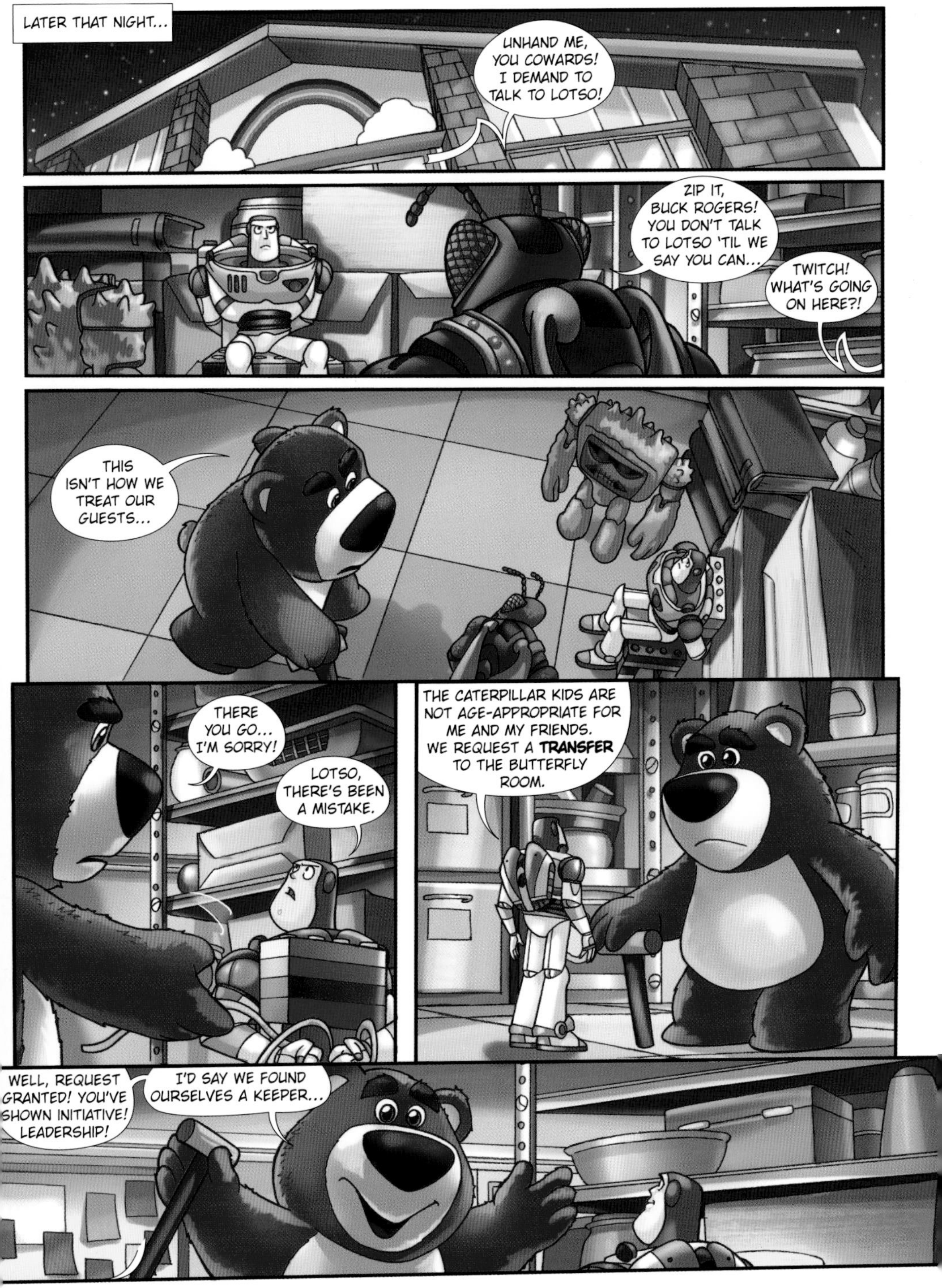
LATER THAT NIGHT...
UNHAND ME, YOU COWARDS! I DEMAND TO TALK TO LOTSO!
ZIP IT, BUCK ROGERS! YOU DON'T TALK TO LOTSO 'TIL WE SAY YOU CAN...
TWITCH! WHAT'S GOING ON HERE?!
THIS ISN'T HOW WE TREAT OUR GUESTS...
THERE YOU GO... I'M SORRY!
LOTSO, THERE'S BEEN A MISTAKE.
THE CATERPILLAR KIDS ARE NOT AGE-APPROPRIATE FOR ME AND MY FRIENDS. WE REQUEST A **TRANSFER** TO THE BUTTERFLY ROOM.
WELL, REQUEST GRANTED! YOU'VE SHOWN INITIATIVE! LEADERSHIP!
I'D SAY WE FOUND OURSELVES A KEEPER...

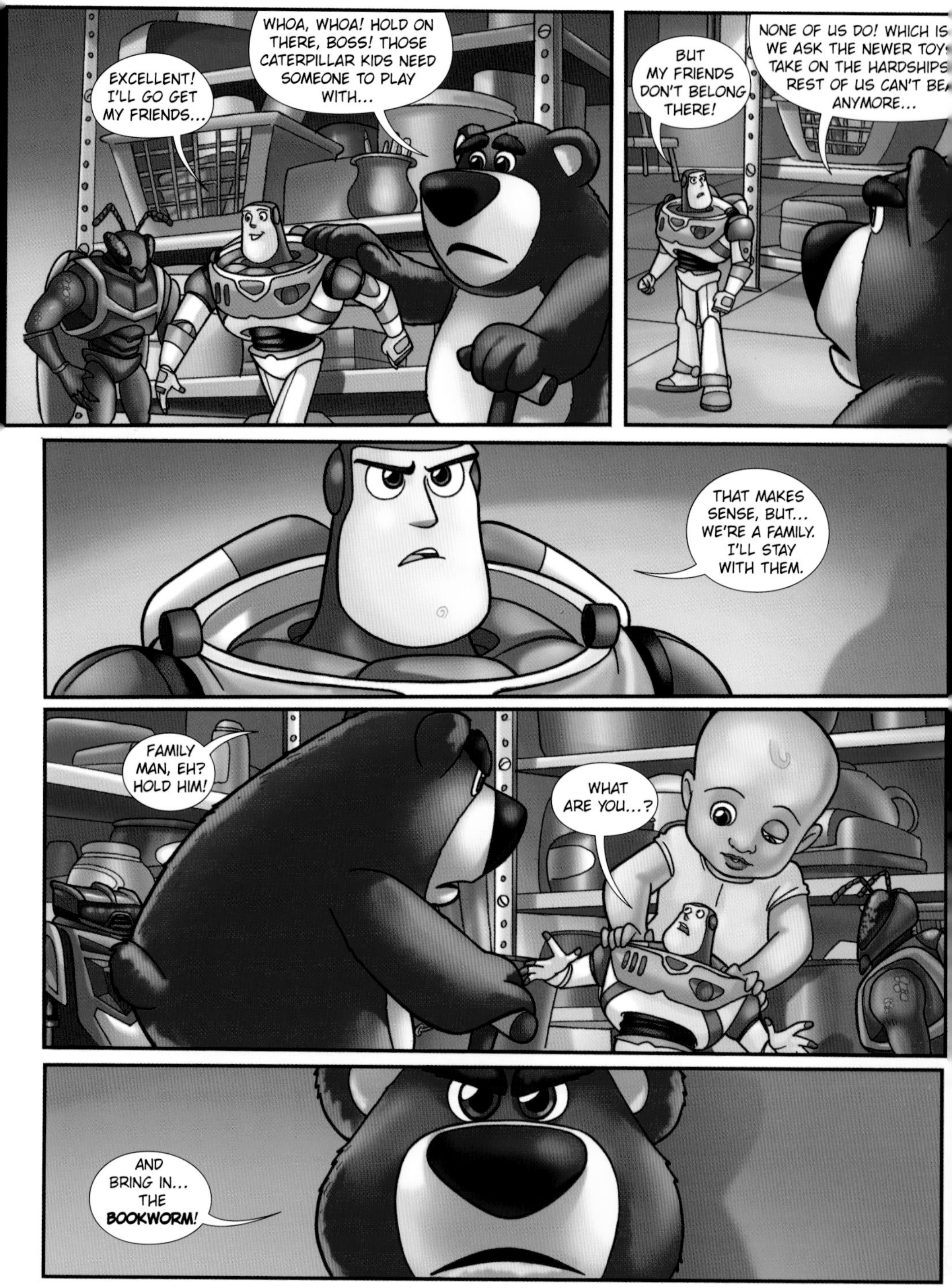
EXCELLENT! I'LL GO GET MY FRIENDS...
WHOA, WHOA! HOLD ON THERE, BOSS! THOSE CATERPILLAR KIDS NEED SOMEONE TO PLAY WITH...
BUT MY FRIENDS DON'T BELONG THERE!
NONE OF US DO! WHICH IS WE ASK THE NEWER TOY TAKE ON THE HARDSHIPS REST OF US CAN'T BE ANYMORE...
THAT MAKES SENSE, BUT... WE'RE A FAMILY. I'LL STAY WITH THEM.
FAMILY MAN, EH? HOLD HIM!
WHAT ARE YOU...?
AND BRING IN... THE **BOOKWORM!**

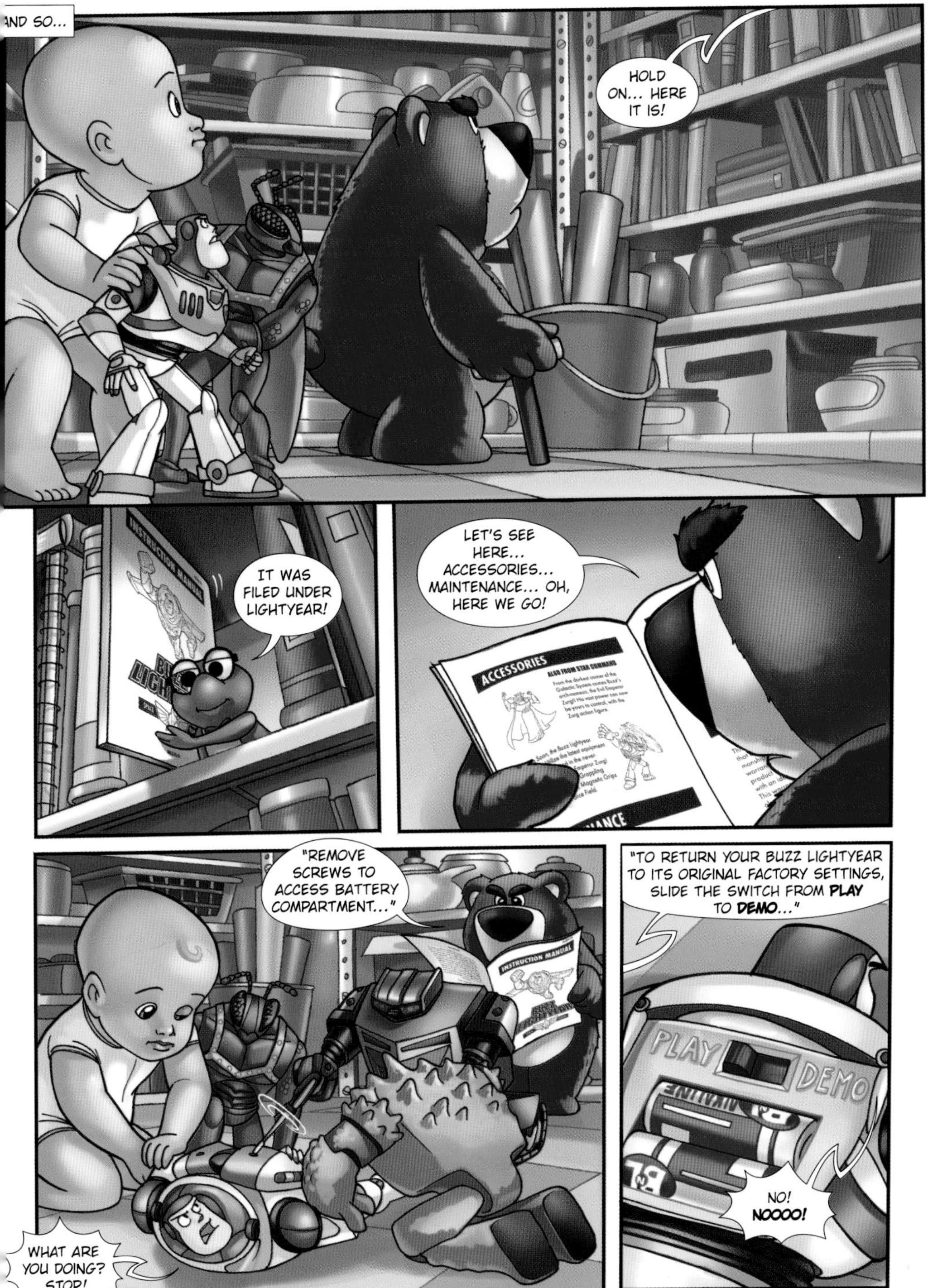
AND SO...
HOLD ON... HERE IT IS!
IT WAS FILED UNDER LIGHTYEAR!
LET'S SEE HERE... ACCESSORIES... MAINTENANCE... OH, HERE WE GO!
"REMOVE SCREWS TO ACCESS BATTERY COMPARTMENT..."
WHAT ARE YOU DOING? STOP!
"TO RETURN YOUR BUZZ LIGHTYEAR TO ITS ORIGINAL FACTORY SETTINGS, SLIDE THE SWITCH FROM **PLAY** TO **DEMO**..."
PLAY
DEMO
NO! **NOOOO!**

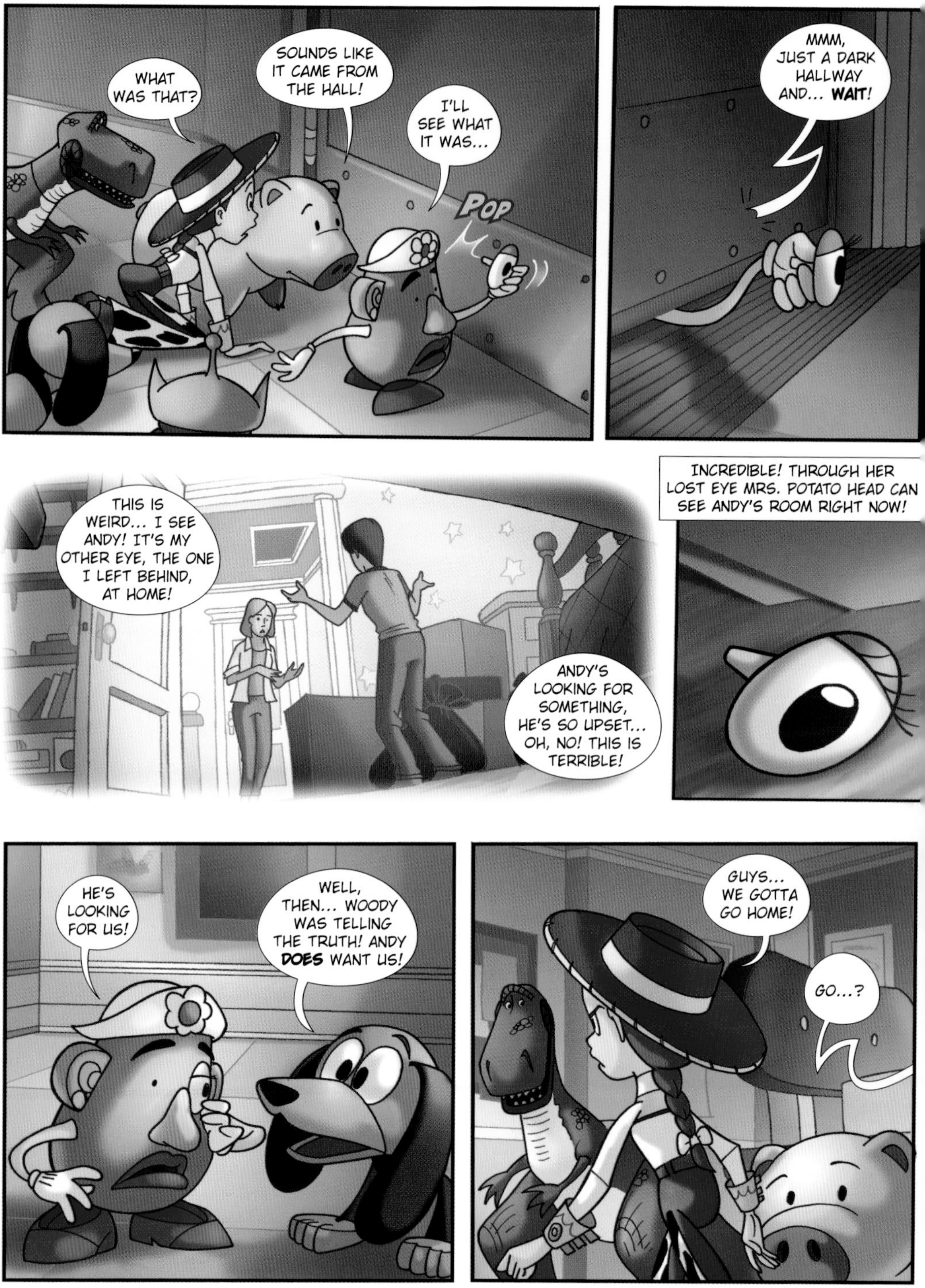
WHAT WAS THAT?
SOUNDS LIKE IT CAME FROM THE HALL!
I'LL SEE WHAT IT WAS...
POP
MMM, JUST A DARK HALLWAY AND... **WAIT**!
THIS IS WEIRD... I SEE ANDY! IT'S MY OTHER EYE, THE ONE I LEFT BEHIND, AT HOME!
ANDY'S LOOKING FOR SOMETHING, HE'S SO UPSET... OH, NO! THIS IS TERRIBLE!
INCREDIBLE! THROUGH HER LOST EYE MRS. POTATO HEAD CAN SEE ANDY'S ROOM RIGHT NOW!
HE'S LOOKING FOR US!
WELL, THEN... WOODY WAS TELLING THE TRUTH! ANDY **DOES** WANT US!
GUYS... WE GOTTA GO HOME!
GO...?

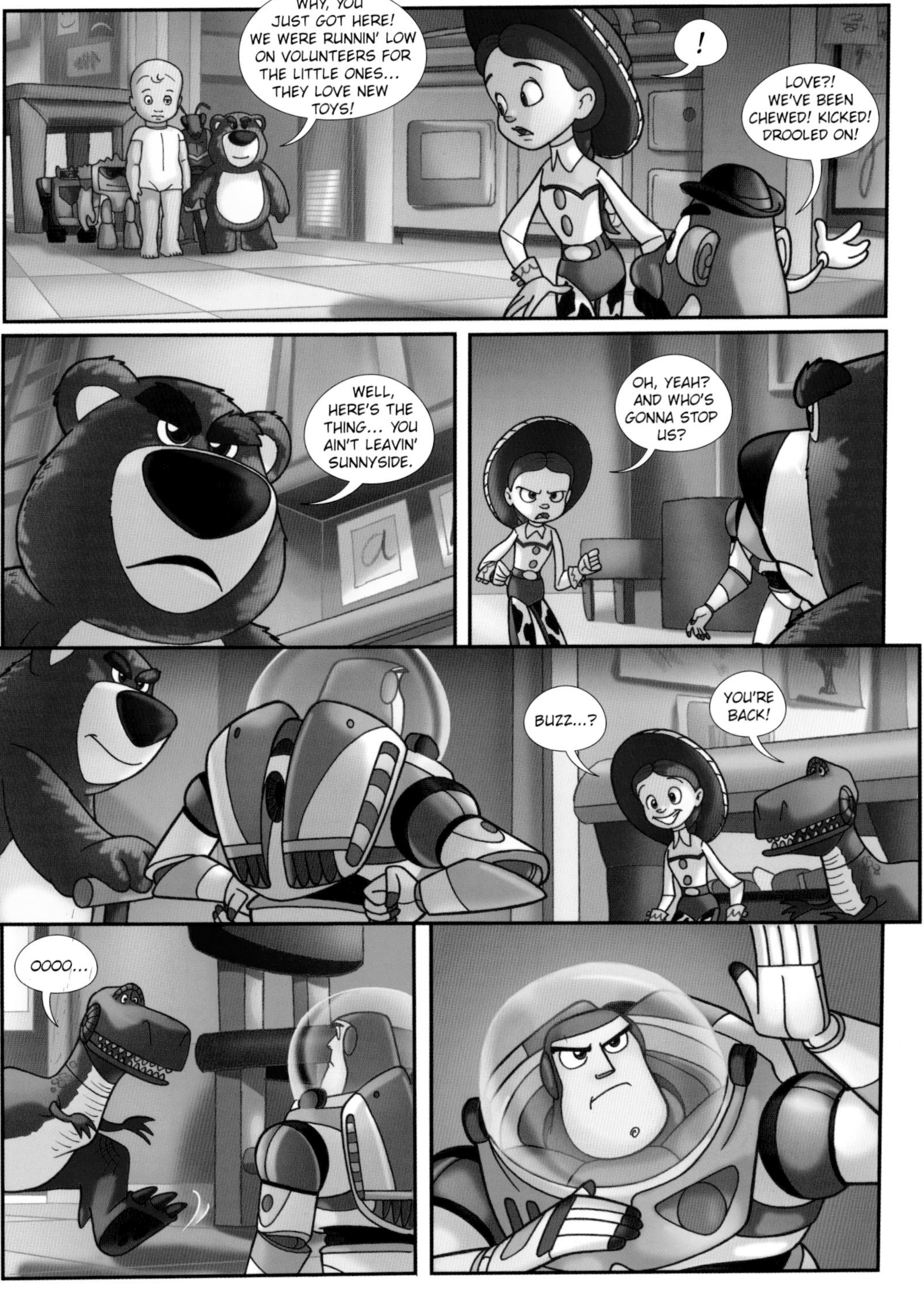
WHY, YOU JUST GOT HERE! WE WERE RUNNIN' LOW ON VOLUNTEERS FOR THE LITTLE ONES... THEY LOVE NEW TOYS!
!
LOVE?! WE'VE BEEN CHEWED! KICKED! DROOLED ON!
WELL, HERE'S THE THING... YOU AIN'T LEAVIN' SUNNYSIDE.
OH, YEAH? AND WHO'S GONNA STOP US?
BUZZ...?
YOU'RE BACK!
OOOO...

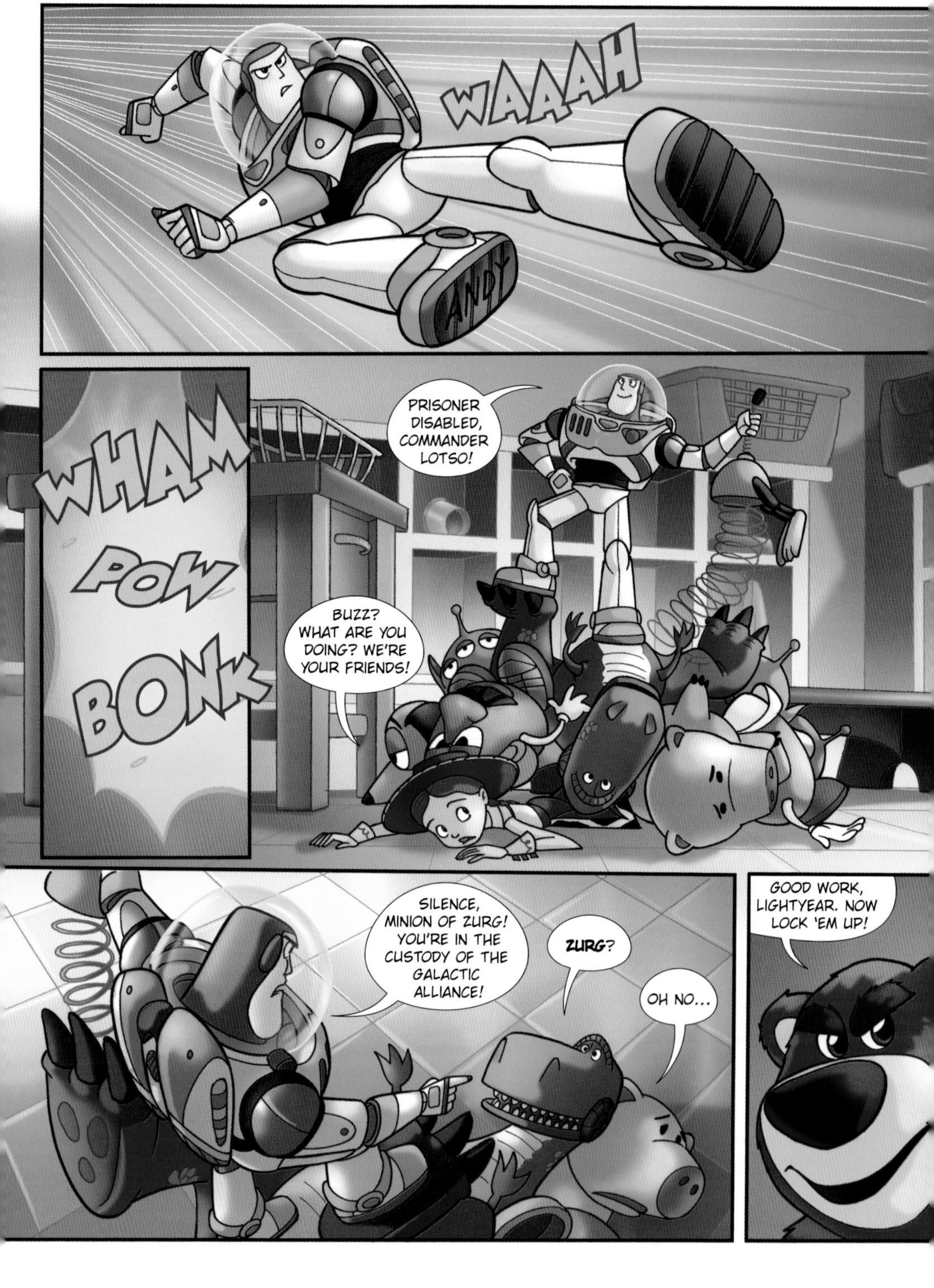
WAAAH
WHAM
POW
BONK
PRISONER DISABLED, COMMANDER LOTSO!
BUZZ? WHAT ARE YOU DOING? WE'RE YOUR FRIENDS!
SILENCE, MINION OF ZURG! YOU'RE IN THE CUSTODY OF THE GALACTIC ALLIANCE!
ZURG?
OH NO...
GOOD WORK, LIGHTYEAR. NOW LOCK 'EM UP!

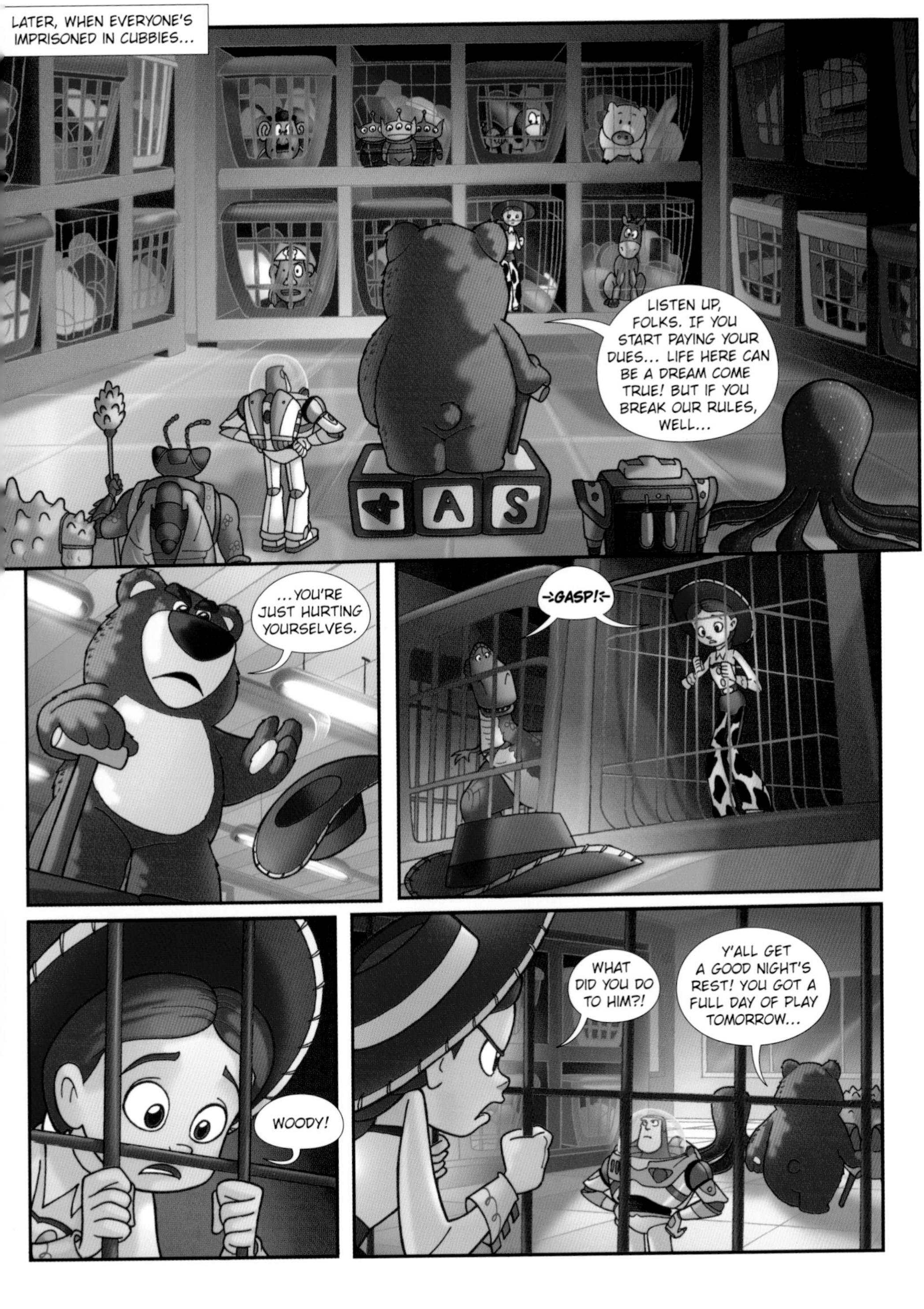
LATER, WHEN EVERYONE'S IMPRISONED IN CUBBIES...
LISTEN UP, FOLKS. IF YOU START PAYING YOUR DUES... LIFE HERE CAN BE A DREAM COME TRUE! BUT IF YOU BREAK OUR RULES, WELL...
...YOU'RE JUST HURTING YOURSELVES.
-GASP!-
WOODY!
WHAT DID YOU DO TO HIM?!
Y'ALL GET A GOOD NIGHT'S REST! YOU GOT A FULL DAY OF PLAY TOMORROW...

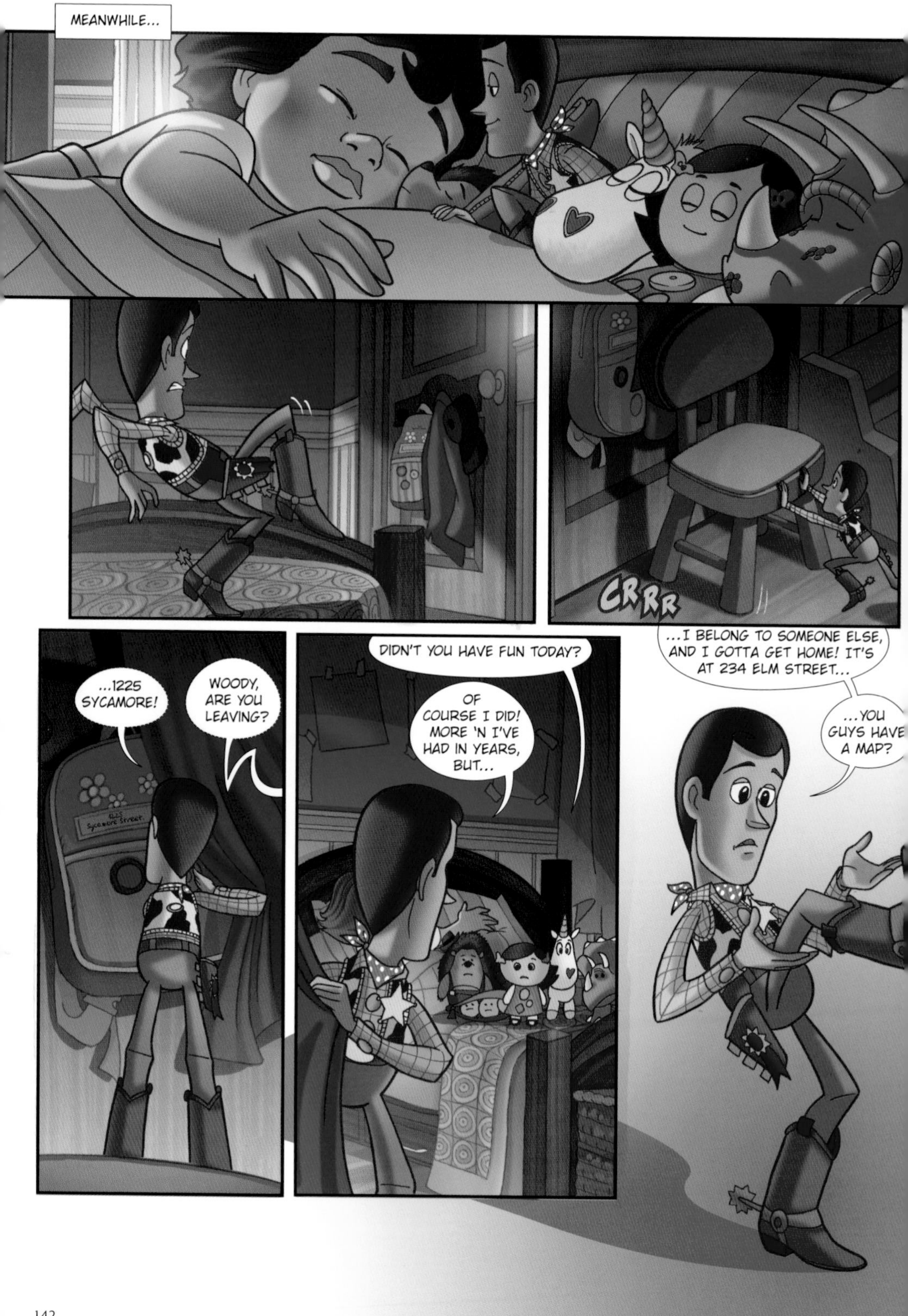
MEANWHILE...
CRRR
...1225 SYCAMORE!
WOODY, ARE YOU LEAVING?
DIDN'T YOU HAVE FUN TODAY?
OF COURSE I DID! MORE 'N I'VE HAD IN YEARS, BUT...
...I BELONG TO SOMEONE ELSE, AND I GOTTA GET HOME! IT'S AT 234 ELM STREET...
...YOU GUYS HAVE A MAP?

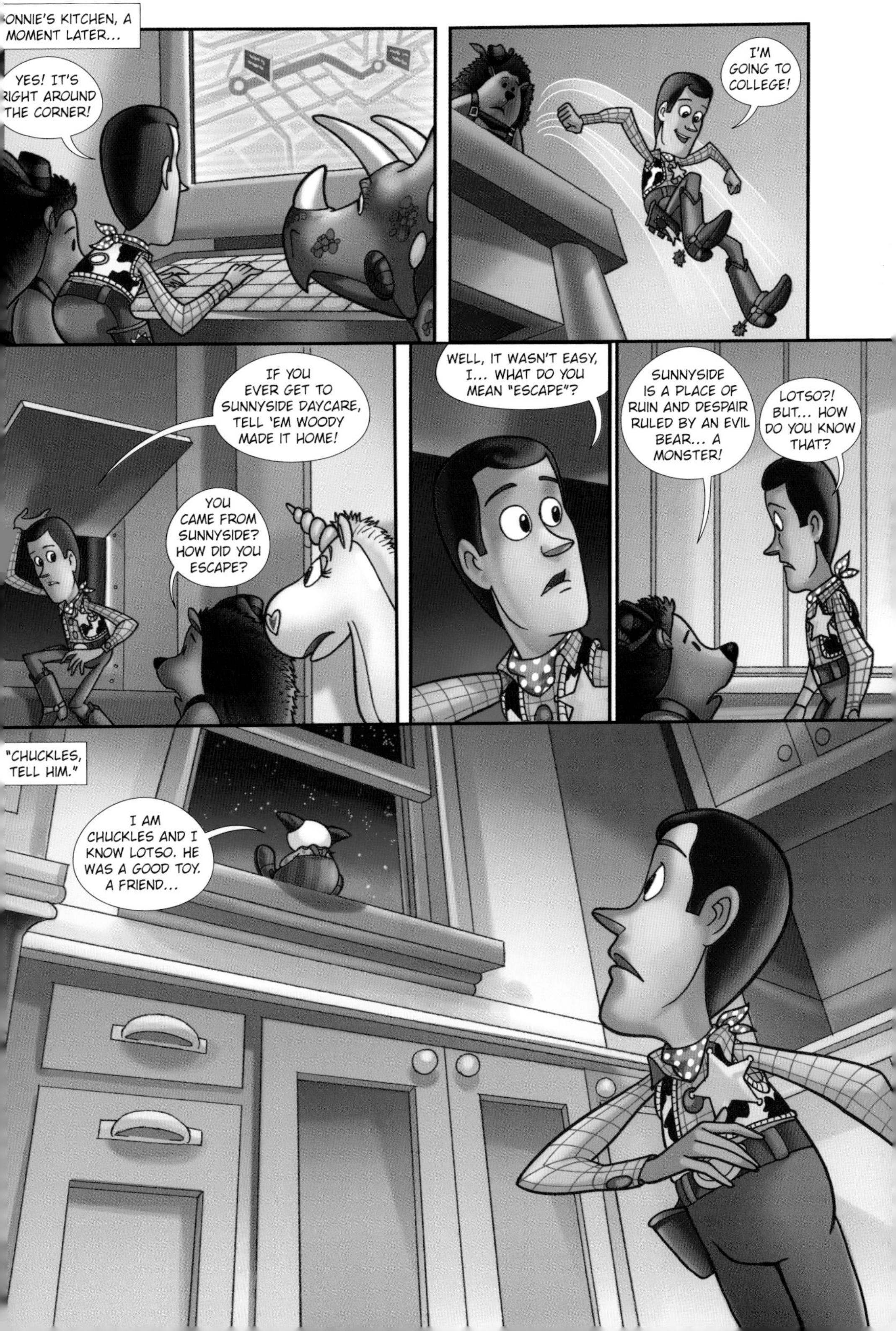
ONNIE'S KITCHEN, A MOMENT LATER...
YES! IT'S RIGHT AROUND THE CORNER!
I'M GOING TO COLLEGE!
IF YOU EVER GET TO SUNNYSIDE DAYCARE, TELL 'EM WOODY MADE IT HOME!
YOU CAME FROM SUNNYSIDE? HOW DID YOU ESCAPE?
WELL, IT WASN'T EASY, I... WHAT DO YOU MEAN "ESCAPE"?
SUNNYSIDE IS A PLACE OF RUIN AND DESPAIR RULED BY AN EVIL BEAR... A MONSTER!
LOTSO?! BUT... HOW DO YOU KNOW THAT?
"CHUCKLES, TELL HIM."
I AM CHUCKLES AND I KNOW LOTSO. HE WAS A GOOD TOY. A FRIEND...

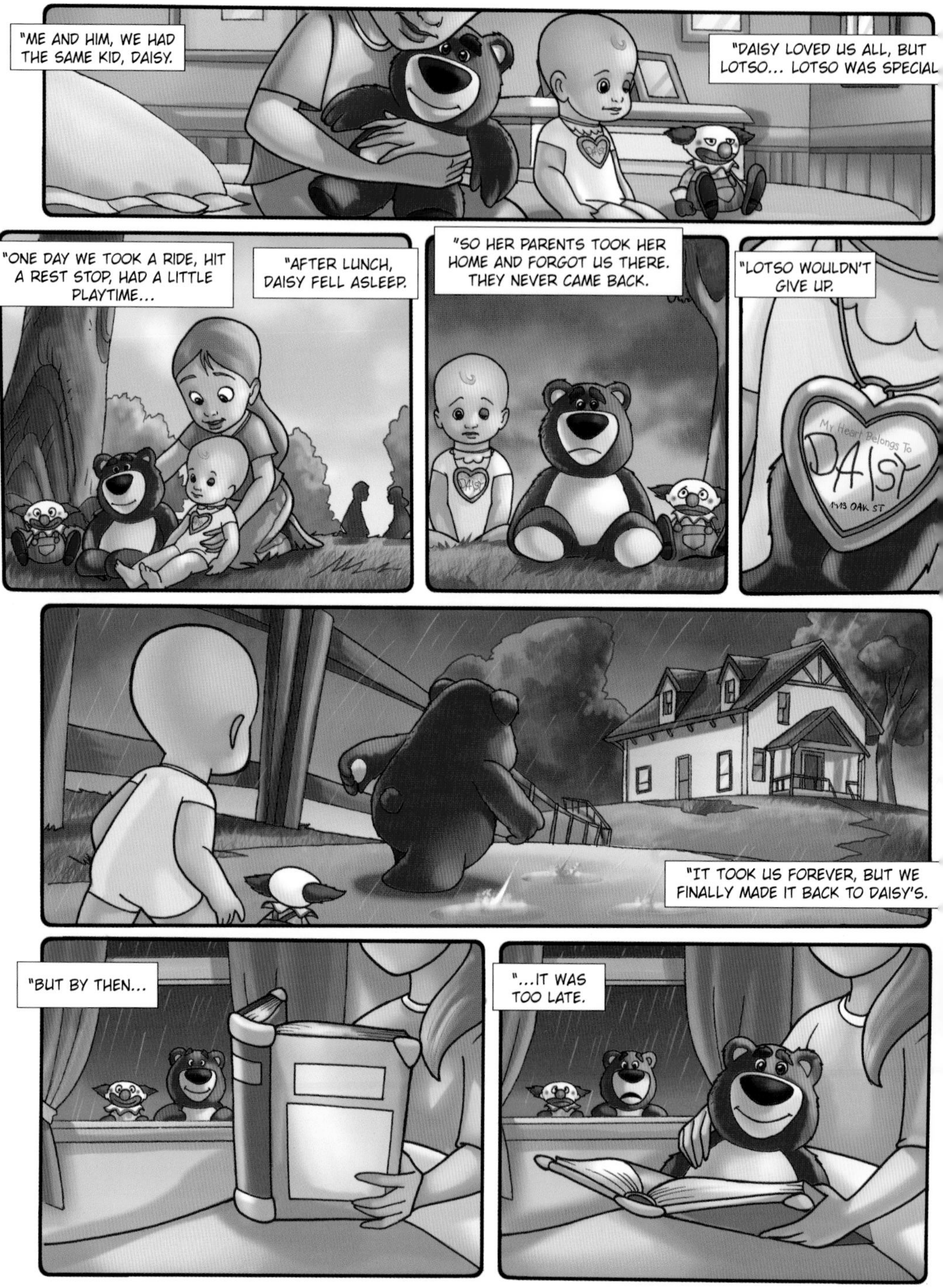
"ME AND HIM, WE HAD THE SAME KID, DAISY.
"DAISY LOVED US ALL, BUT LOTSO... LOTSO WAS SPECIAL
"ONE DAY WE TOOK A RIDE, HIT A REST STOP, HAD A LITTLE PLAYTIME...
"AFTER LUNCH, DAISY FELL ASLEEP.
"SO HER PARENTS TOOK HER HOME AND FORGOT US THERE. THEY NEVER CAME BACK.
"LOTSO WOULDN'T GIVE UP.
My Heart Belongs To
DAISY
1113 OAK ST
"IT TOOK US FOREVER, BUT WE FINALLY MADE IT BACK TO DAISY'S.
"BUT BY THEN...
"...IT WAS TOO LATE.

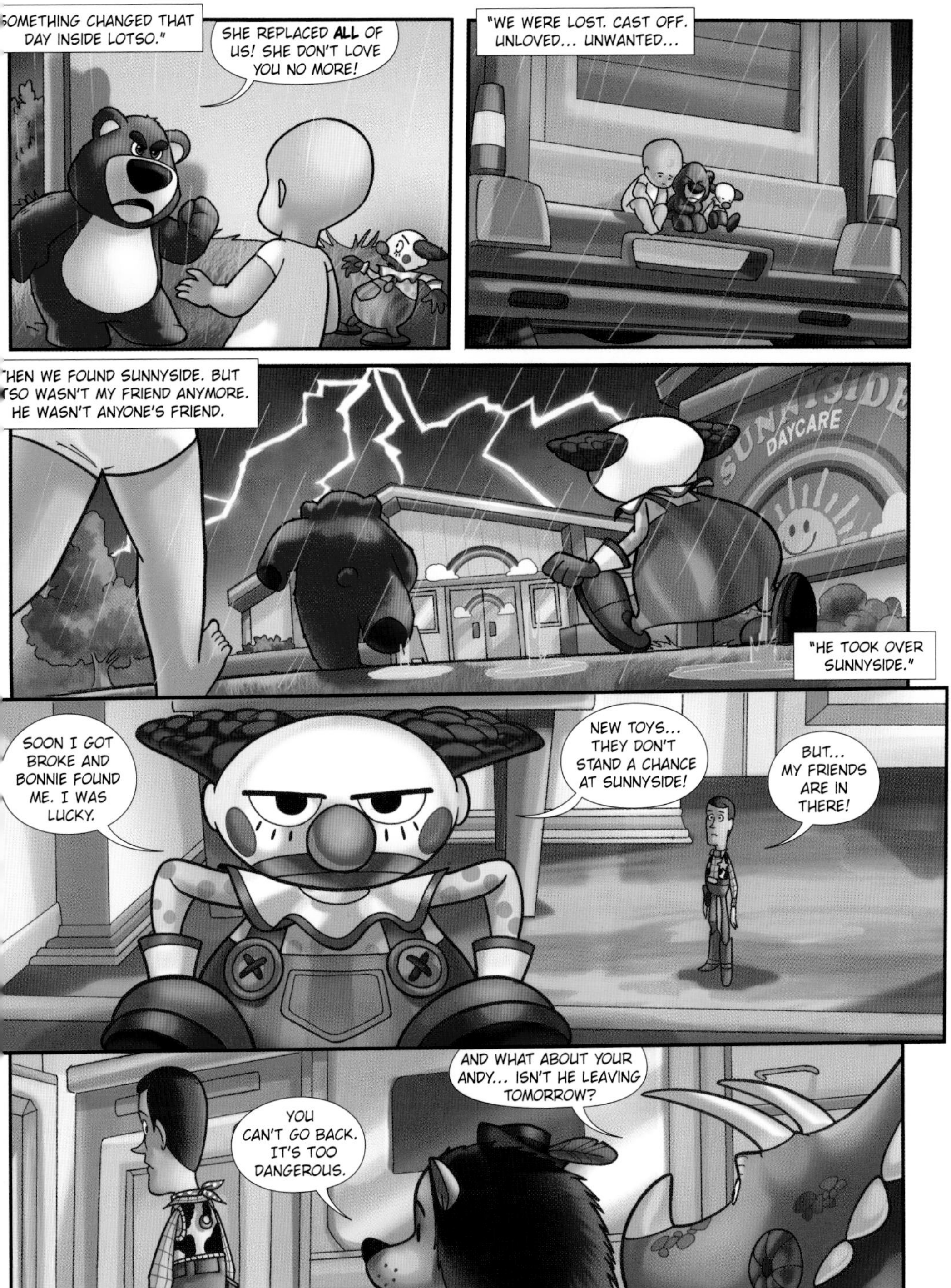
SOMETHING CHANGED THAT DAY INSIDE LOTSO."
SHE REPLACED **ALL** OF US! SHE DON'T LOVE YOU NO MORE!
"WE WERE LOST. CAST OFF. UNLOVED... UNWANTED...
HEN WE FOUND SUNNYSIDE. BUT
TSO WASN'T MY FRIEND ANYMORE.
HE WASN'T ANYONE'S FRIEND.
SUNNYSIDE DAYCARE
"HE TOOK OVER SUNNYSIDE."
SOON I GOT BROKE AND BONNIE FOUND ME. I WAS LUCKY.
NEW TOYS... THEY DON'T STAND A CHANCE AT SUNNYSIDE!
BUT... MY FRIENDS ARE IN THERE!
YOU CAN'T GO BACK. IT'S TOO DANGEROUS.
AND WHAT ABOUT YOUR ANDY... ISN'T HE LEAVING TOMORROW?

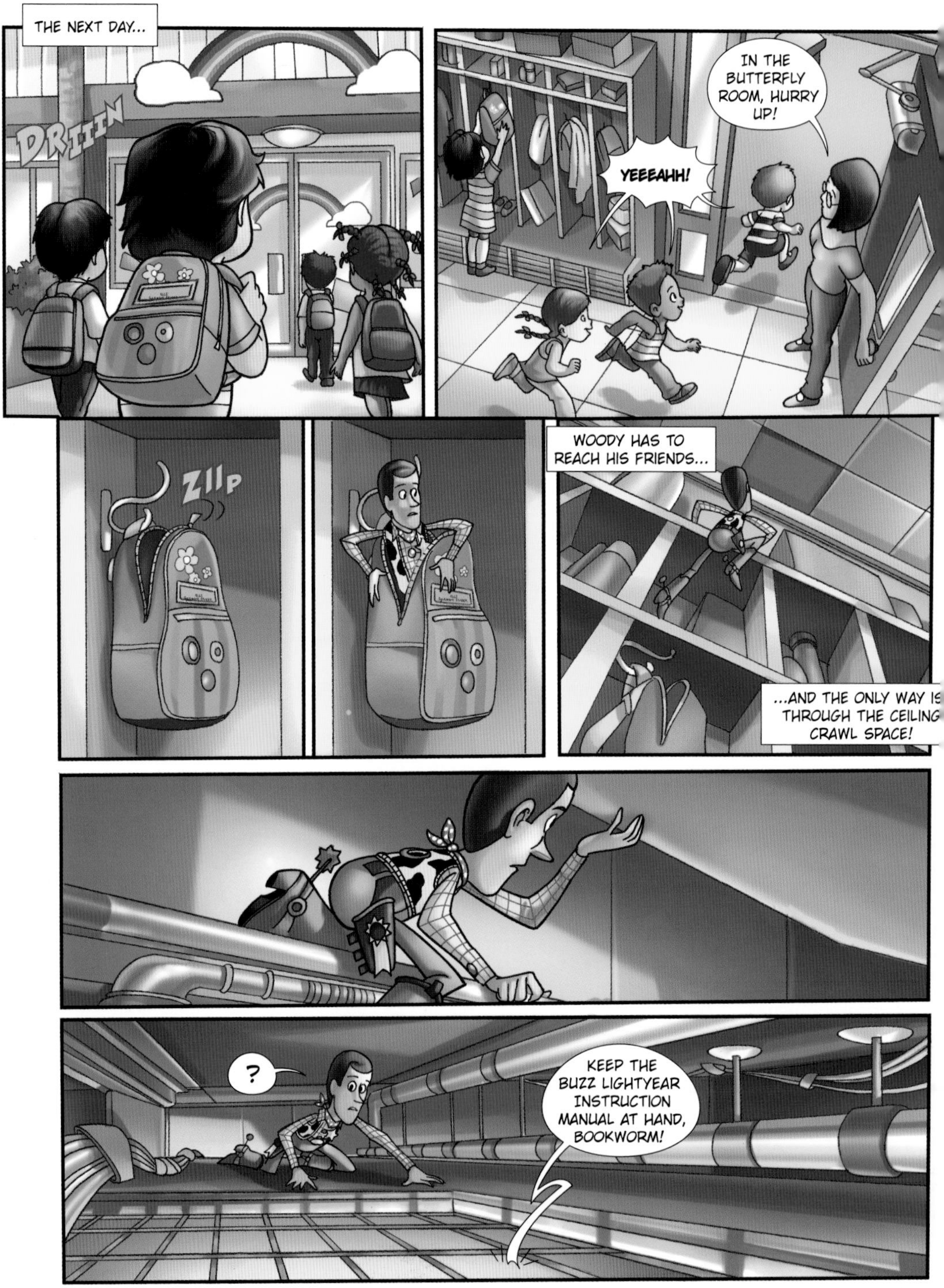
THE NEXT DAY...
DRIIIN
IN THE BUTTERFLY ROOM, HURRY UP!
YEEEAHH!
ZIIP
WOODY HAS TO REACH HIS FRIENDS...
...AND THE ONLY WAY IS THROUGH THE CEILING CRAWL SPACE!
?
KEEP THE BUZZ LIGHTYEAR INSTRUCTION MANUAL AT HAND, BOOKWORM!

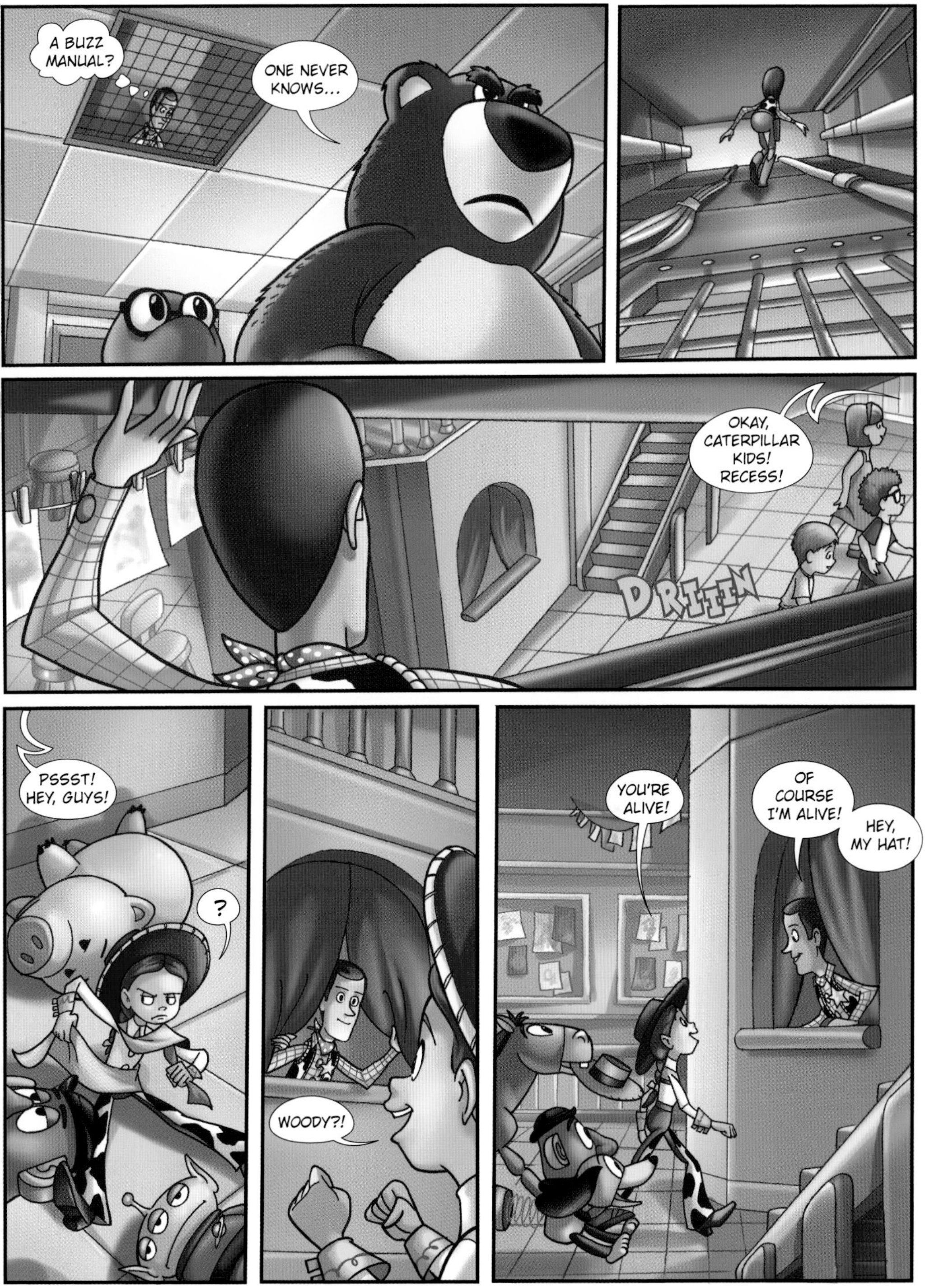
A BUZZ MANUAL?
ONE NEVER KNOWS...
OKAY, CATERPILLAR KIDS! RECESS!
DRIIIN
PSSST! HEY, GUYS!
?
WOODY?!
YOU'RE ALIVE!
OF COURSE I'M ALIVE!
HEY, MY HAT!

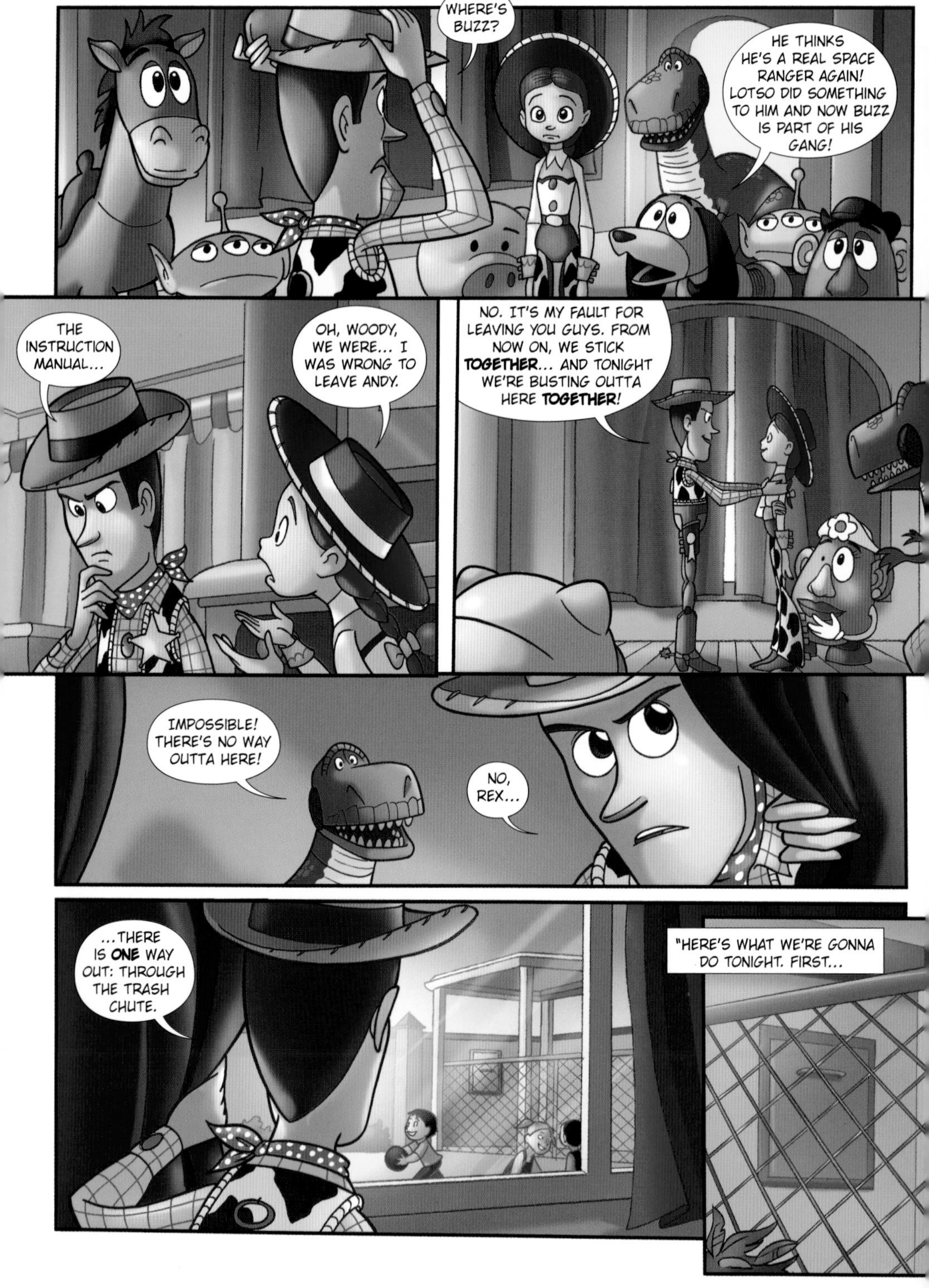
WHERE'S BUZZ?
HE THINKS HE'S A REAL SPACE RANGER AGAIN! LOTSO DID SOMETHING TO HIM AND NOW BUZZ IS PART OF HIS GANG!
THE INSTRUCTION MANUAL...
OH, WOODY, WE WERE... I WAS WRONG TO LEAVE ANDY.
NO. IT'S MY FAULT FOR LEAVING YOU GUYS. FROM NOW ON, WE STICK **TOGETHER**... AND TONIGHT WE'RE BUSTING OUTTA HERE **TOGETHER**!
IMPOSSIBLE! THERE'S NO WAY OUTTA HERE!
NO, REX...
...THERE IS **ONE** WAY OUT: THROUGH THE TRASH CHUTE.
"HERE'S WHAT WE'RE GONNA DO TONIGHT. FIRST...

"...MR. POTATO HEAD WILL CREATE A DIVERSION..."

HEY!

"...WHILE JESSIE AND BULLSEYE GET READY...

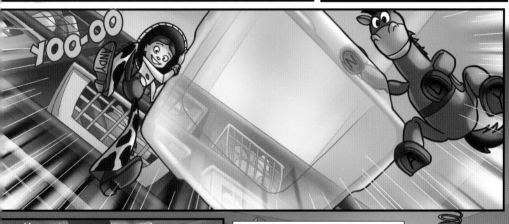

YOO-OO

..TO TRAP BUZZ!

BAM

"ME AND SLINKY WILL BYPASS SURVEILLANCE THROUGH THE CEILING CRAWL SPACE AND GET THE DOOR KEY..."

BINGO!

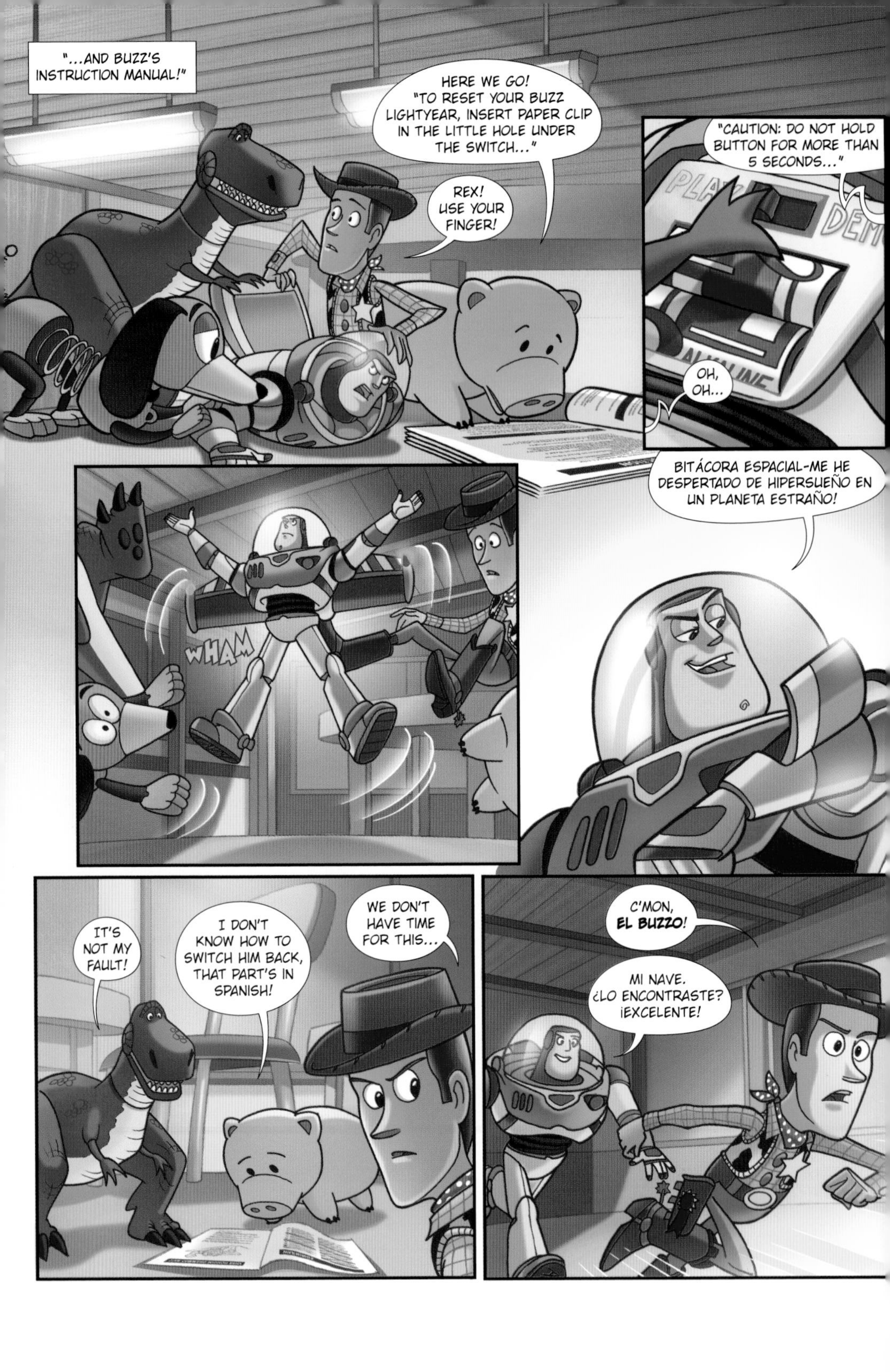
"...AND BUZZ'S INSTRUCTION MANUAL!"
HERE WE GO! "TO RESET YOUR BUZZ LIGHTYEAR, INSERT PAPER CLIP IN THE LITTLE HOLE UNDER THE SWITCH..."
REX! USE YOUR FINGER!
"CAUTION: DO NOT HOLD BUTTON FOR MORE THAN 5 SECONDS..."
OH, OH...
WHAM
BITÁCORA ESPACIAL-ME HE DESPERTADO DE HIPERSUEÑO EN UN PLANETA ESTRAÑO!
IT'S NOT MY FAULT!
I DON'T KNOW HOW TO SWITCH HIM BACK, THAT PART'S IN SPANISH!
WE DON'T HAVE TIME FOR THIS...
C'MON, **EL BUZZO**!
MI NAVE. ¿LO ENCONTRASTE? ¡EXCELENTE!

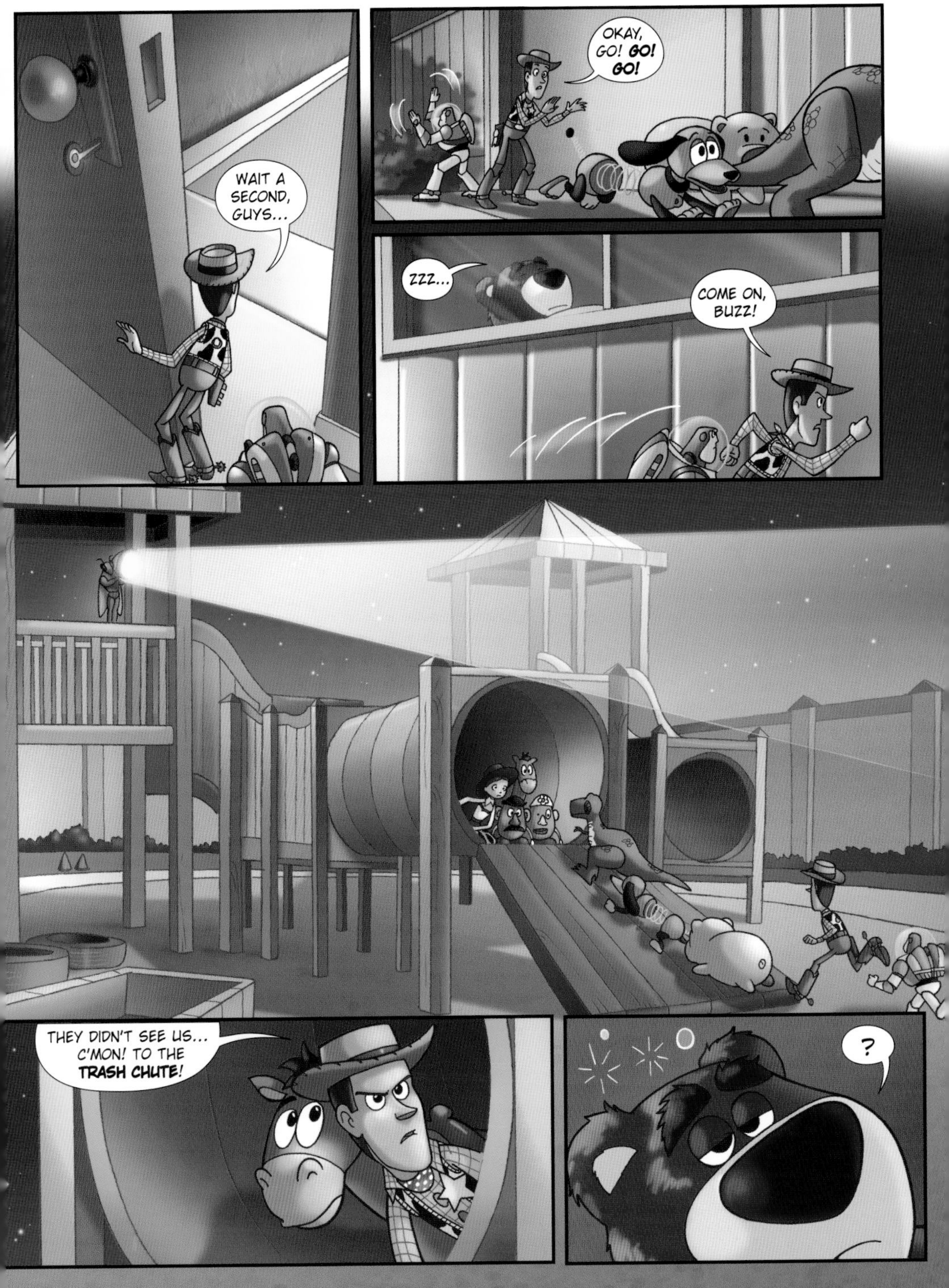
WAIT A SECOND, GUYS...
OKAY, GO! GO! GO!
ZZZ...
COME ON, BUZZ!
THEY DIDN'T SEE US... C'MON! TO THE TRASH CHUTE!
?

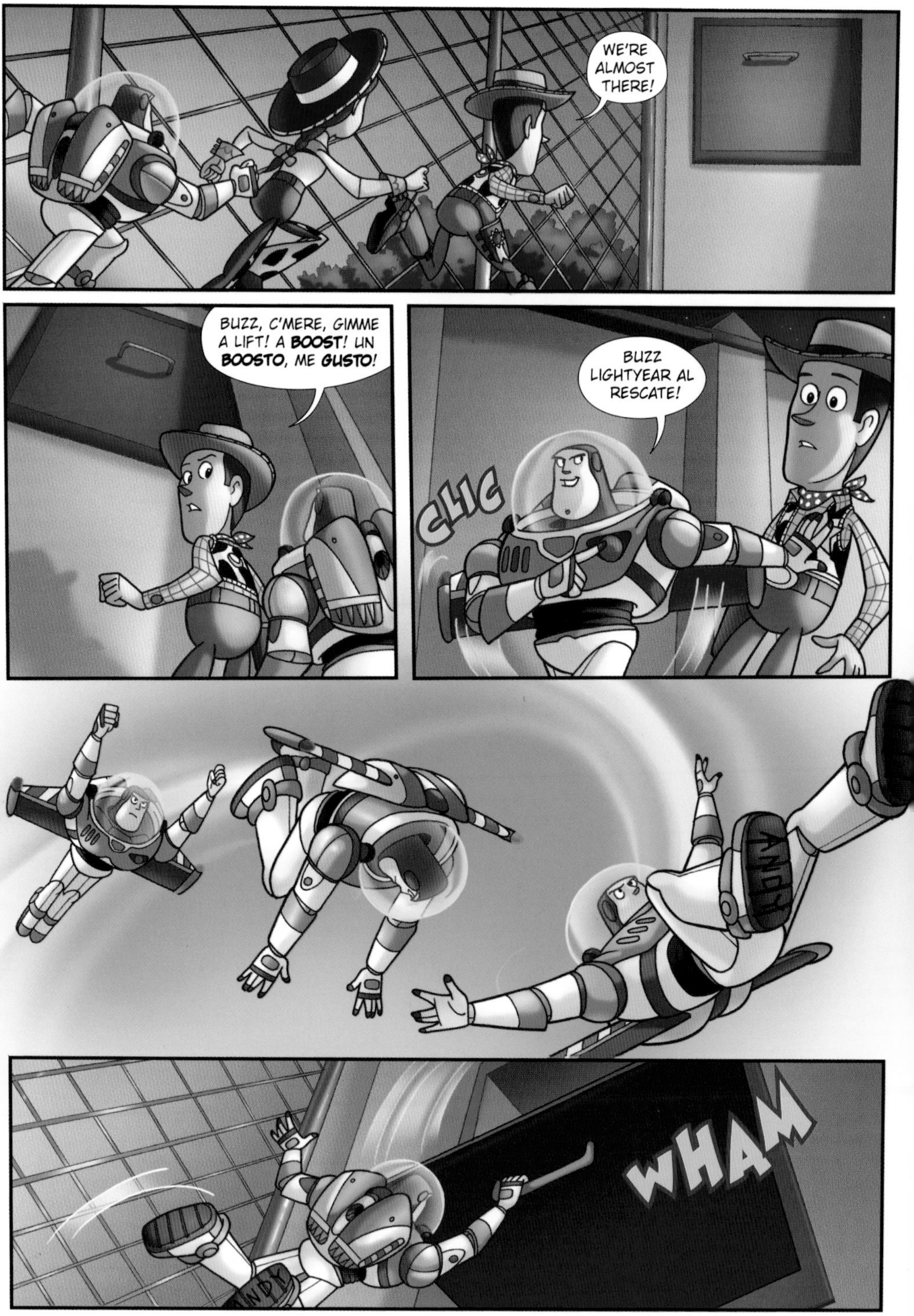
WE'RE ALMOST THERE!
BUZZ, C'MERE, GIMME A LIFT! A **BOOST**! UN **BOOSTO**, ME **GUSTO**!
BUZZ LIGHTYEAR AL RESCATE!
CLIC
ANDY
ANDY
WHAM

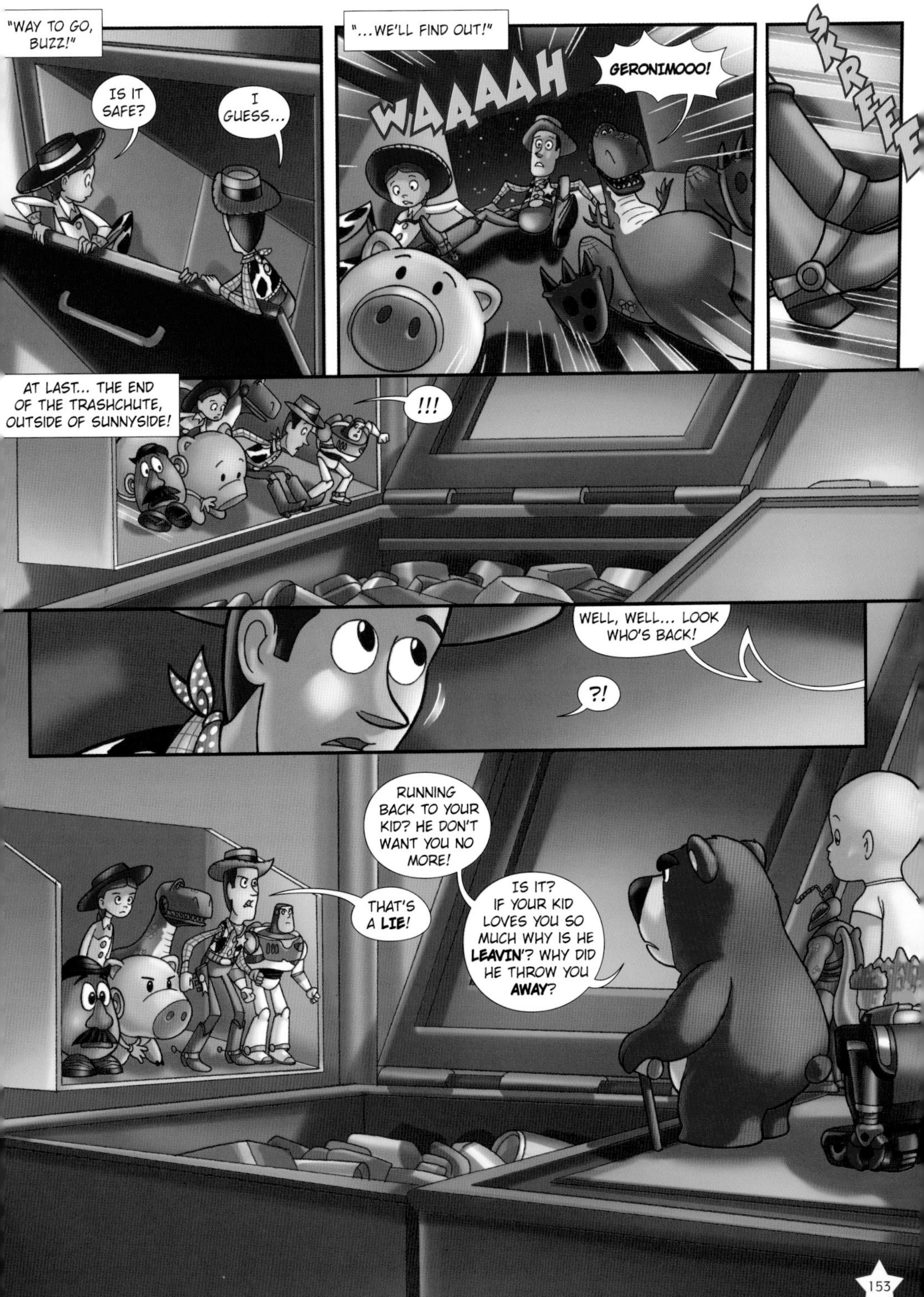
"WAY TO GO, BUZZ!"
IS IT SAFE?
I GUESS...
"...WE'LL FIND OUT!"
WAAAAH
GERONIMOOO!
SKREEEE
AT LAST... THE END OF THE TRASHCHUTE, OUTSIDE OF SUNNYSIDE!
!!!
WELL, WELL... LOOK WHO'S BACK!
?!
RUNNING BACK TO YOUR KID? HE DON'T WANT YOU NO MORE!
THAT'S A **LIE**!
IS IT? IF YOUR KID LOVES YOU SO MUCH WHY IS HE **LEAVIN'**? WHY DID HE THROW YOU **AWAY**?

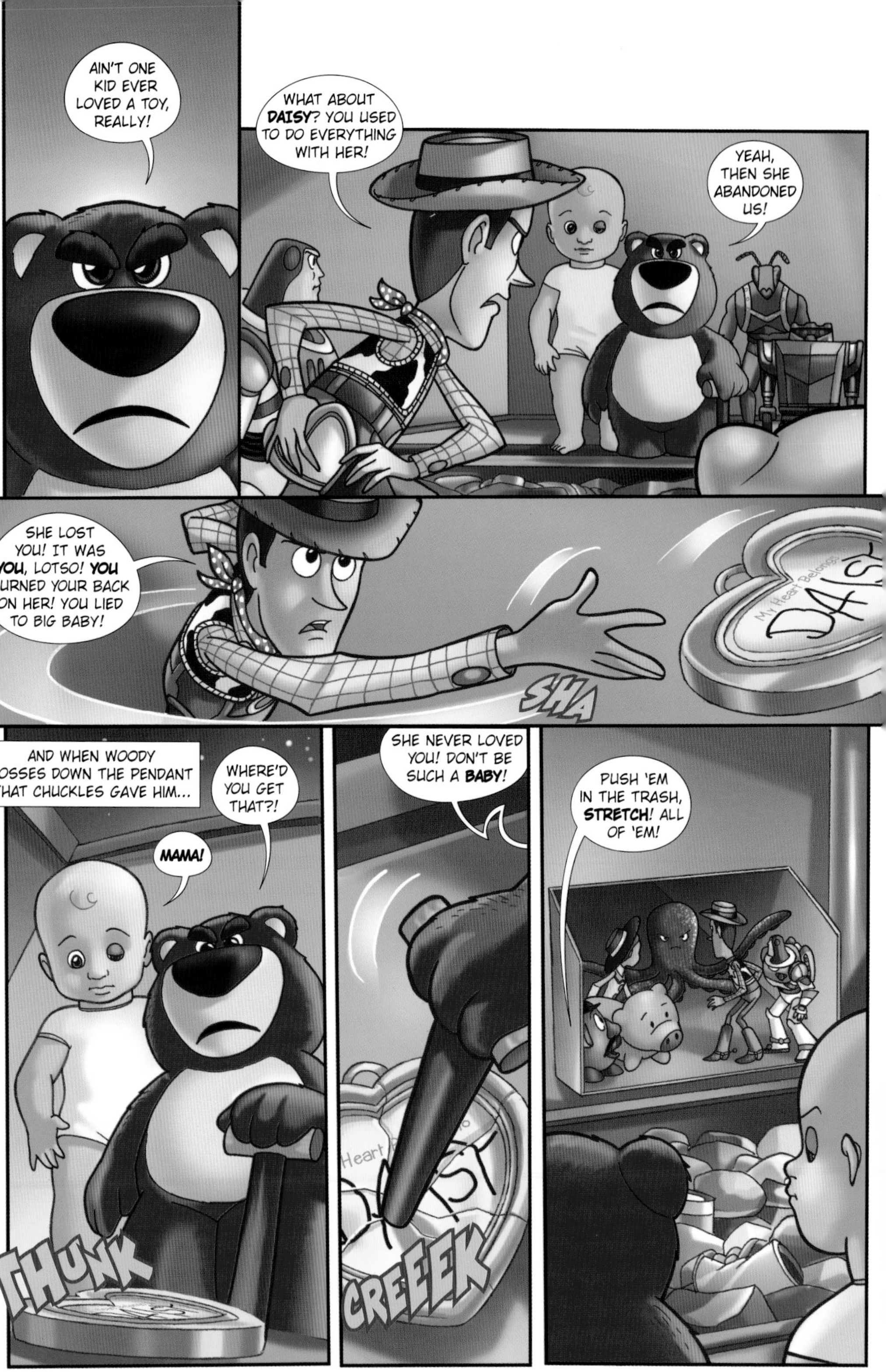
AIN'T ONE KID EVER LOVED A TOY, REALLY!
WHAT ABOUT DAISY? YOU USED TO DO EVERYTHING WITH HER!
YEAH, THEN SHE ABANDONED US!
SHE LOST YOU! IT WAS YOU, LOTSO! YOU TURNED YOUR BACK ON HER! YOU LIED TO BIG BABY!
My Heart Belongs
SHA
AND WHEN WOODY TOSSES DOWN THE PENDANT THAT CHUCKLES GAVE HIM...
WHERE'D YOU GET THAT?!
MAMA!
THUNK
SHE NEVER LOVED YOU! DON'T BE SUCH A BABY!
CREEEK
PUSH 'EM IN THE TRASH, STRETCH! ALL OF 'EM!

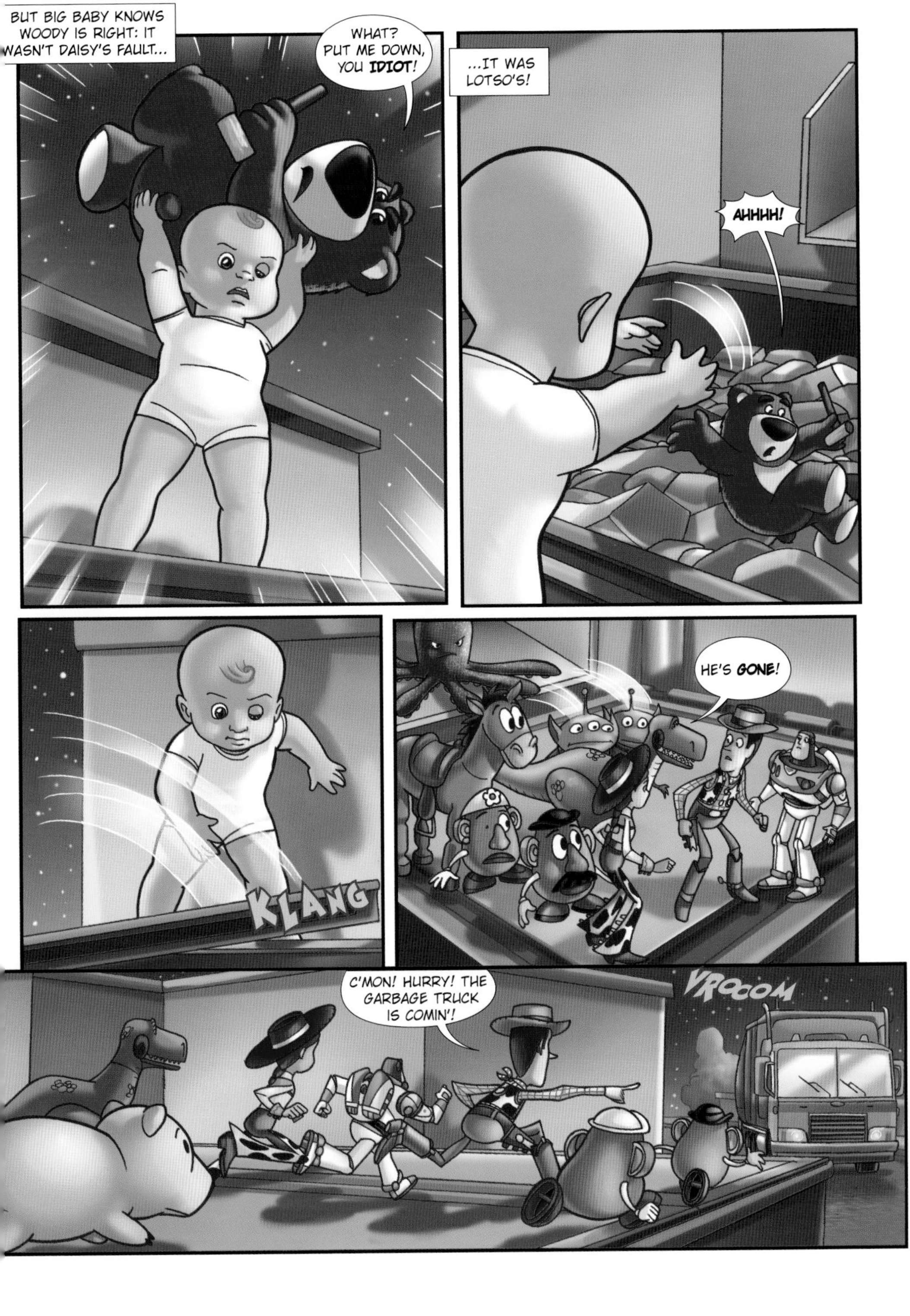
BUT BIG BABY KNOWS WOODY IS RIGHT: IT WASN'T DAISY'S FAULT...
WHAT? PUT ME DOWN, YOU **IDIOT**!
...IT WAS LOTSO'S!
AHHHH!
KLANG
HE'S **GONE**!
C'MON! HURRY! THE GARBAGE TRUCK IS COMIN'!
VROOOM

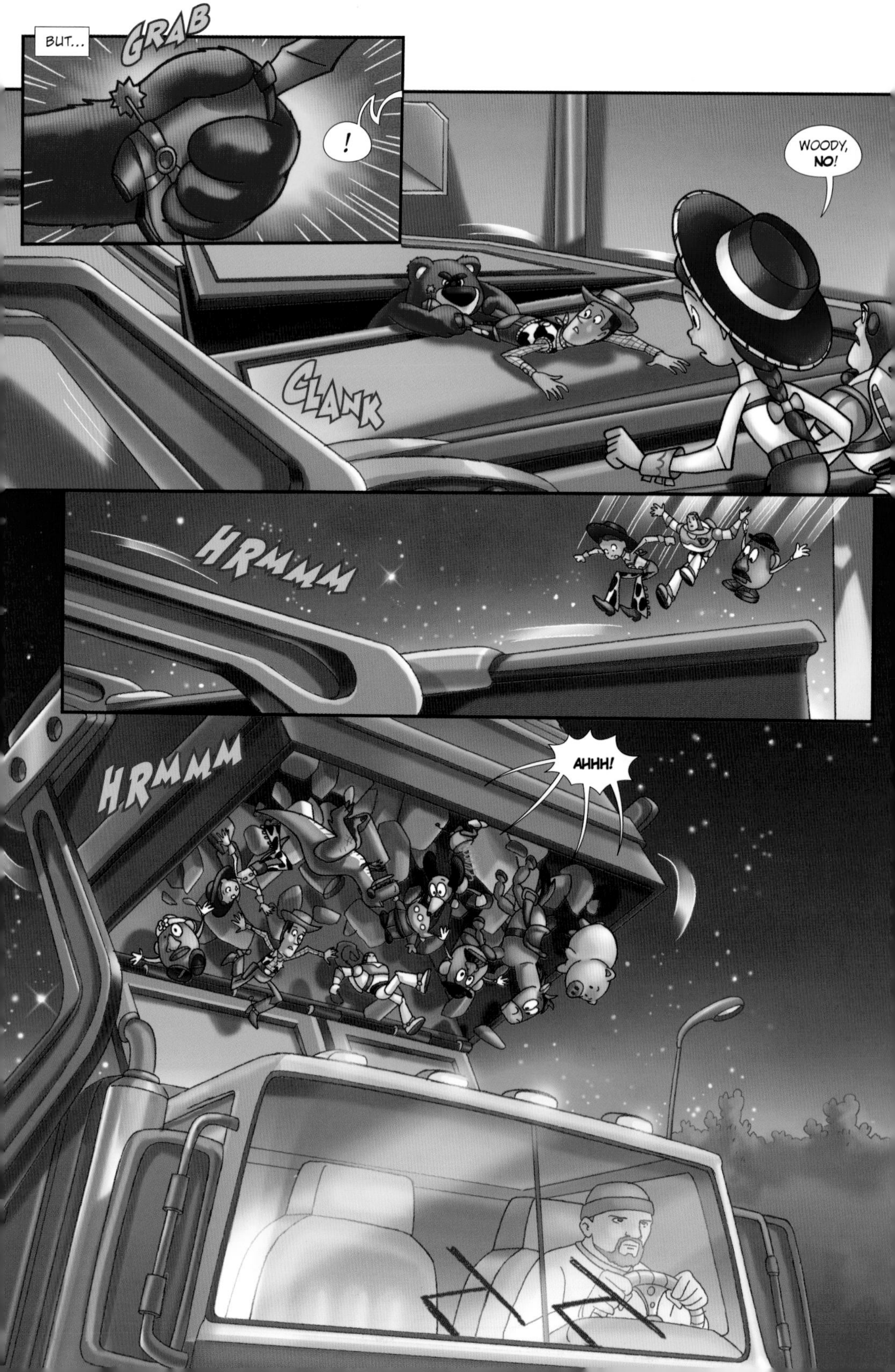
BUT...
GRAB
!
WOODY, NO!
CLANK
HRMMM
HRMMM
AHHH!

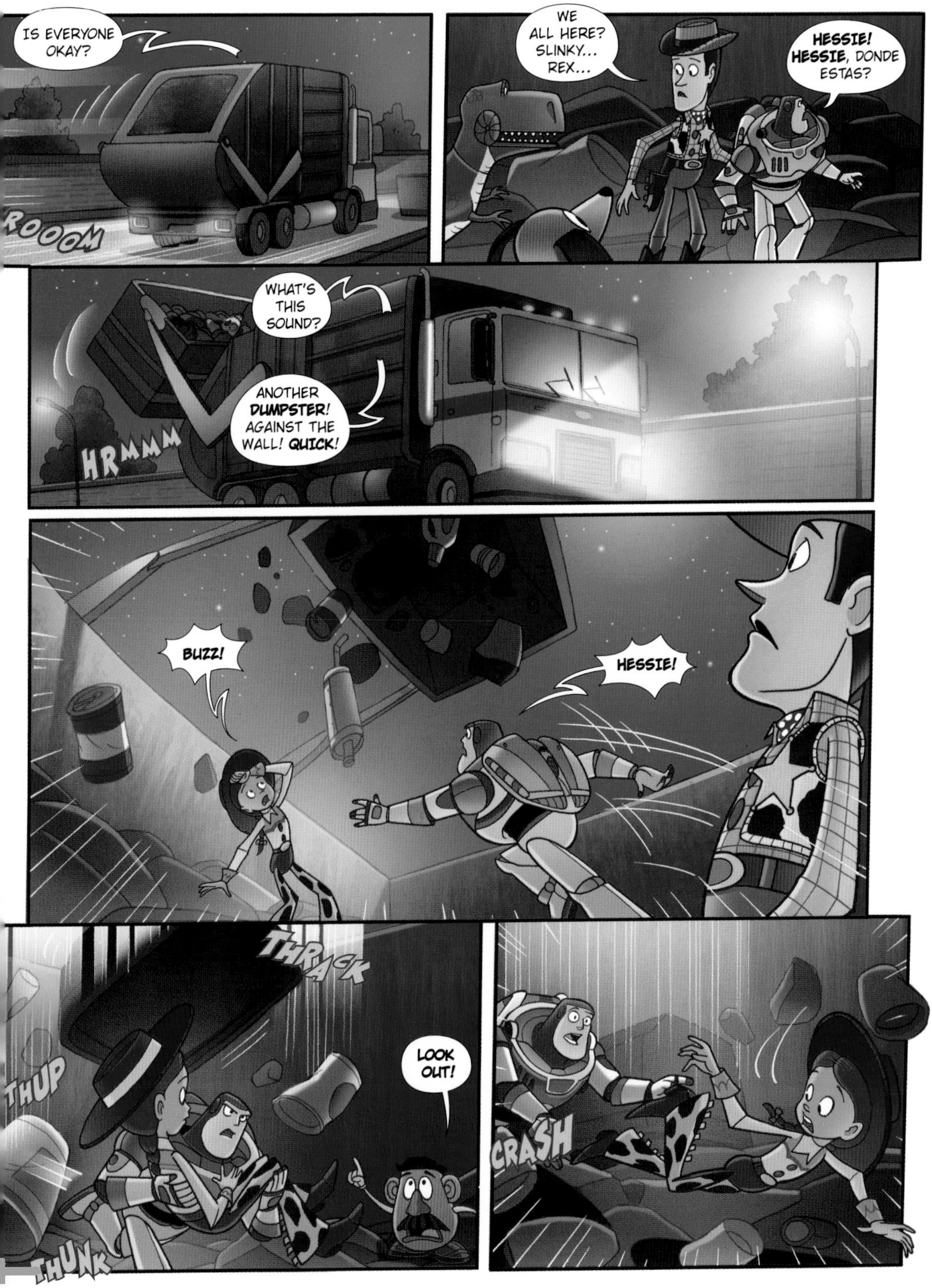

IS EVERYONE OKAY?
ROOOOM
WE ALL HERE? SLINKY... REX...
HESSIE! HESSIE, DONDE ESTAS?
WHAT'S THIS SOUND?
ANOTHER **DUMPSTER**! AGAINST THE WALL! **QUICK**!
HRMMM
BUZZ!
HESSIE!
THRACK
THUP
LOOK OUT!
THUNK
CRASH

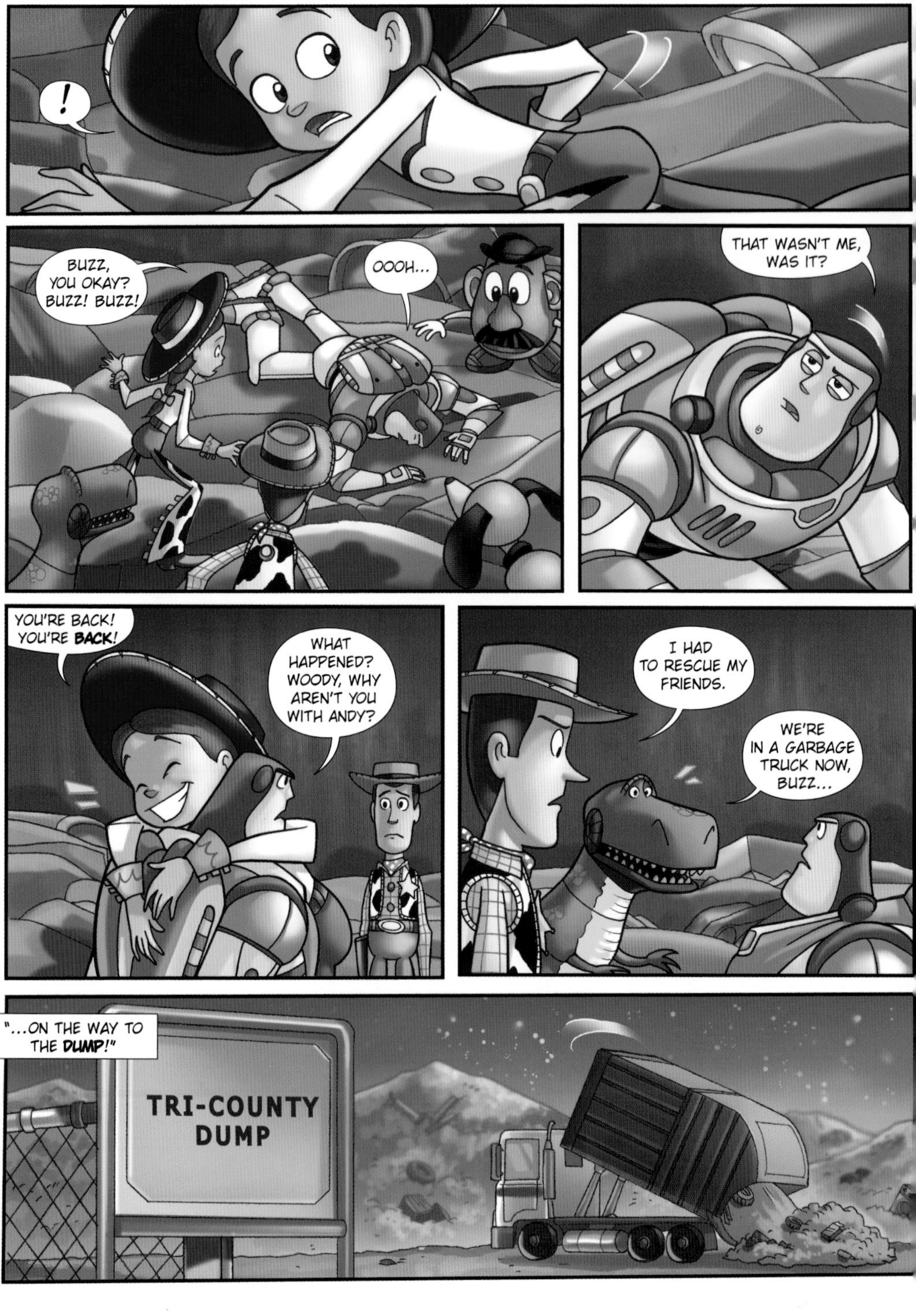
!
BUZZ, YOU OKAY? BUZZ! BUZZ!
OOOH...
THAT WASN'T ME, WAS IT?
YOU'RE BACK! YOU'RE **BACK**!
WHAT HAPPENED? WOODY, WHY AREN'T YOU WITH ANDY?
I HAD TO RESCUE MY FRIENDS.
WE'RE IN A GARBAGE TRUCK NOW, BUZZ...
"...ON THE WAY TO THE **DUMP**!"
TRI-COUNTY DUMP

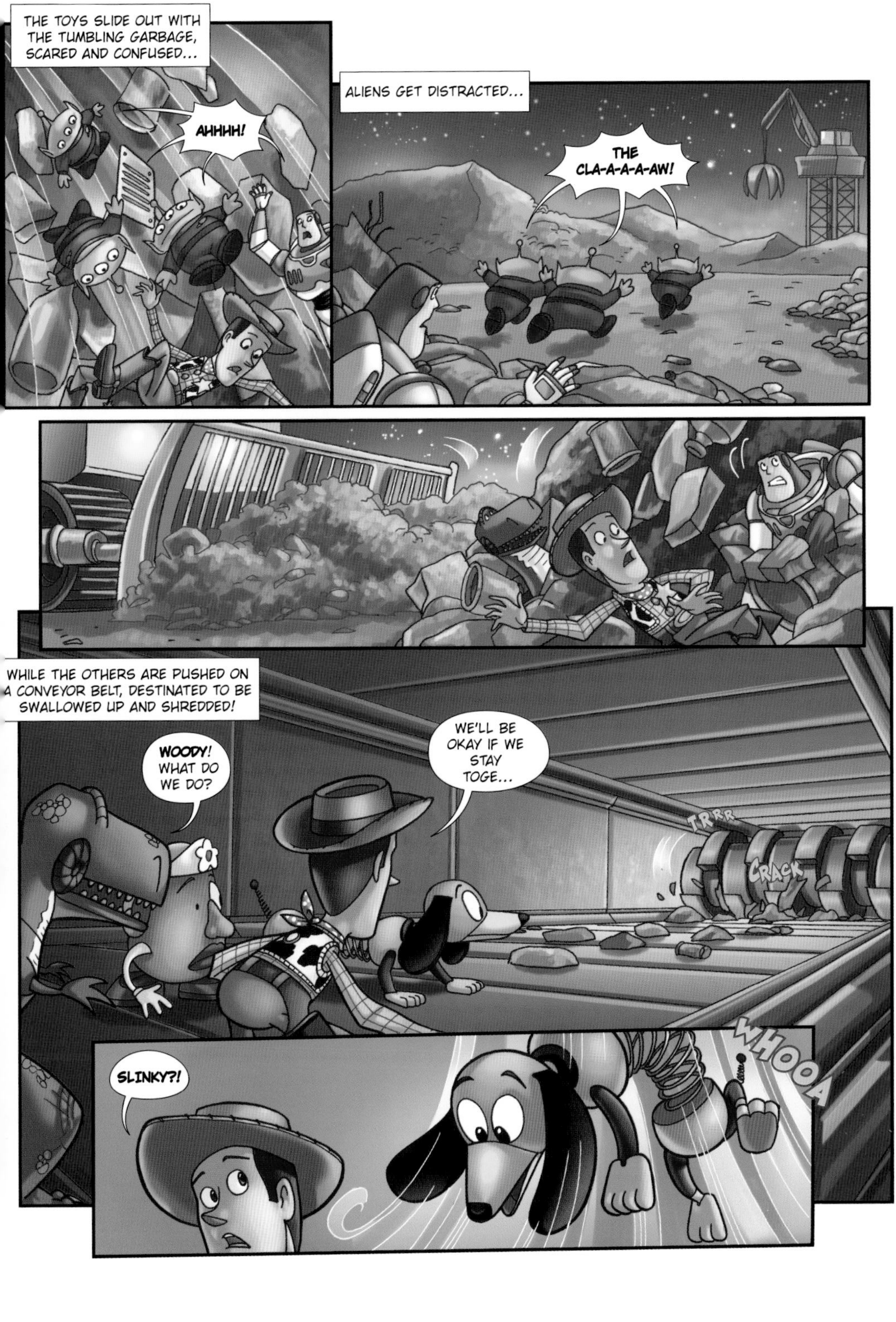
THE TOYS SLIDE OUT WITH THE TUMBLING GARBAGE, SCARED AND CONFUSED...
AHHHH!
ALIENS GET DISTRACTED...
THE CLA-A-A-A-AW!
WHILE THE OTHERS ARE PUSHED ON A CONVEYOR BELT, DESTINATED TO BE SWALLOWED UP AND SHREDDED!
WOODY! WHAT DO WE DO?
WE'LL BE OKAY IF WE STAY TOGE...
TRRR
CRACK
SLINKY?!
WHOOA

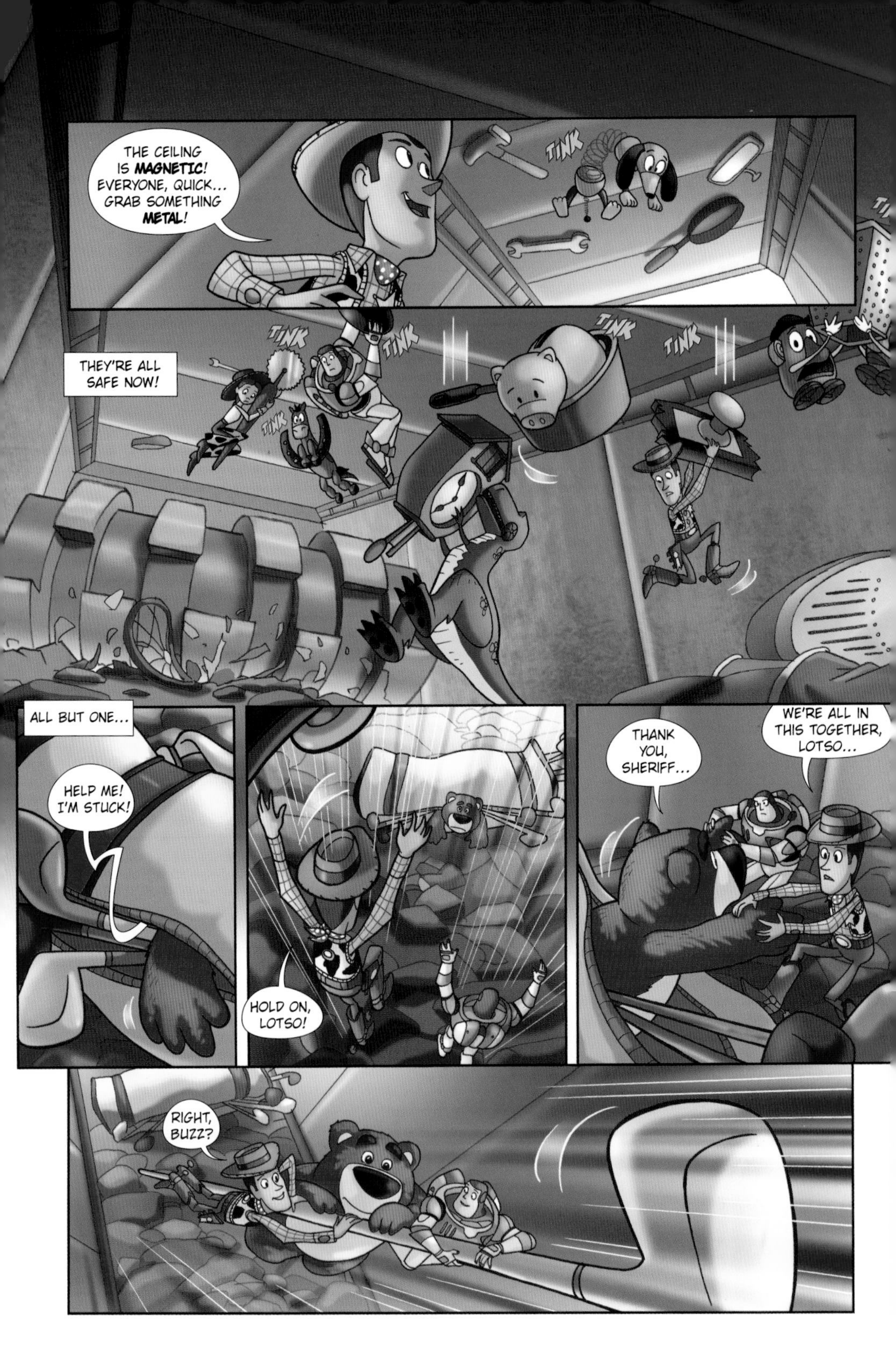
THE CEILING IS MAGNETIC! EVERYONE, QUICK... GRAB SOMETHING METAL!
TINK
THEY'RE ALL SAFE NOW!
TINK
TINK
TINK
TINK
TINK
ALL BUT ONE...
HELP ME! I'M STUCK!
HOLD ON, LOTSO!
THANK YOU, SHERIFF...
WE'RE ALL IN THIS TOGETHER, LOTSO...
RIGHT, BUZZ?

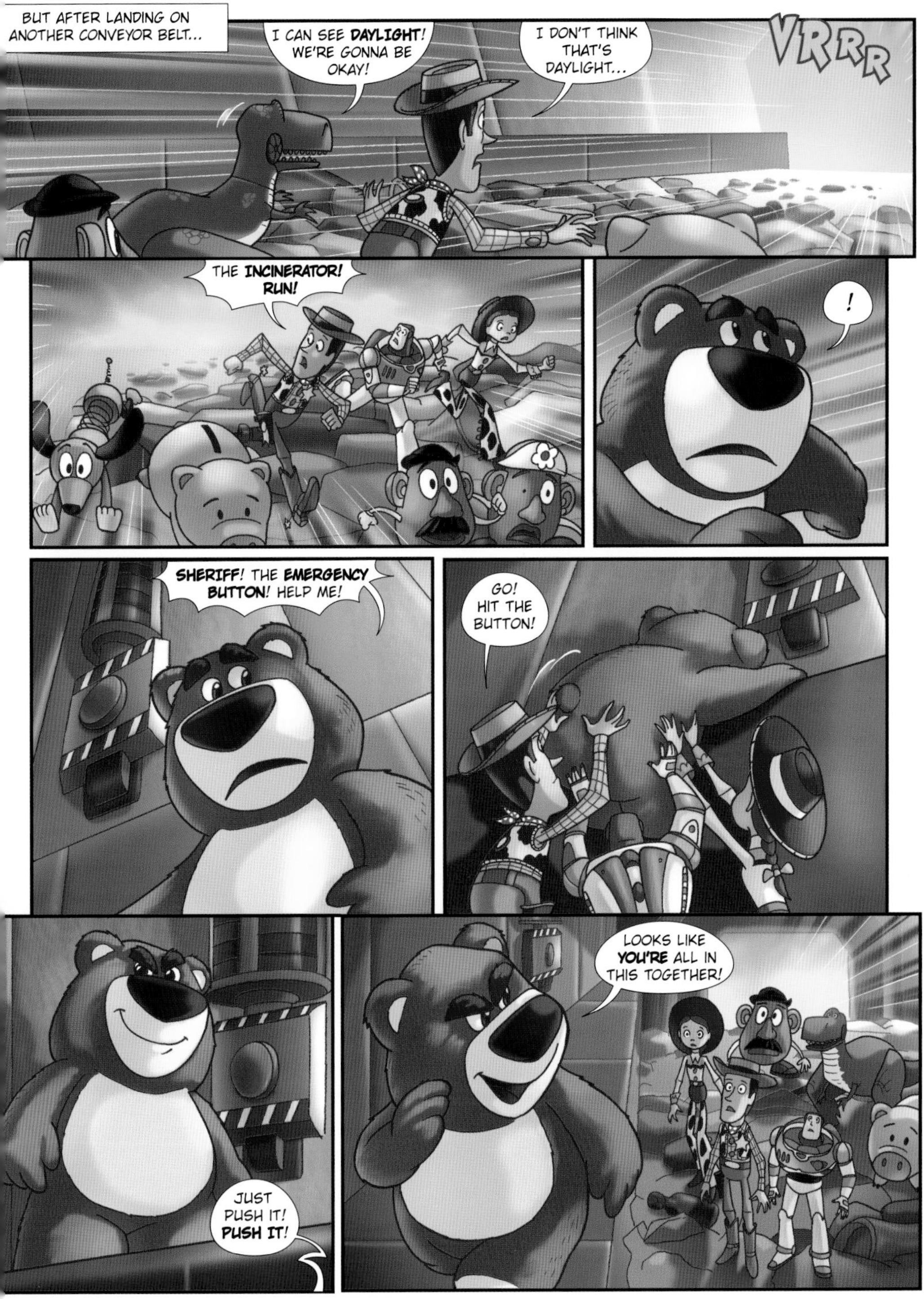
BUT AFTER LANDING ON ANOTHER CONVEYOR BELT...
I CAN SEE DAYLIGHT! WE'RE GONNA BE OKAY!
I DON'T THINK THAT'S DAYLIGHT...
VRRR
THE INCINERATOR! RUN!
!
SHERIFF! THE EMERGENCY BUTTON! HELP ME!
GO! HIT THE BUTTON!
JUST PUSH IT! PUSH IT!
LOOKS LIKE YOU'RE ALL IN THIS TOGETHER!

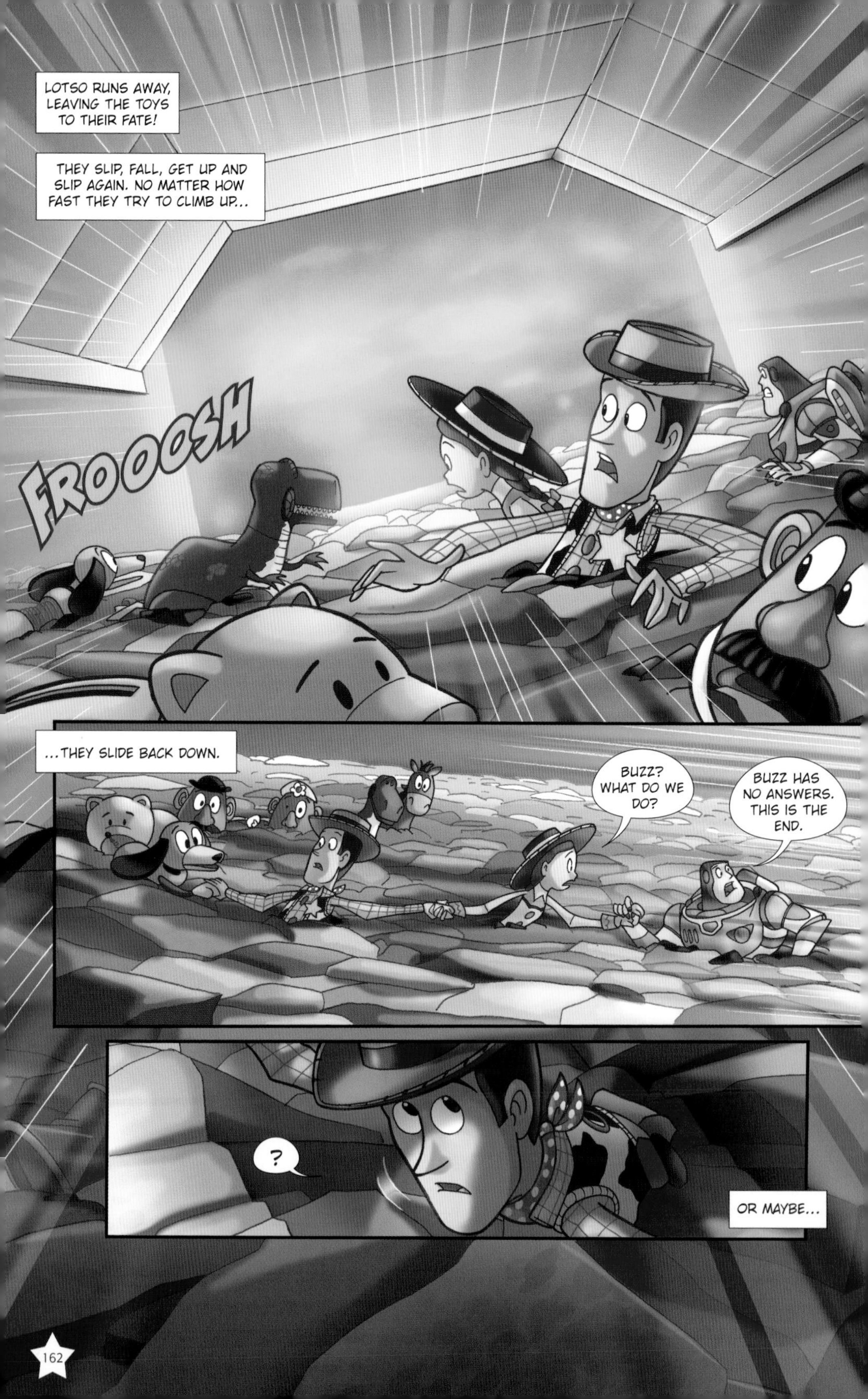
LOTSO RUNS AWAY, LEAVING THE TOYS TO THEIR FATE!
THEY SLIP, FALL, GET UP AND SLIP AGAIN. NO MATTER HOW FAST THEY TRY TO CLIMB UP...
FROOOSH
...THEY SLIDE BACK DOWN.
BUZZ? WHAT DO WE DO?
BUZZ HAS NO ANSWERS. THIS IS THE END.
?
OR MAYBE...

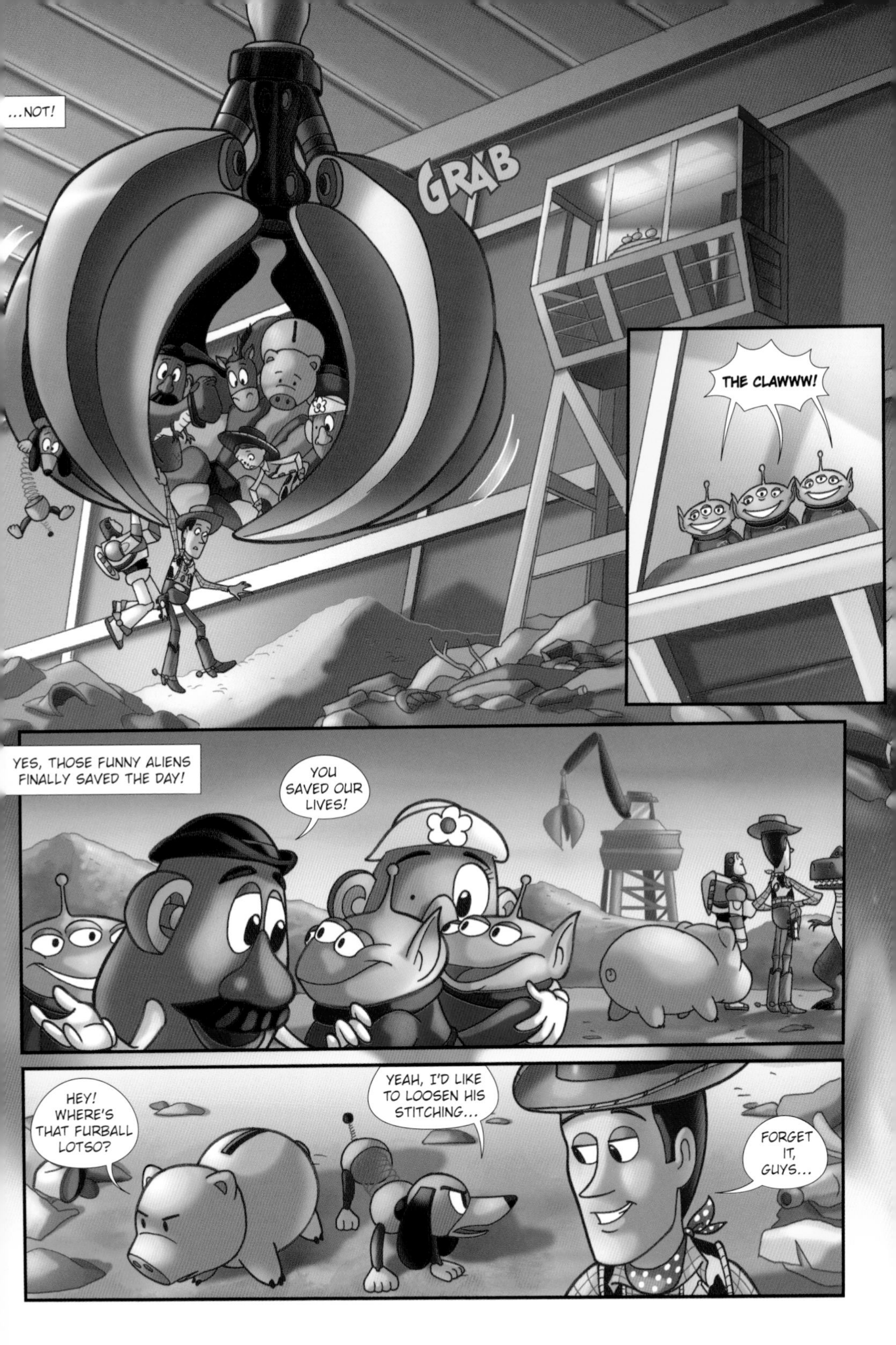
...NOT!
GRAB
THE CLAWWW!
YES, THOSE FUNNY ALIENS FINALLY SAVED THE DAY!
YOU SAVED OUR LIVES!
HEY! WHERE'S THAT FURBALL LOTSO?
YEAH, I'D LIKE TO LOOSEN HIS STITCHING...
FORGET IT, GUYS...

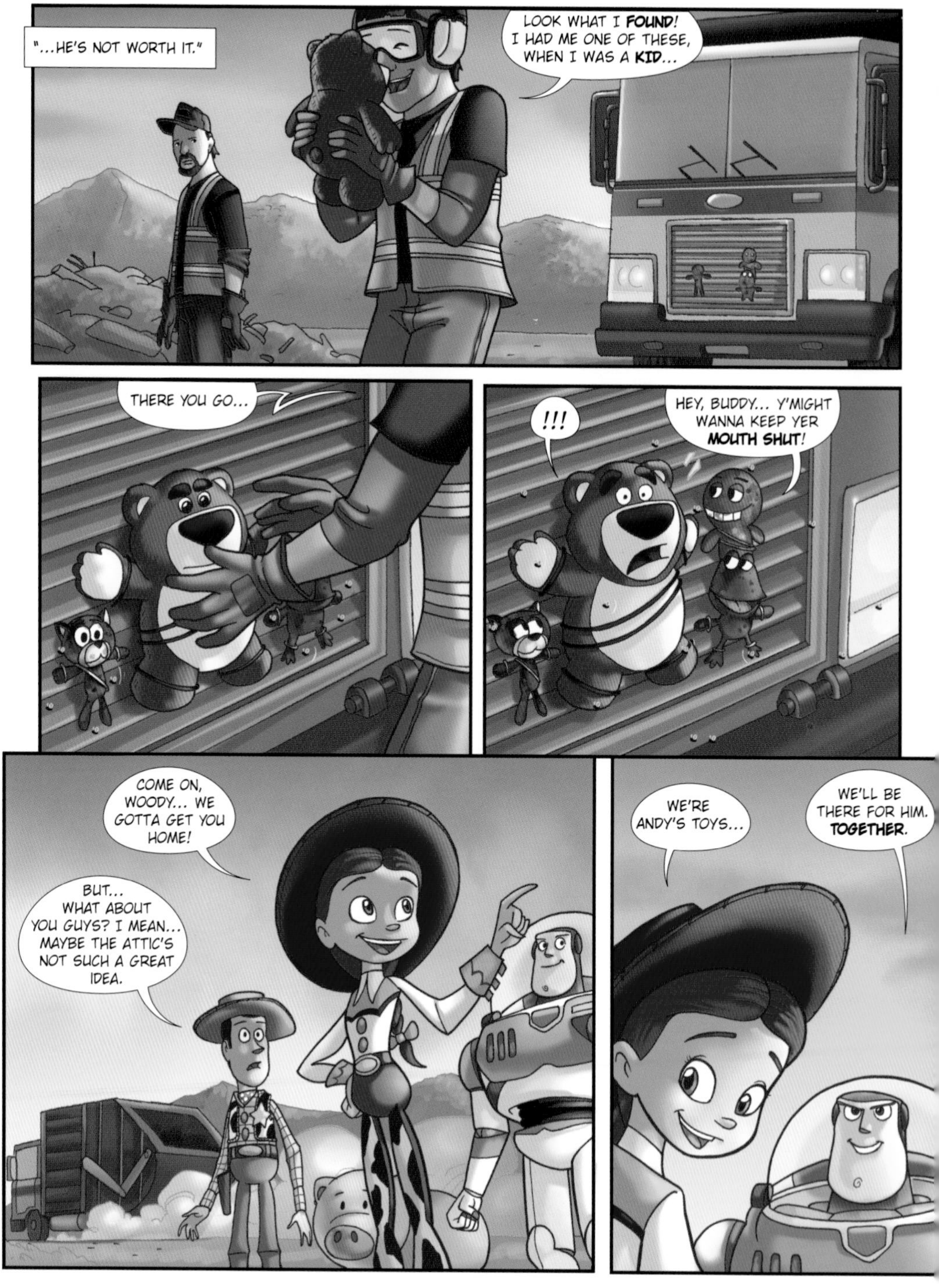
"...HE'S NOT WORTH IT."
LOOK WHAT I **FOUND**! I HAD ME ONE OF THESE, WHEN I WAS A **KID**...
THERE YOU GO...
!!!
HEY, BUDDY... Y'MIGHT WANNA KEEP YER **MOUTH SHUT**!
COME ON, WOODY... WE GOTTA GET YOU HOME!
BUT... WHAT ABOUT YOU GUYS? I MEAN... MAYBE THE ATTIC'S NOT SUCH A GREAT IDEA.
WE'RE ANDY'S TOYS...
WE'LL BE THERE FOR HIM. **TOGETHER**.

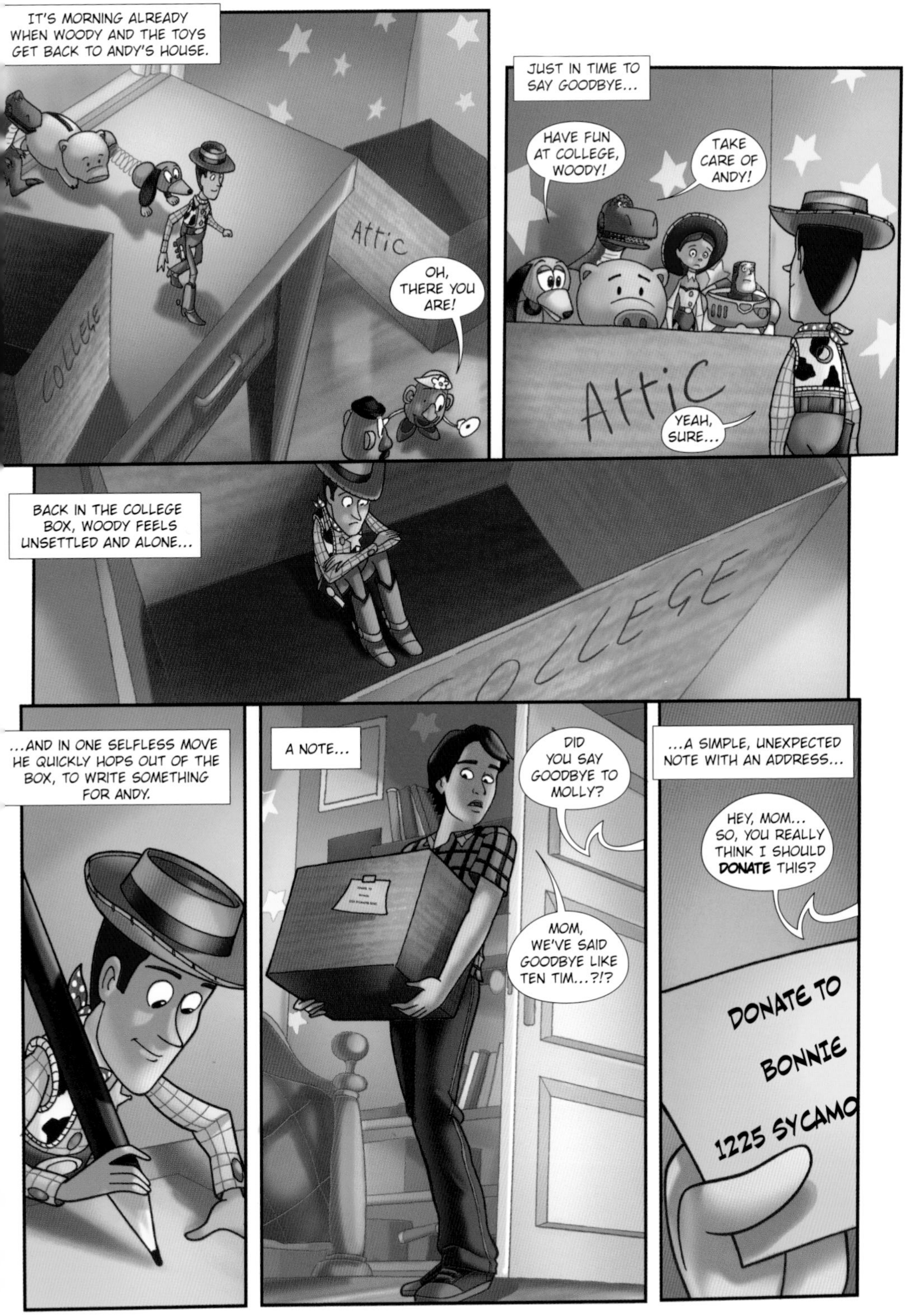
IT'S MORNING ALREADY WHEN WOODY AND THE TOYS GET BACK TO ANDY'S HOUSE.
Attic
COLLEGE
OH, THERE YOU ARE!
JUST IN TIME TO SAY GOODBYE...
HAVE FUN AT COLLEGE, WOODY!
TAKE CARE OF ANDY!
Attic
YEAH, SURE...
BACK IN THE COLLEGE BOX, WOODY FEELS UNSETTLED AND ALONE...
COLLEGE
...AND IN ONE SELFLESS MOVE HE QUICKLY HOPS OUT OF THE BOX, TO WRITE SOMETHING FOR ANDY.
A NOTE...
DID YOU SAY GOODBYE TO MOLLY?
MOM, WE'VE SAID GOODBYE LIKE TEN TIM...?!?
...A SIMPLE, UNEXPECTED NOTE WITH AN ADDRESS...
HEY, MOM... SO, YOU REALLY THINK I SHOULD **DONATE** THIS?
DONATE TO
BONNIE
1225 SYCAMO

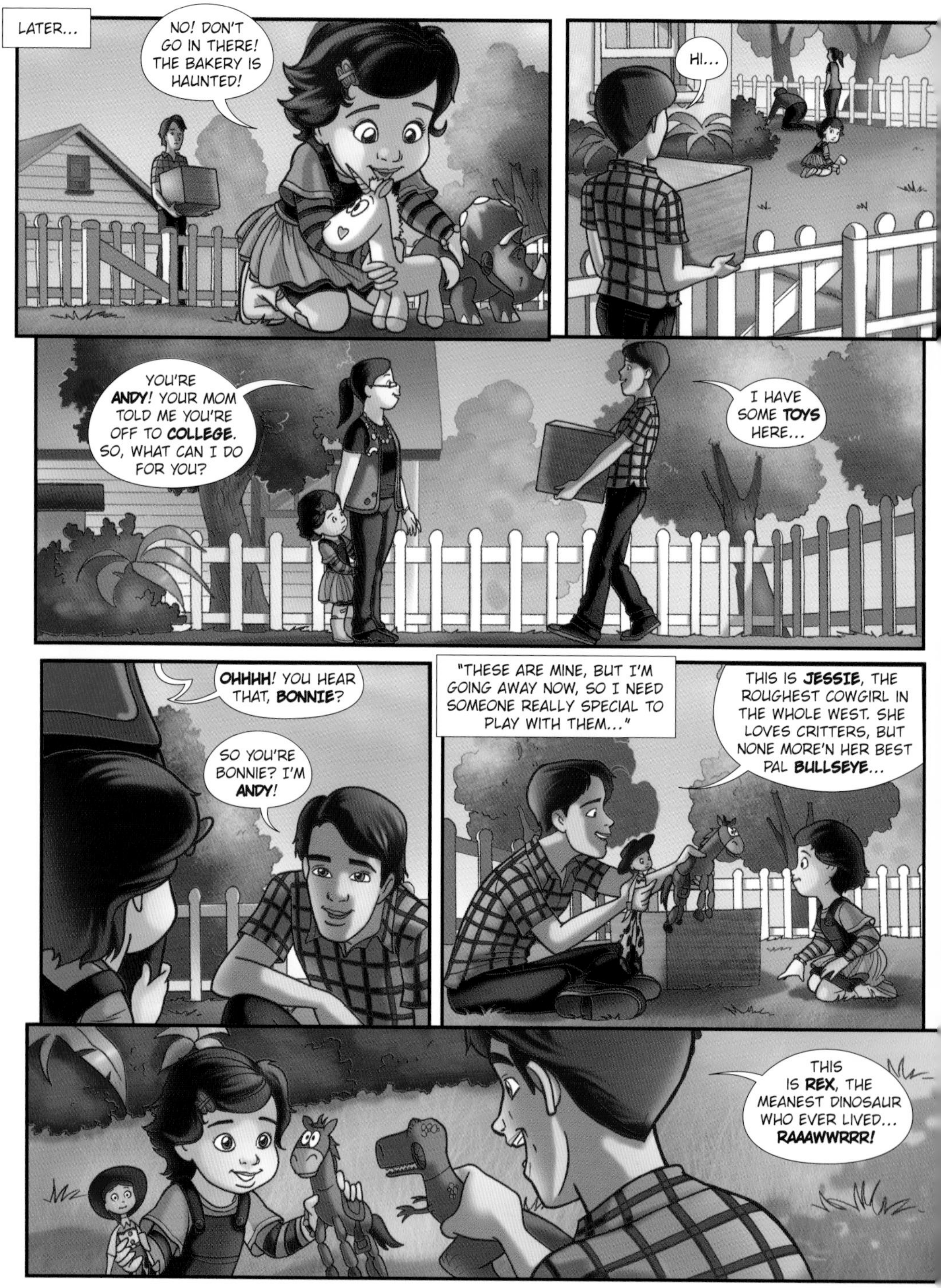
LATER...
NO! DON'T GO IN THERE! THE BAKERY IS HAUNTED!
HI...
YOU'RE ANDY! YOUR MOM TOLD ME YOU'RE OFF TO COLLEGE. SO, WHAT CAN I DO FOR YOU?
I HAVE SOME TOYS HERE...
OHHHH! YOU HEAR THAT, BONNIE?
SO YOU'RE BONNIE? I'M ANDY!
"THESE ARE MINE, BUT I'M GOING AWAY NOW, SO I NEED SOMEONE REALLY SPECIAL TO PLAY WITH THEM..."
THIS IS JESSIE, THE ROUGHEST COWGIRL IN THE WHOLE WEST. SHE LOVES CRITTERS, BUT NONE MORE'N HER BEST PAL BULLSEYE...
THIS IS REX, THE MEANEST DINOSAUR WHO EVER LIVED... RAAAWWRRR!

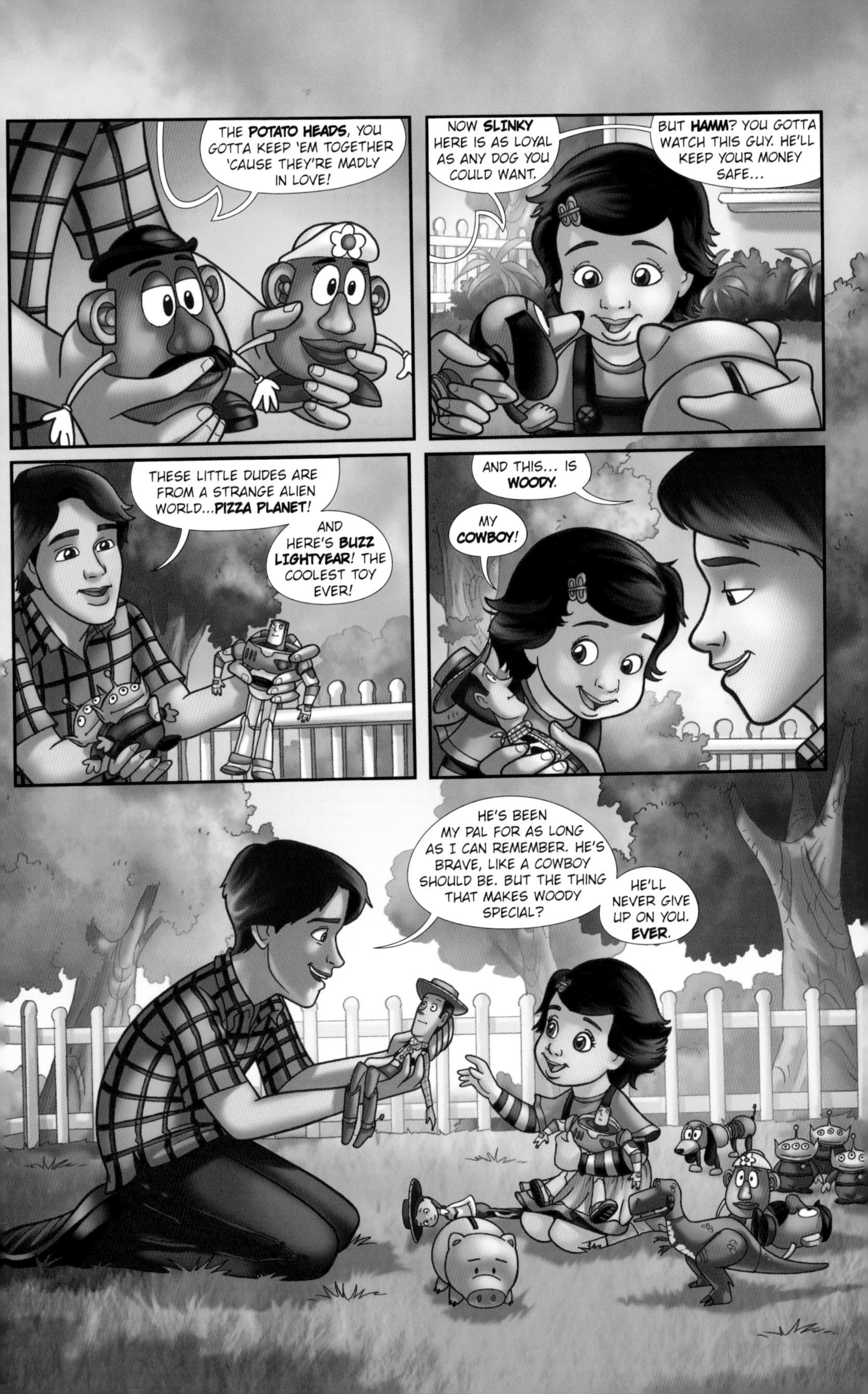
THE **POTATO HEADS**, YOU GOTTA KEEP 'EM TOGETHER 'CAUSE THEY'RE MADLY IN LOVE!
NOW **SLINKY** HERE IS AS LOYAL AS ANY DOG YOU COULD WANT.
BUT **HAMM**? YOU GOTTA WATCH THIS GUY. HE'LL KEEP YOUR MONEY SAFE...
THESE LITTLE DUDES ARE FROM A STRANGE ALIEN WORLD...**PIZZA PLANET**!
AND HERE'S **BUZZ LIGHTYEAR**! THE COOLEST TOY EVER!
AND THIS... IS **WOODY**.
MY **COWBOY**!
HE'S BEEN MY PAL FOR AS LONG AS I CAN REMEMBER. HE'S BRAVE, LIKE A COWBOY SHOULD BE. BUT THE THING THAT MAKES WOODY SPECIAL?
HE'LL NEVER GIVE UP ON YOU. **EVER**.

"Y'THINK YOU CAN TAKE CARE OF HIM FOR ME?"

OH, NO! THE GHOSTS ARE GETTING AWAY! **WOODY TO THE RESCUE!**

BYE, GUYS.

LOOK, MOMMY! THEY'RE ALL PLAYING TOGETHER!

C'MON, LET'S GET SOME LUNCH...

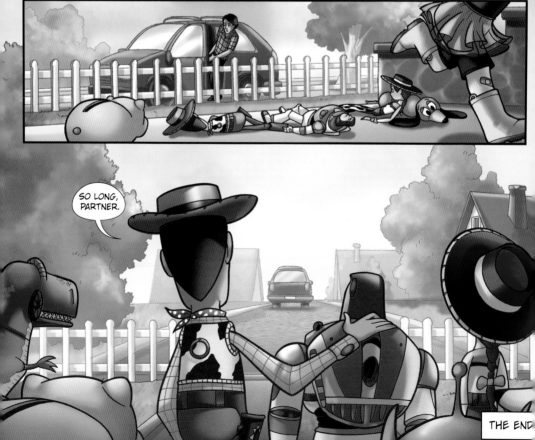

SO LONG, PARTNER.

THE END

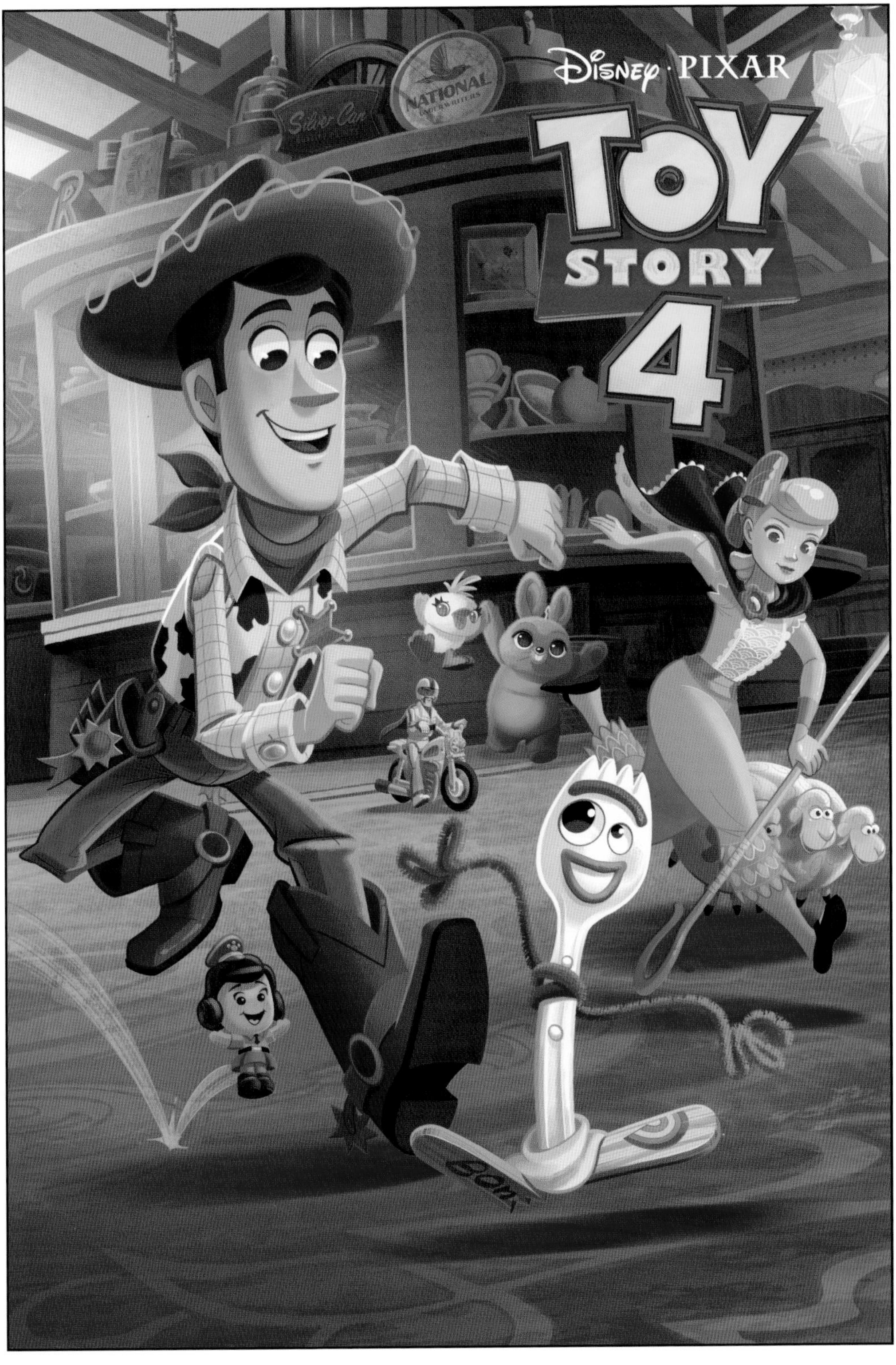
Disney · PIXAR
TOY STORY 4
NATIONAL

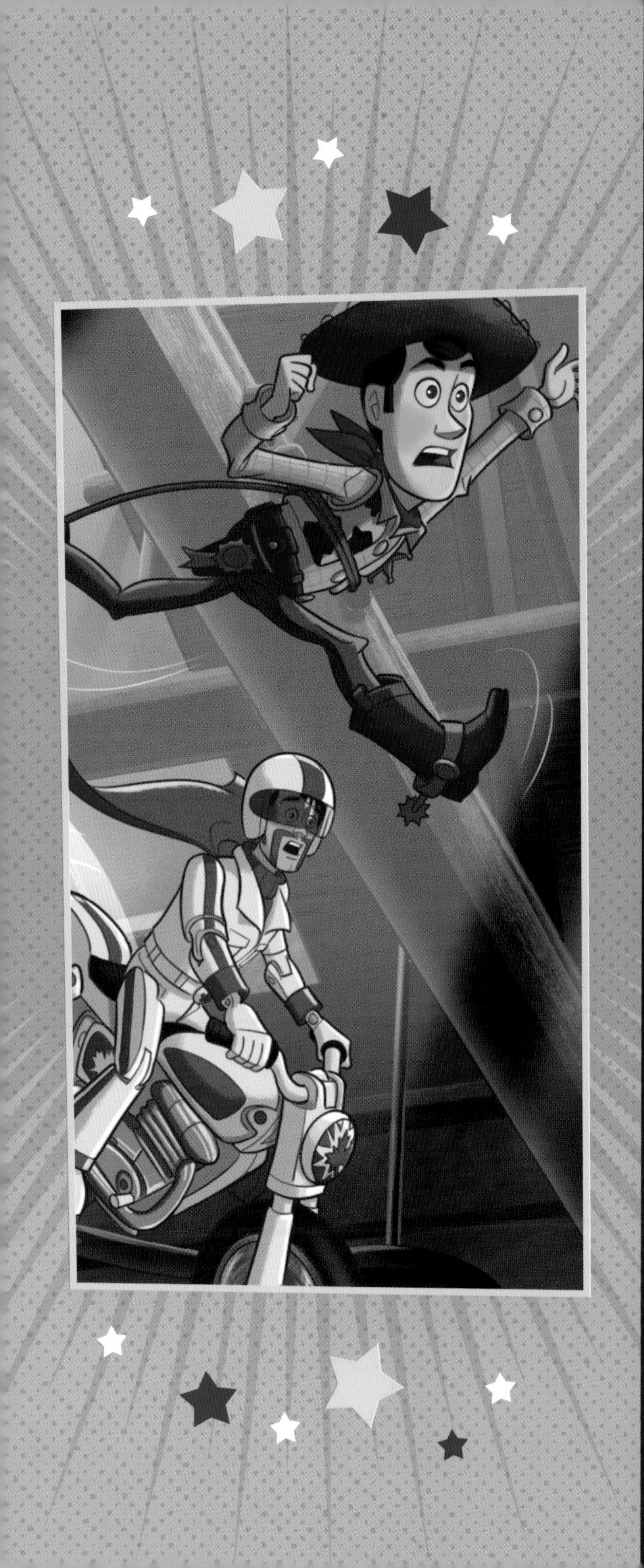

script adaptation
Alessandro Ferrari

layouts
Emilio Urbano

pencils and inks
Andrea Greppi
Marco Forcelloni

color
Angela Capolupo Art Team
Massimo Rocca

letters
Edizioni BD

cover layout
Marco Ghiglione

cover pencils and inks
Marco Forcelloni

cover color
Andrea Cagol

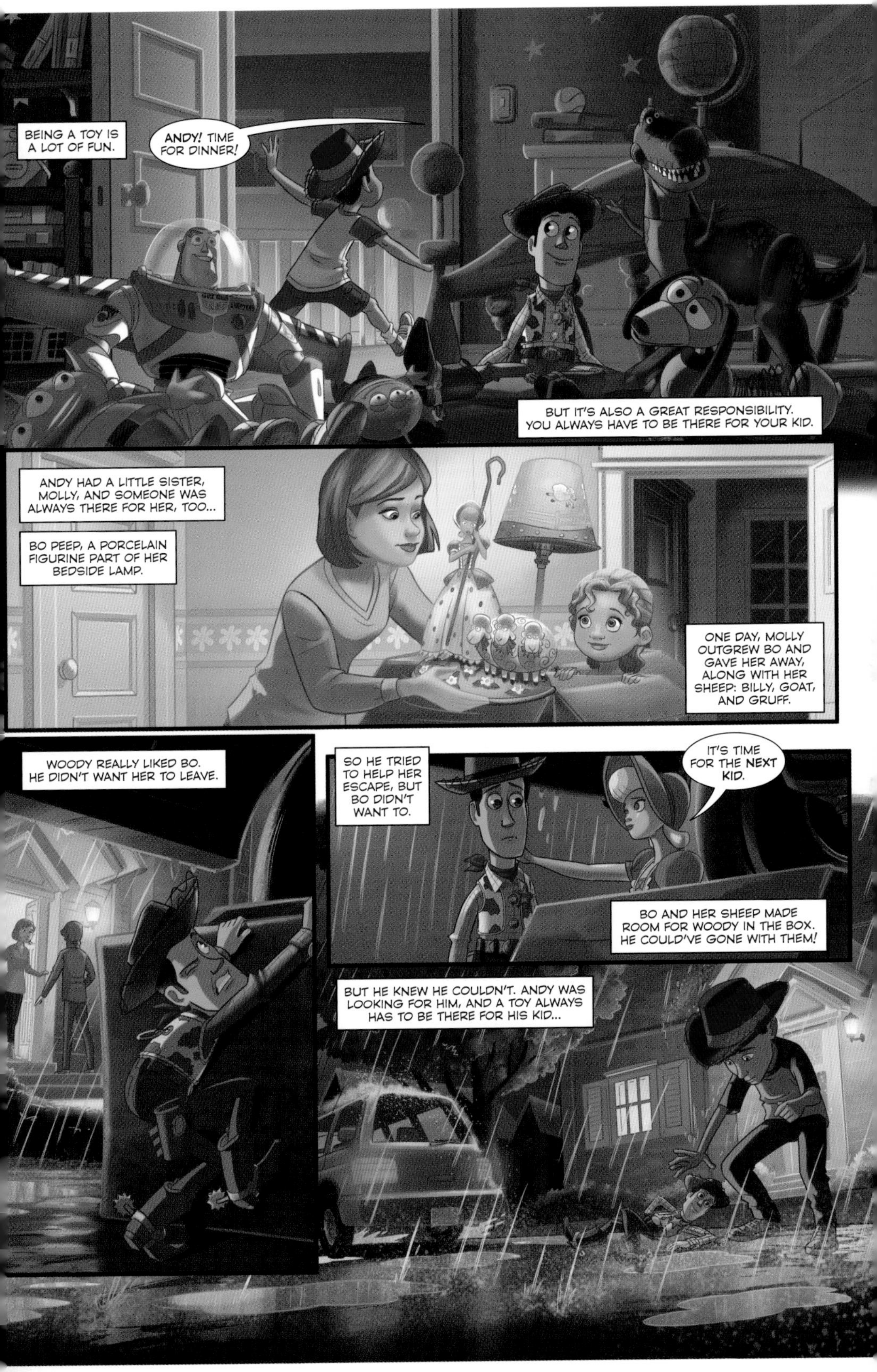
BEING A TOY IS A LOT OF FUN.
ANDY! TIME FOR DINNER!
BUT IT'S ALSO A GREAT RESPONSIBILITY. YOU ALWAYS HAVE TO BE THERE FOR YOUR KID.
ANDY HAD A LITTLE SISTER, MOLLY, AND SOMEONE WAS ALWAYS THERE FOR HER, TOO...
BO PEEP, A PORCELAIN FIGURINE PART OF HER BEDSIDE LAMP.
ONE DAY, MOLLY OUTGREW BO AND GAVE HER AWAY, ALONG WITH HER SHEEP: BILLY, GOAT, AND GRUFF.
WOODY REALLY LIKED BO. HE DIDN'T WANT HER TO LEAVE.
SO HE TRIED TO HELP HER ESCAPE, BUT BO DIDN'T WANT TO.
IT'S TIME FOR THE **NEXT KID**.
BO AND HER SHEEP MADE ROOM FOR WOODY IN THE BOX. HE COULD'VE GONE WITH THEM!
BUT HE KNEW HE COULDN'T. ANDY WAS LOOKING FOR HIM, AND A TOY ALWAYS HAS TO BE THERE FOR HIS KID...

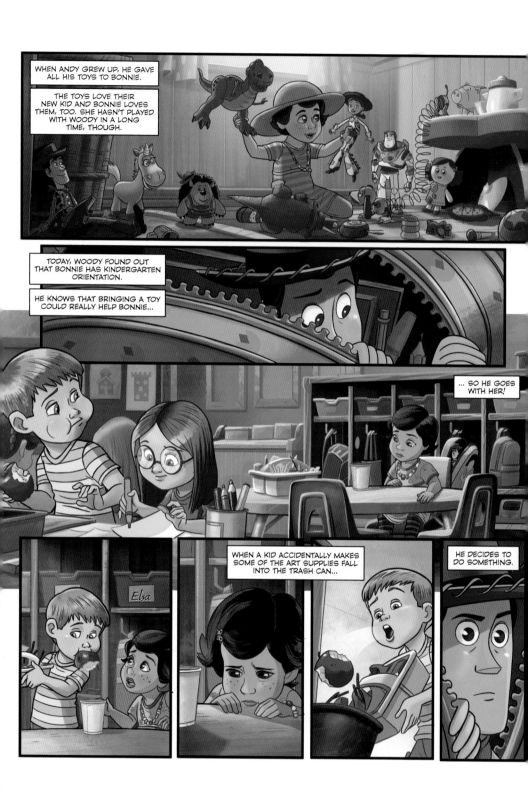

WHEN ANDY GREW UP, HE GAVE ALL HIS TOYS TO BONNIE.

THE TOYS LOVE THEIR NEW KID AND BONNIE LOVES THEM, TOO. SHE HASN'T PLAYED WITH WOODY IN A LONG TIME, THOUGH.

TODAY, WOODY FOUND OUT THAT BONNIE HAS KINDERGARTEN ORIENTATION.

HE KNOWS THAT BRINGING A TOY COULD REALLY HELP BONNIE...

... SO HE GOES WITH HER!

WHEN A KID ACCIDENTALLY MAKES SOME OF THE ART SUPPLIES FALL INTO THE TRASH CAN...

HE DECIDES TO DO SOMETHING.

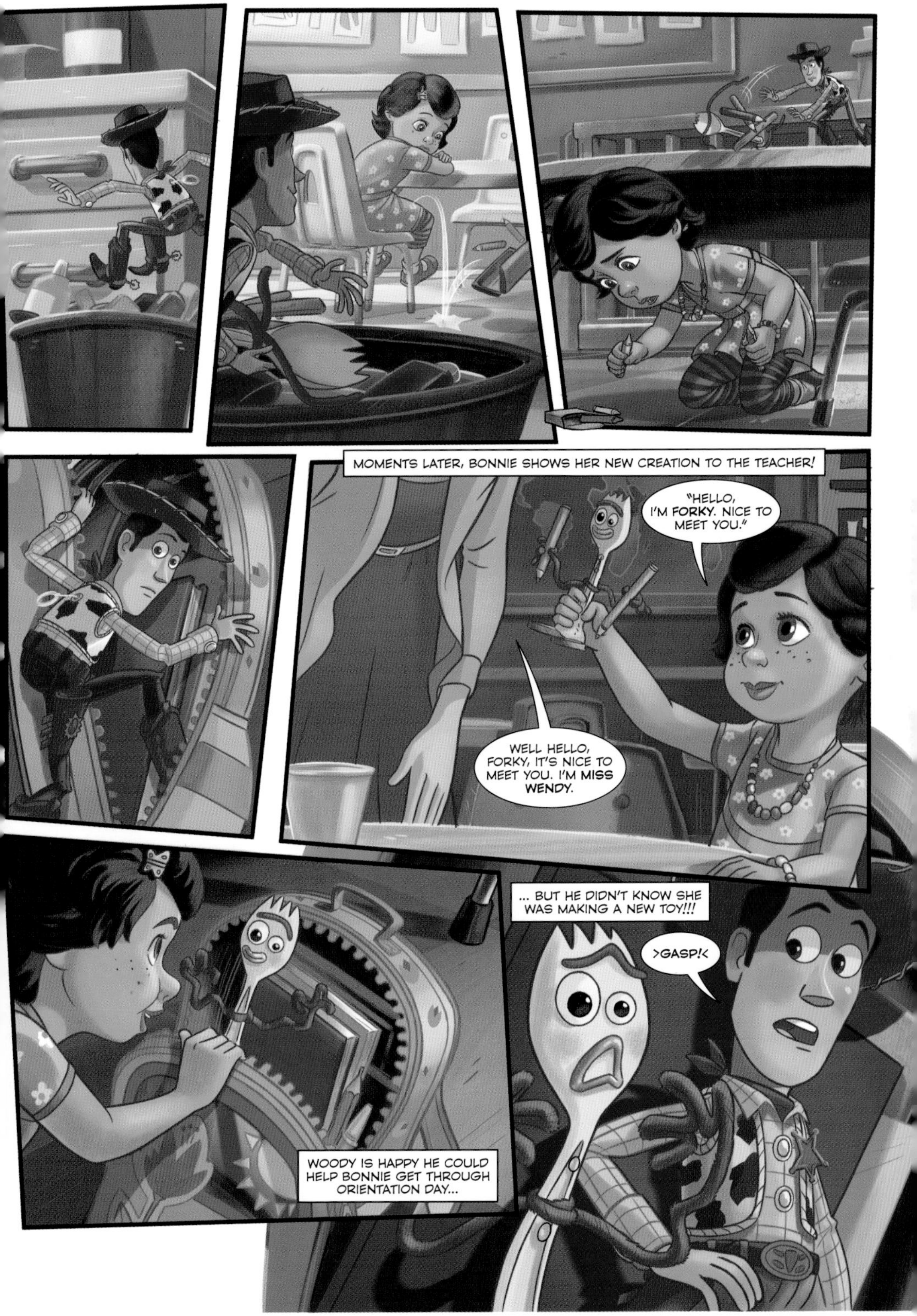
MOMENTS LATER, BONNIE SHOWS HER NEW CREATION TO THE TEACHER!
"HELLO, I'M FORKY. NICE TO MEET YOU."
WELL HELLO, FORKY, IT'S NICE TO MEET YOU. I'M MISS WENDY.
WOODY IS HAPPY HE COULD HELP BONNIE GET THROUGH ORIENTATION DAY...
... BUT HE DIDN'T KNOW SHE WAS MAKING A NEW TOY!!!
>GASP!<

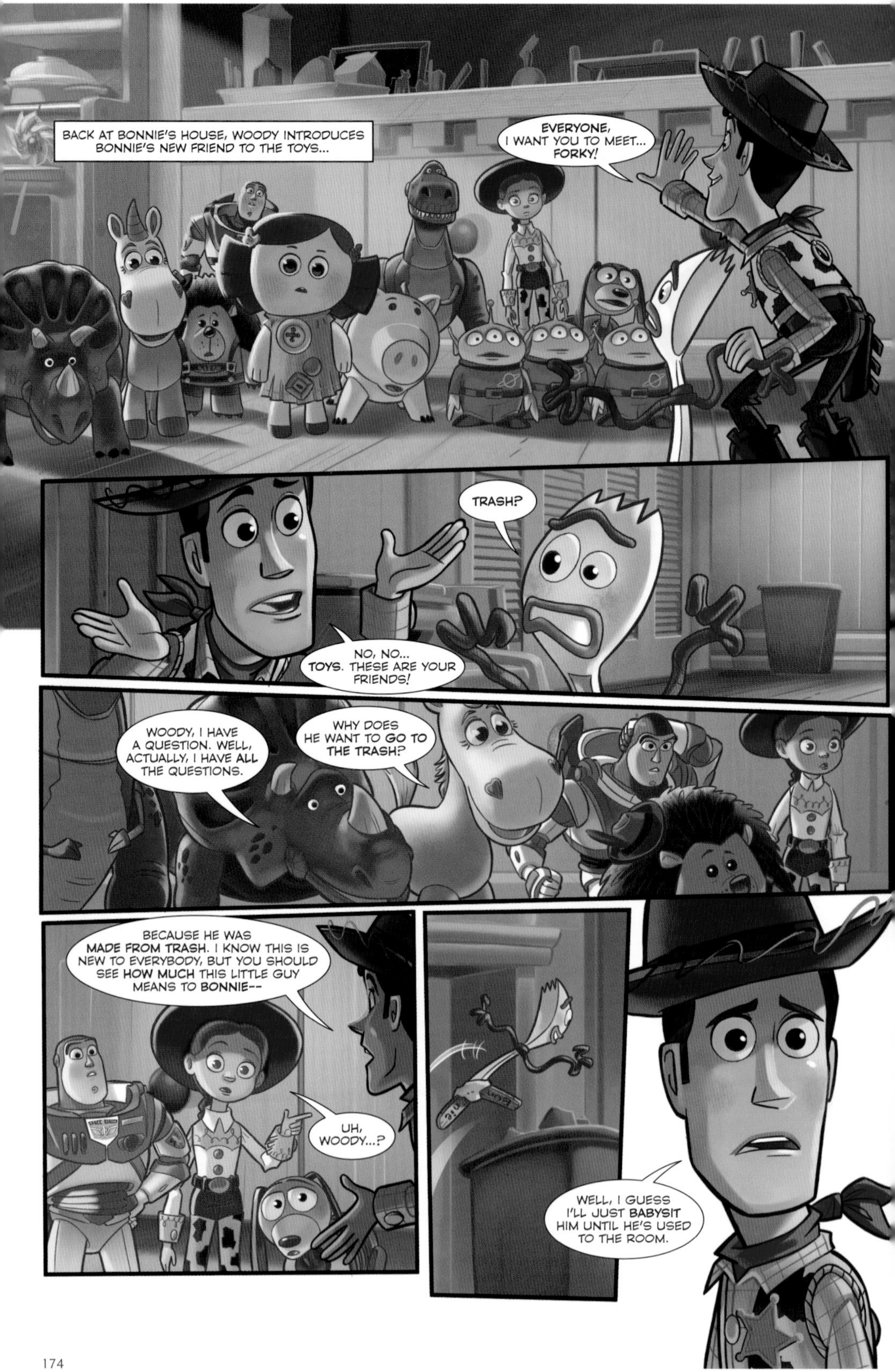
BACK AT BONNIE'S HOUSE, WOODY INTRODUCES BONNIE'S NEW FRIEND TO THE TOYS...
EVERYONE, I WANT YOU TO MEET... FORKY!
TRASH?
NO, NO... TOYS. THESE ARE YOUR FRIENDS!
WOODY, I HAVE A QUESTION. WELL, ACTUALLY, I HAVE ALL THE QUESTIONS.
WHY DOES HE WANT TO GO TO THE TRASH?
BECAUSE HE WAS MADE FROM TRASH. I KNOW THIS IS NEW TO EVERYBODY, BUT YOU SHOULD SEE HOW MUCH THIS LITTLE GUY MEANS TO BONNIE--
UH, WOODY...?
WELL, I GUESS I'LL JUST BABYSIT HIM UNTIL HE'S USED TO THE ROOM.

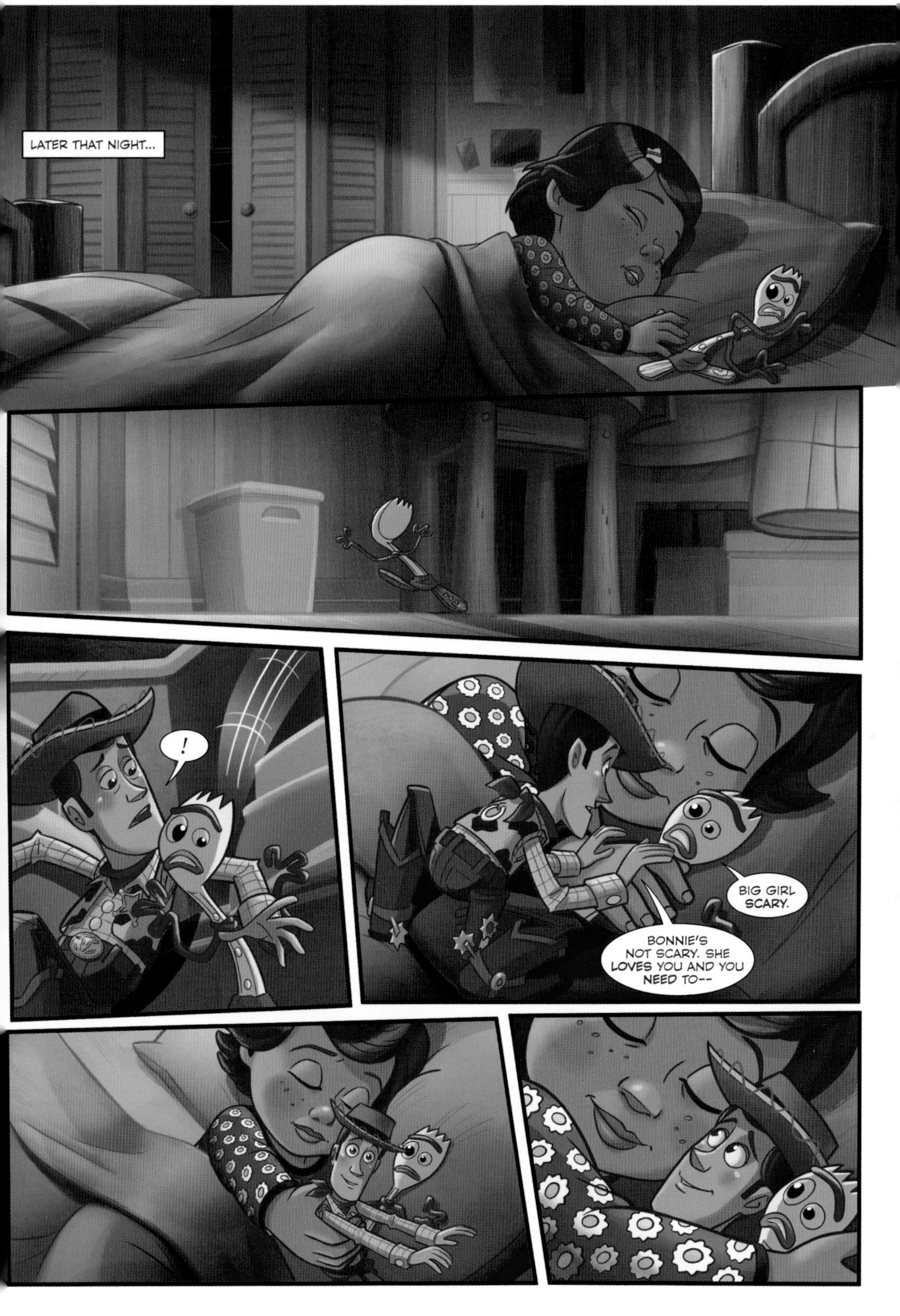
LATER THAT NIGHT...
!
BIG GIRL SCARY.
BONNIE'S NOT SCARY. SHE LOVES YOU AND YOU NEED TO--

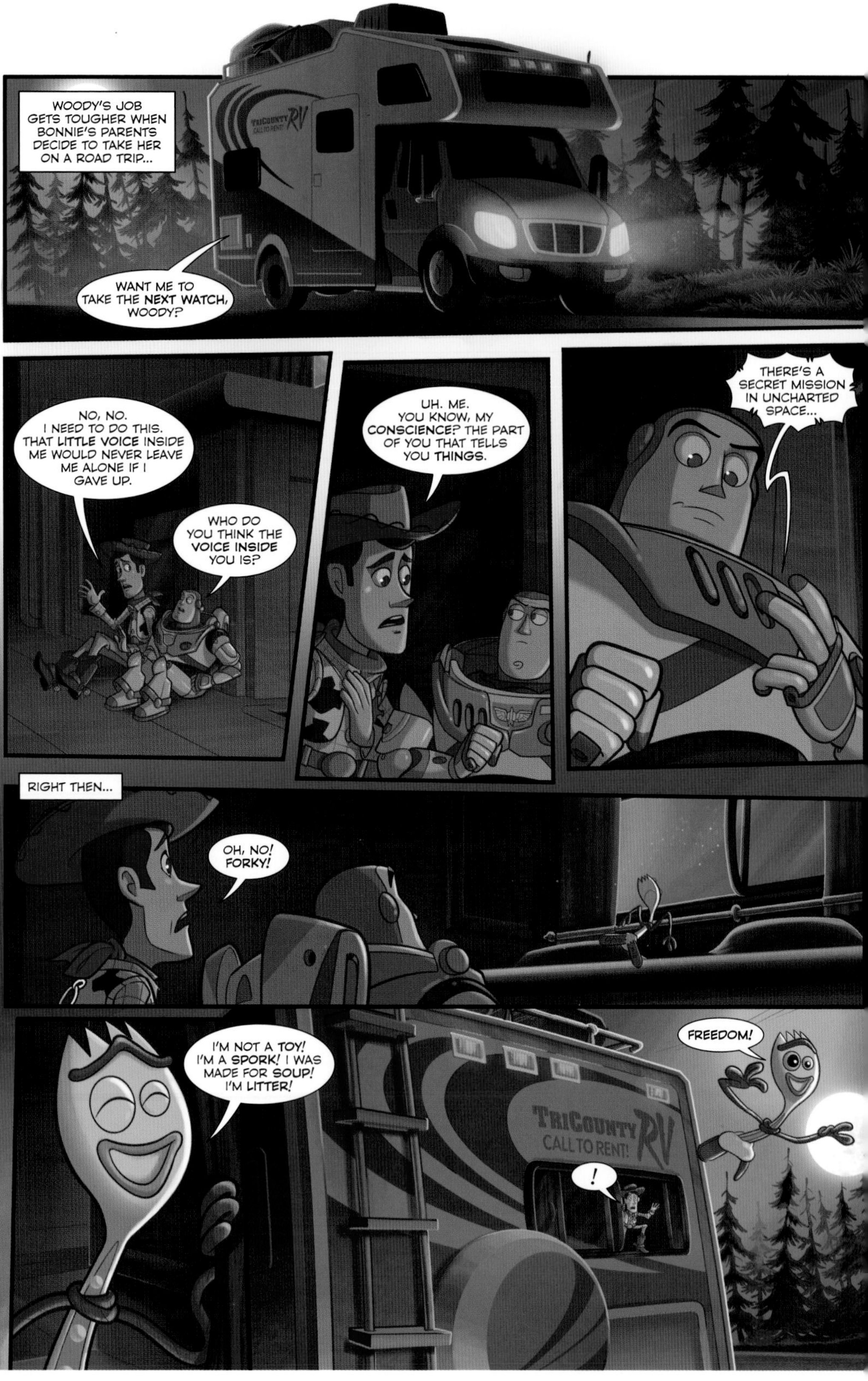
WOODY'S JOB GETS TOUGHER WHEN BONNIE'S PARENTS DECIDE TO TAKE HER ON A ROAD TRIP...
TRICOUNTY RV CALL TO RENT!
WANT ME TO TAKE THE NEXT WATCH, WOODY?
NO, NO. I NEED TO DO THIS. THAT LITTLE VOICE INSIDE ME WOULD NEVER LEAVE ME ALONE IF I GAVE UP.
WHO DO YOU THINK THE VOICE INSIDE YOU IS?
UH. ME. YOU KNOW, MY CONSCIENCE? THE PART OF YOU THAT TELLS YOU THINGS.
THERE'S A SECRET MISSION IN UNCHARTED SPACE...
RIGHT THEN...
OH, NO! FORKY!
I'M NOT A TOY! I'M A SPORK! I WAS MADE FOR SOUP! I'M LITTER!
TRICOUNTY RV CALL TO RENT!
!
FREEDOM!

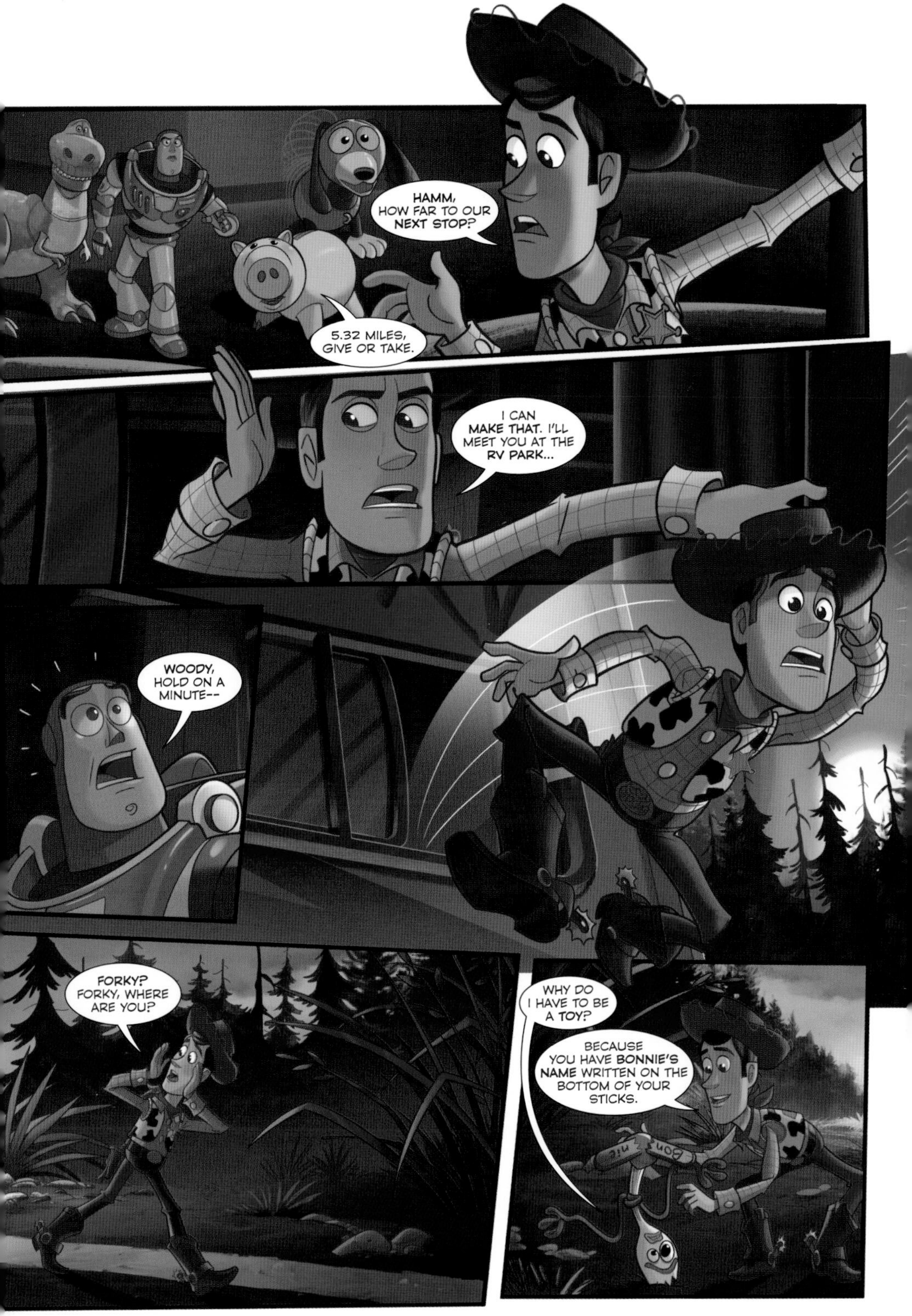
HAMM, HOW FAR TO OUR NEXT STOP?
5.32 MILES, GIVE OR TAKE.
I CAN MAKE THAT. I'LL MEET YOU AT THE RV PARK...
WOODY, HOLD ON A MINUTE--
FORKY? FORKY, WHERE ARE YOU?
WHY DO I HAVE TO BE A TOY?
BECAUSE YOU HAVE BONNIE'S NAME WRITTEN ON THE BOTTOM OF YOUR STICKS.

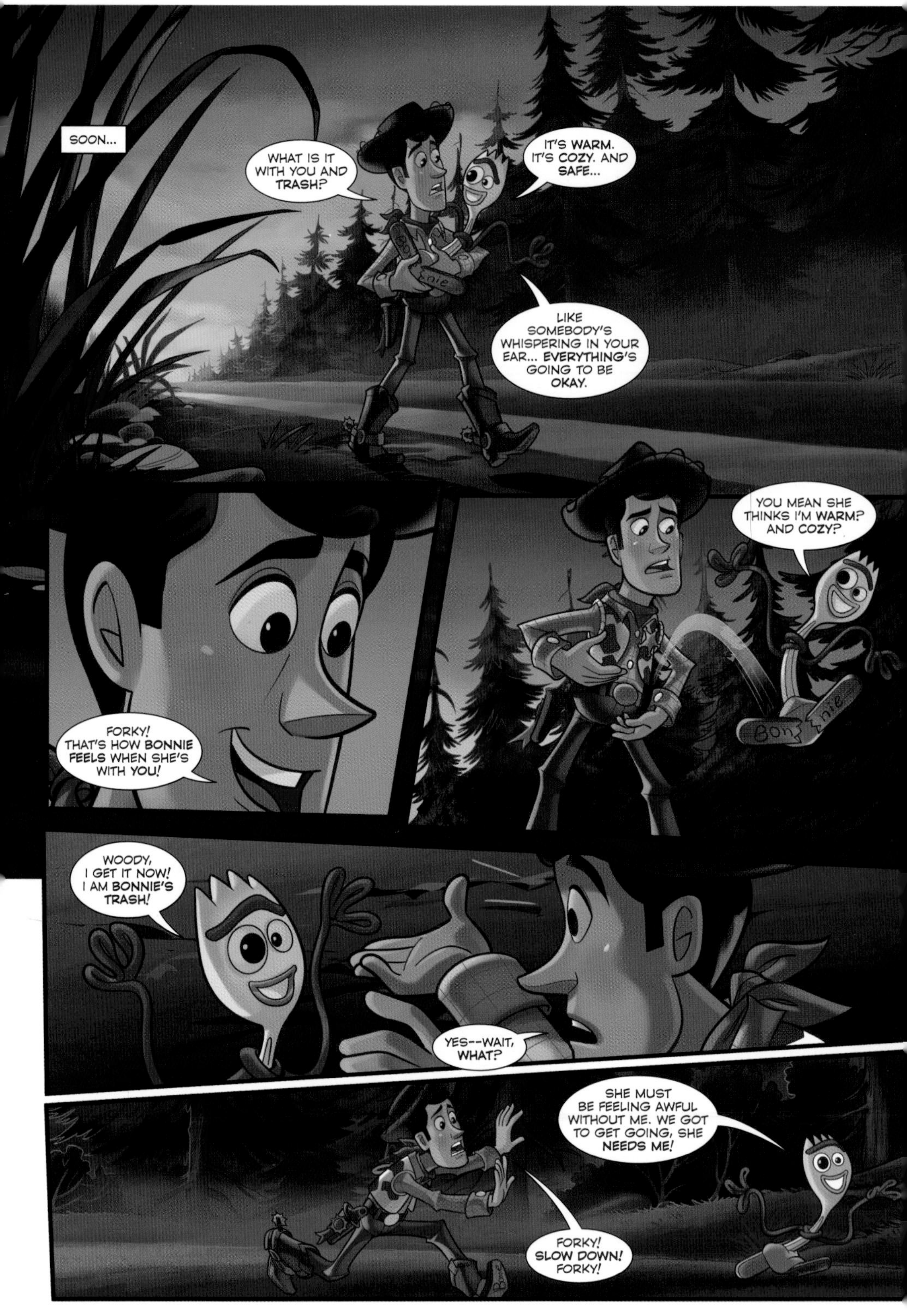
SOON...
WHAT IS IT WITH YOU AND TRASH?
IT'S WARM. IT'S COZY. AND SAFE...
LIKE SOMEBODY'S WHISPERING IN YOUR EAR... EVERYTHING'S GOING TO BE OKAY.
FORKY! THAT'S HOW BONNIE FEELS WHEN SHE'S WITH YOU!
YOU MEAN SHE THINKS I'M WARM? AND COZY?
WOODY, I GET IT NOW! I AM BONNIE'S TRASH!
YES--WAIT, WHAT?
SHE MUST BE FEELING AWFUL WITHOUT ME. WE GOT TO GET GOING, SHE NEEDS ME!
FORKY! SLOW DOWN! FORKY!

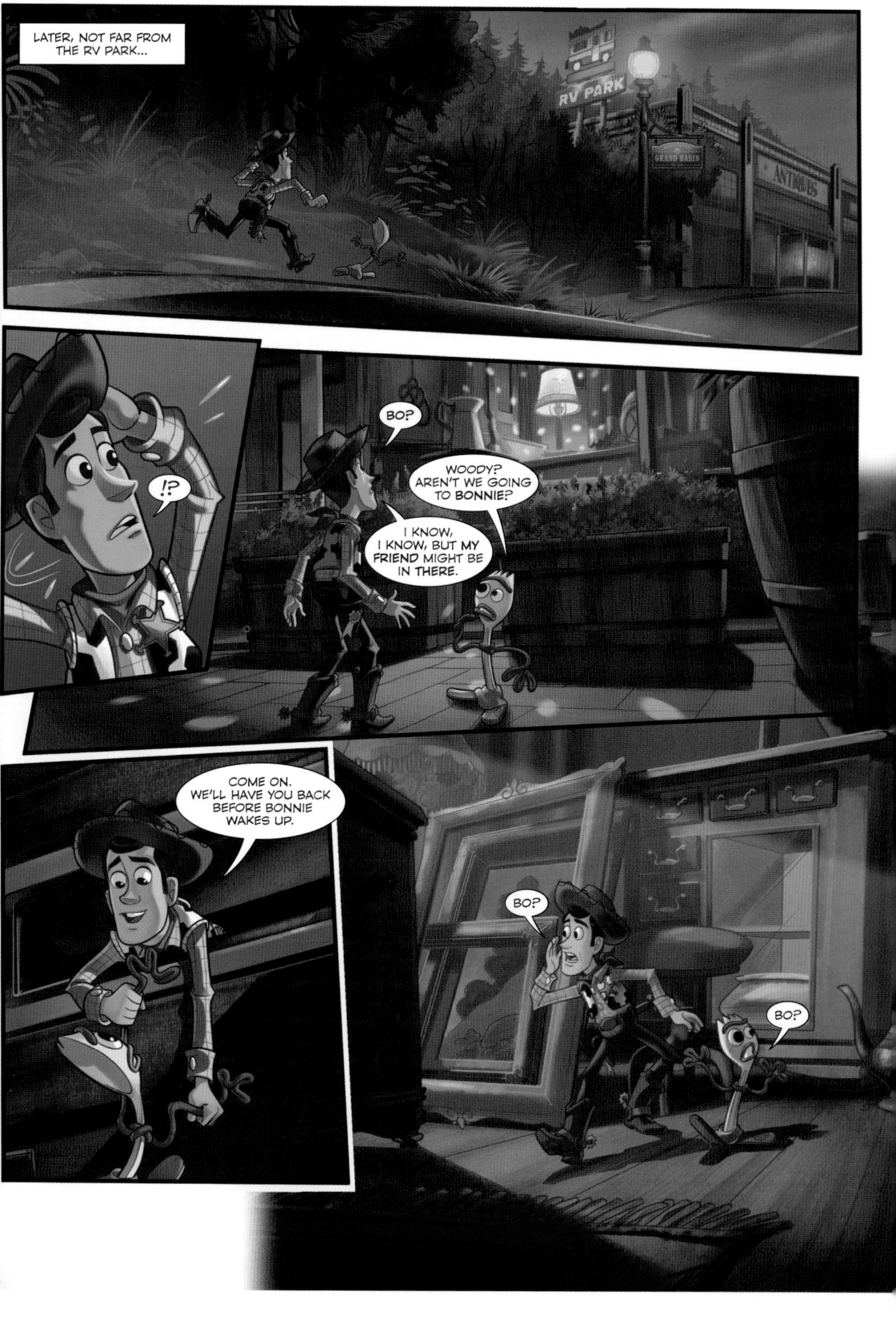
LATER, NOT FAR FROM THE RV PARK...
RV PARK
GRAND BASIN
ANTIQUES
!?
BO?
WOODY? AREN'T WE GOING TO BONNIE?
I KNOW, I KNOW, BUT MY FRIEND MIGHT BE IN THERE.
COME ON. WE'LL HAVE YOU BACK BEFORE BONNIE WAKES UP.
BO?
BO?

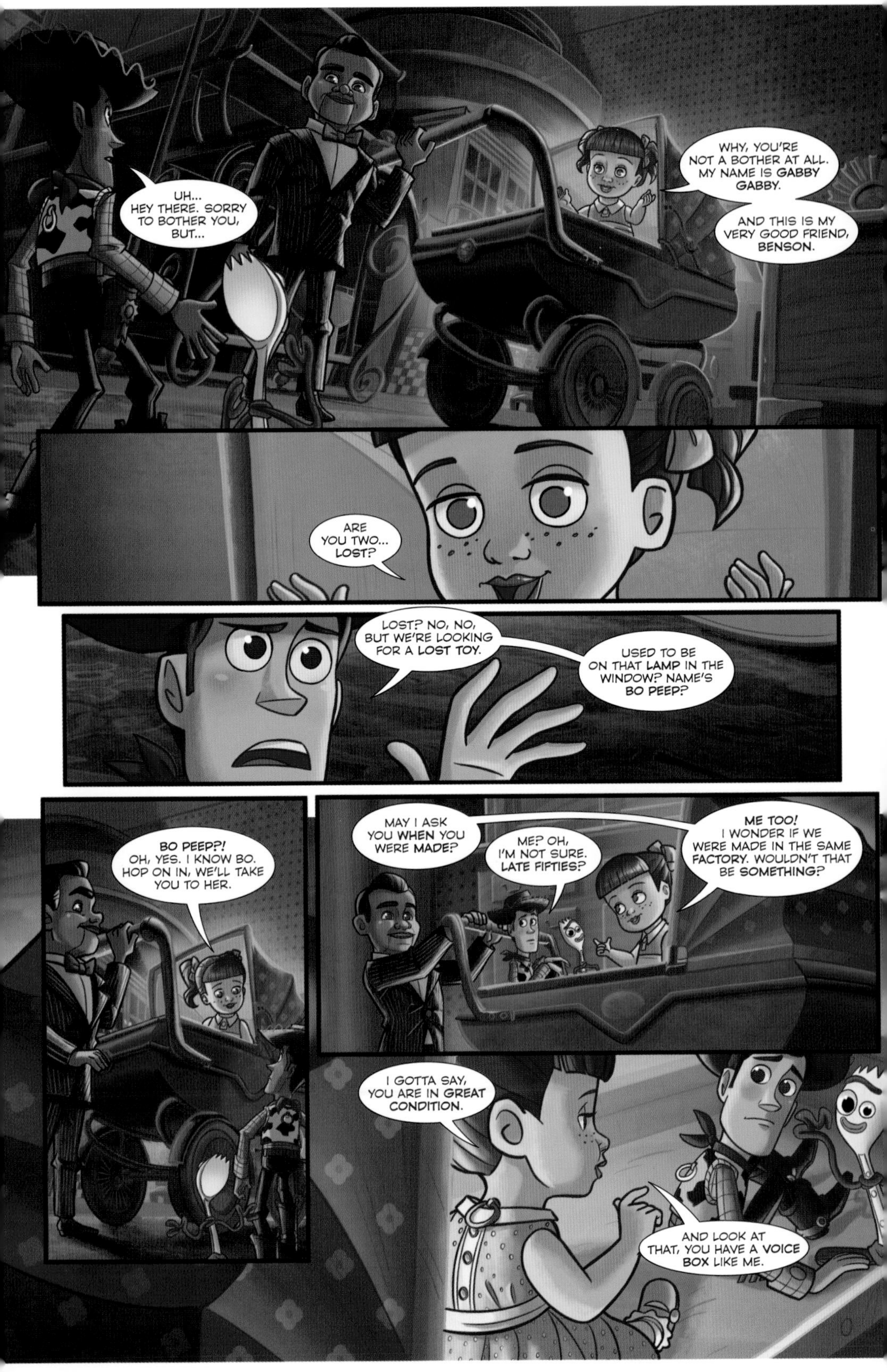
UH... HEY THERE. SORRY TO BOTHER YOU, BUT...
WHY, YOU'RE NOT A BOTHER AT ALL. MY NAME IS GABBY GABBY.
AND THIS IS MY VERY GOOD FRIEND, BENSON.
ARE YOU TWO... LOST?
LOST? NO, NO, BUT WE'RE LOOKING FOR A LOST TOY.
USED TO BE ON THAT LAMP IN THE WINDOW? NAME'S BO PEEP?
BO PEEP?! OH, YES. I KNOW BO. HOP ON IN, WE'LL TAKE YOU TO HER.
MAY I ASK YOU WHEN YOU WERE MADE?
ME? OH, I'M NOT SURE. LATE FIFTIES?
ME TOO! I WONDER IF WE WERE MADE IN THE SAME FACTORY. WOULDN'T THAT BE SOMETHING?
I GOTTA SAY, YOU ARE IN GREAT CONDITION.
AND LOOK AT THAT, YOU HAVE A VOICE BOX LIKE ME.

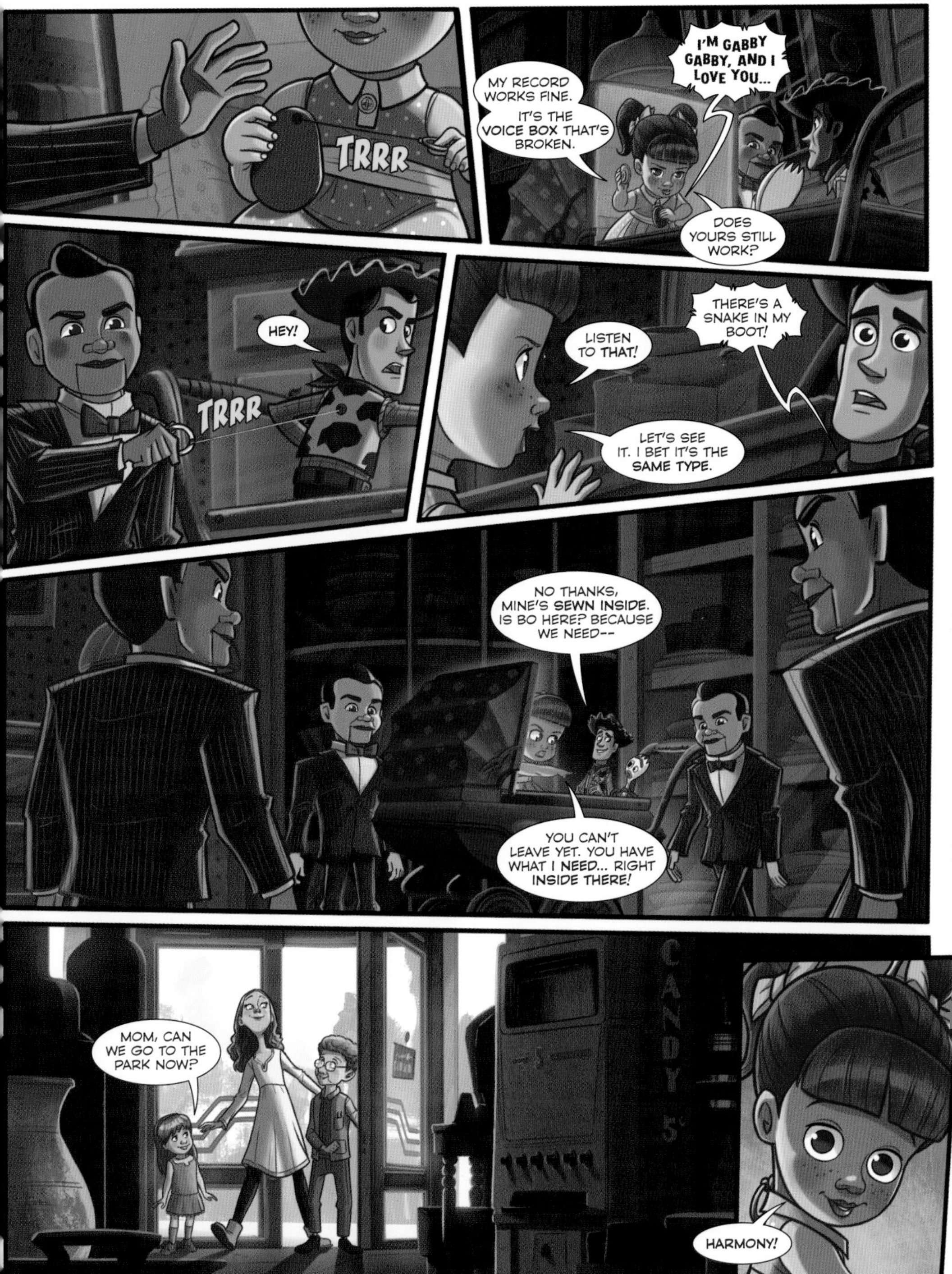

TRRR
MY RECORD WORKS FINE.
IT'S THE VOICE BOX THAT'S BROKEN.
I'M GABBY GABBY, AND I LOVE YOU...
DOES YOURS STILL WORK?
HEY!
TRRR
LISTEN TO THAT!
THERE'S A SNAKE IN MY BOOT!
LET'S SEE IT. I BET IT'S THE SAME TYPE.
NO THANKS, MINE'S SEWN INSIDE. IS BO HERE? BECAUSE WE NEED--
YOU CAN'T LEAVE YET. YOU HAVE WHAT I NEED... RIGHT INSIDE THERE!
MOM, CAN WE GO TO THE PARK NOW?
CANDY 5¢
HARMONY!

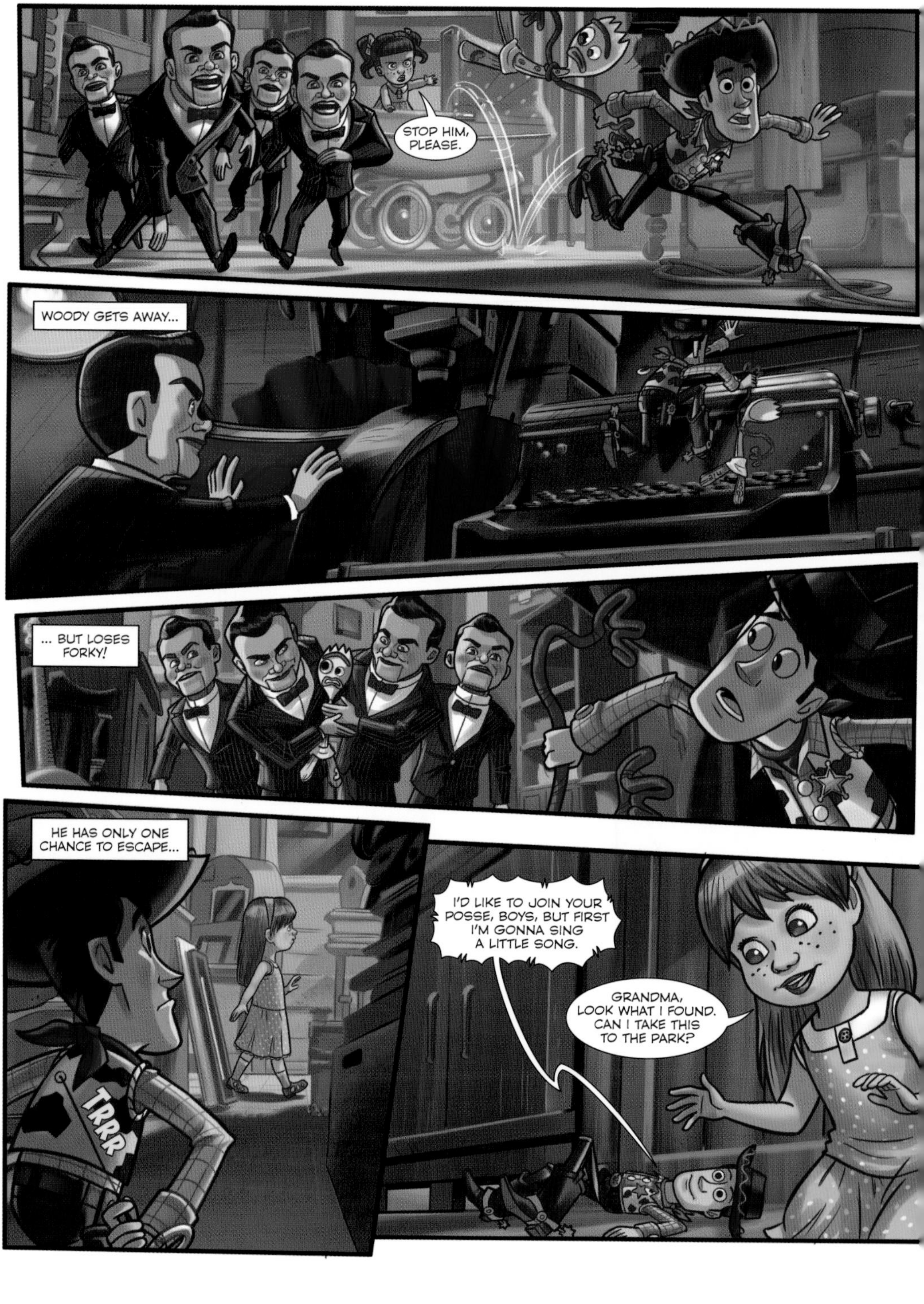
STOP HIM, PLEASE.
WOODY GETS AWAY...
... BUT LOSES FORKY!
HE HAS ONLY ONE CHANCE TO ESCAPE...
TRRR
I'D LIKE TO JOIN YOUR POSSE, BOYS, BUT FIRST I'M GONNA SING A LITTLE SONG.
GRANDMA, LOOK WHAT I FOUND. CAN I TAKE THIS TO THE PARK?

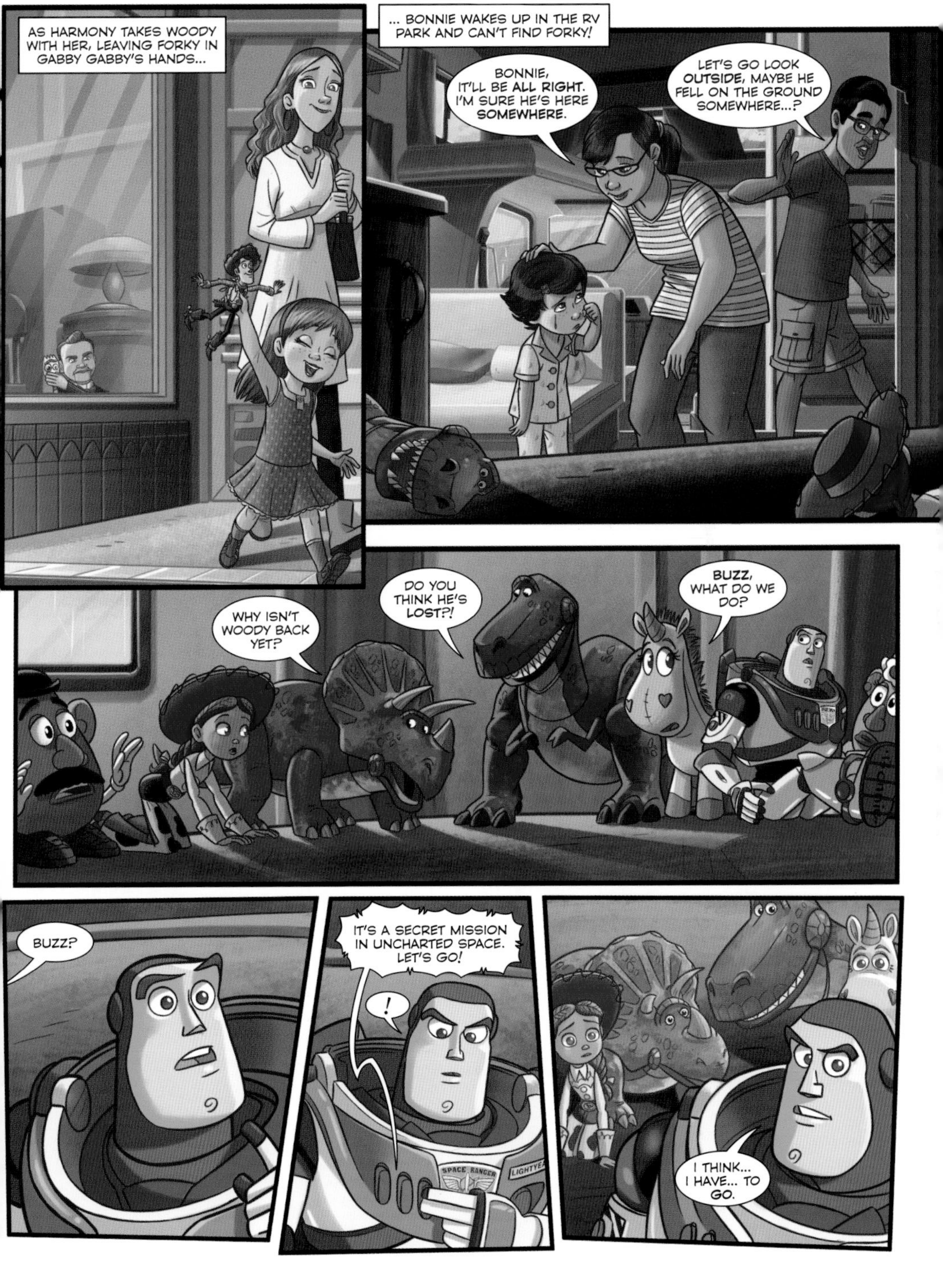

AS HARMONY TAKES WOODY WITH HER, LEAVING FORKY IN GABBY GABBY'S HANDS...
... BONNIE WAKES UP IN THE RV PARK AND CAN'T FIND FORKY!
BONNIE, IT'LL BE **ALL RIGHT**. I'M SURE HE'S HERE **SOMEWHERE**.
LET'S GO LOOK **OUTSIDE**, MAYBE HE FELL ON THE GROUND SOMEWHERE...?
WHY ISN'T WOODY BACK YET?
DO YOU THINK HE'S **LOST**?!
BUZZ, WHAT DO WE DO?
BUZZ?
IT'S A SECRET MISSION IN UNCHARTED SPACE. LET'S GO!
!
I THINK... I HAVE... TO **GO**.

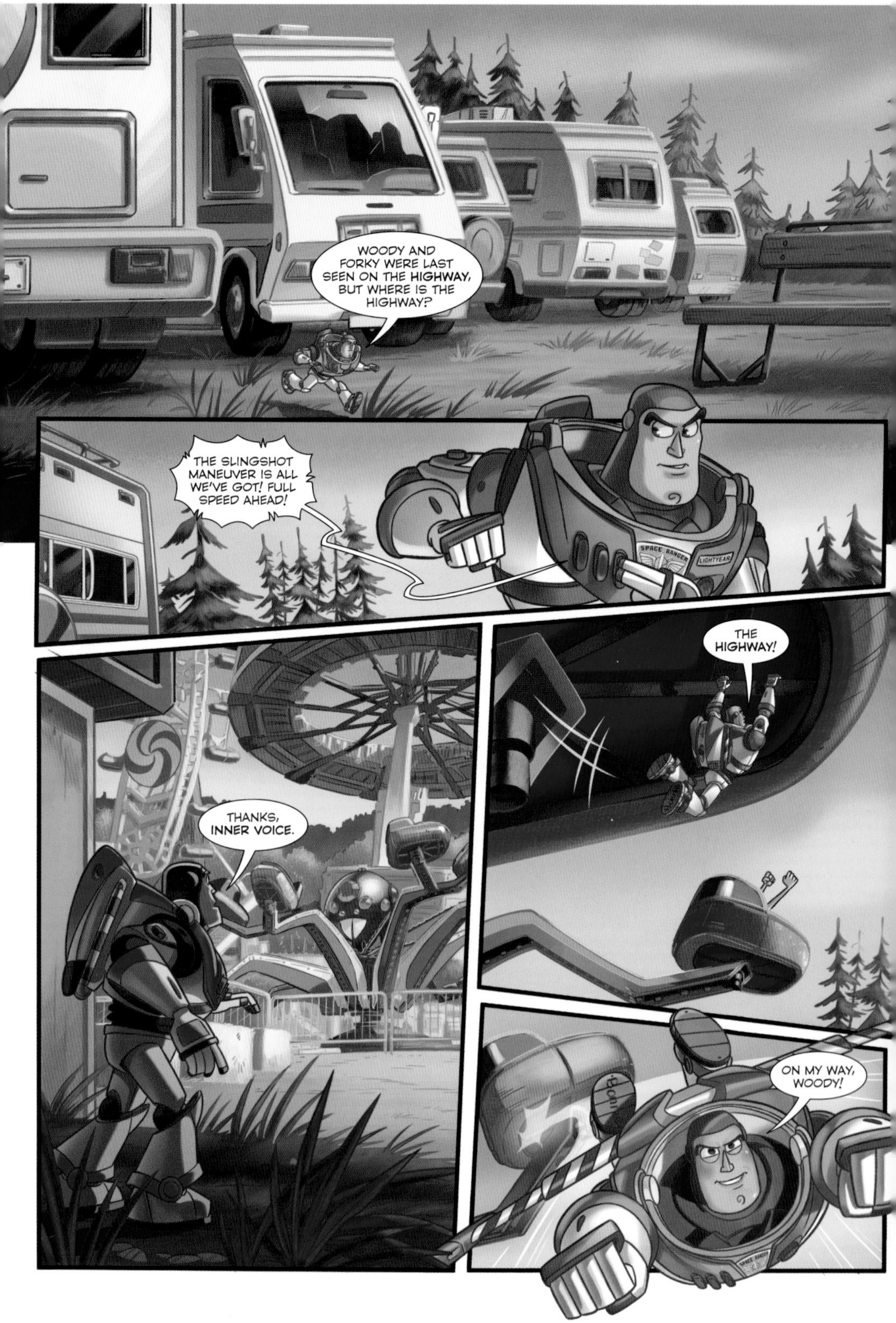

WOODY AND FORKY WERE LAST SEEN ON THE HIGHWAY, BUT WHERE IS THE HIGHWAY?
THE SLINGSHOT MANEUVER IS ALL WE'VE GOT! FULL SPEED AHEAD!
THANKS, INNER VOICE.
THE HIGHWAY!
ON MY WAY, WOODY!

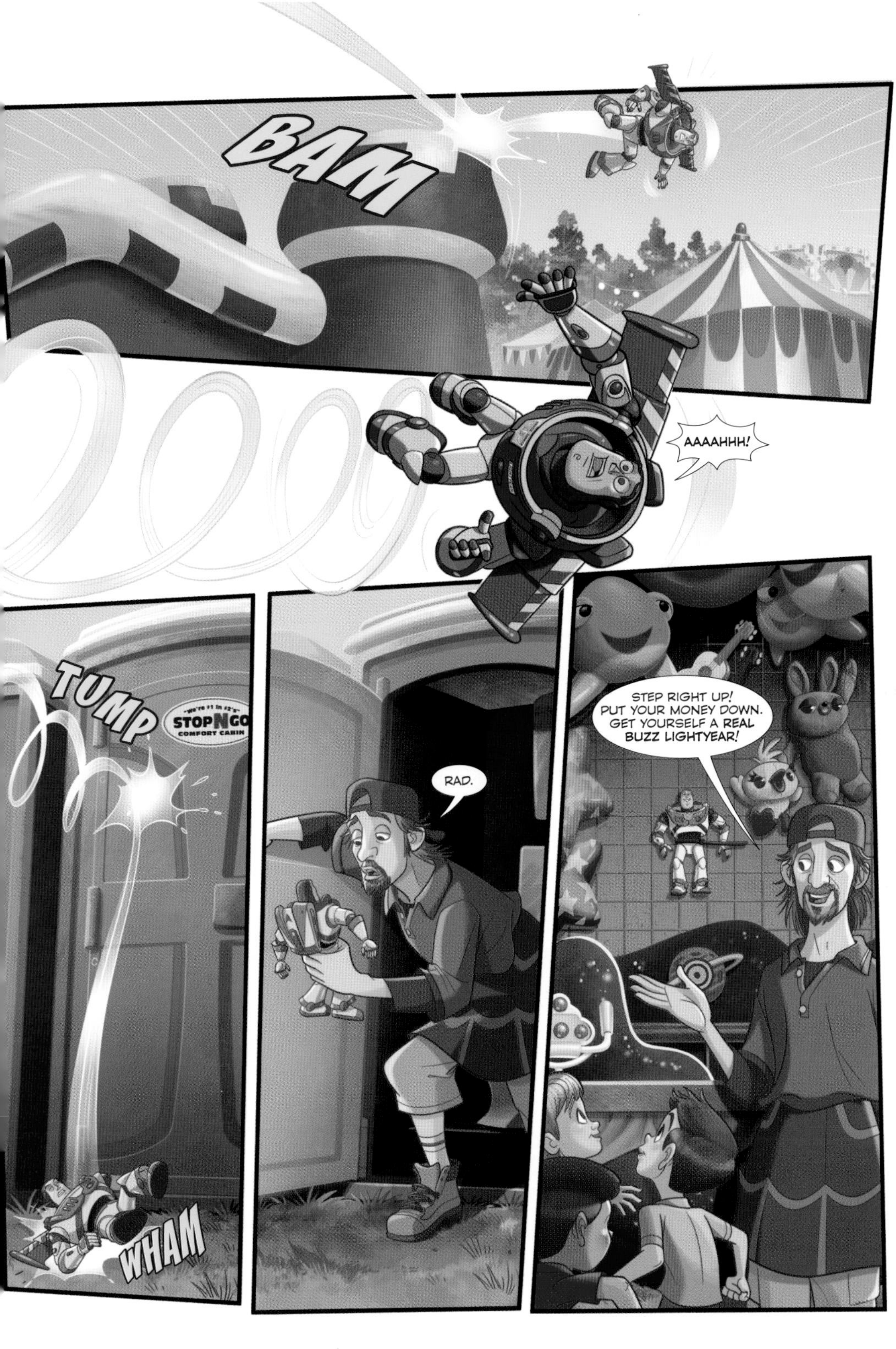
BAM
AAAAHHH!
TUMP
We're #1 in #2's
STOPNGO
COMFORT CABIN
WHAM
RAD.
STEP RIGHT UP! PUT YOUR MONEY DOWN. GET YOURSELF A REAL BUZZ LIGHTYEAR!

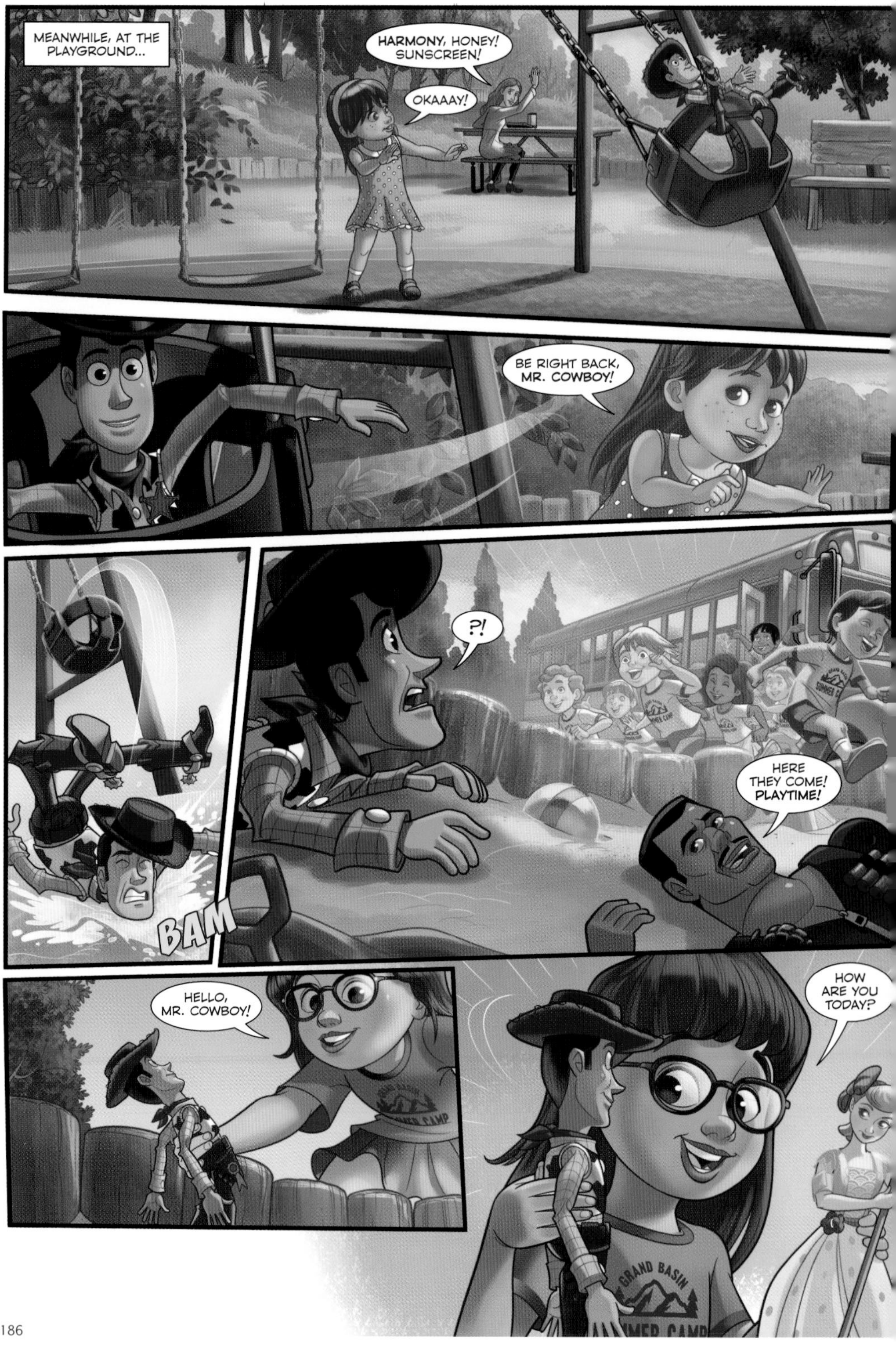
MEANWHILE, AT THE PLAYGROUND...
HARMONY, HONEY! SUNSCREEN!
OKAAAY!
BE RIGHT BACK, MR. COWBOY!
BAM
?!
HERE THEY COME! PLAYTIME!
HELLO, MR. COWBOY!
HOW ARE YOU TODAY?
GRAND BASIN SUMMER CAMP

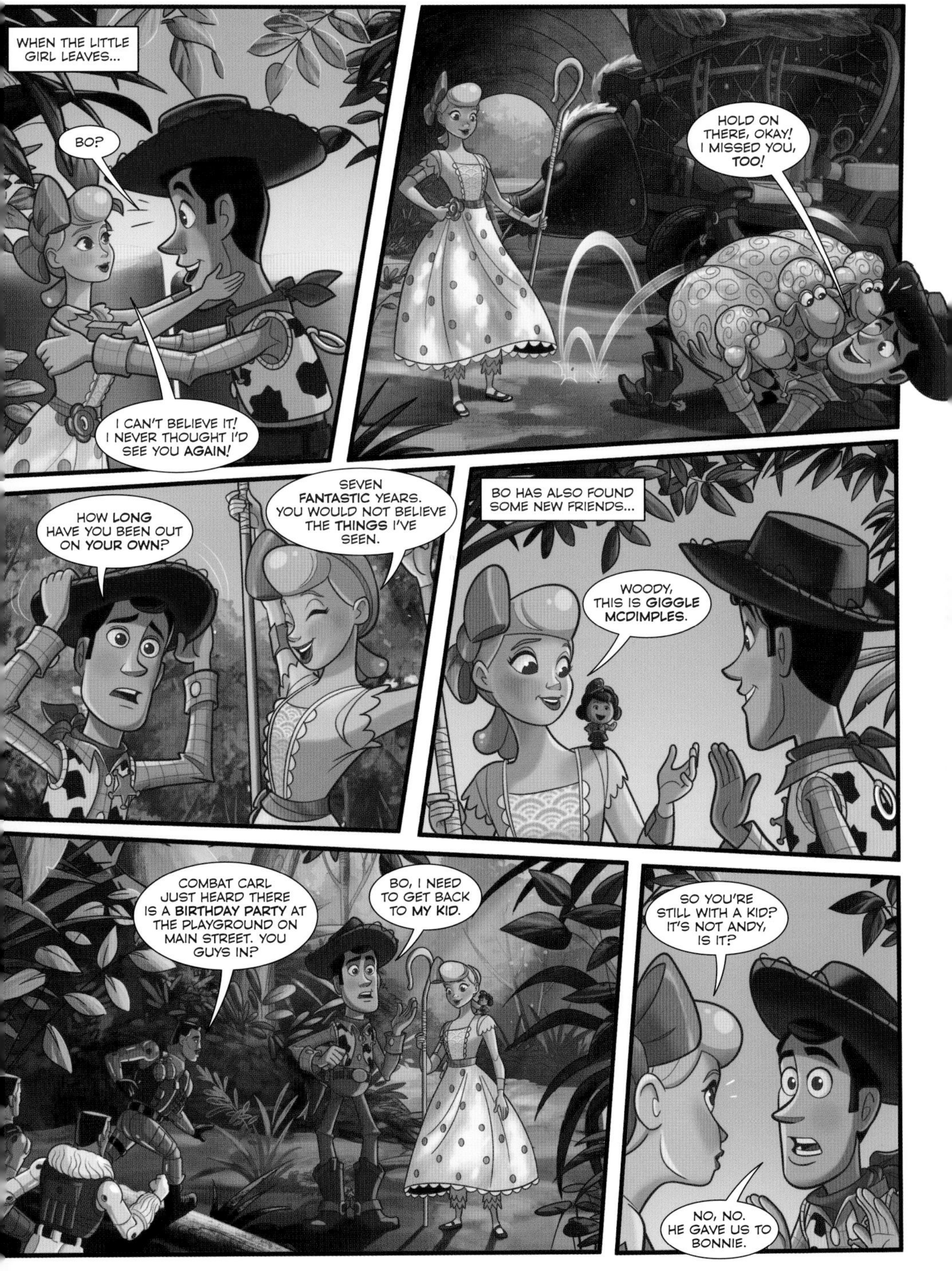
WHEN THE LITTLE GIRL LEAVES...
BO?
I CAN'T BELIEVE IT! I NEVER THOUGHT I'D SEE YOU AGAIN!
HOLD ON THERE, OKAY! I MISSED YOU, TOO!
HOW LONG HAVE YOU BEEN OUT ON YOUR OWN?
SEVEN FANTASTIC YEARS. YOU WOULD NOT BELIEVE THE THINGS I'VE SEEN.
BO HAS ALSO FOUND SOME NEW FRIENDS...
WOODY, THIS IS GIGGLE MCDIMPLES.
COMBAT CARL JUST HEARD THERE IS A BIRTHDAY PARTY AT THE PLAYGROUND ON MAIN STREET. YOU GUYS IN?
BO, I NEED TO GET BACK TO MY KID.
SO YOU'RE STILL WITH A KID? IT'S NOT ANDY, IS IT?
NO, NO. HE GAVE US TO BONNIE.

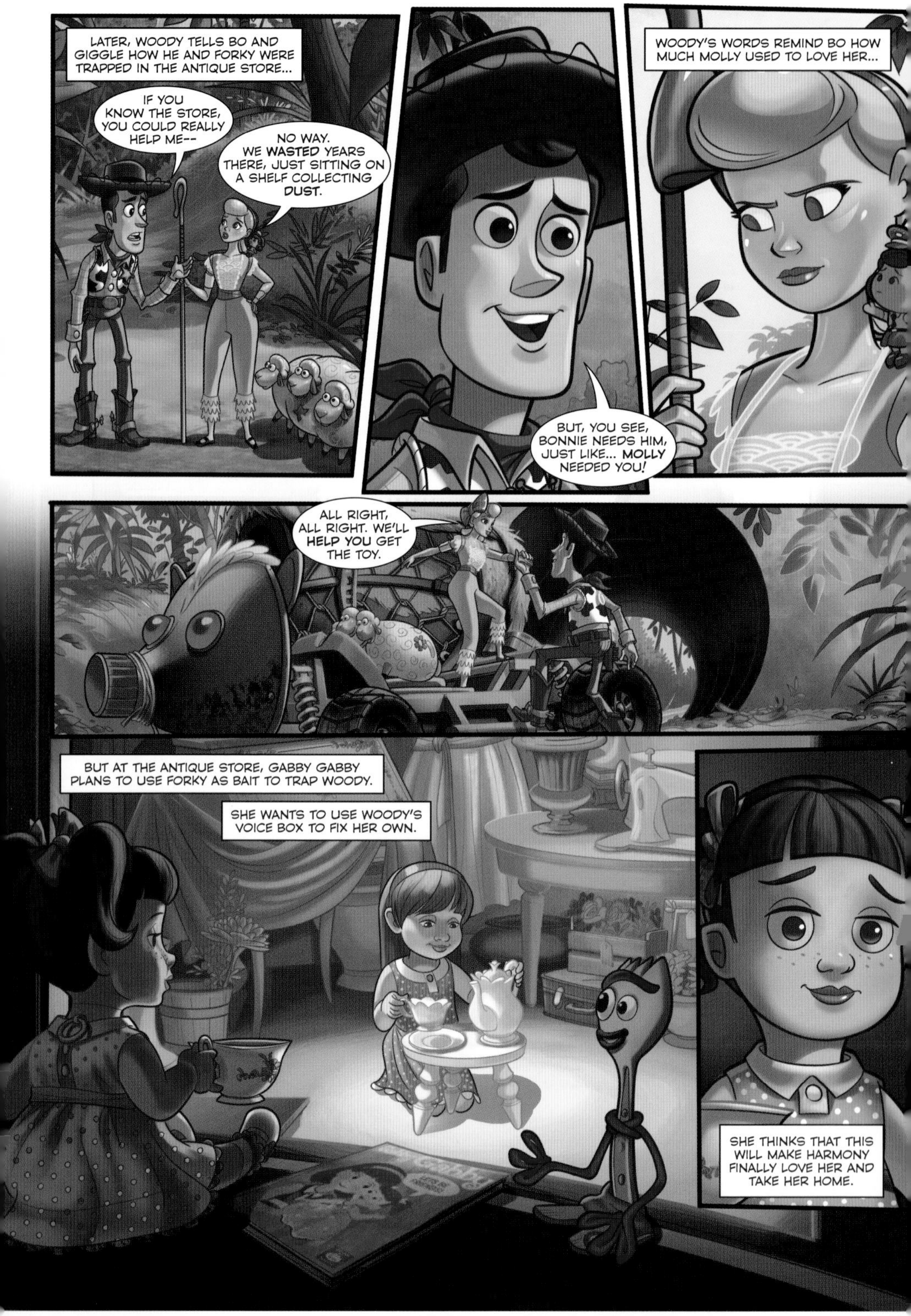
LATER, WOODY TELLS BO AND GIGGLE HOW HE AND FORKY WERE TRAPPED IN THE ANTIQUE STORE...
IF YOU KNOW THE STORE, YOU COULD REALLY HELP ME--
NO WAY. WE WASTED YEARS THERE, JUST SITTING ON A SHELF COLLECTING DUST.
BUT, YOU SEE, BONNIE NEEDS HIM, JUST LIKE... MOLLY NEEDED YOU!
WOODY'S WORDS REMIND BO HOW MUCH MOLLY USED TO LOVE HER...
ALL RIGHT, ALL RIGHT. WE'LL HELP YOU GET THE TOY.
BUT AT THE ANTIQUE STORE, GABBY GABBY PLANS TO USE FORKY AS BAIT TO TRAP WOODY.
SHE WANTS TO USE WOODY'S VOICE BOX TO FIX HER OWN.
SHE THINKS THAT THIS WILL MAKE HARMONY FINALLY LOVE HER AND TAKE HER HOME.

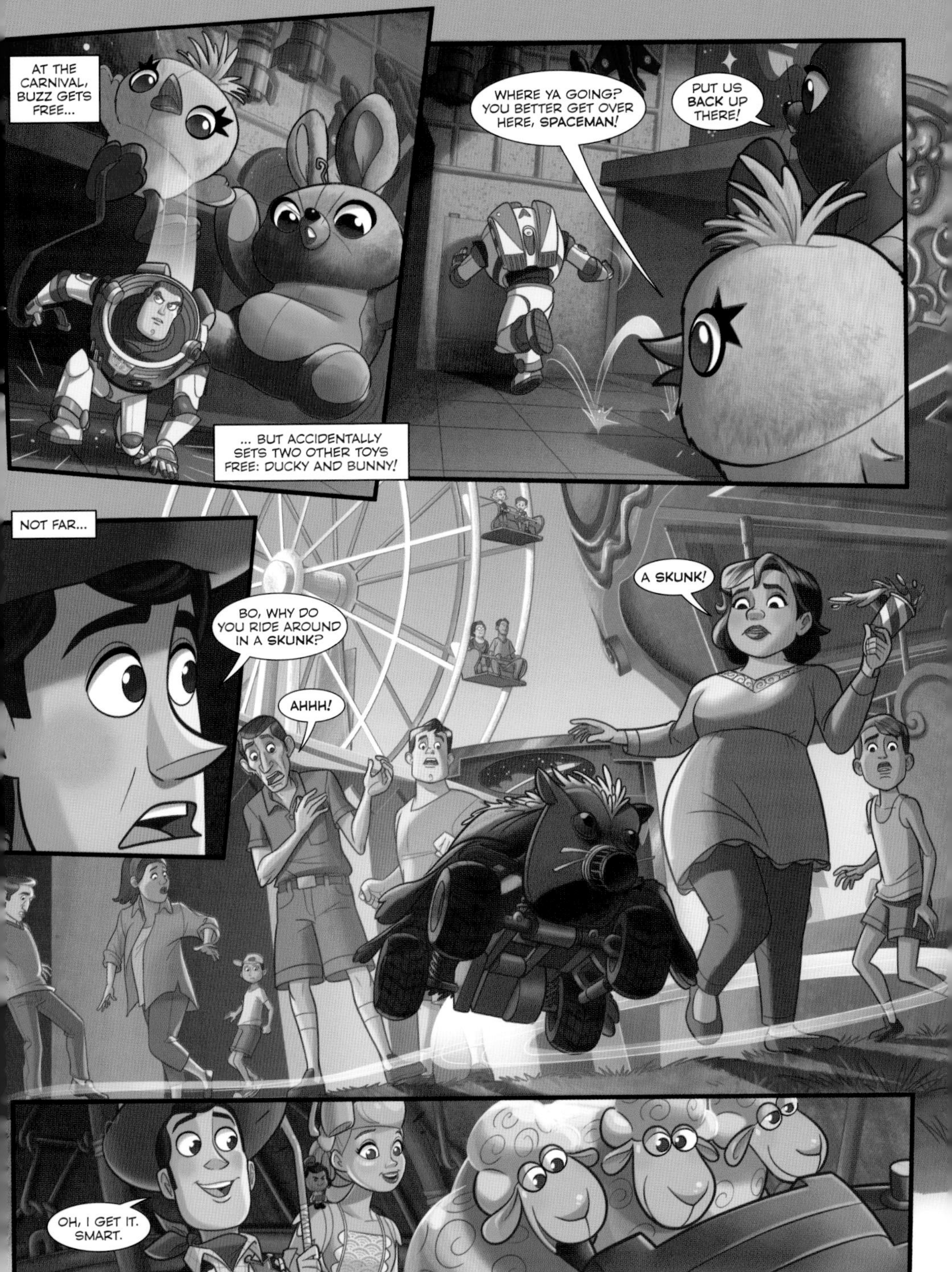
AT THE CARNIVAL, BUZZ GETS FREE...
... BUT ACCIDENTALLY SETS TWO OTHER TOYS FREE: DUCKY AND BUNNY!
WHERE YA GOING? YOU BETTER GET OVER HERE, SPACEMAN!
PUT US BACK UP THERE!
NOT FAR...
BO, WHY DO YOU RIDE AROUND IN A SKUNK?
AHHH!
A SKUNK!
OH, I GET IT. SMART.

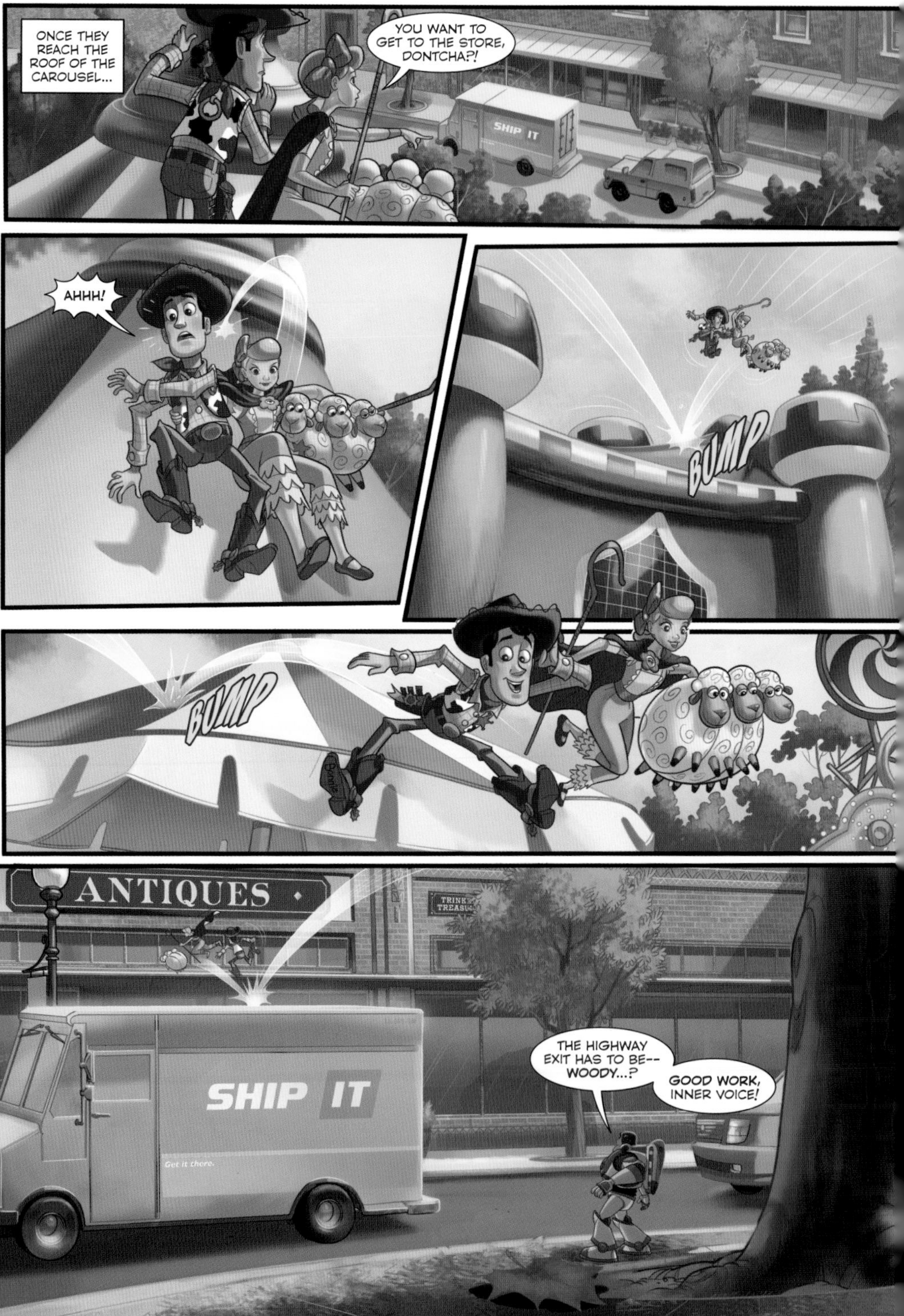
ONCE THEY REACH THE ROOF OF THE CAROUSEL...
YOU WANT TO GET TO THE STORE, DONTCHA?!
SHIP IT
AHHH!
BUMP
BUMP
ANTIQUES
SHIP IT
Get it there.
THE HIGHWAY EXIT HAS TO BE-- WOODY...?
GOOD WORK, INNER VOICE!

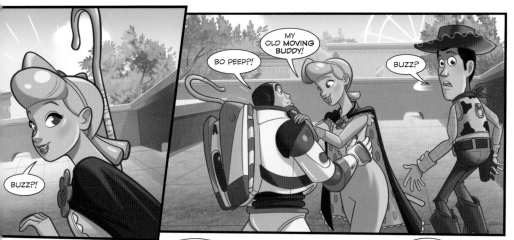

BUZZ?!

BO PEEP?!

MY OLD MOVING BUDDY!

BUZZ?

WOODY, IT'S *BO!!!* WHAT ARE YOU DOING OUT HERE?

WHAT ARE YOU DOING HERE?

AAAAHHH!

SBAM

YOU'VE RUINED OUR LIVES!

THREE YEARS! THAT'S HOW LONG WE'VE BEEN HANGING UP THERE WAITING FOR A KID!

COME ON, STOP IT!

LOOK, I'M SORRY ABOUT THAT...

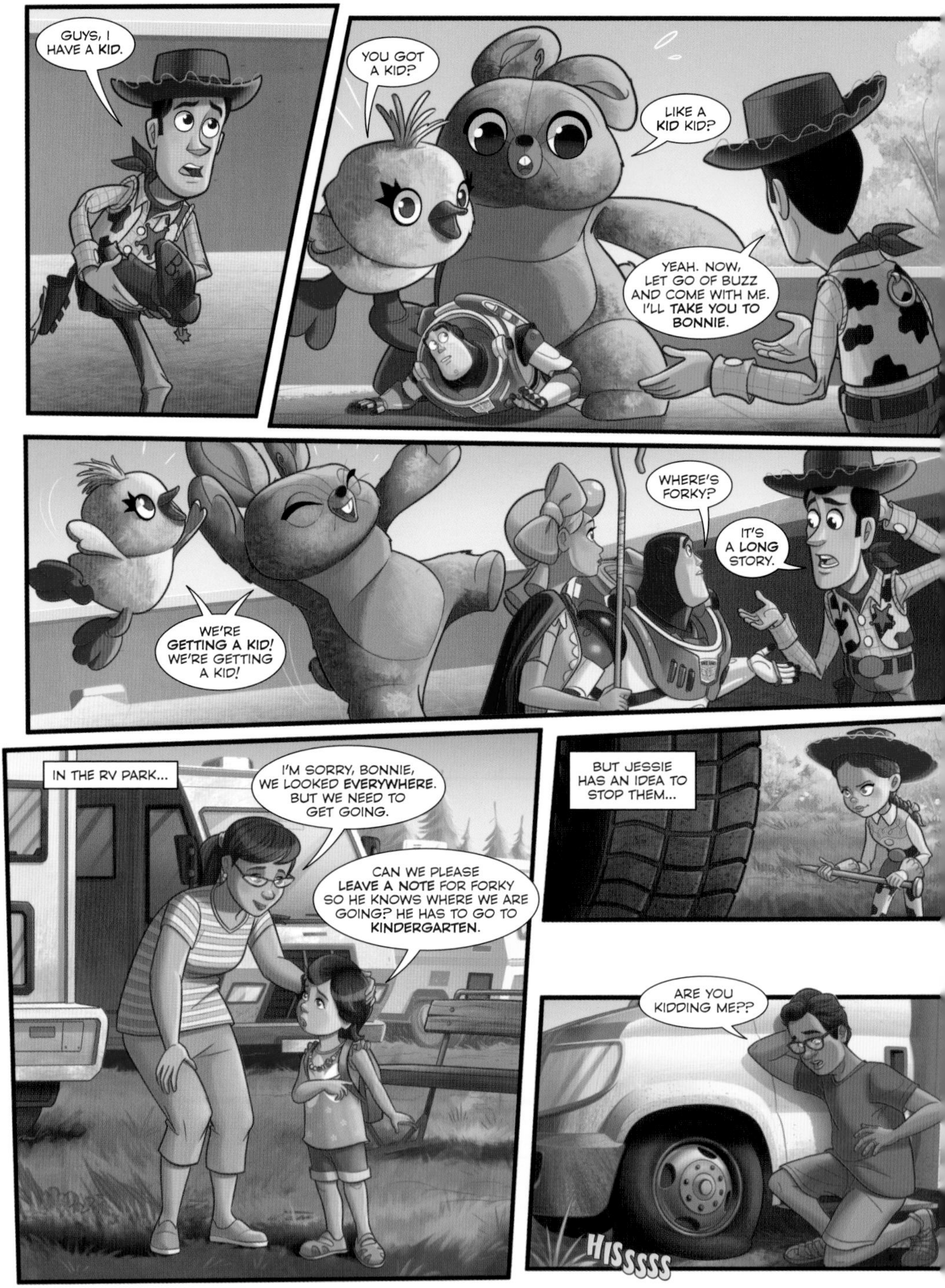
GUYS, I HAVE A KID.
YOU GOT A KID?
LIKE A KID KID?
YEAH. NOW, LET GO OF BUZZ AND COME WITH ME. I'LL TAKE YOU TO BONNIE.
WE'RE GETTING A KID! WE'RE GETTING A KID!
WHERE'S FORKY?
IT'S A LONG STORY.
IN THE RV PARK...
I'M SORRY, BONNIE, WE LOOKED EVERYWHERE. BUT WE NEED TO GET GOING.
CAN WE PLEASE LEAVE A NOTE FOR FORKY SO HE KNOWS WHERE WE ARE GOING? HE HAS TO GO TO KINDERGARTEN.
BUT JESSIE HAS AN IDEA TO STOP THEM...
ARE YOU KIDDING ME??
HISSSSS

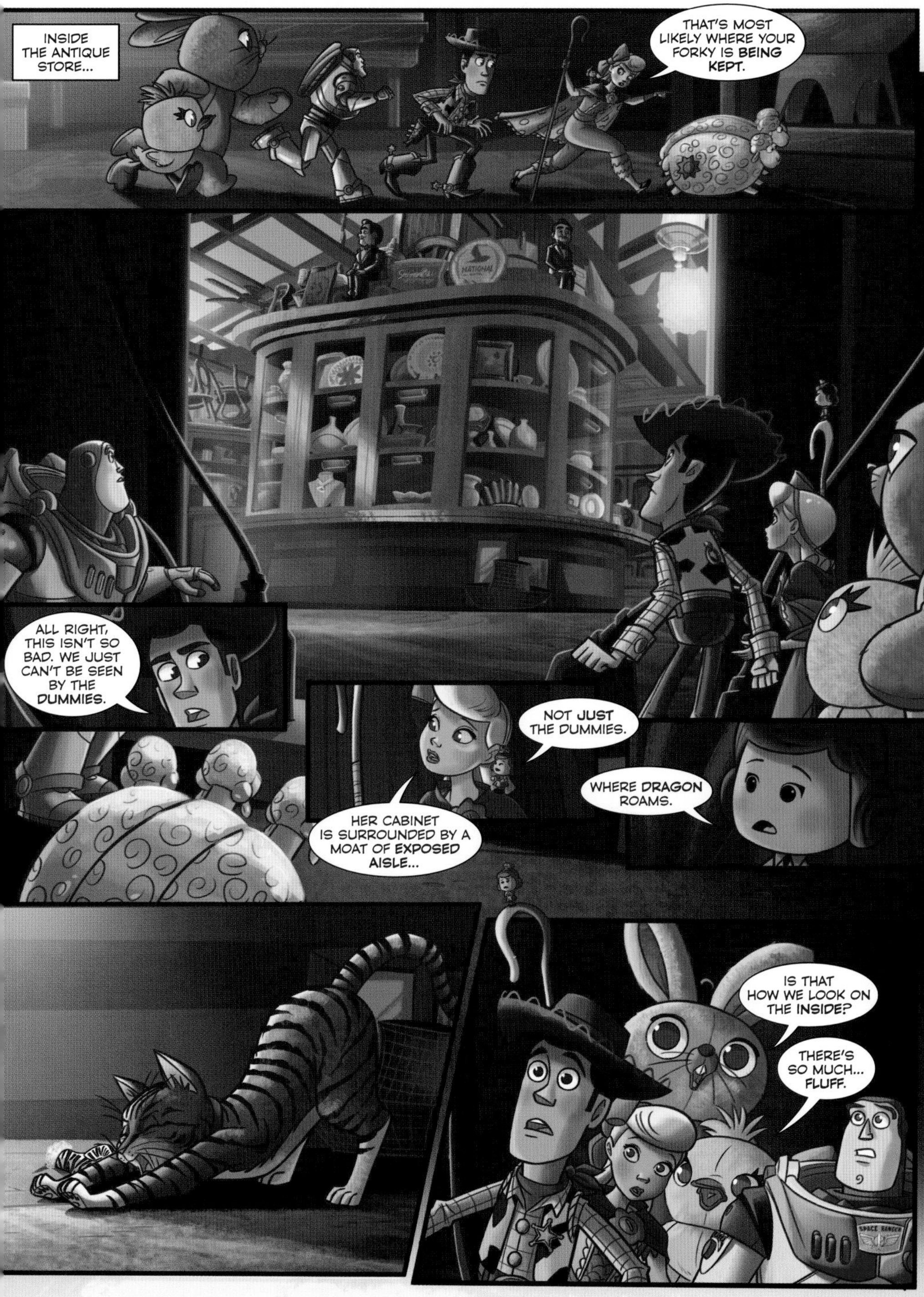
INSIDE THE ANTIQUE STORE...
THAT'S MOST LIKELY WHERE YOUR FORKY IS **BEING KEPT**.
ALL RIGHT, THIS ISN'T SO BAD. WE JUST CAN'T BE SEEN BY THE **DUMMIES**.
NOT **JUST** THE DUMMIES.
HER CABINET IS SURROUNDED BY A MOAT OF **EXPOSED AISLE**...
WHERE **DRAGON** ROAMS.
IS THAT HOW WE LOOK ON THE **INSIDE**?
THERE'S SO MUCH... **FLUFF**.

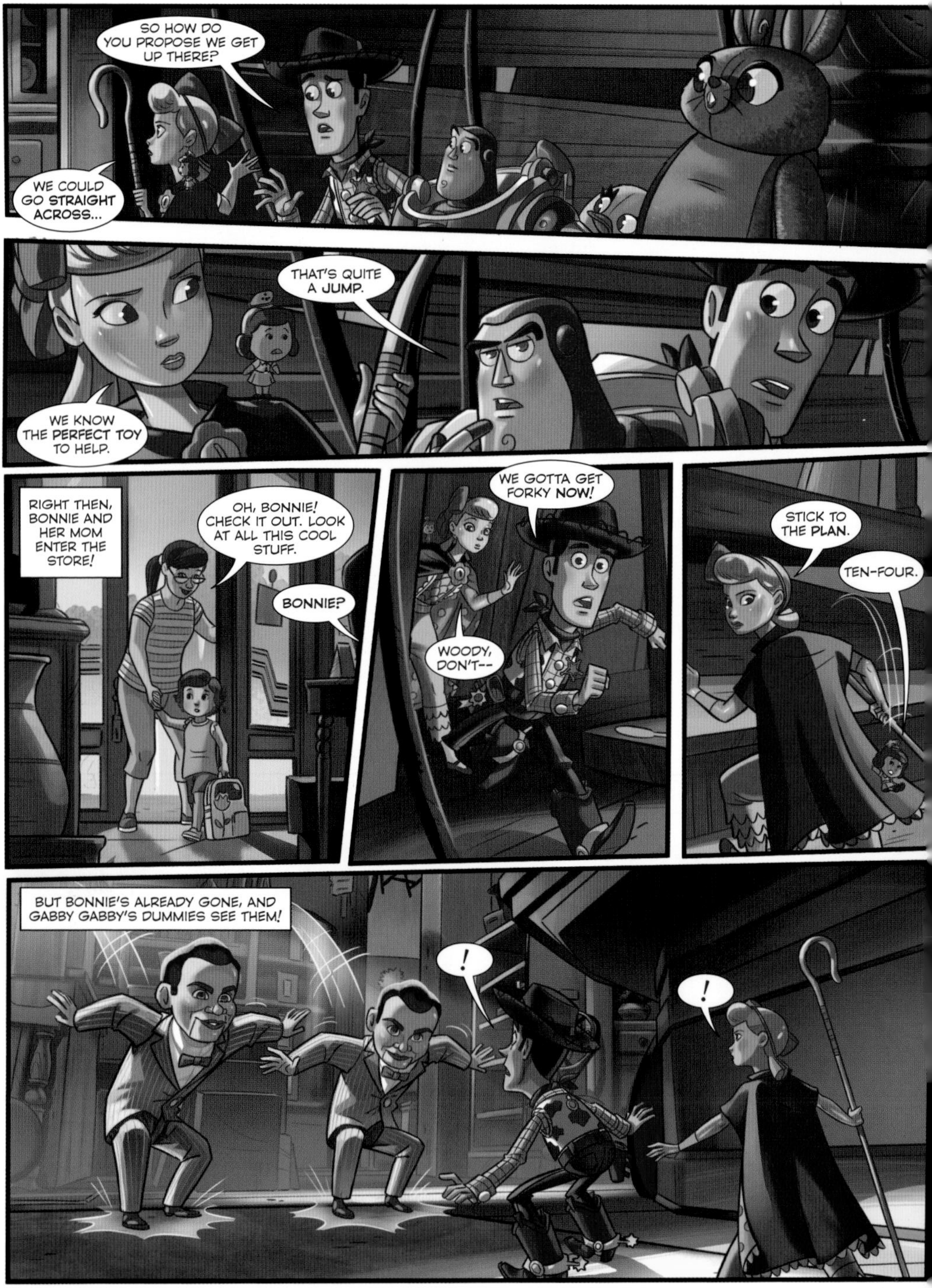
SO HOW DO YOU PROPOSE WE GET UP THERE?
WE COULD GO STRAIGHT ACROSS...
THAT'S QUITE A JUMP.
WE KNOW THE PERFECT TOY TO HELP.
RIGHT THEN, BONNIE AND HER MOM ENTER THE STORE!
OH, BONNIE! CHECK IT OUT. LOOK AT ALL THIS COOL STUFF.
BONNIE?
WE GOTTA GET FORKY NOW!
WOODY, DON'T--
STICK TO THE PLAN.
TEN-FOUR.
BUT BONNIE'S ALREADY GONE, AND GABBY GABBY'S DUMMIES SEE THEM!
!
!

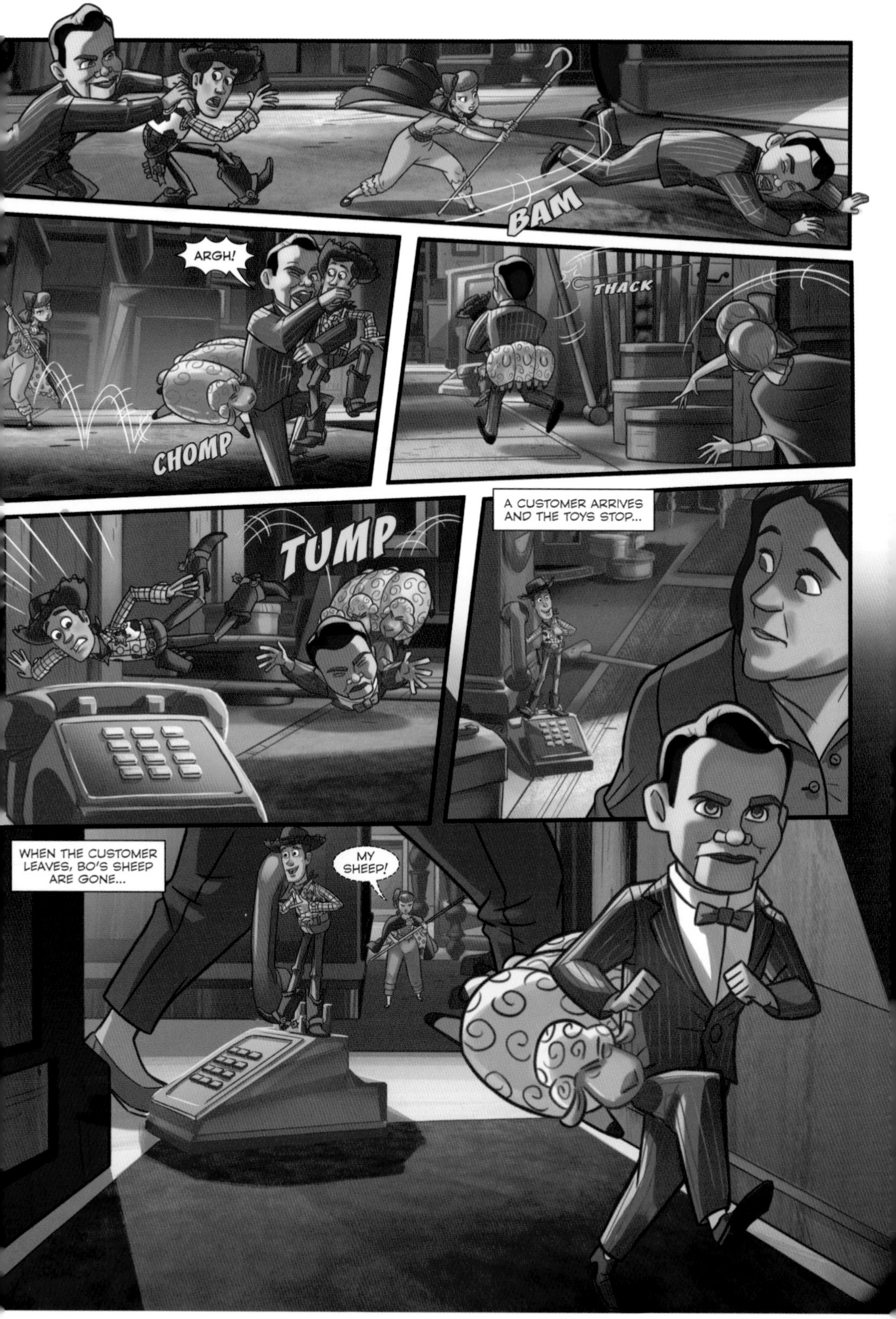
BAM
ARGH!
CHOMP
THACK
TUMP
A CUSTOMER ARRIVES AND THE TOYS STOP...
WHEN THE CUSTOMER LEAVES, BO'S SHEEP ARE GONE...
MY SHEEP!

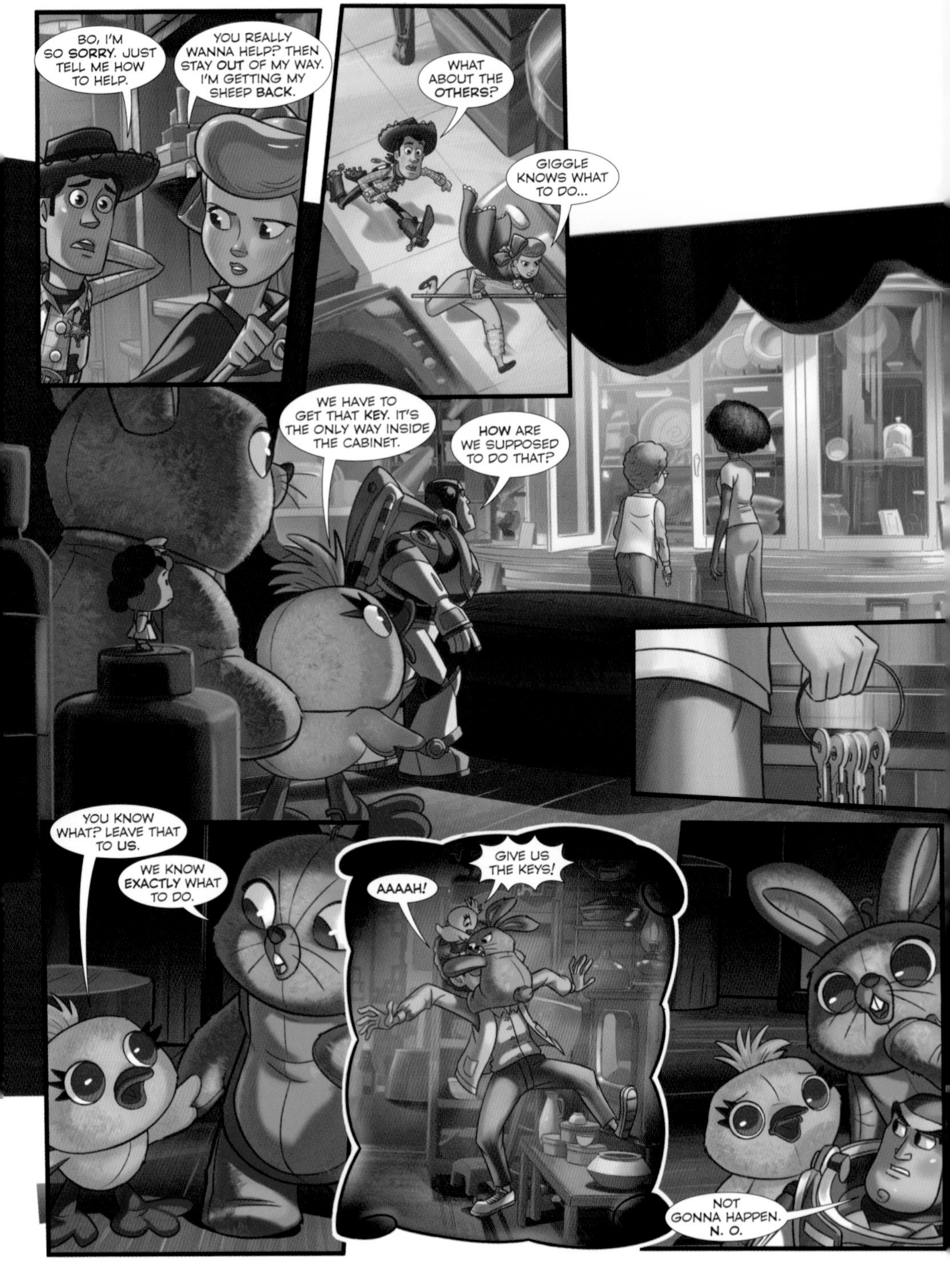
BO, I'M SO SORRY. JUST TELL ME HOW TO HELP.
YOU REALLY WANNA HELP? THEN STAY OUT OF MY WAY. I'M GETTING MY SHEEP BACK.
WHAT ABOUT THE OTHERS?
GIGGLE KNOWS WHAT TO DO...
WE HAVE TO GET THAT KEY. IT'S THE ONLY WAY INSIDE THE CABINET.
HOW ARE WE SUPPOSED TO DO THAT?
YOU KNOW WHAT? LEAVE THAT TO US.
WE KNOW EXACTLY WHAT TO DO.
GIVE US THE KEYS!
AAAAH!
NOT GONNA HAPPEN. N. O.

NOT FAR, BO TAKES WOODY INSIDE A PINBALL MACHINE...

BO! COULDN'T TAKE IT OUT THERE, HUH?

...TO MEET HER OLD FRIEND DUKE CABOOM, CANADA'S GREATEST STUNTMAN!

WHAT BRINGS YOU BACK, PEEP?

WE NEED YOUR HELP. GABBY GABBY HAS HIS TOY AND MY SHEEP. WE NEED TO JUMP OVER THE AISLE TO HER CABINET. AND YOU ARE THE TOY TO DO IT.

NOPE.

BUT--

NO WAY!

BUT--

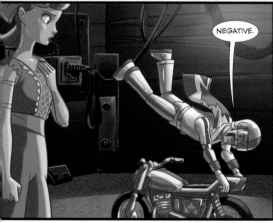

NEGATIVE.

PLEASE, MR. DUKE CABOOM, THIS IS REALLY IMPORTANT. MY KID--

YOU HAVE A KID?

I HAD A KID... REJEAN.

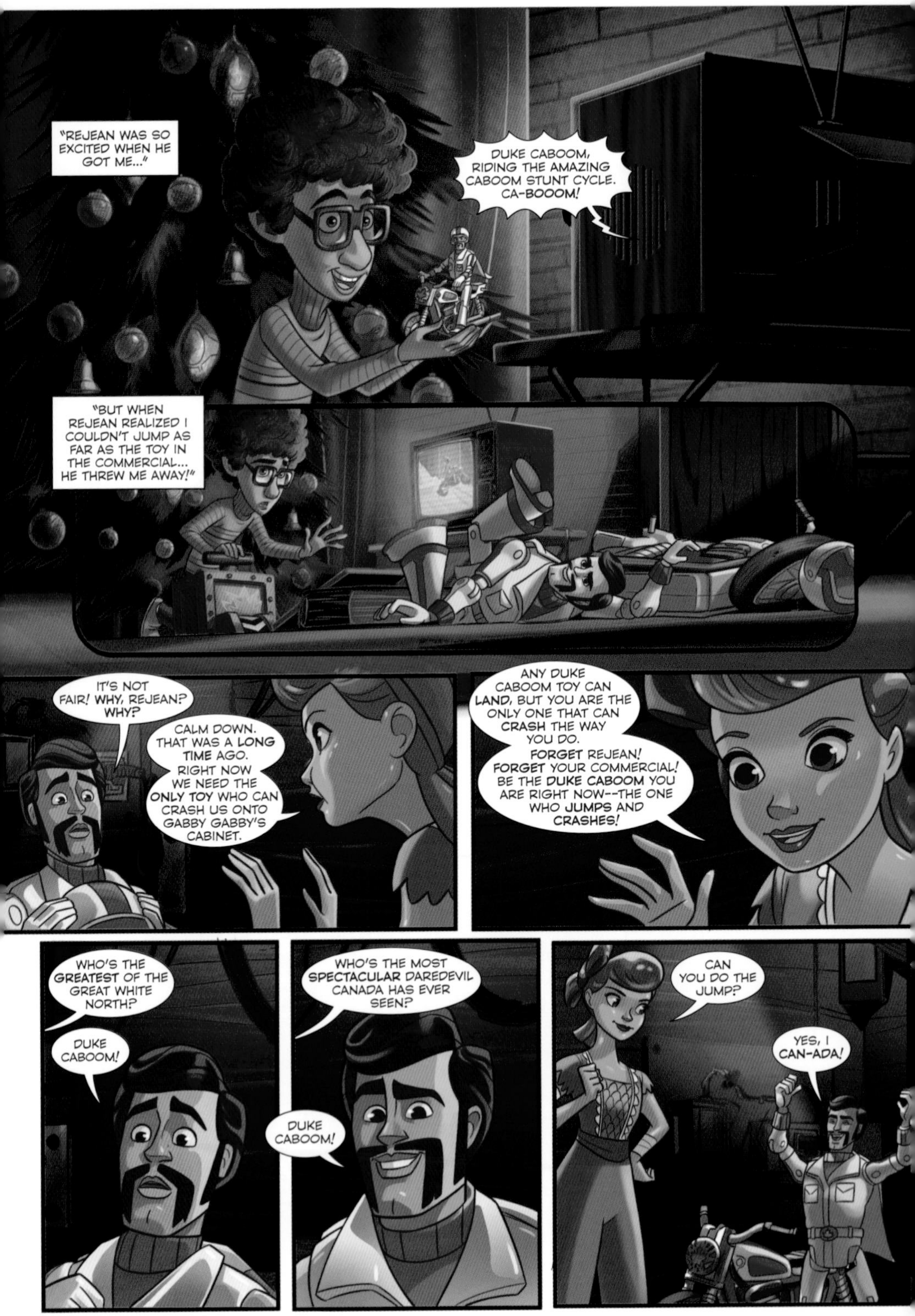
"REJEAN WAS SO EXCITED WHEN HE GOT ME..."
DUKE CABOOM, RIDING THE AMAZING CABOOM STUNT CYCLE. CA-BOOOM!
"BUT WHEN REJEAN REALIZED I COULDN'T JUMP AS FAR AS THE TOY IN THE COMMERCIAL... HE THREW ME AWAY!"
IT'S NOT FAIR! WHY, REJEAN? WHY?
CALM DOWN. THAT WAS A LONG TIME AGO. RIGHT NOW WE NEED THE ONLY TOY WHO CAN CRASH US ONTO GABBY GABBY'S CABINET.
ANY DUKE CABOOM TOY CAN LAND, BUT YOU ARE THE ONLY ONE THAT CAN CRASH THE WAY YOU DO.
FORGET REJEAN! FORGET YOUR COMMERCIAL! BE THE DUKE CABOOM YOU ARE RIGHT NOW--THE ONE WHO JUMPS AND CRASHES!
WHO'S THE GREATEST OF THE GREAT WHITE NORTH?
DUKE CABOOM!
WHO'S THE MOST SPECTACULAR DAREDEVIL CANADA HAS EVER SEEN?
DUKE CABOOM!
CAN YOU DO THE JUMP?
YES, I CAN-ADA!

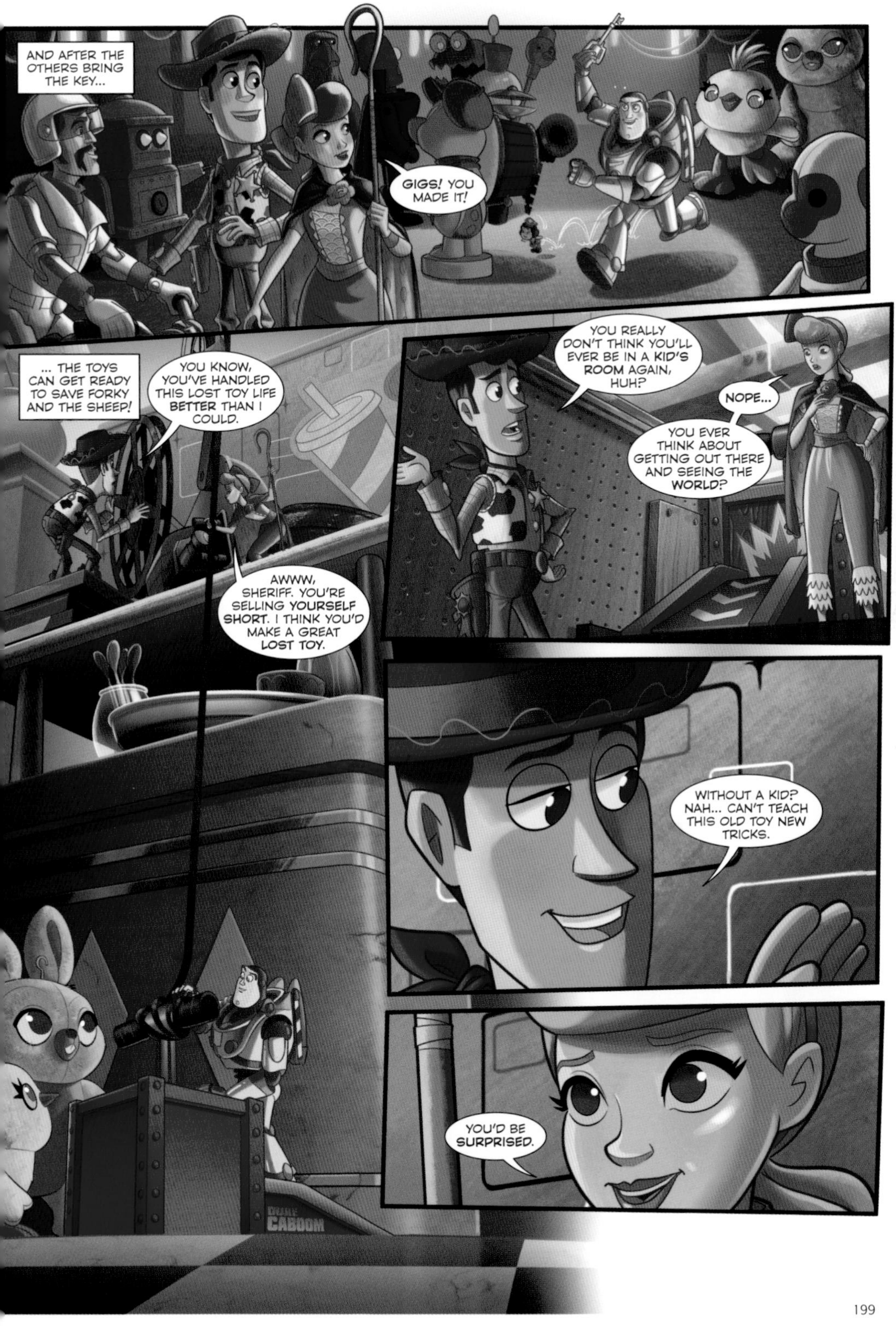
AND AFTER THE OTHERS BRING THE KEY...
GIGS! YOU MADE IT!
... THE TOYS CAN GET READY TO SAVE FORKY AND THE SHEEP!
YOU KNOW, YOU'VE HANDLED THIS LOST TOY LIFE BETTER THAN I COULD.
AWWW, SHERIFF. YOU'RE SELLING YOURSELF SHORT. I THINK YOU'D MAKE A GREAT LOST TOY.
YOU REALLY DON'T THINK YOU'LL EVER BE IN A KID'S ROOM AGAIN, HUH?
NOPE...
YOU EVER THINK ABOUT GETTING OUT THERE AND SEEING THE WORLD?
WITHOUT A KID? NAH... CAN'T TEACH THIS OLD TOY NEW TRICKS.
YOU'D BE SURPRISED.
DUKE CABOOM

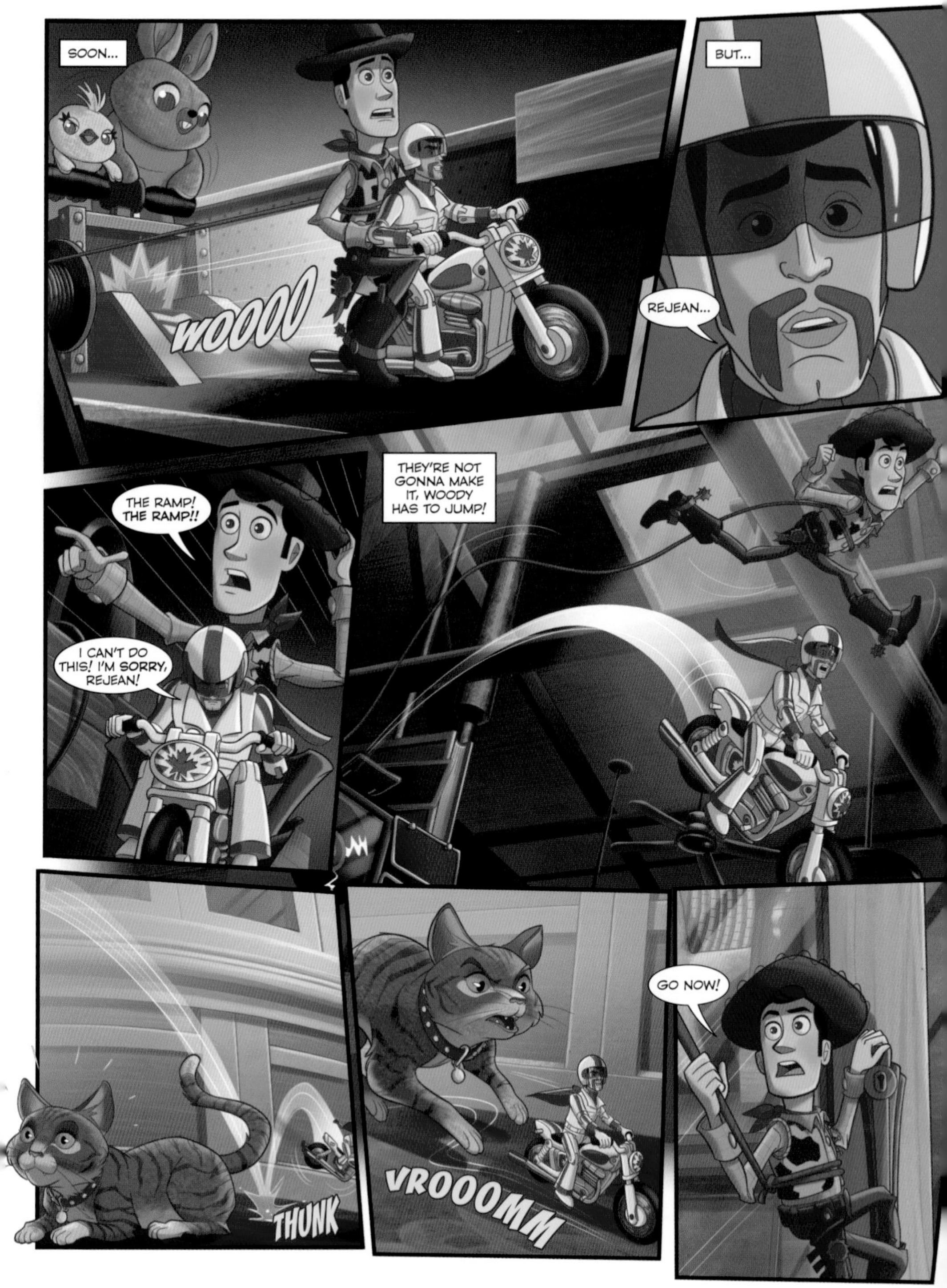
SOON...
WOOOO
BUT...
REJEAN...
THE RAMP! THE RAMP!!
I CAN'T DO THIS! I'M SORRY, REJEAN!
THEY'RE NOT GONNA MAKE IT, WOODY HAS TO JUMP!
THUNK
VROOOMM
GO NOW!

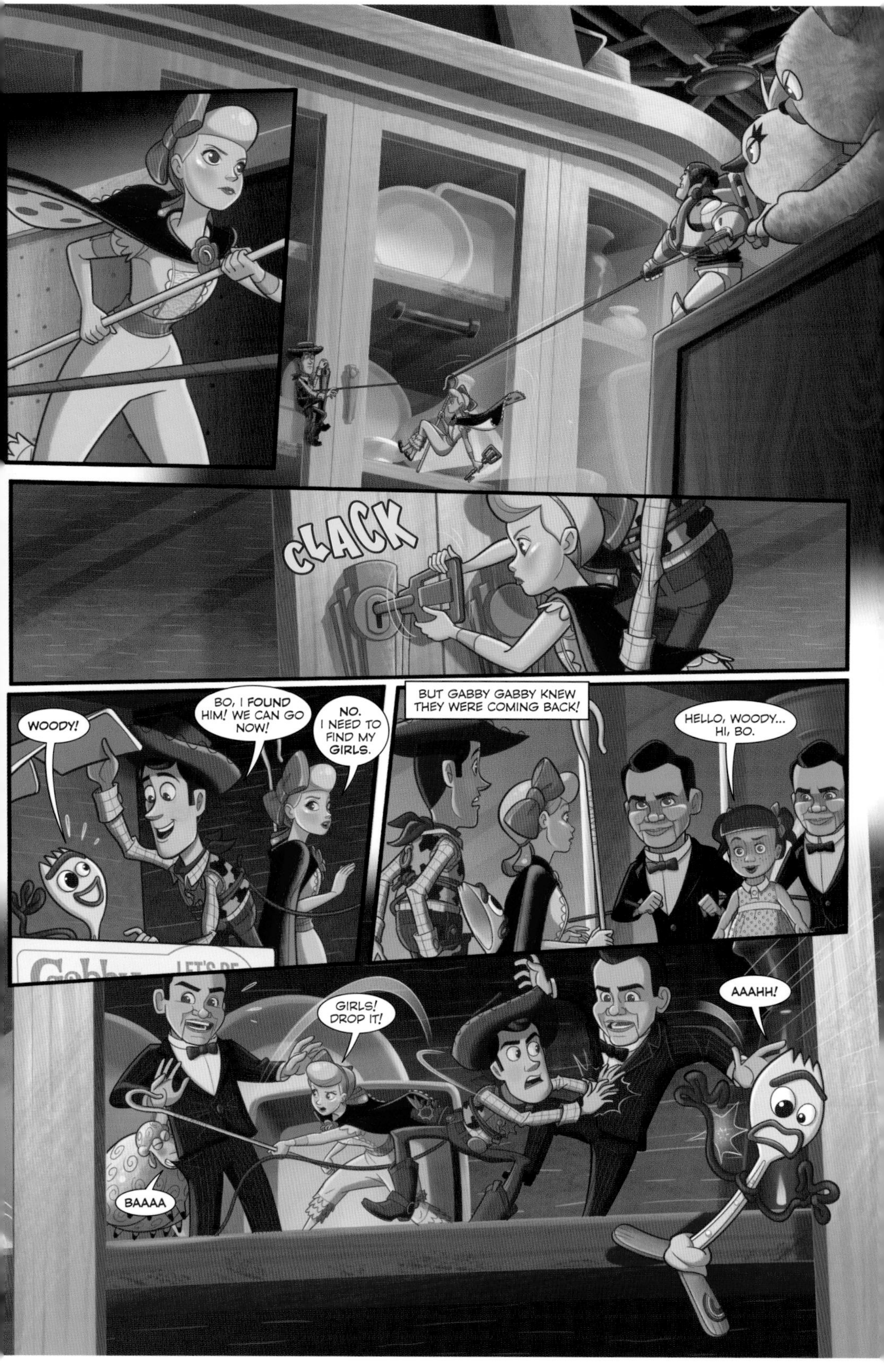
CLACK
WOODY!
BO, I FOUND HIM! WE CAN GO NOW!
NO. I NEED TO FIND MY GIRLS.
BUT GABBY GABBY KNEW THEY WERE COMING BACK!
HELLO, WOODY... HI, BO.
GIRLS! DROP IT!
AAAHH!
BAAAA

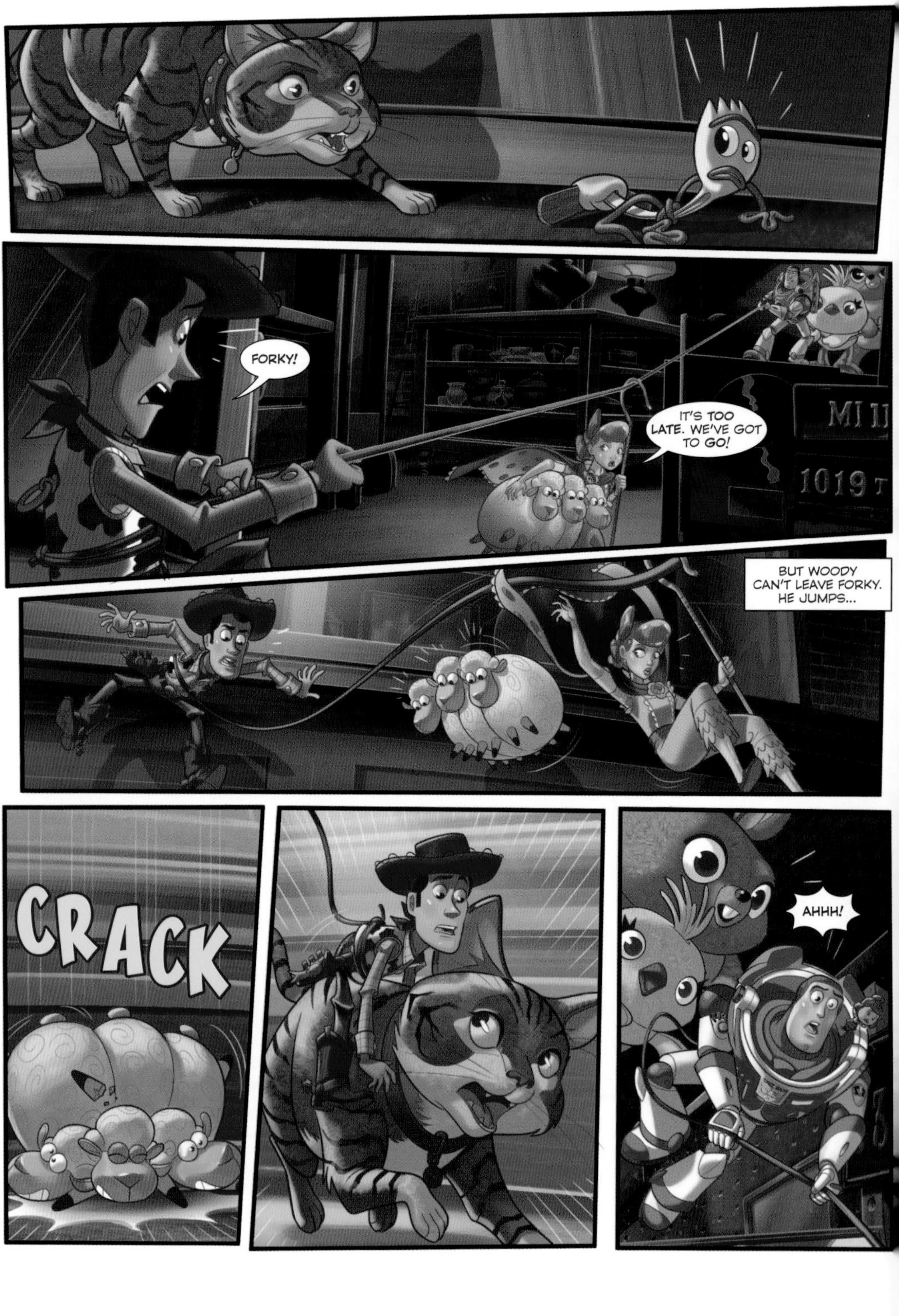
FORKY!
IT'S TOO LATE. WE'VE GOT TO GO!
BUT WOODY CAN'T LEAVE FORKY. HE JUMPS...
CRACK
AHHH!

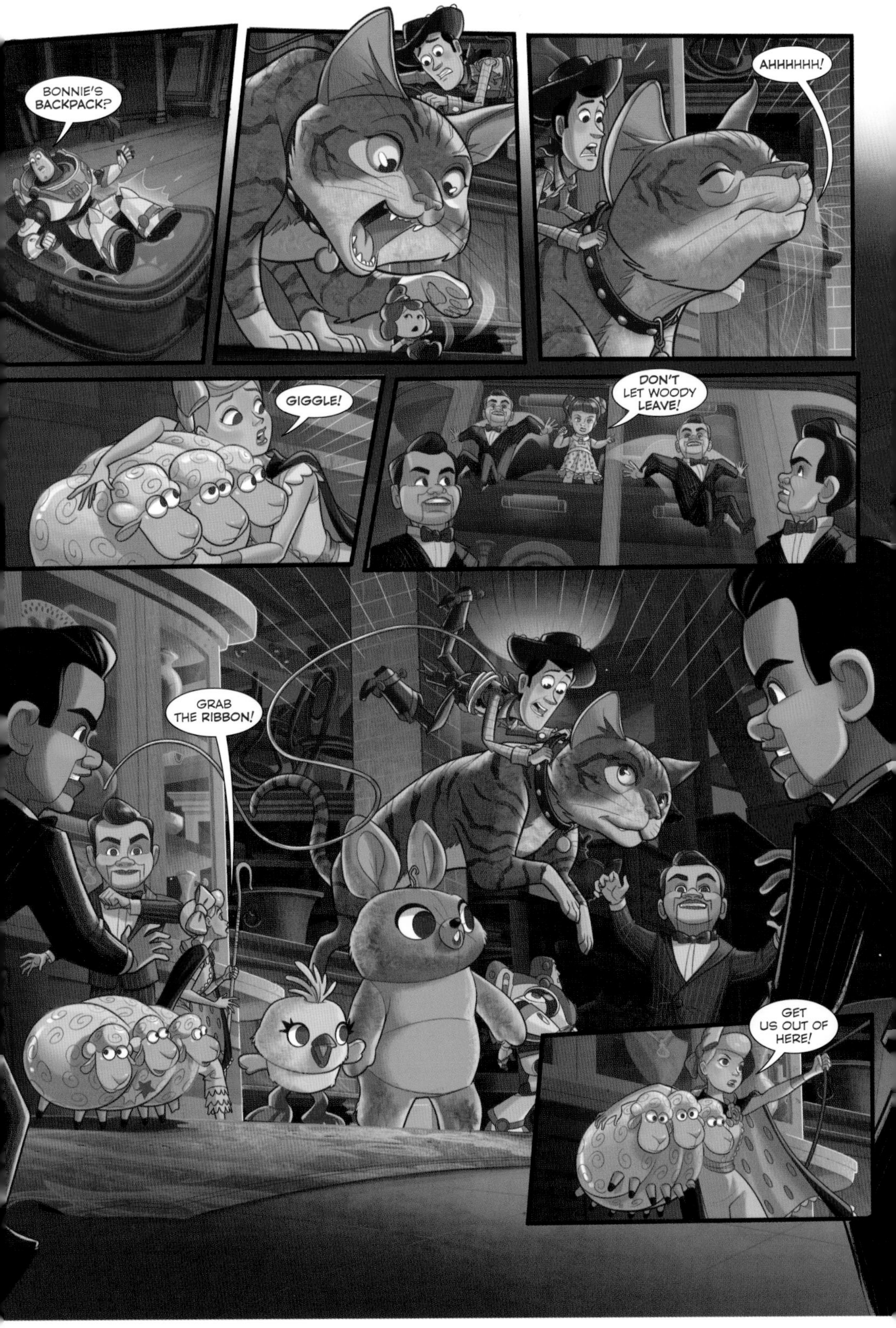
BONNIE'S BACKPACK?
AHHHHHH!
GIGGLE!
DON'T LET WOODY LEAVE!
GRAB THE RIBBON!
GET US OUT OF HERE!

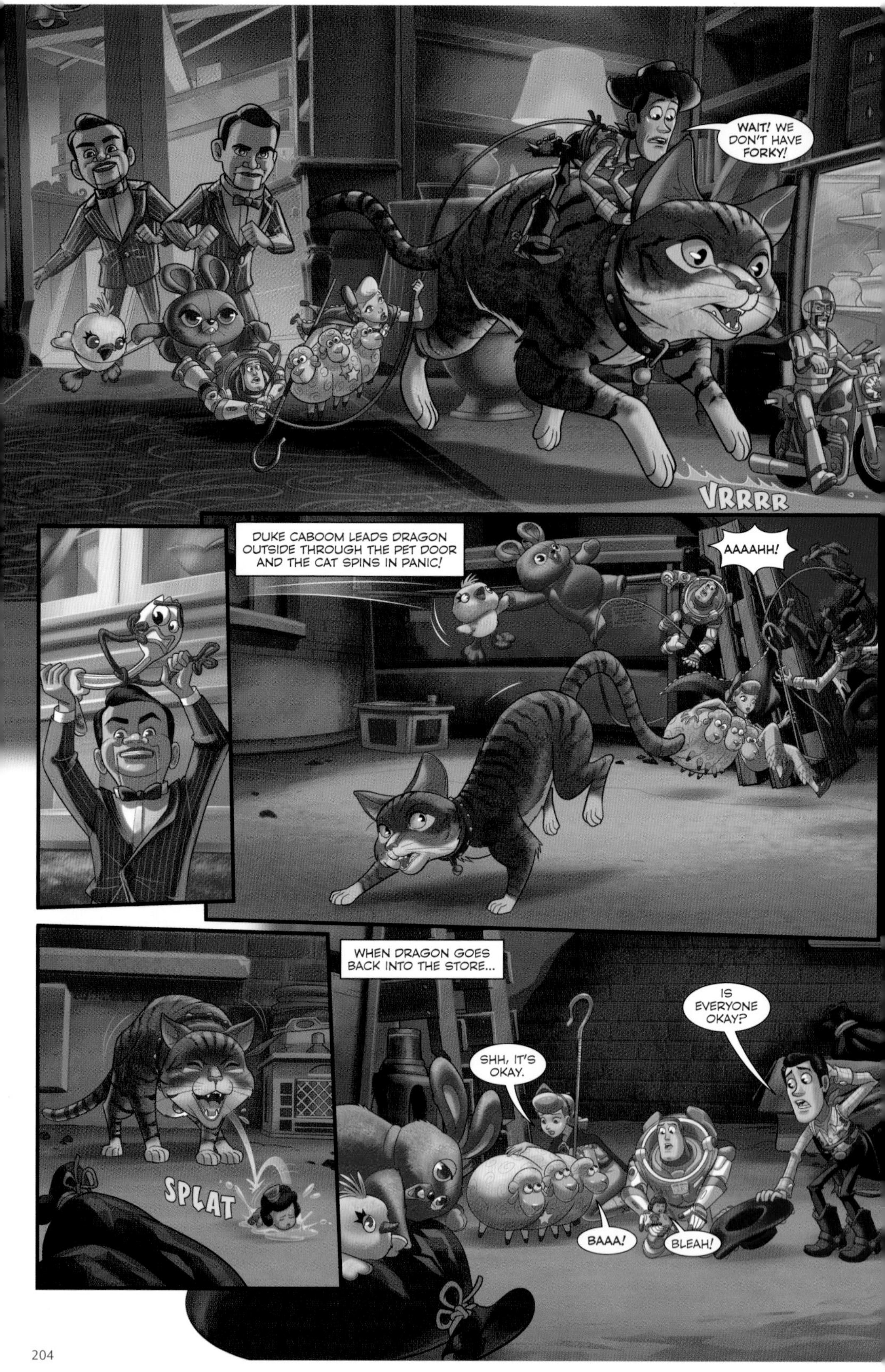
WAIT! WE DON'T HAVE FORKY!
VRRRR
DUKE CABOOM LEADS DRAGON OUTSIDE THROUGH THE PET DOOR AND THE CAT SPINS IN PANIC!
AAAAHH!
SPLAT
WHEN DRAGON GOES BACK INTO THE STORE...
SHH, IT'S OKAY.
IS EVERYONE OKAY?
BAAA!
BLEAH!

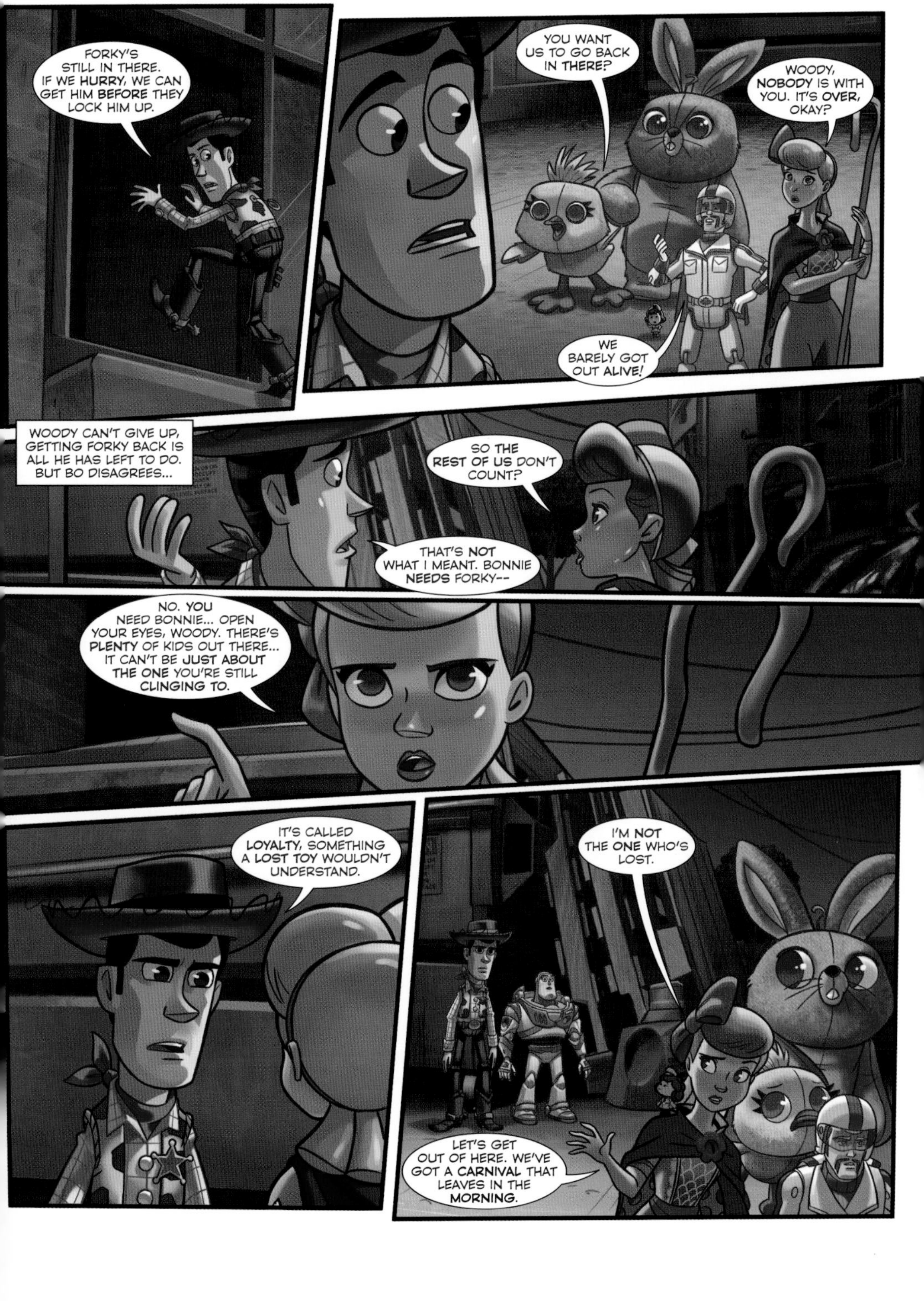
FORKY'S STILL IN THERE. IF WE HURRY, WE CAN GET HIM BEFORE THEY LOCK HIM UP.
YOU WANT US TO GO BACK IN THERE?
WOODY, NOBODY IS WITH YOU. IT'S OVER, OKAY?
WE BARELY GOT OUT ALIVE!
WOODY CAN'T GIVE UP, GETTING FORKY BACK IS ALL HE HAS LEFT TO DO. BUT BO DISAGREES...
SO THE REST OF US DON'T COUNT?
THAT'S NOT WHAT I MEANT. BONNIE NEEDS FORKY--
NO. YOU NEED BONNIE... OPEN YOUR EYES, WOODY. THERE'S PLENTY OF KIDS OUT THERE... IT CAN'T BE JUST ABOUT THE ONE YOU'RE STILL CLINGING TO.
IT'S CALLED LOYALTY, SOMETHING A LOST TOY WOULDN'T UNDERSTAND.
I'M NOT THE ONE WHO'S LOST.
LET'S GET OUT OF HERE. WE'VE GOT A CARNIVAL THAT LEAVES IN THE MORNING.

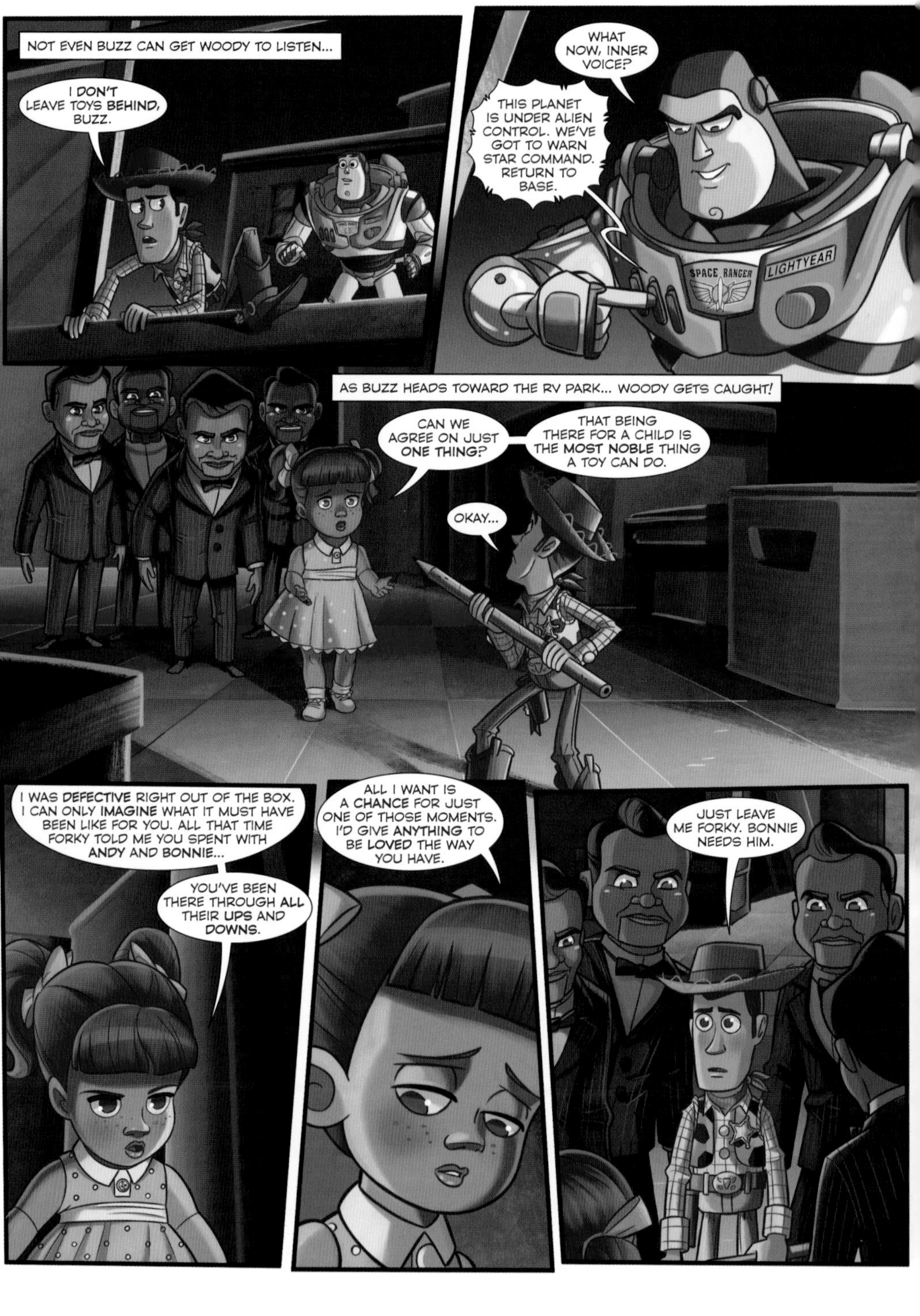
NOT EVEN BUZZ CAN GET WOODY TO LISTEN...
I DON'T LEAVE TOYS BEHIND, BUZZ.
WHAT NOW, INNER VOICE?
THIS PLANET IS UNDER ALIEN CONTROL. WE'VE GOT TO WARN STAR COMMAND. RETURN TO BASE.
SPACE RANGER
LIGHTYEAR
AS BUZZ HEADS TOWARD THE RV PARK... WOODY GETS CAUGHT!
CAN WE AGREE ON JUST ONE THING?
THAT BEING THERE FOR A CHILD IS THE MOST NOBLE THING A TOY CAN DO.
OKAY...
I WAS DEFECTIVE RIGHT OUT OF THE BOX. I CAN ONLY IMAGINE WHAT IT MUST HAVE BEEN LIKE FOR YOU. ALL THAT TIME FORKY TOLD ME YOU SPENT WITH ANDY AND BONNIE...
YOU'VE BEEN THERE THROUGH ALL THEIR UPS AND DOWNS.
ALL I WANT IS A CHANCE FOR JUST ONE OF THOSE MOMENTS. I'D GIVE ANYTHING TO BE LOVED THE WAY YOU HAVE.
JUST LEAVE ME FORKY. BONNIE NEEDS HIM.

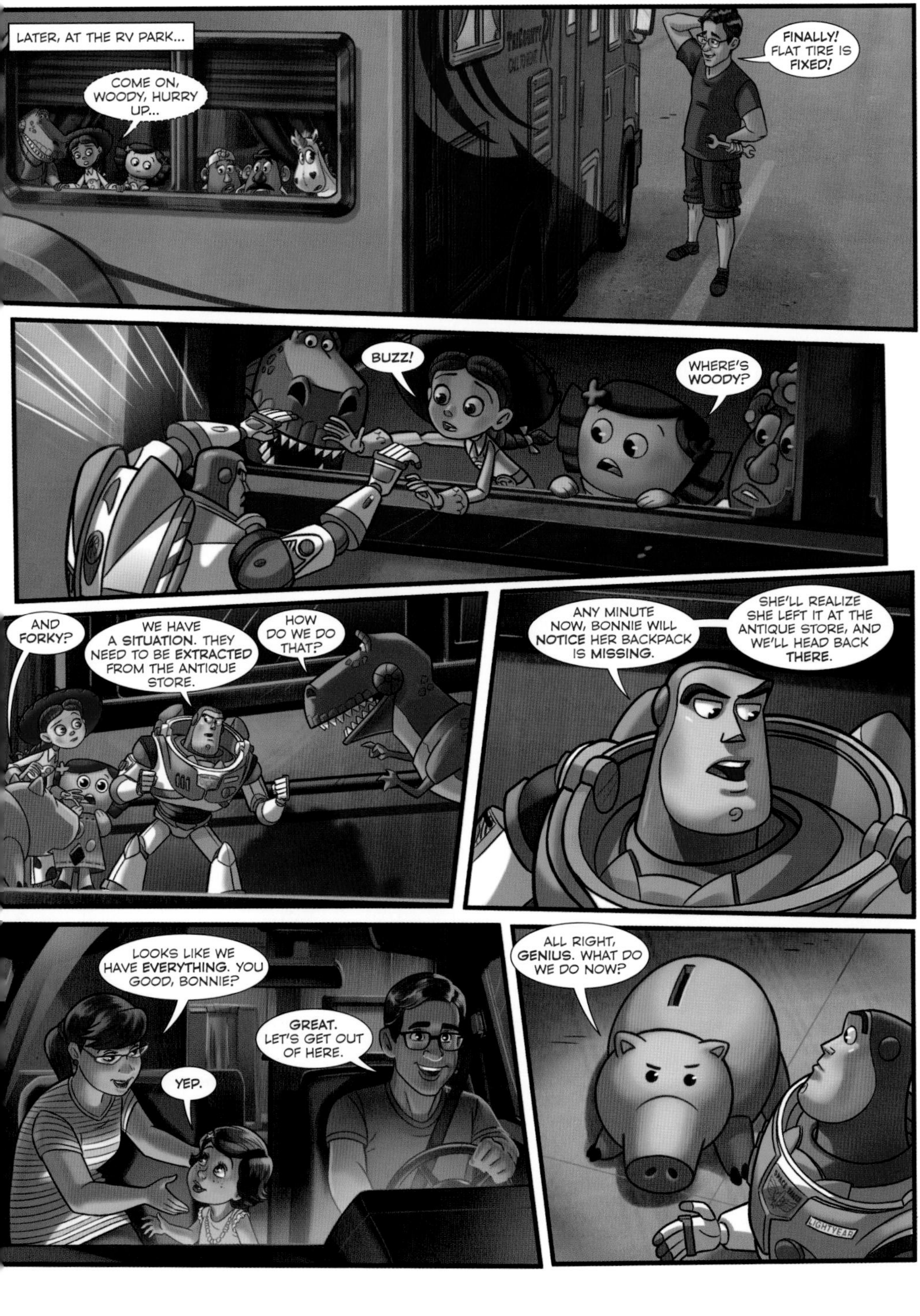

LATER, AT THE RV PARK...
COME ON, WOODY, HURRY UP...
FINALLY! FLAT TIRE IS FIXED!
BUZZ!
WHERE'S WOODY?
AND FORKY?
WE HAVE A SITUATION. THEY NEED TO BE EXTRACTED FROM THE ANTIQUE STORE.
HOW DO WE DO THAT?
ANY MINUTE NOW, BONNIE WILL NOTICE HER BACKPACK IS MISSING.
SHE'LL REALIZE SHE LEFT IT AT THE ANTIQUE STORE, AND WE'LL HEAD BACK THERE.
LOOKS LIKE WE HAVE EVERYTHING. YOU GOOD, BONNIE?
YEP.
GREAT. LET'S GET OUT OF HERE.
ALL RIGHT, GENIUS. WHAT DO WE DO NOW?

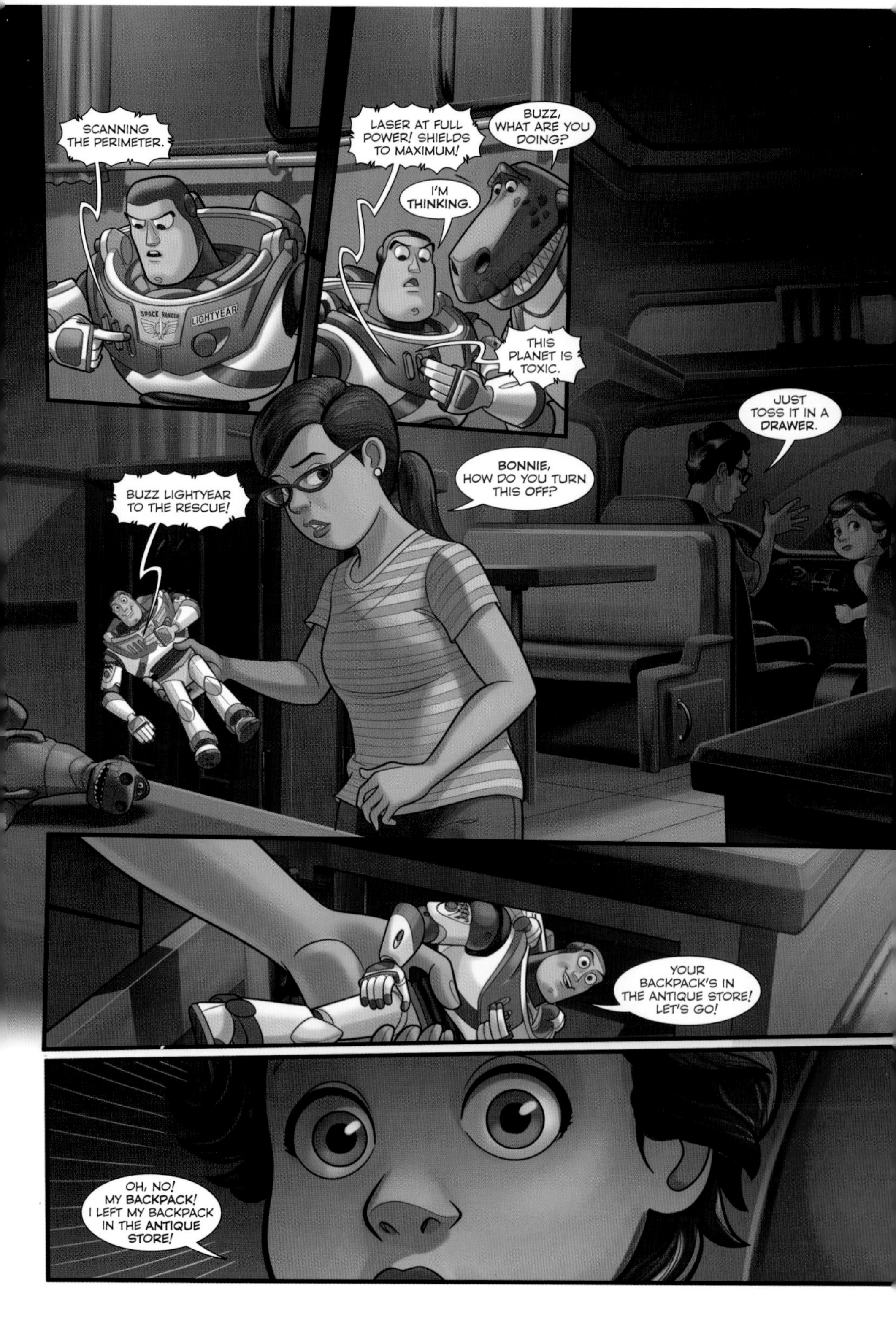
SCANNING THE PERIMETER.
LASER AT FULL POWER! SHIELDS TO MAXIMUM!
BUZZ, WHAT ARE YOU DOING?
I'M THINKING.
THIS PLANET IS TOXIC.
SPACE RANGER
LIGHTYEAR
JUST TOSS IT IN A DRAWER.
BONNIE, HOW DO YOU TURN THIS OFF?
BUZZ LIGHTYEAR TO THE RESCUE!
YOUR BACKPACK'S IN THE ANTIQUE STORE! LET'S GO!
OH, NO! MY BACKPACK! I LEFT MY BACKPACK IN THE ANTIQUE STORE!

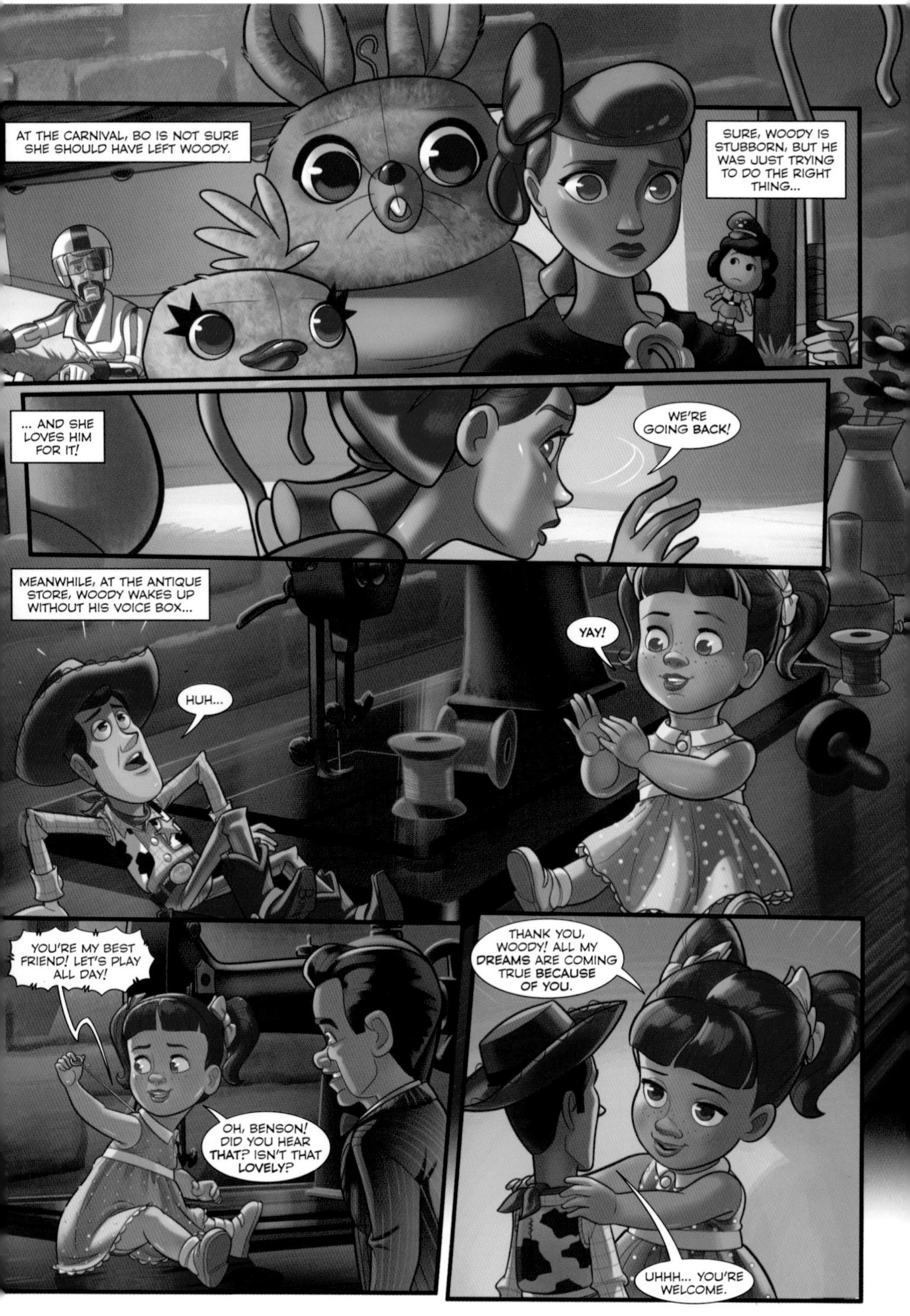
AT THE CARNIVAL, BO IS NOT SURE SHE SHOULD HAVE LEFT WOODY.
SURE, WOODY IS STUBBORN, BUT HE WAS JUST TRYING TO DO THE RIGHT THING...
... AND SHE LOVES HIM FOR IT!
WE'RE GOING BACK!
MEANWHILE, AT THE ANTIQUE STORE, WOODY WAKES UP WITHOUT HIS VOICE BOX...
YAY!
HUH...
YOU'RE MY BEST FRIEND! LET'S PLAY ALL DAY!
OH, BENSON! DID YOU HEAR THAT? ISN'T THAT LOVELY?
THANK YOU, WOODY! ALL MY DREAMS ARE COMING TRUE BECAUSE OF YOU.
UHHH... YOU'RE WELCOME.

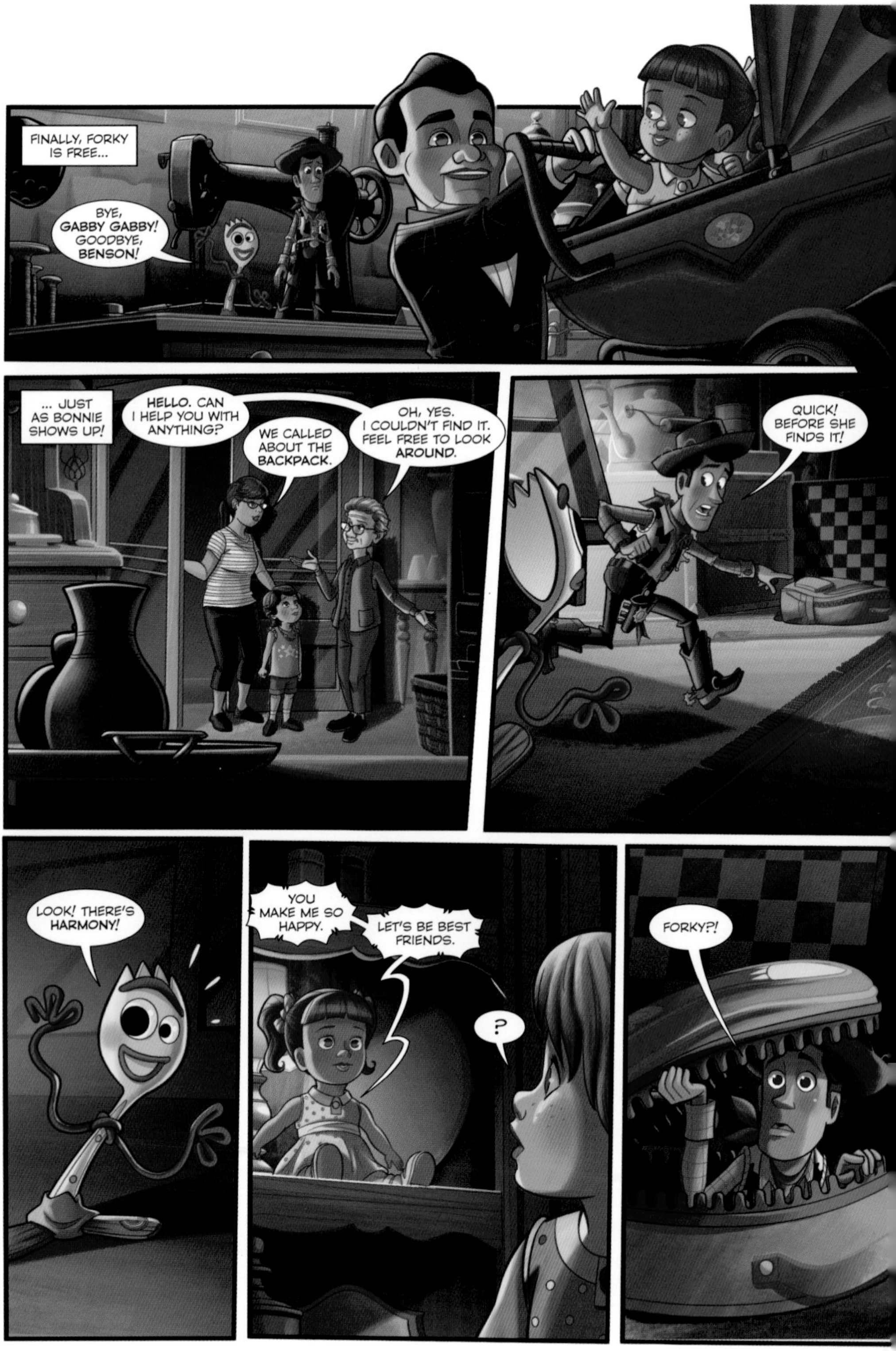

FINALLY, FORKY IS FREE...
BYE, GABBY GABBY! GOODBYE, BENSON!
... JUST AS BONNIE SHOWS UP!
HELLO. CAN I HELP YOU WITH ANYTHING?
WE CALLED ABOUT THE BACKPACK.
OH, YES. I COULDN'T FIND IT. FEEL FREE TO LOOK AROUND.
QUICK! BEFORE SHE FINDS IT!
LOOK! THERE'S HARMONY!
YOU MAKE ME SO HAPPY.
LET'S BE BEST FRIENDS.
?
FORKY?!

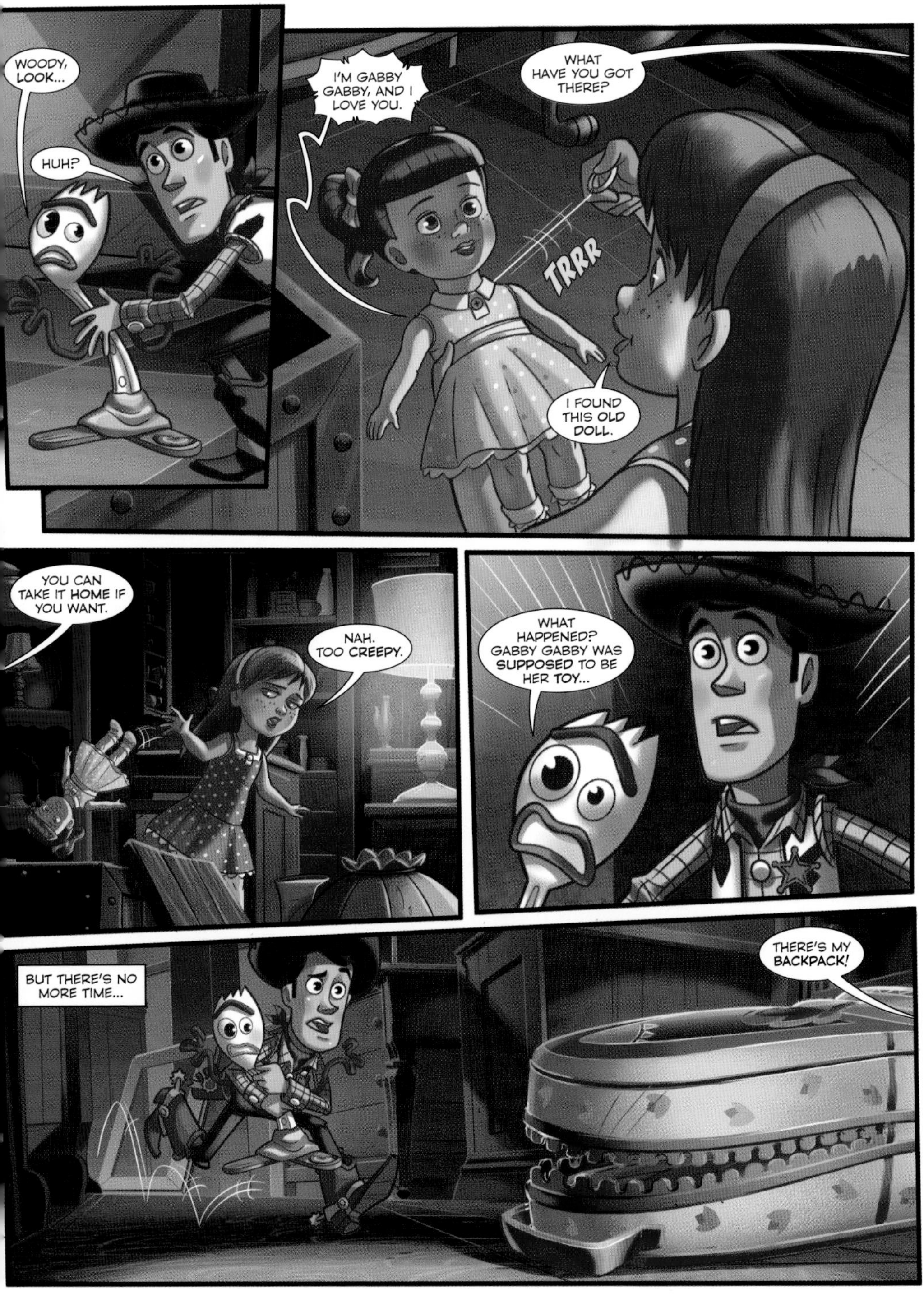
WOODY, LOOK...
HUH?
I'M GABBY GABBY, AND I LOVE YOU.
WHAT HAVE YOU GOT THERE?
TRRR
I FOUND THIS OLD DOLL.
YOU CAN TAKE IT HOME IF YOU WANT.
NAH. TOO CREEPY.
WHAT HAPPENED? GABBY GABBY WAS SUPPOSED TO BE HER TOY...
BUT THERE'S NO MORE TIME...
THERE'S MY BACKPACK!

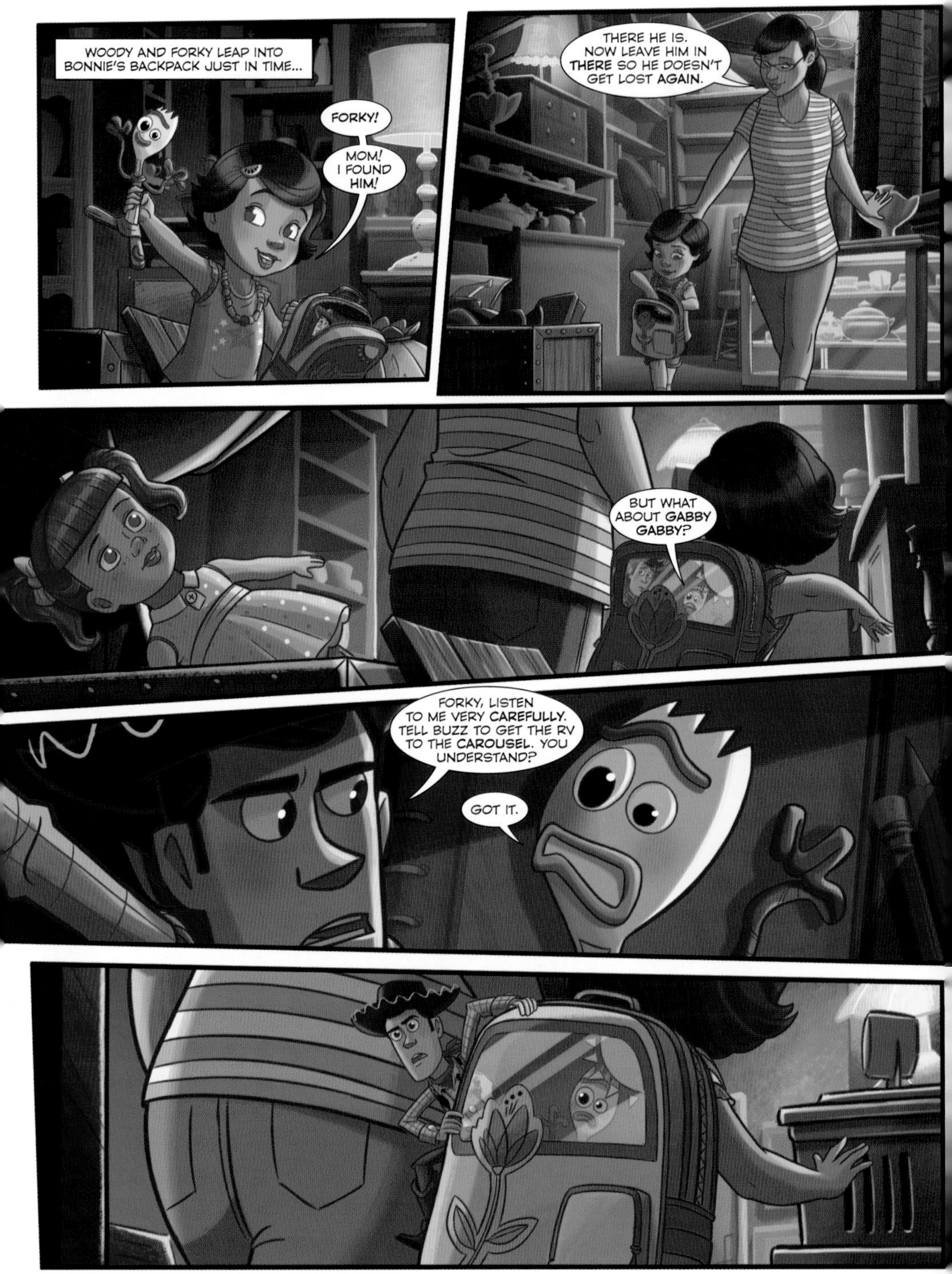
WOODY AND FORKY LEAP INTO BONNIE'S BACKPACK JUST IN TIME...
FORKY!
MOM! I FOUND HIM!
THERE HE IS. NOW LEAVE HIM IN THERE SO HE DOESN'T GET LOST AGAIN.
BUT WHAT ABOUT GABBY GABBY?
FORKY, LISTEN TO ME VERY CAREFULLY. TELL BUZZ TO GET THE RV TO THE CAROUSEL. YOU UNDERSTAND?
GOT IT.

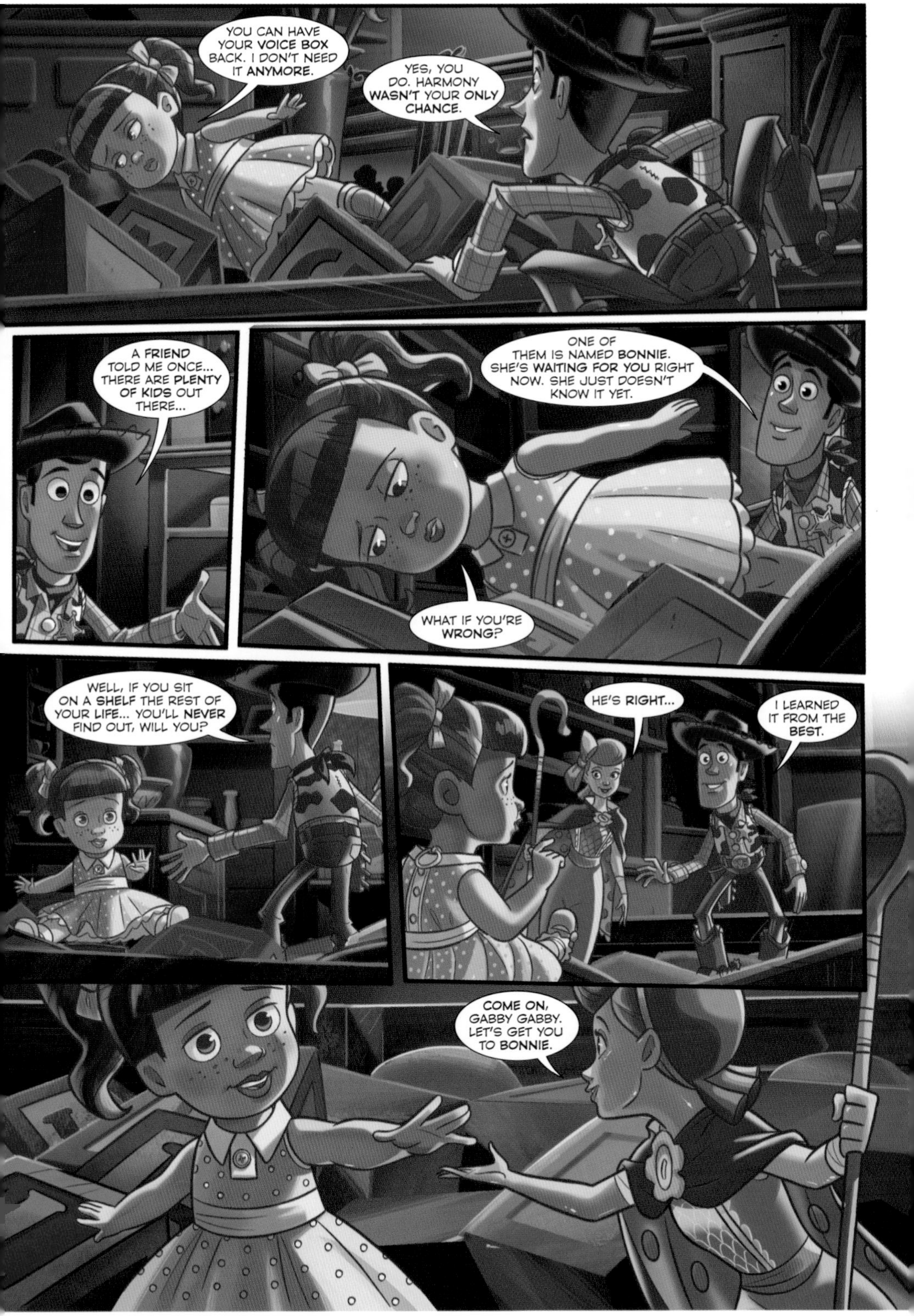
YOU CAN HAVE YOUR VOICE BOX BACK. I DON'T NEED IT ANYMORE.
YES, YOU DO. HARMONY WASN'T YOUR ONLY CHANCE.
A FRIEND TOLD ME ONCE... THERE ARE PLENTY OF KIDS OUT THERE...
ONE OF THEM IS NAMED BONNIE. SHE'S WAITING FOR YOU RIGHT NOW. SHE JUST DOESN'T KNOW IT YET.
WHAT IF YOU'RE WRONG?
WELL, IF YOU SIT ON A SHELF THE REST OF YOUR LIFE... YOU'LL NEVER FIND OUT, WILL YOU?
HE'S RIGHT...
I LEARNED IT FROM THE BEST.
COME ON, GABBY GABBY. LET'S GET YOU TO BONNIE.

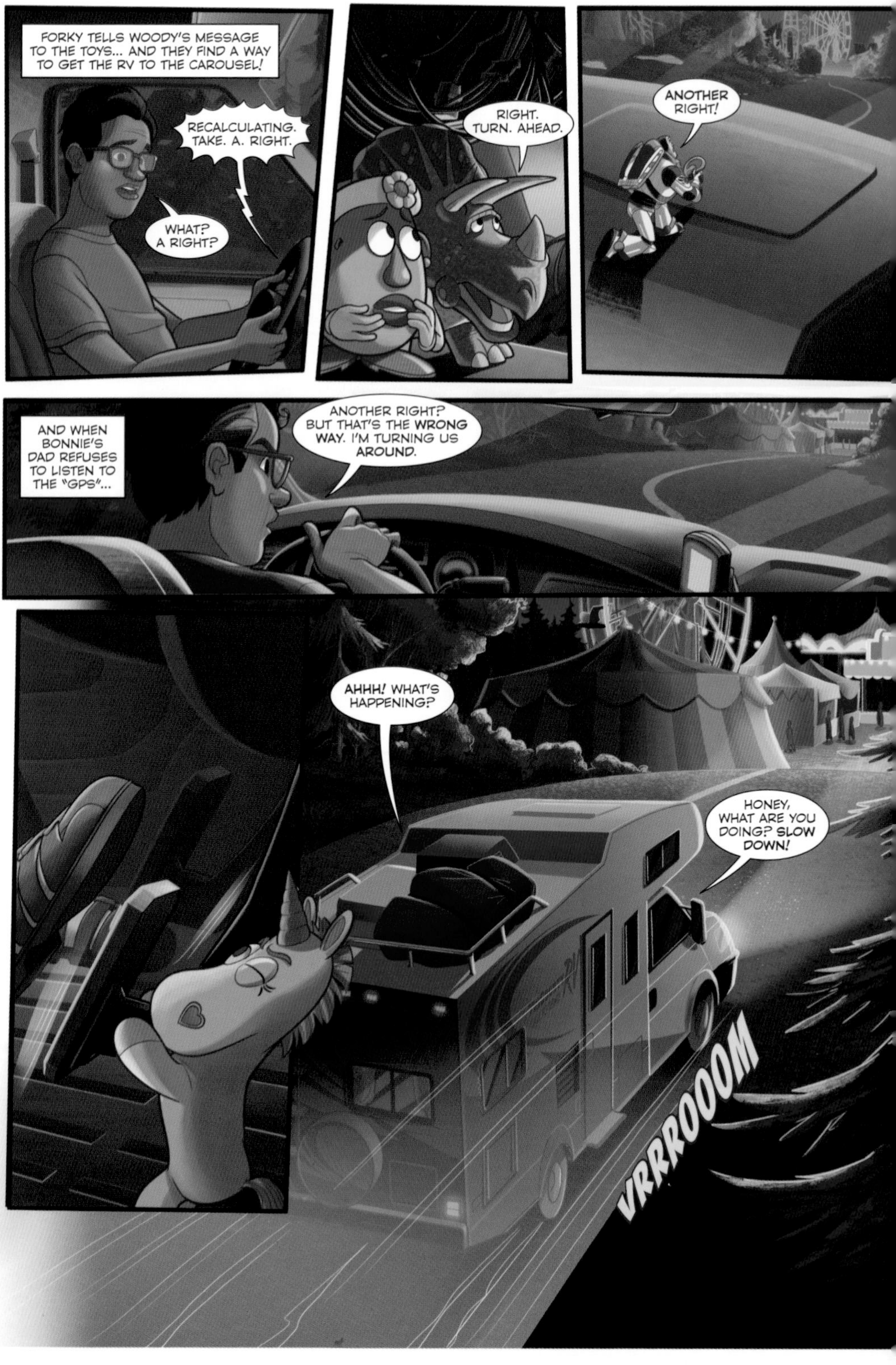
FORKY TELLS WOODY'S MESSAGE TO THE TOYS... AND THEY FIND A WAY TO GET THE RV TO THE CAROUSEL!
RECALCULATING. TAKE. A. RIGHT.
WHAT? A RIGHT?
RIGHT. TURN. AHEAD.
ANOTHER RIGHT!
AND WHEN BONNIE'S DAD REFUSES TO LISTEN TO THE "GPS"...
ANOTHER RIGHT? BUT THAT'S THE WRONG WAY. I'M TURNING US AROUND.
AHHH! WHAT'S HAPPENING?
HONEY, WHAT ARE YOU DOING? SLOW DOWN!
VRRROOOM

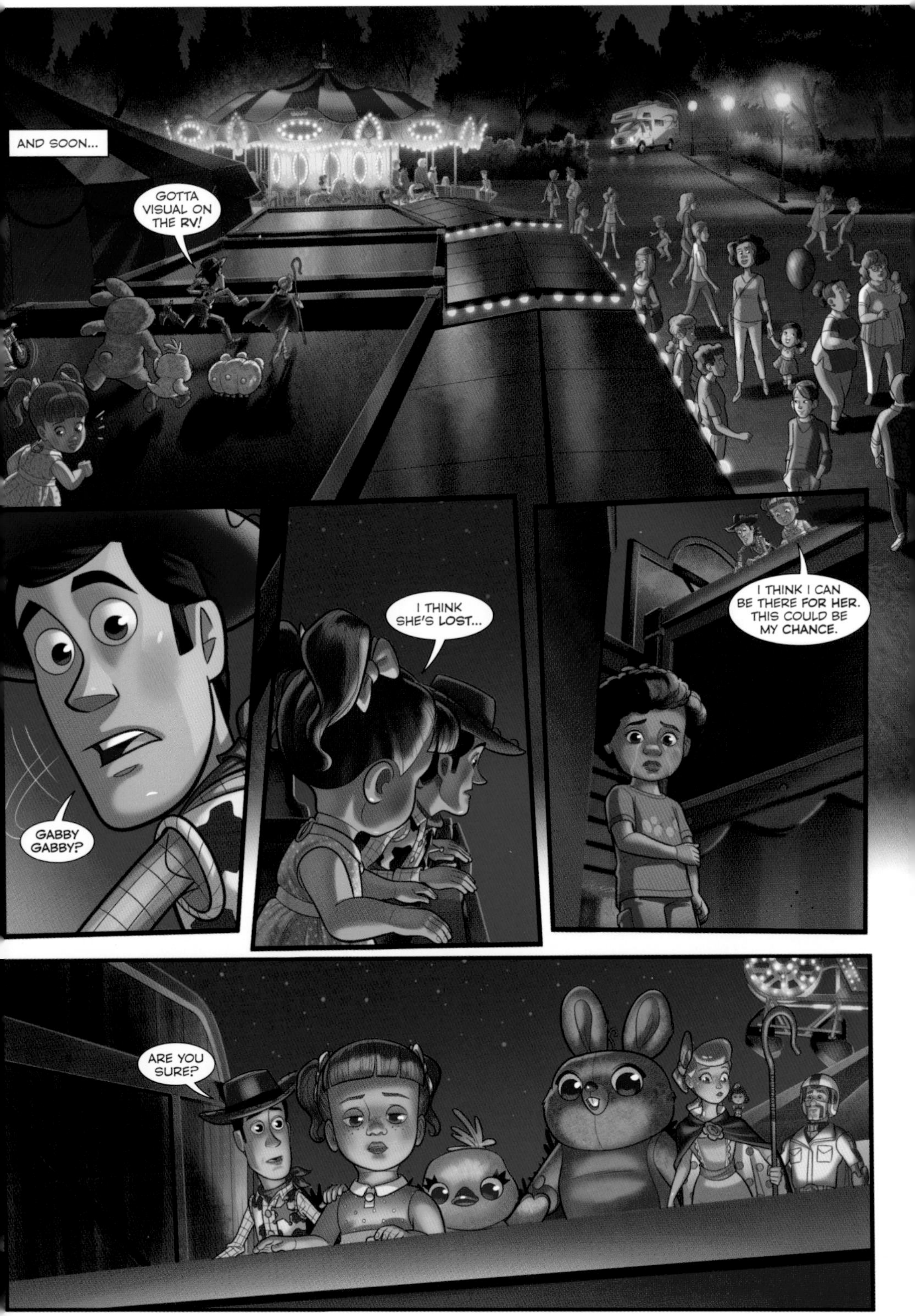
AND SOON...
GOTTA VISUAL ON THE RV!
GABBY GABBY?
I THINK SHE'S LOST...
I THINK I CAN BE THERE FOR HER. THIS COULD BE MY CHANCE.
ARE YOU SURE?

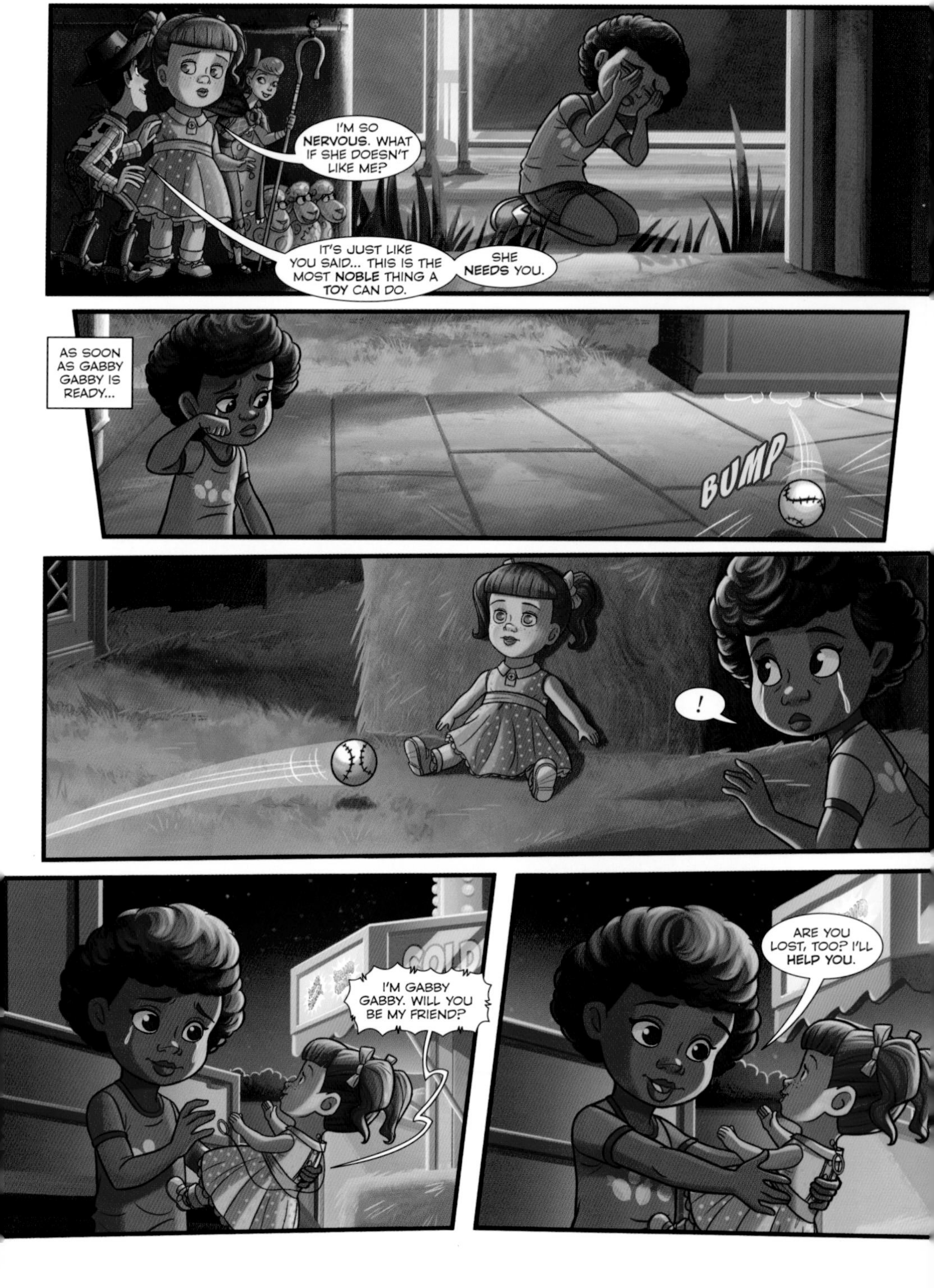
I'M SO NERVOUS. WHAT IF SHE DOESN'T LIKE ME?
IT'S JUST LIKE YOU SAID... THIS IS THE MOST NOBLE THING A TOY CAN DO.
SHE NEEDS YOU.
AS SOON AS GABBY GABBY IS READY...
BUMP
!
I'M GABBY GABBY. WILL YOU BE MY FRIEND?
ARE YOU LOST, TOO? I'LL HELP YOU.

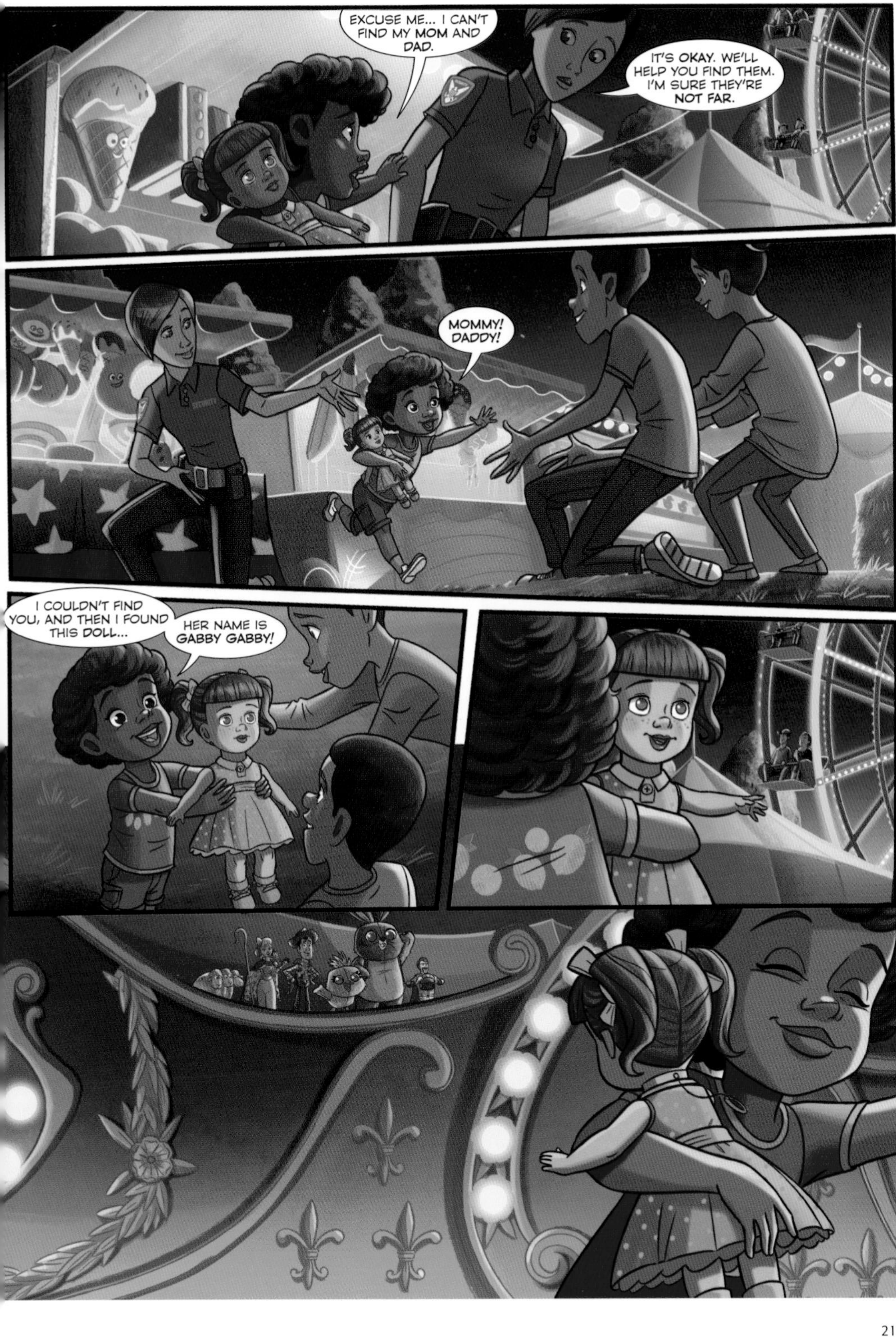
EXCUSE ME... I CAN'T FIND MY MOM AND DAD.
IT'S OKAY. WE'LL HELP YOU FIND THEM. I'M SURE THEY'RE NOT FAR.
MOMMY! DADDY!
I COULDN'T FIND YOU, AND THEN I FOUND THIS DOLL...
HER NAME IS GABBY GABBY!

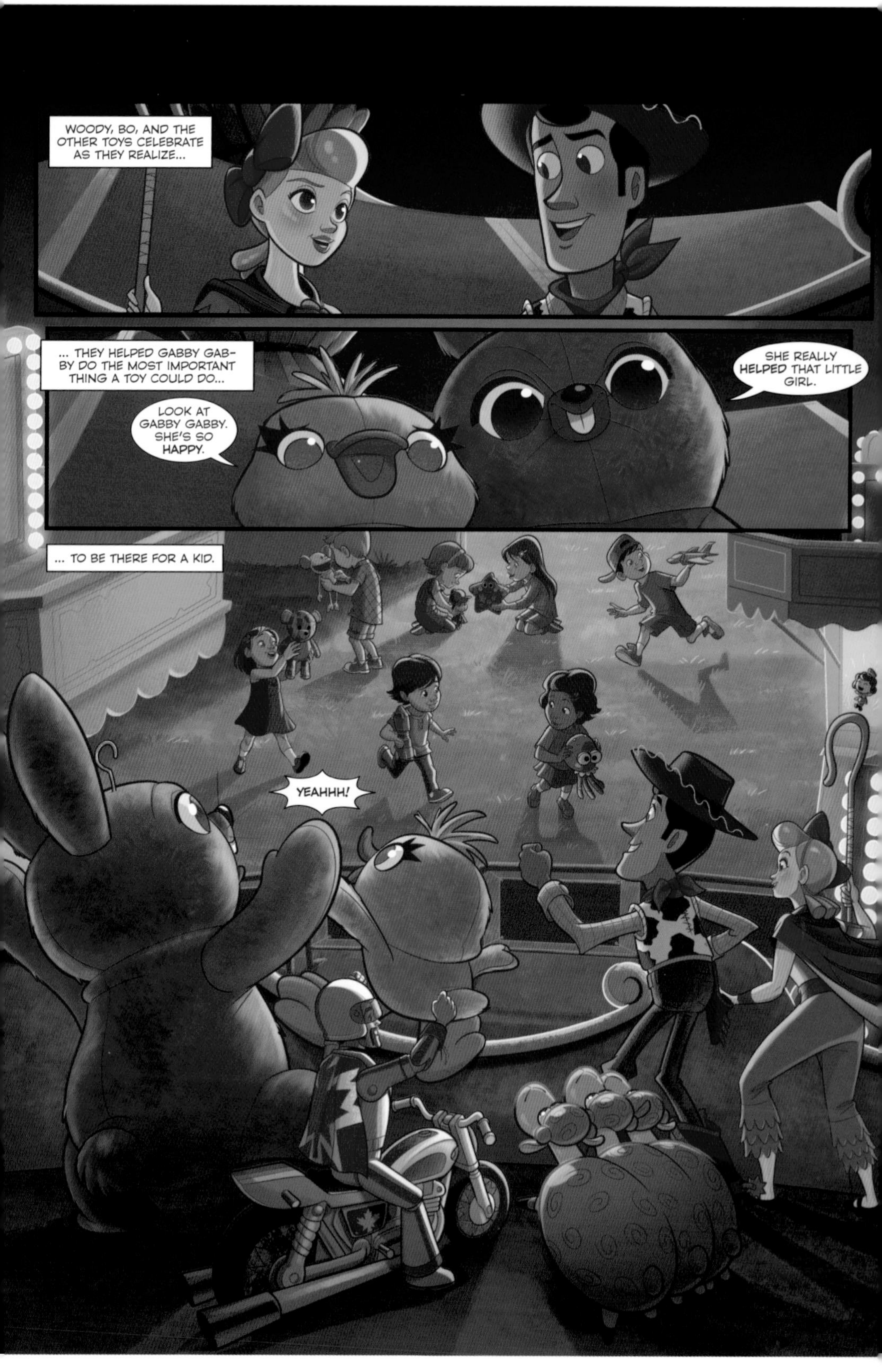
WOODY, BO, AND THE OTHER TOYS CELEBRATE AS THEY REALIZE...
... THEY HELPED GABBY GAB-BY DO THE MOST IMPORTANT THING A TOY COULD DO...
LOOK AT GABBY GABBY. SHE'S SO HAPPY.
SHE REALLY HELPED THAT LITTLE GIRL.
... TO BE THERE FOR A KID.
YEAHHH!

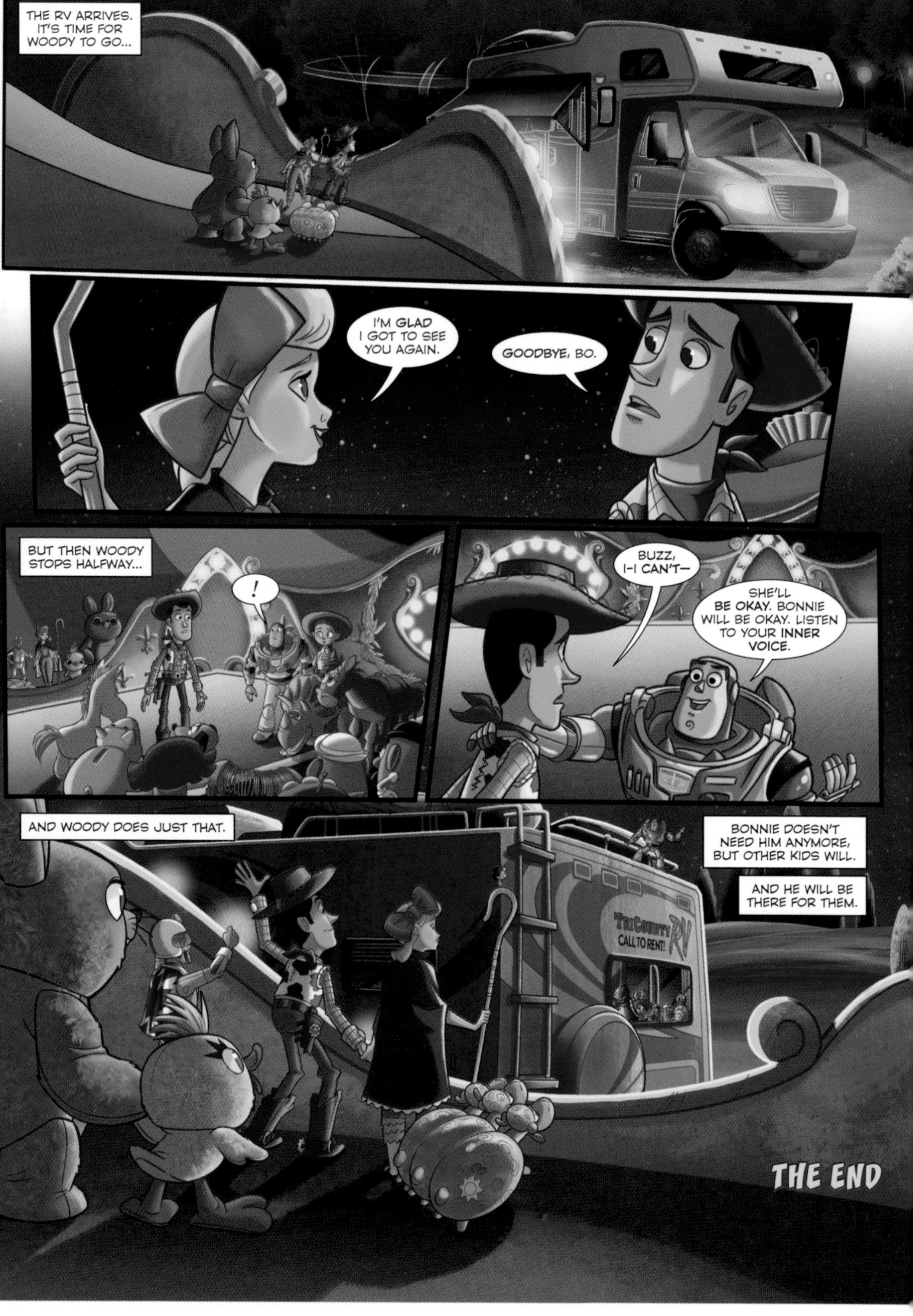
THE RV ARRIVES. IT'S TIME FOR WOODY TO GO...
I'M GLAD I GOT TO SEE YOU AGAIN.
GOODBYE, BO.
BUT THEN WOODY STOPS HALFWAY...
!
BUZZ, I–I CAN'T—
SHE'LL BE OKAY. BONNIE WILL BE OKAY. LISTEN TO YOUR INNER VOICE.
AND WOODY DOES JUST THAT.
BONNIE DOESN'T NEED HIM ANYMORE, BUT OTHER KIDS WILL.
AND HE WILL BE THERE FOR THEM.
TRICOUNTY RV
CALL TO RENT!
THE END

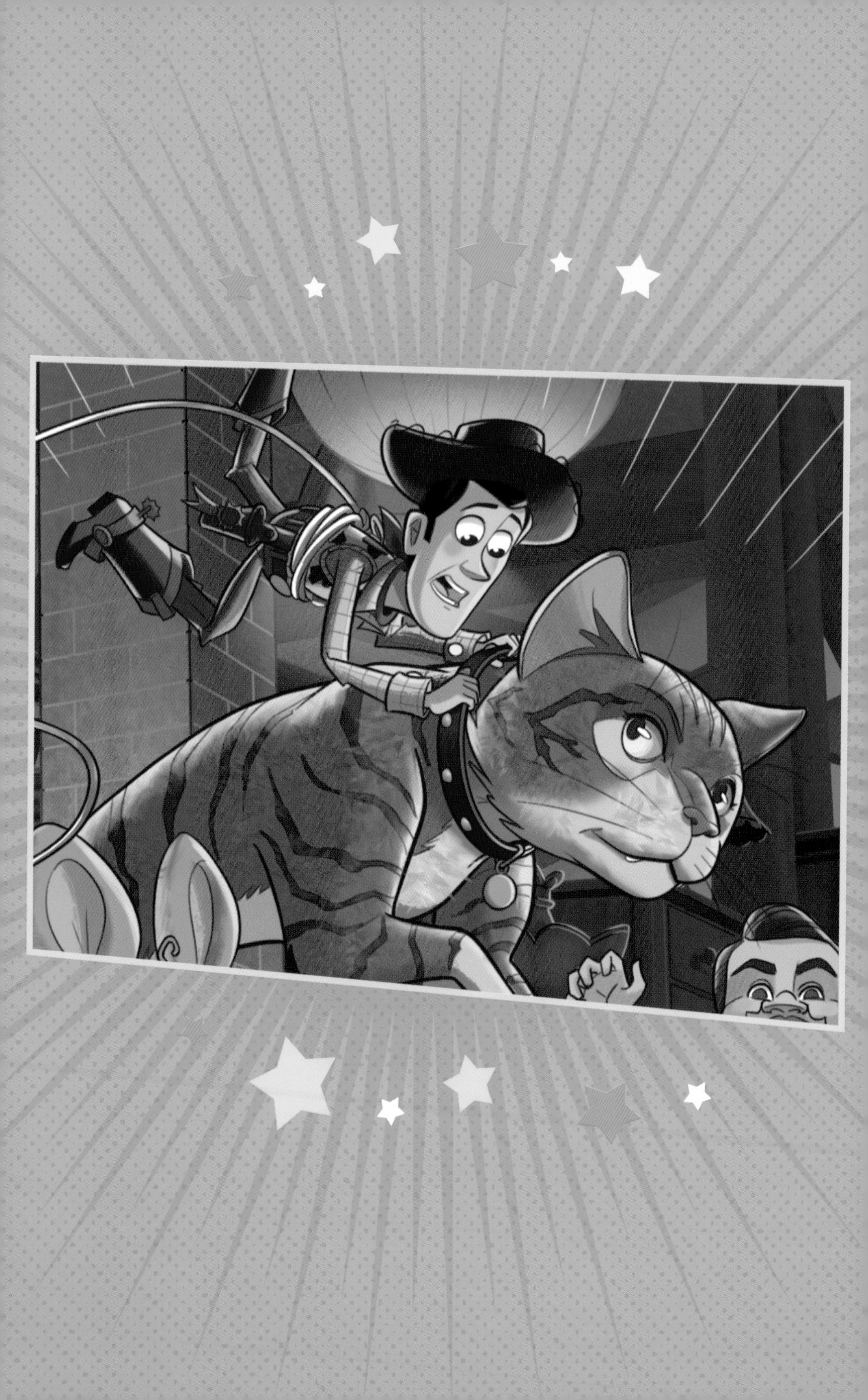

CATCH UP WITH WOODY AND FRIENDS FROM DISNEY·PIXAR'S *TOY STORY*!

Disney·Pixar Toy Story: Adventures

A collection of short comic stories based on the animated films Disney·Pixar *Toy Story*, *Toy Story 2*, and *Toy Story 3*!

Set your jets for adventure. Join Woody, Buzz, and all of your *Toy Story* favorites in a variety of fun and exciting comic stories. Get ready to play with your favorite toys with Andy and Bonnie, join the toys as they take more journeys to the outside, play make-believe in a world of infinite possibilities, meet new friends, and have a party or two—experience all of this and more!

Volume 1 | 978-1-50671-266-6 | $10.99
Volume 2 | 978-1-50671-451-6 | $10.99

Disney·Pixar Toy Story 4

A graphic novel anthology expanding on the animated blockbuster Disney·Pixar *Toy Story 4*.

Join Woody and the *Toy Story* gang in four connecting stories set before and after Disney·Pixar's *Toy Story 4*.

978-1-50671-265-9 | $10.99

AVAILABLE AT YOUR LOCAL COMICS SHOP OR BOOKSTORE!

To find a comics shop in your area, visit **comicshoplocator.com** For more information or to order direct: On the web: **DarkHorse.com** Email: **mailorder@darkhorse.com** Phone: **1-800-862-0052** Mon.–Fri. 9 a.m. to 5 p.m. Pacific Time

CATCH UP WITH DISNEY•PIXAR'S INCREDIBLES 2!

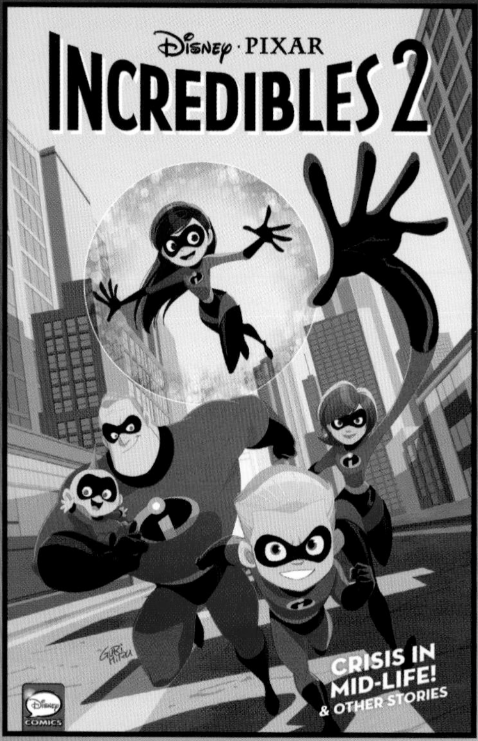
DISNEY · PIXAR
INCREDIBLES 2
CRISIS IN MID-LIFE! & OTHER STORIES
DISNEY COMICS

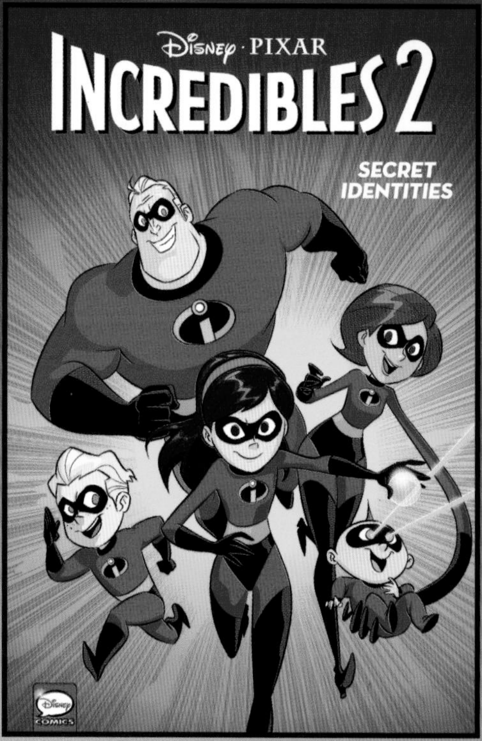
DISNEY · PIXAR
INCREDIBLES 2
SECRET IDENTITIES
DISNEY COMICS

DISNEY · PIXAR INCREDIBLES 2

CRISIS IN MID-LIFE! & OTHER STORIES

An encounter with villain Bomb Voyage inspires Bob to begin training the next generation of Supers, Dash and Violet. Mr. Incredible will find himself needing to pull his family back together . . . because Bomb Voyage is still at large! In another story, Bob tells the kids about a battle from his glory days that seems too amazing to be true—but they never imagined the details would include their mom and dad's super secret first date . . . Finally, in two adventures all his own, baby Jack-Jack and his powers are set to save the day.

978-1-50671-019-8 • $10.99

DISNEY · PIXAR INCREDIBLES 2

SECRET IDENTITIES

It's tough being a teenager, and on top of that, a teenager with powers! Violet feels out of place at school and doesn't fit in with the kids around her . . . until she meets another girl at school—an outsider with powers, just like her! But when her new friend asks her to keep a secret, Violet is torn between keeping her word and doing what's right.

978-1-50671-392-2 • $10.99

DARK HORSE BOOKS

AVAILABLE AT YOUR LOCAL COMICS SHOP OR BOOKSTORE! TO FIND A COMICS SHOP IN YOUR AREA, VISIT COMICSHOPLOCATOR.COM

FOR MORE INFORMATION OR TO ORDER DIRECT: ON THE WEB: DARKHORSE.COM • EMAIL: MAILORDER@DARKHORSE.COM • PHONE: 1-800-862-0052 MON.–FRI. 9 AM TO 5 PM PACIFIC TIME

DISNEY COMICS

PULP ADVENTURES AROUND THE WORLD!

"THIS IS A FEEL-GOOD ADVENTURE LOADED WITH PERILOUS MOMENTS AND TENSION-FILLED SITUATIONS THAT KEEP THE PAGES FLYING BY." –GEEK DAD

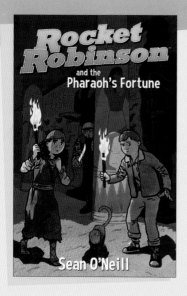

Rocket Robinson
and the
Pharaoh's Fortune
Sean O'Neill

ROCKET ROBINSON AND THE PHARAOH'S FORTUNE

The Egyptian capital is a buzzing hive of treasure-hunters, thrill-seekers, and adventurers, but to 12-year-old Ronald "Rocket" Robinson, it's just another sticker on his well-worn suitcase. But when Rocket finds a strange note written in Egyptian hieroglyphs, he stumbles into an adventure more incredible than anything he's ever dreamt of.

ISBN 978-1-50670-618-4 • $14.99

ROCKET ROBINSON AND THE SECRET OF THE SAINT

Rocket, Nuri, and Screech find themselves in the French capital, where a rare and mysterious painting from the middle ages has been stolen from the Louvre Museum! The young adventurers are soon hot on the trail and the secret contained within may lead all the way to the most mysterious and sought-after treasure in history.

ISBN 978-1-50670-679-5 • $14.99

Rocket Robinson
and the Secret
of the Saint
Sean O'Neill

AVAILABLE AT YOUR LOCAL COMICS SHOP OR BOOKSTORE! **To find a comics shop in your area, visit comicshoplocator.com. For more information or to order direct: On the web: DarkHorse.com • Email: mailorder@darkhorse.com • Phone: 1-800-862-0052 Mon.–Fri. 9 AM to 5 PM Pacific Time**

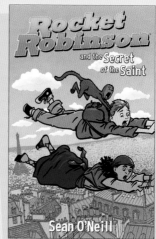

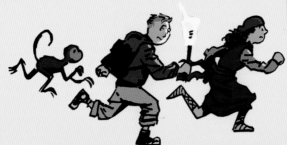

A LOVE THAT CROSSES LIGHT YEARS . . .

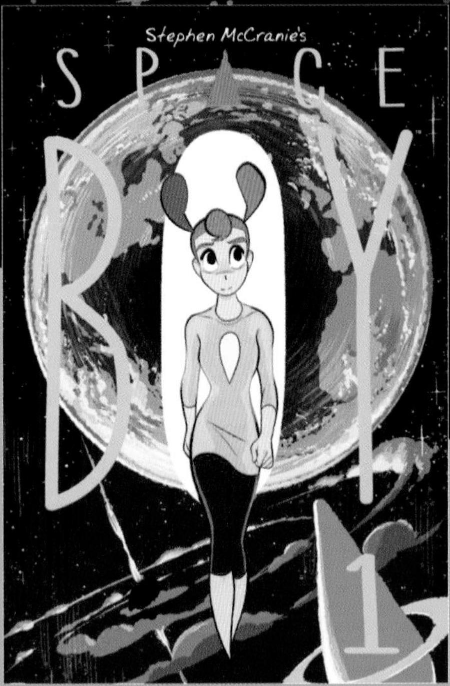
Stephen McCranie's
SPACE
BOY
1

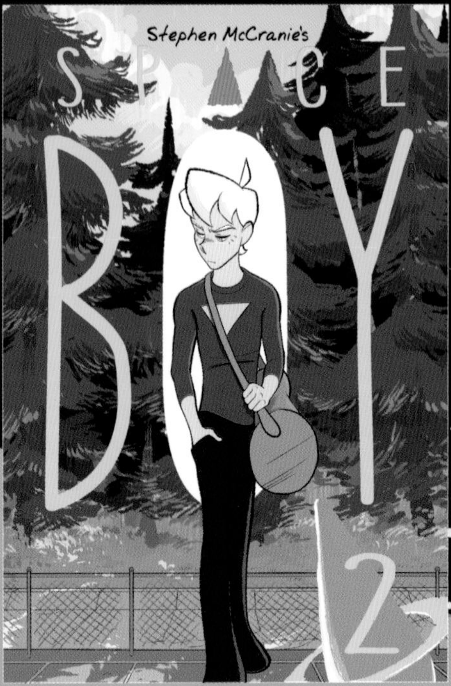
Stephen McCranie's
SPACE
BOY
2

Stephen McCranie's

SPACE BOY VOLUME 1

When Amy's entire family is forced to move back to Earth, Amy says goodbye to her best friend Jemmah and climbs into a cryotube to spend the next thirty years frozen in suspended animation, heading toward her new home. Her life will never be the same . . . and Jemmah is going to grow up without her.

ISBN 978-1-50670-648-1 $10.99

Stephen McCranie's

SPACE BOY VOLUME 2

High school seemed difficult at first, and a close group of friends has made the transition to Earth easier for Amy, but now she finds herself falling down a rabbit hole in her relationship with Oliver—the boy with no flavor.

ISBN 978-1-50670-680-1 $10.99

"TRULY ONE OF THE MOST THOUGHTFUL EXAMPLES I'VE EVER SEEN OF A TEENAGED GIRL IN FICTION."

—NARRATIVE INVESTIGATIONS

Available at your local comics shop or bookstore! To find a comics shop in your area, visit comicshoplocator.com

For more information or to order direct:
on the web DarkHorse.com
email mailorder@darkhorse.com
phone 1-800-862-0052
Mon.-Fri. 9 AM to 5 PM Pacific Time